SOWING SPELLS

Book and Cover Design by: Cay Fletcher
Edited by: Gabriel Hargrave

ISBN: 978-1-959916-36-9 (paperback)
978-1-959916-38-3 (hardcover)
978-1-959916-37-6 (e-book)
First Edition 2025

Printed in the United States of America

Fox Fern Books, LLC

www.foxfernbooks.com

www.cayfletcher.com

Sowing Spells

A Field Guide to Becoming a Wizard's Apprentice

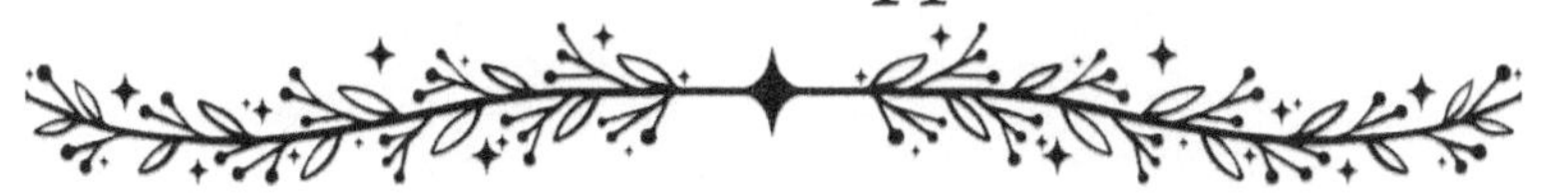

Cay Fletcher

Fox Fern Books, LLC

Copyright © 2025 by Cay Fletcher

This book is for all the readers that wanted more of Sil & Anders' adventures. Your love for them is the reason Sowing Spells exists.

XOXO

P.S. they're 'roommates'!

In loving memory of our fuzzy book dragon and writing assistant, Satsuki.

2001-2025

ALSO BY
CAY FLETCHER

ADULT FANTASY

Queer Windows: Volume 1 Spring

Queer Windows: Volume 2 Summer

The Kingdom Asleep in Thorns

Masked

TTRPG JOURNALS

The Chronicle Diary

The Chronicle Diary: Pocket-Sized

The Ultimate Chronicle Diary

The Storyteller's Chronicle Diary

ANTHOLOGIES

"Sir Rexington's Bookshop", Illusion, Northwest
Independent Writers Association

CONTENTS

AUTHOR'S NOTES

CONTENT WARNINGS

Sowing Spells is a cozy fantasy, but there are a couple of content warnings I'd like to make readers aware of:

Bullying | Dead-Naming

THE WIZARD'S GARDEN

Q. Do I need to read the original short story before I read *Sowing Spells?*
A. No! *Sowing Spells* includes an expanded version of "The Wizard's Garden" as the first story.

ON THE TOPIC OF STORIES...

Sewing Spells is a collection of interconnected short stories or vingettes rather than traditional chapters. Don't be alarmed when the 'chapters' go on longer than expected!

THE MAGIC OF THE URSHIRE COUNTRYSIDE

If you come across an animal, plant, or some other strange termominology you don't recognize, don't fret! While much of Sil and Anders' world looks and feels like ours, there is a touch of magic in it. Some of the plants are sentient. There are pipe dragons and dust mites intent on blanketing gardens with dust. While some things are inspired by real life, they are sadly, fictional. If you have questions about something in particular, check the glossary!

THE RECIPES

The recipes included in the Field Notes are ones we use in our household on a regular basis. They've been adapted to our tastes. Please feel free to try them out and adjust them as needed!

AI

No AI (Artificial Intelligence), generative or otherwise, was used in the writing, editing, design or art in this book. Everything was human created.

FORWARD

I wrote the original short story, "The Wizard's Garden" without too much fuss in January of 2022, to be the opener for my first short story collection. I'd been doing a lot of gardening during a certain global event, so it was easy to pour my desire to be arms deep in the dirt into a cozy little story about a grouchy plant shop manager and the wizard that takes a shine to him.

What I didn't expect was for so many readers to fall in love with them. Because the writing process was so quick for the original short, I never thought that people would gravitate towards it so much. Somehow it's always those projects you don't think too hard about that attract the most love in my experience.

Sil and Anders were never even supposed to be a couple, they were just friends, since its so rare to see male platonic friendships where they are close and intimate. But the readers saw them as a couple, and wanted more of them together and more of the world I'd started building. One of the most common responses to that original story that I get is that its *too* short.

So, while I didn't see myself writing cozy fantasy, here we are, almost four years later. My hopes for *Sowing Spells* are that previous readers reconnect with Sil and Anders on their continued adventures. And that new readers learn to love their silly antics.

Enjoy!

BEGINNINGS & BOTANY

STANDING IN FRONT OF THE OLD STONE shop, Sil sucked in a chest full of the crisp morning air. He had already inspected the old wooden sign hanging above the door and made certain that the flower boxes hanging below the windows looked perfect.

The opening of the garden shop was a signal that spring was close at hand.

Beren, the easy-going owner, had taken over the shop, with its huge glass greenhouse, from her parents almost a decade ago, and Sil had spent the last several years learning everything he could about the unique selection of plants they sold. He had been promoted to the senior clerk at the end of last season. Though, "promoted" might be a strong term, as the previous senior clerk had retired after a nasty tangle with an octopus bramble bush. But all the same, Sil was determined to prove that he was a valuable asset to the shop.

All the usual herbs were out in pots, trimmed to be perfectly appealing to anyone looking to add a little spice to their potions. The flowers were slowly waking up, petals stretching out as the early morning sun rose higher in the sky, light streaming in through the greenhouse glass. Sil carefully inspected each pot, pressing a finger into the cool soil and watering the ones that felt dry. Everything needed to go perfectly. A good opening day would show Beren that he had everything under control.

With the watering done, Sil straightened his apron and looked over the tables of plants. He leaned over a display of carnivorous plants and put on his bossiest tone. "Today is very important. I don't think any of you want to ruin it, so be on your best behavior."

Magda, donning a sweatshirt with her university's pixie mascot on the front, sipped loudly at her iced coffee, "Are you going to berate them if they're bad?"

Sil pushed his glasses up the bridge of his nose. "What good would that do?"

With a shrug, Magda replied, "You're the 'expert.' You tell me."

"I don't have time to go over the theories for keeping plants happy and harmonious in a shop setting," Sil said dismissively and walked over to the snapdragons. A part of him preened at the title of "expert," even if it was meant as a jab.

Most of the brightly colored blooms were still snoozing, but a few were awake and nuzzling each other. The bell that signaled the door opening rang brightly, and he heard Magda mumble a greeting.

"You lot, no biting anyone today," Sil softly instructed the sleepy flowers.

He could feel someone standing behind him. They leaned over and let the snapdragons nip at their dirt-stained fingers. "You know, if you give them a little honey, they listen better."

The man's deep voice was warmly familiar. Standing stiff as a board, Sil slipped out of the man's way, his optimistic mood suddenly darkened by the man's foreboding arrival.

"We can't spoil them in a shop setting," he told the man. "They might turn on a new owner if they don't keep up with the care that we provide. You of all people should know that, Anders."

Smiling at the snapdragons, Anders shook his head in amusement. "Honey wouldn't spoil you, would it?"

They nipped more at his fingers and rustled together in agreement.

"Is there something I can help you with, sir?" Sil snapped at the wizard.

Somehow, the man always looked disheveled. His velvet cloak was tattered at the hem and worn down to the threads in some places. The cuffs of his shirt sleeves were fraying and stained with ink and dirt. Not to mention the bits of leaves and mulch that stuck in the wizard's pale brown hair or the scruffy appearance of his stubble.

"Sir? No need to be so formal, Sil. I've been shopping here for years," Anders said as he continued tickling the snapdragons. "But I suppose you might be able to assist me with finding something."

Bristling, Sil readied himself for another of Anders' outrageous requests. He was in the shop almost every week buying plant after plant. Surely, the wizard had an entire graveyard full of the poor things. Sil could picture the stacks of pots, the soil dried out and hydrophobic, the withered remains of once lush, green foliage shivering in the breeze. Beren wouldn't have kept selling to him if she knew that the wizard was in the business of killing plants, right? It was a truly horrid image, and he shook his head to banish it from his thoughts.

He certainly hadn't anticipated Anders being their first customer of the season, and he felt it cast a bad omen over his new position. At least the man hadn't gone to Magda for help; she hardly knew the difference between the uses of lemon balm and lavender, and she was likely to let him buy whatever he wanted.

"What is it you're looking for, Mr. Anders?" Sil asked him.

Wincing at the mangling of his name, the wizard replied, "Just Anders is okay, Sil. Though I wish you'd tell me your full name." The wizard chuckled. "Sil seems so…silly."

Sil was certain that anyone nearby could sense his disdain at the pun. "And let you cast all kinds of spells on me? No. I think not."

"I'm not of the fae persuasion. I just like to address people properly. Is it Sylvestre?" There was a knowing twinkle in Anders' eyes.

"It's not short for anything," Sil replied firmly for probably the hundredth time.

"I'll figure it out eventually." Anders stroked his chin for a moment before pulling a small glass bottle out of a hidden pocket in his cloak. When Anders held it up to the light, Sil could see tiny specks of what looked like dirt flitting around. "My garden has recently been infested with dust mites. I was hoping you might have something to repel them, given the garden is my workspace."

Sil's eyes widened a bit. "And you brought them *here?*"

"They're quite contained, don't worry." Anders shook the bottle gently. "Oh, and I need something new for the front herb garden. I have all the usual things, but plain herbs are a little boring. I think we could spice things up a little."

"Salt and vinegar are the best thing to get rid of dust mites," Sil said, bristling at the thought that anyone could be bored with their garden. Plants were living things, even if they weren't as "interesting" as pets. "We have spray bottles over with the supplies."

"I don't want to kill them, just encourage them to move along."

Sil blinked at the wizard for a moment. "Are you intent upon making up headstones for your poor plants, then?"

The wizard shrugged. "Even pests have their place in the world, just as anyone does. I just don't want them dusting every plant I'm using for research. I've tried planting ivy; I heard they like that, but they haven't taken to it."

"My gram used to leave out candy near where she was okay with them living," Magda said in a bored tone. "Though, I'm pretty sure the gnomes ate most of it. They got rather fat not long after."

Anders chuckled. "I don't have gnomes yet. I'm working on cultivating some mushrooms for them first."

"Why would you want to encourage gnomes to live in your garden? They'll attract even more pests!" Sil said, horrified.

The situation was far worse than he could have imagined. Was Anders wrangling every pest and animal to feast on the poor plants he purchased every week like an open buffet?

"Pests?" Anders shook his head. "Y'know, humans are probably pests to them. Always chasing them out of their homes or blocking off their usual food. I think we should try to live more harmoniously with them."

"Why don't we come back to the dust mites?" Sil suggested, starting to feel exasperated. "What types of herbs were you looking for?"

"I thought fire curry might be fun. I don't have much time to cook, but I enjoy the smell of them," Anders said, leaning over the display of walking succulents and tickling one. The succulent curled up its plump leaves much like an anemone.

"We don't keep fire curry in the shop. It's only available on special order, as it's too dangerous." He could just imagine the scorched remains of an herb bed that was unprepared to be living next to something so volatile.

"Drat, I was really hoping for some. Spicy food makes the gray days all the better, and it's been so rainy and dull lately. I don't think I have the space for creeping oregano. Maybe some catnip? I might be able to enlist the neighborhood cats into helping with the dust mites."

Crossing his arms, Sil said, "The cats will probably chase away your other pests. If they're good mousers at least. We can order the fire curry for you to pick up. If you have an appropriate planting space for it."

"Hrm, I much prefer the cats that lie in sunspots all day. For the fire curry, though, can you deliver it?" Anders asked.

"That's not usually—"

Sil felt a hand on his shoulder and turned to find his boss smiling gently, curly moss dangling from her own salt and pepper curls. "Of course we can, Anders. You've always been one of our best customers, and I think Sil would enjoy visiting your garden."

"Thank you, Beren. I think I'll see what else you have that's new and then make that order," Anders said with a grin. "By the way, your moss is lovely."

Beren gently stroked the moss cascading down her curls, "I thought it would be a nice change from the mushrooms. They're enjoying their new log out back."

"I'm sure they are. I'll be sure to say goodbye before I'm finished shopping," Anders said before he wandered off.

"He's always so sweet," Beren said. "He once helped me save a whole crop of angry dandelions from being mowed over in a park."

"I guess a wizard would be perfect for that sort of thing," Sil grumbled. "But we don't deliver. And I don't think we should be selling him fire curry. He's not on the registry of approved owners, and he's always buying new plants. Do we really know he's properly taking care of them? His garden could be a graveyard for everything we've let him buy, for all we know."

Smiling, Beren started tickling the leaves of a new fennec fern. "If you're that concerned about the state of his plants, then you should make the delivery. Then you can see for yourself. As for the registry, wixen have exceptions. Especially ones with specialties in plants like Anders."

"Alright," Sil replied reluctantly, glancing over at the wizard who was now bent over, examining a pallet of herbs rather intently. Maybe he could rescue a few tormented plants.

Anders was pleased with the fact that he'd soon have a fire curry plant to add to his slightly neglected herb garden. Really, he'd been meaning to give the whole bed more attention. But his journal commitments had kept him holed up inside, chipping away at his editor's notes for weeks. Beren kept suggesting he employ someone to help with some of the regular chores, but he hadn't found anyone suitable. It was always a delicate matter to invite someone new into your workflow.

Striding down the lane to another row of shops, Anders glanced at the windows. The bookshop had a full display of new gardening and cookbooks. He was tempted to stop in and see if there was anything he might be interested in. But then he spotted a green cover with gold lettering propped up in the window. *M.H. Cershaw's Guide to a Green Garden.* The title was horribly boring. But then Cershaw was an unimaginative prick who was more interested in signing books than research or useful information.

Anders shuffled past the bookshop and instead popped into the sleepy café at the end of the lane. A lazy firefox was sprawled out on the counter, taking full advantage of the sun filtering through the transom above the door. Its fur shifted colors in the light, and tiny sparks flew off its tail when it flicked back and forth, only hinting at its magical inclinations.

"And how are you today, Brandr?" he asked the firefox, carefully scratching behind his ears.

Stretching out further, Brandr's paws batted at the loose threads of Anders' cuffs. With a large yawn, he chuffed, his tail twitching.

"Clearly well," the owner responded, appearing from the back room, wiping her hands on her apron. "Your usual, Anders?"

"That would be wonderful. Thank you."

She nodded, reddish curls bouncing as she started on his lavender and mint coffee. With a touch of her fingers, the milk pitcher began to steam. He always preferred oat milk, to help give the coffee an earthly undertone. But there was always a magical flair to Wendy's drinks, an indescribable touch that no one else could replicate. That was one of the brilliant things about magic. It was so personal and unique.

"What are you up to today?" she asked him, stripping lavender buds off the stem.

"Just dropped by Beren's to put in an order for a fire curry plant. I have some experiments I want to try out."

"Of the plant kind or the food kind?"

Anders chuckled. "Both?"

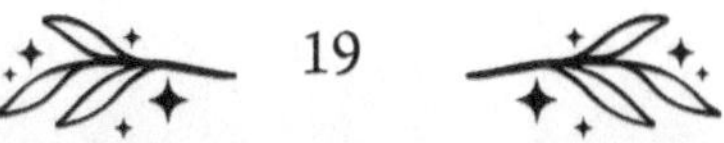

"Good luck with that, then. My brother-in-law tried adding fire curry to a holiday meal once. He's not allowed to cook family dinners anymore."

"Well, no one else has to suffer through trying my cooking at least."

Wendy held out a to go cup with his drink along with a flyer. "The bookshop asked if we'd hand these out."

He wrinkled his nose and shoved the green flyer into his pocket. "Thanks." A couple of coins manifested into his hand, and he held them out for Wendy.

"Thought you'd be interested 'cause it's your field…" she said, taking the coins.

"Eh, Cershaw's not my cup of tea."

Shrugging, Wendy picked up the firefox and nuzzled his head. "No worries. Good luck with the fire curry. See you next time."

He nodded in appreciation as he headed out the door to take the long way home. Fog still clung to the country roads, hiding fence posts and causing the animals to appear as strange apparitions in the distance. Normally, he didn't mind his solitude. It allowed Anders to live how he wished, without the interference of others or their expectations. His plants and garden were plenty enough company. But on rare occasions, he yearned for someone to be waiting for him at home.

When he reached his mailbox, he fished out his post and sorted through it as he walked up the cobblestone path to the cottage. One of the letters was from his editor, probably lamenting that Anders still owed him half a manuscript and a handful of articles. But by Anders' calculations, he still had a few weeks on those deadlines before the poor man became desperate enough to show up on his doorstep.

There were some postcards from his parents. And a notice from the Mycological Society for Wixen. He tore the letter open as he hurried into the cottage and plopped down in the sitting room to scan through its contents. He'd been petitioning the society to be allowed to study some of the fungi native to the moors for months. Given how close it was to the full moon, he was relieved that the letter finally contained permission for the study.

It would be a bit of a whirlwind trip. And of course he'd have to bring the cottage along. The letter was too short notice not to. Luckily, the grounds already had the correct sigils marked out to move the cottage to a new temporary home. It would be like shepherds and farmers bringing out little sheds to stay in while they watched over livestock in far off fields and grazing land. Only, he'd have the comfort of his own bed.

The fire curry plant delivery would have to be planned around this excursion. But that shouldn't be too difficult. If he had an assistant or apprentice, they could handle the delivery. But there was no sense in wishing for the unlikely. He had a garden to prepare.

Sil slid off his bicycle and leaned it against the fence once he reached the address scribbled down on the order pad. A neglected mailbox stood atop a post being choked by ivy, but there was no sign of a house or even a hut beyond the old wooden gate. He double-checked the number on the pad and the one on the mailbox, and they seemed to match. If the wizard had somehow gotten his address wrong, Sil wouldn't be surprised. Beren had made it sound like the wizard had an extensive garden, but all Sil could see was a poorly tended lawn and some scrappy shrubs along the fence line.

Stepping over the worst of the mud puddles in the road, he tried to see if maybe there was another house hidden behind the collection of scraggly oak trees, but the countryside was only broken up by wandering lines of fencing and the occasional hedge.

"Well, this is perfect," Sil said to himself.

Going back to the gate, he noticed a small sign which had flipped over in the wind.

"'State your name for deliveries?'" Sil read out loud, glancing at the empty lot beyond the fence.

He desperately hoped this wasn't some kind of joke.

Eventually, he called out, "Sil here with your fire curry plant, Wixen Kessel."

Nothing happened as he stood there on the quiet, empty lane. The longer he stood there, the dumber he felt. Clearly, this was Anders somehow getting back at him for the years of underhanded comments, and he was going to have to bike all the way back to the shop with a chilly, grumpy fire curry plant.

"Oh, you're early," Anders' voice came from down the lane.

Sil jumped, catching himself against the gate as he turned to see Anders striding down the lane without a care in the world. The wizard was attempting to wrestle something

back under his cloak.

"Where did you come from?"

"I was visiting my neighbor," Anders said, grinning at him as if appearing from thin air was a normal thing.

"So, this is the right address?"

"Of course!" Anders opened the gate and started walking before stopping abruptly. "Damn, I forgot the cottage out on the moors. That's a bit inconvenient."

"I would think so. I'll just get the fire curry out and be on my way, Wixen Kessel," Sil said.

The last thing he wanted was to be involved in whatever wizarding problems Anders was currently having. That was how someone ended up a wizard's apprentice—or worse, friend.

"No, no, at least have some tea for your trouble. Just give me a moment to call back the cottage," Anders said.

As he wandered off the stone path and into the front garden, a tiny, almost fuzzy, black head popped up out of his collar. Little tendrils of smoke twisted around its whiskers as the pipe dragon's golden eyes fixated on Sil.

"It's really alright; no need to go out of your way-" Sil insisted, hurriedly pulling on the oven mitts and fireproof apron he'd brought with him. The faster he could hand over the fire curry, the better. All hopes of rescuing any suffering plants had vanished from his thoughts.

"Ah, found it!" Anders declared, either ignoring Sil's protests or not hearing him. He held up a brick and waved it for Sil to see.

"Oooookay, time to get the hell out of here," Sil mut-

tered to himself, unzipping the heat-proof grocery bag that was strapped into the basket on the front of his bicycle. "Don't burn me. I'm just giving you over to a crazy wizard. You'll be fine. He has a pipe dragon, so I'm sure that will go over well."

He could feel something looming over him, and he jumped again, nearly dropping the fire curry as he turned to find Anders standing next to him

"You like talking to them, don't you?" Anders asked.

"I, um…" Sil hoped that Anders hadn't heard him calling the wizard crazy.

The pipe dragon wrapped its narrow, snake-like body around Anders' neck so it could watch Sil more closely. He was impressed that Anders had a pipe dragon, seeing as how they'd nearly disappeared after being treated as common pests.

"Don't worry, they can hear you at least," Anders assured him. "And more people talk to 'inanimate' objects than you think. It's not that strange." Chirping, the pipe dragon tried coiling down Anders' arm. "Ah, ah, ah, leave the nice garden clerk alone. He doesn't need you biting him."

"I'm sure he doesn't bite too hard," Sil said.

Anders snorted. "Maybe not, but he tends to get attached to strangers."

"I didn't think pipe dragons were still around."

"They're pretty rare. I rescued this guy from a drainpipe a few years ago. I'm hoping to start up a new colony of them here."

"That would be nice. I know a lot of gardeners like them around to help keep mites and rodents out of their gardens."

Anders rubbed the little dragon's head "Hear that? You

should be helping me with the dust mites." It chirped inno-cently before retreating under Anders collar. "I'm afraid he's no good at mite hunting. I've got flower mites now, too."

Sil frowned. "They shouldn't be out this time of year. It's still too chilly."

"True, but they're around all the same. Speaking of, let's get that fire curry settled before it catches its death," Anders said, heading back towards the gate.

Carefully holding the fire curry out in front of him, Sil gaped at the moss-covered, thatched cottage sitting where previously there had been an empty lot. Smoke filtered from the chimney, and a large stone bed of herbs lay under the front windows. Lush greenery surrounded the cottage, filling the yard to the point of bursting.

"Are you alright?" Anders asked him, concern in his tone.

Nodding slowly, Sil looked back and forth between the neighboring lots and the newly appeared cottage. A robin landed on the edge of the roof and sang happily, as if the house had in fact been there the whole time. It was a cute little house, and it fit with Anders' personality. Though, there was no possibility that all the tender, tropical and rare plants that Sil had witnessed Anders purchase over the years could fit in it. Unless it was bigger on the inside.

"Sil?" Anders was peering at him, hand outstretched as if he was ready to shake Sil's shoulder.

Coming back to his senses, Sil cleared his throat. "Where do you want it?"

Anders held open the gate for Sil and pointed towards

the herb bed. "I think out front might be best."

"It might enjoy a warmer spot. This bed is east facing."

"Hrm, well, the south side of the garden is pretty full. And the herb bed is warmed."

"The soil is warmed?"

"Yes, I have ceramic pipes with warm water running through them throughout the bed. No magic required. It's a bit of an experiment."

Sil wasn't familiar with the technique, but it could work in theory, even if it was unconventional. He set the fire curry on the stone edge of the bed and pulled off one of the oven mitts so he could rest his hand on the soil. It was warmer than he would have expected, almost like the sun had been shining on it all day.

"I guess that might be okay. Though, really, you should have a soil thermometer to ensure the bed is keeping the right temperature. If you mulched this bed, it would help keep that heat in better."

Anders nodded. "I keep forgetting to do that. Maybe I could pay you for some yard work? If you're interested, I mean."

"You'd pay me to do yard work?" Sil asked skeptically, moving the fire curry to a spot in the bed where it might do well and was far enough from the other plants. He could always use the extra money. But was working for Anders worth it?

"Yes, Beren clearly trusts you. And you seem to care a lot about plants. It would give me more time for research. And the plants would enjoy the extra attention," Anders said, wandering around the corner of the house towards the back garden.

Sil followed him, surprised by the sheer amount of rare and unusual plant life all seemingly coexisting in such a temperate area. Half of the plants—large, brightly colored flowers; towering palms; and other tender-stemmed plants—thrived in tropical or arid climates, which were very different from the cool, dreary, gray days of early spring in the rolling hills of Guinen. The path along the side of the house even seemed pleasantly warm compared to the front, which couldn't all be due to the sun.

"How do you have so many plants out of season?" Sil asked, pushing his glasses up his nose to examine a dragon orchid growing from the trunk of a palm. It was thriving against all odds. Maybe Anders wasn't just letting his plants die. The cost of replacing them would be enormous given the selection.

"A micro-climate spell. Come, I want to show you where the mites have been troublesome," Anders said, waving him along the moss-covered path.

"Leave it to a wizard to figure out that kind of spell, I guess," Sil muttered to himself, a bit jealous. He'd never be able to keep even a fraction of what was in Anders' garden in his tiny apartment. Anders' freedom to buy and keep whatever he liked had always upset Sil, who was limited by both budget and space.

As he entered the back garden, Sil stopped and stared at what appeared to be a forest of every plant he'd ever seen or heard of. Sections were marked off by woven fences and paths winding around and disappearing behind taller, bushier vegetation. He wanted to spend the hours it would take to wander Anders' backyard with his notebook, scribbling down all the varieties he wanted to look up.

"How? All this wasn't here before."

Anders grinned. "The garden is connected to the cottage, so if I move, the garden doesn't get left behind to fall into disrepair. It's a rather simple translocation spell, actually."

He knelt and motioned along with one of the paths which curved off to the left. As Sil followed it with his eyes, he realized that the connecting paths helped form a large magical inscription.

"The spell is built into the garden?" Sil asked.

He quickly let it sink in that someone who had taken the time to magically connect their garden to their house so it wouldn't be left behind was unlikely to be a bad plant-parent on purpose. In fact, Anders had always asked questions about the plants before he ended up purchasing them. It left Sil feeling uncomfortable about judging the man so harshly based on their limited interactions at the shop.

"Yes, clever, don't you think?" Anders asked enthusiastically.

"I would think so. But I don't know that much about magic."

"I could teach you some of the basic things."

"Like the micro-climate spell?" Sil asked hopefully.

"Probably. Though, it might benefit you to learn the fundamentals first. A watering spell might be a good start…" Anders said before trailing off into thought.

"I can start next week," Sil found himself saying before

he could stop himself.

"Are you sure?"

"So long as you're fine with me working around my usual shifts at the shop."

"I don't see why that would be a problem. I'm usually around doing one thing or another."

Sil held out his hand to shake. "Great! I'll see you next week, then."

"Not so worried about entering a contract with a wizard now, are you?" Anders asked as he took Sil's hand in agreement.

"You're paying me. If anything, you should be more concerned about what my rate is," Sil said smugly, though Anders' comment did start his mind spinning into an infinite number of possibilities.

Anders shook his head with a smile. "True. Maybe I should have negotiated that first."

"You've agreed, so you'll just have to suffer knowing you didn't."

"Are you certain you're not a wizard looking to bespell someone?"

Sil shrugged. "We haven't had a wizard in the family before."

Turning Sil's hand over in his own, Anders examined the lines on Sil's palm. "If you say so. There's never a bad time to add a wixen to the family."

Sil shivered as Anders' finger traced a line from his palm up to his wrist. What could Anders tell from his hand that he couldn't tell just looking at him? He doubted he would be any

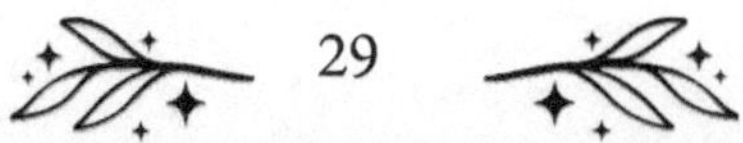

good at whatever magic Anders tried to teach him anyway. His talents lay strictly with raising plants and his mediocre cooking.

Pulling his hand away, Sil cleared his throat and straightened his glasses, "Well, we have an agreement, so…I'll see you next week."

"Yes. Be sure to bring a hat. The weather is supposed to be sunny, and I wouldn't want you to get sunburnt."

Sil rolled his eyes as he followed the path back around the cottage and down to the gate. He looked up at the cottage and the garden before stuffing his oven mitts and apron into the basket and turning down the muddy road.

He wished he had anything close to the garden that Anders had. Instead, he had a lonely shelf over his kitchen sink stuffed with an array of tiny pots of herbs and a pothos his mother had given him to nurse back to health. It was ninety-five percent function, and he had nowhere to expand in his tiny flat.

The garden had started to pick up on Anders' giddy mood. Or maybe it was just happy to have another set of hands to tend to it. Either way, the garden had been lusher and buzzing with energy since Sil's visit and his agreement to come and assist with some chores.

Anders had gone through every little section and bed one-by-one, making lists of what each one needed done. Weeding was a general chore. But spring brought fertilizing, pruning, thinning out, transplanting, reseeding—and there were the dust mites to keep an eye on. Not to mention the gnomes, and the neighbor's flock of geese that liked to sneak into the garden. Plus, there was the upkeep on all the micro-climate spells. Sil probably couldn't take that on, but the other things were perfectly doable for the non-magically inclined. Not that Anders believed that Sil was completely unmagical. Most people had some spark buried under their self-doubt.

The young man just had something about him, the way plants reacted to him, that made Anders certain that he had some underutilized magical talent. But they could worry about testing Sil's aptitude later. To start with, there was the chore list, top of which was settling in the new fire curry.

After gathering some tools and a bucket, Anders looked over the unruly state of the herb bed. He really had let his maintenance grow lax over the early part of the year. The mint was out of control. But then that was its happiest state, taking over every inch of space and strangling out everything else. Repotting it was the best option, then he wouldn't have to worry about the fire curry burning it. He could keep it in the kitchen window for now.

Trimming and pruning along, it didn't take long to tidy the herb bed up. Anders got the fire curry planted and was happy to have a visit from the little pipe dragon once it discovered Anders had stirred up all the worms. It had started coming out more recently, which Anders hoped was a good sign. Pipe dragons brought luck, according to the old wives' tales.

"Anders!"

He dropped the bucket of clippings and debris and froze at the sound of his editor screaming his name. Looking down the path to the road, Torlind was climbing out of a cab, fighting against the tangle of the seatbelt in her haste.

"Don't you dare move!"

Looking down at the little pipe dragon happily munching on a worm, Anders sighed, so much for the old wives' tales.

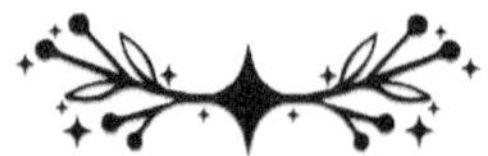

An ominous quiet had settled over the cottage. Torlind had planted herself in the sitting room, glaring across the hall into Anders' office. Every time he moved as if he might get up from his desk, she tapped her foot loudly. At least he could refill his tea mug with a gentle caress of the stoneware handle. But he hated being watched while he worked. The silence was broken by the flutter of pages every so often, as Torlind worked through what Anders had finished with her red pen.

"If only you were done, I'd say we would be on track to hit our deadlines," Torlind muttered mostly to herself.

"I'm nearly done…" Anders said, re-reading a paragraph for what felt like the hundredth time. He carefully moved the page over to his "finished" pile.

"*Nearly* isn't done, though, is it?"

Anders sucked in a deep breath. "I told you I had to take that trip to the moors—"

Torlind pointed the end of her pen at him and asked, "Is your current book about mushrooms?"

"No, but—"

"Then it could have waited!"

Spinning around in his chair to face her, Anders waved vaguely towards the window. "The season would have ended." It was a beautifully misty, cool morning that would be perfect for mushroom studies.

"You could have gone in the fall."

"I'm a mood researcher, you know that, Torlind!"

Gritting her teeth, Torlind replied, "Yes, I know. And I'd love to be able to snap my fingers and make you an all-the-time researcher."

"I mean, someone might be able to figure that out…" Anders mused.

"If you don't get at least ten more pages done today, I'm calling in Auda to ghost write for you."

Dropping his pen, Anders grabbed his mug and stomped into the kitchen. "Don't you *dare* call her!"

"Your sister would be more than willing to help."

"I don't need her help. Especially with 'ghost writing.' I write my own books, do my own research, etc. I'm not going to stoop so low!"

Following Anders into the kitchen, Torlind refilled her coffee mug. "You can't do everything all on your own, Anders! The garden is overgrown, the cottage is in an absolute state, and I could hardly even find your articles buried under all your books and papers! You need help."

"And I'm getting it," he argued, "Just not in the form of a ghost writer."

Torlind gaped at him. "Really?"

"Yes, I just hired an assistant to help with the garden."

"You're letting someone else touch the garden? Are you

sure you're not ill?"

"Yes. Why?"

"You hardly let *anyone* in the garden. You made me go through hours of 'plant training' before I was allowed to water anything. And you still shoo Auda and your parents out of it whenever they're here to visit."

"That's because Auda always brings along Crusher, and he tries to dig up half the garden."

"And my plant training?"

"You knew nothing about them. So, I needed to make sure you wouldn't ruin any of my experiments," Anders replied matter of factly.

"So, who is it?" Torlind asked.

"His name is Sil. He works for Beren at the plant shop."

Torlind looked like she was trying to place the name. "Is that the one with glasses or the one who always has the iced coffee?"

"The glasses."

"Ahhhh…" Torlind nodded into her coffee mug, eyebrows raising.

"What's that mean?" Anders demanded.

"Nothing. Just interesting. He's very prickly."

"He's good with plants. He talks to them."

"Riiiiight," his editor grabbed a muffin from a box that she'd brought with her.

"I know you're trying to insinuate things."

"Not at all. Now excuse me, I need to call your sister to gossip."

Anders startled away from the counter. "What! No!

Don't you dare tell Auda anything!"

Torlind smirked. "Finish your pages and I won't."

Anders opened his mouth to argue but instead grumbled something about abusing their working relationship and retreated to his office.

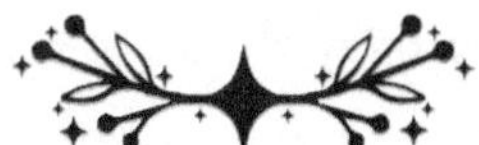

Anders' garden was quickly becoming Sil's favorite place, even if Anders' promise to teach him a few spells wasn't going well. After not even a week, he had already managed to chase the dust mites from the lily patch back to a specially prepared fern patch at the rear of the garden. Though he suspected that without a more permanent solution, they would likely move back. He'd also discovered a family of gnomes living under an old willow and convinced them that stealing the red caps for haberdashery purposes wouldn't be needed if Anders provided some tiny wool caps. Anders had been a bit miffed, but Sil insisted that leaving the mushrooms alone would be better for the garden's overall ecosystem.

The pipe dragon had decided that Sil's apron pocket was the perfect nap spot and would often scurry out of a bush to slip into it. Anders had assured him that it was good luck to keep a sleeping dragon on you and that the risk of burns was minimal.

One of the many strange things about his new job, though, was Anders' insistence that he always leave before dark. The wizard never gave an explanation, and while Sil was curious, he didn't want to risk upsetting him and losing the opportunity to work in the garden.

"You've been here every day for the last week. Shouldn't you take a day off?" Anders asked him as he handed over a warm cup of tea.

Sil shrugged and sipped at the tea absently with one hand and pruned an unruly rhododendron that was overgrowing one of the paths with the other. "I'd just be at home. Reading. Or taking care of my own plants."

"Oh, you shouldn't neglect them," Anders said worriedly.

"They're fine. They don't need nearly as much attention as your garden does." Namely due to their inferior number in comparison, he didn't add out loud.

Anders sighed and leaned his head back. "Okay, just don't exhaust yourself. Beren wouldn't forgive me if I wore out her favorite employee."

"Favorite?" Sil asked, a bit surprised.

"Of course. Why else would she promote you? No offense, but you're a little young to be the lead clerk. And grumpy."

"I'm not that young. I live by myself, thank you." He couldn't refute the grumpy comment, though Anders didn't seem to mind his disposition much.

"You're twenty."

Sil rounded on the wizard. "Twenty-one! And you're not much older than me. And besides, you're a wizard! Who says you should have that much power and responsibility?"

Setting aside his tea, Anders leaned in towards Sil. "I've been training since I was a child."

"And I've been raising plants since I was a child."

"What was your first rare plant, then?" Anders asked,

challenging him.

"Tuft tails. They only grow along a single riverbank and only flower for about a week. I had one when I was ten and kept it alive in my bedroom window."

"Tuft tails?" the wizard asked while inspecting the leaves of a fern.

"Commonly known as feather duster plants," Sil explained smugly.

"Ahhhhh, alright, not bad."

"Not bad?" Any normal plant enthusiast would be impressed, but of course, Anders was far from normal.

"It's not as if you were raising fire curry at age ten."

"That's because fire curry shouldn't be raised by a child!" Sil said, outraged.

Anders chuckled. "You're very talented Sil."

"Don't patronize me," Sil said, setting down his tea to chop away at the rhododendron. At least the woody branches could afford to withstand Sil's annoyance.

Gently moving a few fern fronds out of the way of Sil's clippers, he said, "I'm not patronizing you. You *are* talented."

"Then why can't I make that stupid watering spell work?" Sil asked.

"You've only been practicing it for a week. It's expected that you wouldn't be able to make it work yet."

"How long did it take you?" Sil asked him.

"A couple...days."

"See?"

"That's only because I already knew other spells. It goes quicker once you know a bit more. You'll get the hang of it."

Anders smiled at him with that stupid grin of his.

Sil snipped off the last few rhododendron branches that were intruding on the walkway. "I'm going to go mulch the front herb bed. Unless you need to torment me with something else."

Anders smiled, "I'm not tormenting you."

"Uh-huh."

"You agreed to work for me, might I remind you."

"For the *plants*."

"You wound me, Silvan," Anders replied dramatically.

"It's not Silvan. Just Sil," he grumbled, careful not to drop the shears on the pipe dragon's head in his apron pocket in his annoyance.

"Okay, okay. I'll be back here looking over the spider plants. They seem out of sorts."

Taking his tea, Sil went around to the front of the house where the herb bed was. There were all the usual suspects—rosemary, oregano, six types of basil, marjoram, thyme, and of course the new fire curry—among numerous other plants Sil wasn't familiar with. Some spearmint was taking over the back corner of the raised planting bed, threatening to encroach on the rest of the plants. At least everything had been trimmed recently, and most of the weeds had been pulled. The mulch would help keep future weeds from taking over and the bed looking neat.

He set aside his tea and started trimming back the mint, making sure to toss the leaves into a bowl for Anders to use later. With all of Anders' spells, Sil was surprised that he hadn't cast one to prune all the plants at the correct times.

Though it did give him something to do. And a chance to play in Anders' garden.

The pipe dragon slithered out of his apron pocket and coiled around his neck, its whiskers tickling his jaw.

"Hey, stop that!" Sil tried to rearrange the pipe dragon. "Settle down or you have to go back into the apron."

Chirping at him, the pipe dragon finally settled on his shoulder.

Sighing, Sil started on the oregano. "Why is he so impossible?"

The pipe dragon trilled almost in understanding.

"And why can't I get this damn spell to work?" Sil asked, setting down the shears and mimicking the hand motions that Anders had shown him.

A few tiny drops of water appeared between Sil's hands, and the pipe dragon raised its head and chirped happily before the drops fizzled into steam.

"See? I'm useless."

The pipe dragon nuzzled his neck.

"It's fine. I'll always have plants."

Nipping at his neck, the pipe dragon twirled its body around Sil's upper arm.

"And you. So long as you stop chewing on me," Sil told it, getting back to tidying up the herb bed. "Now, all of you, how is the fire curry fitting in? I don't see any scorch marks, so that's good. Though, mint, if you keep trying to choke out the other herbs, I'm going to take a trowel to you and move you to your own pot. So, behave, won't you?"

He sighed when there was no response from the mint.

There was never an expectation they would talk back, though some of the more magically inclined plants would respond in other ways. Sil was getting far too used to Anders talking back. Even in the week he'd been there, he was finding Anders' company enjoyable, and his life away from the garden incredibly lonely. That might have been the largest contributor to Sil being willing to ride his bike across town and out into the country lanes to Anders' cottage.

As he finished pruning and put a layer of mulch on the soil, his mind began to wander, and he stared at his reflection in the window that the herb bed stood under. He unconsciously pushed his glasses back up his nose and grumbled at the sight of leaves and twigs stuck in his hair. His parents always complained about his penchant to drag the outdoors inside.

The window above the herb bed was home to a spider who had taken it upon itself to weave a web that could only be rivaled by the best lacemakers. Spiders were always a good sign in a garden, as they helped take care of flies and other pests. Though, a thought struck him. Growing up, his tuft tail had always prevented the house spiders from making their webs in his bedroom window. If they tried, the tuft tails would sweep their fibrous flowers across the corners of the window, gently removing the webs but not harming the spider.

Tuft tails might be the answer to Anders' dust mite problem. The pests were bound to make their way back to the lilies if left to their own devices, if not spread to any number of other plants. But a line of tuft tails around their current home in the ferns would gently prevent them from leaving the area. Anders might have to create a new micro-climate spell to keep them happy, but it was worth a try.

As Sil ran around to the backyard, the pipe dragon slipped under his collar so it wouldn't lose its grip.

Sil skidded to a stop in front of Anders and said, "I need tuft tails."

Anders stopped mid-spell and blinked up at him. "Right now?"

"To keep the dust mites contained."

The spark of realization dawned over Anders' face. "Of course! Why didn't I think of that?"

"Because you didn't raise one when you were ten."

Anders pulled Sil into a hug and spun him around. "And that's why I have you, Sirik."

"Still just Sil," Sil said, too surprised to push Anders away.

"I can probably have Beren order some."

"You'll need a micro-climate spell for them to do well," Sil said, finally escaping the hug.

"Right, you can give me the details on that. Tomorrow, though. It's almost dark, so you should get going."

Sil hadn't even noticed how late it had gotten, "I still have things to put away. I don't mind it being a little dark."

Anders frowned. "It's not ready for you to see yet."

"What isn't ready?" Maybe Anders had mentioned something and Sil had just tuned him out.

"Your surprise."

Sil snorted. "Surprise? Why would you have a surprise for me?"

Anders scratched the back of his neck sheepishly. "Because you've been such a big help."

"I've been working for you for a week."

"At Beren's shop, too, though. You always have ideas for new varieties of plants, or how to help them grow healthier. You've worked there for almost five years, right?"

"Yes, but I help everyone there. It's my job."

"Even slightly crazy wizards."

Sil felt his face grow hot. "I shouldn't have called you crazy."

Anders shrugged. "It's okay. It happens a lot."

"That doesn't make it okay."

"I guess not, but I'd rather have a friend than dwell on that."

He turned towards the garden and clapped his hands together twice. As if on command, every plant and bloom in the garden stood at attention, looking their best and brightest. A swarm of fireflies flew into the middle of the garden and began blinking, spelling out, "Thank you Sil."

"I wanted to give them more time to practice, but..."

"You did all this for me?" Sil asked, tears starting to well up.

"Of course."

Sil wiped at his eyes and wrapped his arms around Anders' neck. "You're not a crazy wizard. You're a silly one."

"So...does this mean we're friends?"

"Yes, so long as you don't have plans of making me an apprentice."

Anders started to laugh. "You're the one that wanted to

learn magic! And somehow, I think you already are."

"I am *not* your apprentice, learning magic or not. I'm just an assistant."

"Don't worry about the label so much. What do you want to learn next?"

Sil nearly started a retort, but stopped himself. "As much as possible."

field Notes
1

Garden Mites

the mites will often congregate
around a favorite food source to
dust it with their spores

Family: Pyroglyphidae

Habitat: humid, dark spaces, overgrown hedges, burrows, and nests of larger fauna

Native to: Most gardens and wild areas.

Common Names: Garden Soot, Dust Sprite, Garden Dust Mite, Black Spot Mite

Or just HORRIBLE, plant destroying _pests!!!_

Sil suggested Tuft Tails as a solution for the garden mites infesting the northern corner of the garden. Since he's raised them before, I'm not horribly worried.

Though they do need a lot of specialized care and can be temperamental until they get used to you. I think they'll have plenty of space in that spot and shouldn't bother the mushrooms nearby.

I wouldn't count on it.

Check the moss for sporophytes they're a little overdue...

Things To-Do!

- ✦ Speak with Beren about ordering Tuft Tails
- ✦ Visit original habitat in Urshire
- ✦ Develop micro-climate spell for them
- ✦ Test creek soil for any diseases
- ✦ ~~Figure out something to do about the gnomes before they become a problem~~
- ✦ Investigate cost of tiny hats ← *Absolutely not!*
- ✦ Reorganize to-do list for Sil (garden tasks) as requested

Don't forget anything.

Oh and you need to show me where all your tools and supplies are kept.

SOWING SPELLS

At least Sil liked his surprise. Even if it wasn't fully ready. The fireflies really were good sports. It helps that the pipe dragon hasn't been chasing them since Sil started coming over. Someone down the road mentioned they might have spotted another pipe dragon in their garden bed. I'll have to go check on that next week and see. Oh, and make sure to feed the hedge animals.

I really need to finish up that paper on moss life cycles, I don't think Torlind will allow me another extension on it. And it's that time of year, so my sister could show up at any moment! Maybe I should warn Sil about her. Though they'll probably get along...in tormenting me. Sadly I don't think my schedule could accommodate a sudden months-long trip. And leaving would make Sil's work more complicated. I'm not sure he's familiar with portal travel.

Tuft Tails

Sil,
You can draw the tuft tails in here! If you know the classification info, can you add it?

My drawing is terrible. So no.

Thanks!

Classification info goes here!

I added what I know for sure

Family: *Typhaceae*

Habitat: *rich, swampy soil and riverbanks*
Some also like the edges of bogs

Native to: *Northern shore of the Ingary River outside of Urshire*

~~Sil's childhood windowsill!~~

Tuft Tails are not NATIVE to my windowsill! I had them in a pot!

Common Names: *Feather Duster Plant, Dragon Tails*

REMEDIES & ROOMATES

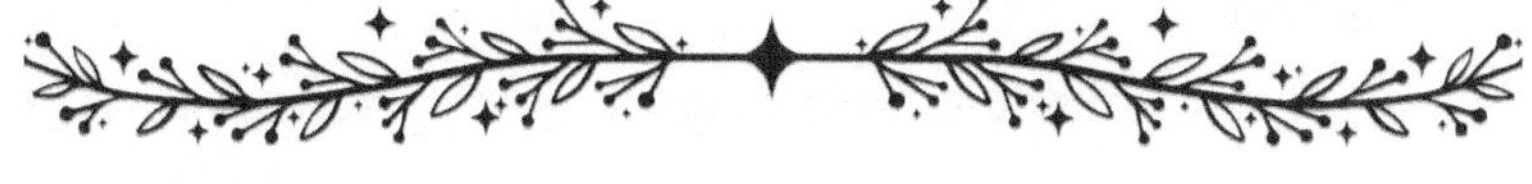

THE NOTICE HAD BEEN SITTING ON SIL'S kitchen counter for a week now, looming over his thoughts every time he watered the herbs in the kitchen window or reheated his coffee. A red circle had been scribbled around the date that his lease ended to ensure he didn't miss it. As if the impending thought of no longer having a place to live in less than three weeks would really leave his brain. He had options, which were, in no particular order: to move back in with his parents, beg an acquaintance to put him up, set up a tent on the side of the road, or cross his fingers that one of the housing applications he'd submitted in a panic would pan out.

There was still plenty of time to find a solution. Three weeks was more than enough. He didn't have much when it came to possessions to begin with. The moving timeline might be tricky, though. Working for the garden shop and for

Anders meant he didn't have a lot of free time to search for a new apartment or pack, but he had a few free days saved up that he could use to move...once he figured out where he'd be moving to.

Sil was leaning back against the sink, trying not to think too much, when Anders' voice startled him. "Sil? Do you have a moment?"

Turning around slowly to face the window, Sil was greeted by the wizard instead of the drizzle dripping down the windowpane. Anders' nose and cheeks were red, as if he'd been out in the cold, and he raised a pair of thick goggles to his forehead.

"I'm a bit waylaid with inspecting the roof moss," Anders said, "so I was hoping you had some time to come by and tend to a few things in the garden."

Blinking stupidly, Sil's brain tried to process the fact that his friend had opened a portal in his kitchen window rather than call him on the phone.

"The roof moss?"

"Yes, it hasn't sent up its sporophytes yet, and I was getting concerned."

Peering into the portal, Sil realized that Anders was laid out on the thatch of his roof, surrounded by an array of tweezers and sample jars.

"You're on the roof on your own! What if you fall?"

Anders shrugged, propping himself up on his elbows. "I cast a movement arrest spell all along the roof line. It's quite fun to roll off of actually. You just float down to the ground."

"You still didn't tell anyone you were going on the roof."

"Well, you know now."

"Now!"

"Can you come over?"

Sil pinched the bridge of his nose, pushing up his glasses. "Yeah. I'll be there in forty minutes or so."

"Oh, you don't have to bike all the way here." Anders reached out his hand. "Just come through here."

"Through what?"

"The portal, you silly gooseberry!"

The wizard had gotten up on his knees, reaching through the portal into Sil's kitchen. Anders' hand traversed the portal, sending ripples across its surface. As he took Anders' clammy hand, Sil's feet lifted off the floor, and he nearly split his coffee.

"Careful," the wizard said. "Just relax. Step up and through."

His feet pedaled in the air for a few moments before Sil was able to get purchase on the edge of his sink. Anders gently pulled him forward, and Sil tumbled through the portal and onto Anders' roof, dropping his coffee mug before clinging to the wizard as a sudden rush of vertigo and the sweet smell of recent rain washed over him.

"I've got you."

"Get me down this instant," Sil said quietly.

"Alright. You're not afraid of heights, are you?" Anders asked, careful to avoid the moss as he got to his feet.

"I wasn't!" Sil snapped, squeezing his eyes shut.

"The quickest way down is to jump."

"Jump? How about a ladder?"

Anders had nudged them to the edge of the roof. "It'll

be fine."

Sil looked up at the roiling clouds to avoid looking down. "Anders, magic me a ladder. I am not ju—"

He felt Anders' hand slowly slipping out of his as the wizard stepped off the roof and began sinking.

"What happens if that spell fails and you break your neck?" Sil demanded. "I'll have to take care of all the plants all by myself while you recover!"

Anders chuckled until he began sneezing. "Don't worry about that. The spell is flawless."

Sil knelt, clinging to the thatch with one hand and trying to grab onto Anders with the other. "You've been out in all the rain we've been having, haven't you?"

"No, I'm fine!" Anders insisted, pulling out his handkerchief. "Will you just come down?"

After a long moment, Sil stretched his foot over the edge of the roof, feeling the air as if there might be some invisible structure there to support him. While there wasn't a ladder or a step, there was a strange feeling of resistance and warmth that swirled around his leg. He inched further over the ledge, both feet dangling over the drop. Anders was now looking up at him from the ground, having floated down to safety. With his mind still boggling at the strangeness of it, Sil closed his eyes and slid off the roof, his legs treading air as he sank to the cobbled path.

"See?" Anders asked him.

"You still could've gotten the ladder."

"Or you could trust—" He was cut off by a loud sneeze as he held his handkerchief to his nose.

"I'll get the kettle on," Sil sighed and headed towards the back door into the kitchen.

Dishes were stacked precariously in and around the sink. He didn't understand why Anders didn't just use a spell to have the dishes wash themselves. That was a far more useful application of magic than a spell to make you float off a roof. Then again, logic wasn't Anders' strong suit.

Finding the kettle behind a stack of pots, Sil filled it and shooed the pipe dragon off the top of the wood stove so he could set it down. It sneezed as it wrapped affectionately up his arm, spraying a puff of soot against Sil's sleeve. Sil scratched under its chin once it settled across his shoulders.

"You're not getting sick, too, are you, little guy?"

It simply nuzzled Sil's neck, its fluffed up scales a bit colder than usual. That was worrying, especially since it had just been curled up on the stove.

"The poor little garden noodle's been sniffling for days," Anders lamented as he dropped his goggles and notebook on top of a mess of papers before sinking into a chair.

Sil crossed his arms over his chest, leaning back against the edge of the stove. "You need to take better care of yourself. I don't have time to work at the garden shop, take care of things here, *and* deal with you being sick."

"Stop saying that," Anders grumbled.

"What? That you're sick because you spend more time out in the rain with the moss than you do taking care of your-self?"

"Yes! That! Once you say it, you can't take it back." Anders sneezed again, nearly falling out of his chair.

"You're being ridiculous. If you're sick, you need to rest."

"I have work to finish."

"Work that can't be delayed?" Sil asked skeptically.

"Yes." He pouted.

"Like what?"

Pointing to the roof, Anders said, "The sporophytes, for one!"

"I'm sure they'll come out when they're ready," Sil replied.

"Then the burping lilies. I haven't mulched the tropical beds yet. And my editor keeps hounding me about some paper that's due next week," Anders said as he ticked off the items one-by-one on his fingers.

Sil rubbed his temples. "You hired me to do the extra work like mulching the garden so you could focus on your research."

"I know, but I still like getting my hands dirty."

"Look, focus on the paper so your editor doesn't get mad and let me deal with the garden," Sil said as he poured them both a cup of tea. "If you're inside, maybe you can get rid of this cold or whatever it is."

Anders gave him a guilty look. "Well, the paper is on the magical applications of moss, and while I was checking on the roof colony is when I realized that they hadn't put up their sporophytes yet. So, I still need to finish some preliminary field notes…"

It was like dealing with a child! Sil shoved papers out of the way in front of Anders so he could set down the mug of tea in front of him. "I hope for your sake your editor is willing to take the paper late, then. Because you're not going back up on that roof in this weather. I'd like you not to die from pneumonia so I still at least have an employer if I need to move back in with my parents."

Sil's off-handed comment seemed to pique Anders' interest. "You're moving?"

"That's not the point. What things need done in the garden? Did you get around to making that to-do list for me?"

"I think I'm missing some things on it," Anders said, shifting a stack of papers and pulling out a tea-stained notebook.

Snatching the notebook out of Anders' hand, Sil skimmed the list. "Right, you drink your tea, and I'll get on with this."

"I need to—"

Sil glared at Anders. "Drink. Your. Tea."

"Fine, but I'm telling my editor you're not letting me finish my work."

"Go ahead." Sil coaxed the little pipe dragon from around his neck and handed it off to Anders. "Keep an eye on this one. I don't want anyone out in the rain today."

When Sil returned to Anders' cottage the next day after his shift at the garden shop, he was surprised to find the kitchen dark. The fire had died down to the coals, and the stacks of papers and dishes were all in the same place. The little sitting room, with the corner where Anders had a little worktable covered in more papers and jars of various experiments, was also empty. He stared at the closed door to Anders' room for a long moment before knocking on it.

"Anders?"

There was a sneeze from inside, so Sil cracked the door open. The wizard's room was just as covered in all manner of stuff as the rest of the cottage. Framed awards filled the space above the wainscoting on the few walls that weren't lined with bookshelves stuffed with books, scrolls, and strange instruments. Hanging from the ceiling, heavy velvet curtains surrounded the bed.

"Anders?" Sil asked again.

The curtain pulled back slightly, revealing a mass of tangled, mousy hair poking out from a pile of blankets. "Oh, Sil?"

Sil shook his head as he yanked the curtains back.

Anders shrunk back under the blankets with a groan. "Too bright..." His voice cracked like a stick being crushed under foot.

"Your windows aren't even open," Sil said with a sigh. There were abandoned cups of tea stacked on the end table.

The wizard groaned miserably. "Still too bright."

"Look, you're clearly sick. Is there a doctor I can call for you?"

Shifting under the blankets, Anders shook his head and snaked a hand from under the covers out to try to tug the curtains closed again. "I just need some tea."

"Tea is not a magical cure-all. Have you eaten anything in the last twenty-four hours?"

"A couple of ginger biscuits?"

"So, nothing then." Sil rubbed his temples, willing the

universe to stop testing his patience and sanity. "Okay, I'm going to make you something to eat, then I'll get started on the garden chores."

"Talk to the moss…" Anders said. "It needs attention."

The idea of climbing back up onto the cottage roof was even less appealing than dealing with Anders in his current state. But Sil also knew how important Anders' research was to him.

"Yeah, I'll check on it," he said, picking up a stack of mugs to deliver to the sink.

Papers and books littered every surface in the kitchen, including the stove top. Anders insisted that he'd fireproofed everything in the cottage to minimize accidents, but Sil found himself removing stacks of books from the cook top constantly. He set the mugs in the sink and replaced a couple notebooks that were open on the stove with the kettle before rummaging around for something to make for Anders.

His dad always made lintel soup for him when he had a cold, but Sil knew from experience that Anders' pantry was a bit lacking. The wizard had a bad habit of using magic to acquire his groceries. Opening the cupboard door, he stared at the dim shelves, remembering that he still needed to pack up his own kitchen in the milk crates Beren had lent him. Even if he hadn't heard back about any apartments he'd applied to yet, it was still a good idea to be ready to move.

Taking out a can of beans, he wondered if Anders would eat it. It would, of course, require finding a can opener somewhere in the chaos of the kitchen. Sil put the can of beans back and wondered if he could bike to the little cafe in the next town over. His fingers brushed a jar of something with a peeling label shoved in the back of the pantry. It was a clear glass canning jar filled with dried or dehydrated something. Smoothing out the label, he read, "*Red Pepper Chicken & Potato Soup. For emergencies only. Recite incantation to reconstitute, then serve.*"

Sil figured it was worth a try. If nothing else, he could probably dump the contents into a pot of hot water and come up with something edible. It couldn't be worse than those dehydrated meals meant for backpacking trips. The magically inclined had it so much easier. There was no need to haul a heavy pack of food and water and supplies if everything could be conjured at the campsite.

The incantation was scrawled in red ink on the back of the label but was luckily still readable. He set the jar on the counter, and read out the words, doing his best to will the magic into working, "*Bubble, bubble, soup be doubled. Warm and transform into something yummy. Make it go down, just like honey.*"

For a long moment, nothing happened, and Sil was willing to bet the poor rhyming had something to do with it. Then the jar rattled. The contents jumped and twirled together. Liquid appeared inside and started to bubble, causing the jar to topple over and roll off the counter. It jumbled over the clay tile floor, finally coming to a stop when it knocked into the door mat laying in front of the back door.

There was a sharp rapping at the door before it blew open with burst of cold air. In the door frame stood a tall woman wrapped in a plaid cloak. Her tawny-colored hair was wild and frizzy under a pointed wool hat.

She looked down her nose at Sil. "Well, where is he?"

"Who?" Sil asked, wondering if he'd read the spell wrong. He'd needed soup, not this strange woman who'd appeared on a mysterious east wind. Given his luck, the woman had some grudge or was plotting to curse them.

"Anders, my hopeless brother. I assume he finally resigned himself to needing my assistance."

"You're his—"

"Sister. Elder sister to be precise." She bent down and picked up the now steaming jar of soup. "Is he ill again? He must be. It was raining earlier in the week. I imagine he spent all day out in it, up to his elbows in mud."

"Moss actually," Sil replied, seeing the similarities between them.

While Sil knew logically that Anders hadn't popped out of the ground as the fully fledged wizard he was today, he'd never wondered about his family. And the wizard had certainly never hinted at having a sister. It was still to be seen if she planned to curse them, though. Families were complicated.

She clicked her tongue and pushed by Sil, plopping a large carpet bag on the kitchen table. "This place is certainly in a state, isn't it? Nothing for it. I'll stay and get him back on his feet." With a flourish, she removed her cloak, tossing it up in the air to float over to the hook next to the door. "Now, who are you?"

He suddenly felt like one of Anders' moss samples as she looked him up and down.

"You really don't need to stay," he said.

"That isn't what I asked. At least you're cuter than a the last one." She glanced in the pantry and shook her head. "What's he eaten?"

"Um…"

"Exactly. Now, your name? Or do I need to come up with one for you?"

Pushing his glasses up his nose, Sil grumbled, "It's Sil."

"Sil? Short for Sylvester?"

"Not short for anything. It's just Sil."

"Strange."

"You haven't given me your name," Sil countered.

"Auda?" Anders croaked, standing in the doorway, wrapped pathetically in a blanket.

"Ande, darling, why didn't you call me?"

"Why are you here?"

Holding up the jar of soup, his sister grinned. "To take care of you, of course. You're an absolute wreck, and this slip of a thing clearly can't manage you, the cottage, and the garden all alone."

"No, no, no! The last time you were here, I couldn't find my work for months!" Anders wagged a finger at her before doubling over with a sneeze.

"Go back to bed," she insisted. "I'll bring you the soup and a fresh cup of tea in a moment."

"I can handle it, really," Sil tried to argue.

"Don't let your pride get in the way of someone offering a helping hand," she said, and Sil was sure she meant it for both of them. "Now, you probably have garden chores to handle, if your apron is anything to go by?"

"I do, but—"

"No buts. I'll deal with Ande so you can work."

"You can't order my assistant around, Auda."

Auda turned to Anders with a look that begged him to try arguing further. "Anders, to bed with you before I carry you there myself."

The wizard gave Sil a pitiful look as he shuffled back to his room, the door slamming behind him.

Sighing, Auda surveyed the kitchen. "It's more of a mess then when I was here last."

"He's busy. Things that aren't an immediate concern sometimes get overlooked."

"Well, if he'd get himself some help or an apprentice…" She pushed up her sleeves and began unpacking her bag. "You should get to your chores, otherwise you'll be put to work cleaning."

Sil grabbed his gloves from the little cubby by the door he'd managed to claim and hurried out the back door before any more strangeness could happen.

There was a chirp from one of the piles of pots and various garden supplies as the pipe dragon poked its head out of the drain hole of one of the upturned pots and looked towards the cottage.

"There you are," Sil said, letting the little dragon slither up his arm and settle on his shoulder. "I'd stay out here with me for now. I doubt she'll be done cleaning any time soon."

He finished up the swath of things needing done in the garden as slowly as possible, but he'd streamlined the list too well in the last few weeks. After checking on the feather duster plants to make sure they were adapting to the garden well, Sil looked up at the roof. Putting off the moss wouldn't do him any good, even if he would much rather have braved Auda's wrath to try and ferret out a few books from Anders' collection to read. Sil was slowly making his way through Anders' library of botany focused tomes, both magical and non-magical.

Clinging tightly to the ladder, which wobbled as he started to climb, he made his way up to the roof. Anders had marked out sections of the roof with different colored twine, but Sil had no idea what the difference between them was.

"So, do you just need talking to, then?" he asked.

The rain dripped softly from the roof line to the ground below.

"Okay, well, Anders went and got himself sick," he told the plants, "so you're going to have to put up with me."

"What on earth are you doing up there?" Anders' sister asked, looking up at him with her hands bunched up on her hips.

Sil did his best not to fall off the ladder in surprise. "Talking to the moss."

"Just cast a yapping spell, then. I need your help inside."

"A yapping spell?" He'd never heard of such a thing.

"Yes," Auda shook her head in annoyance. "'Yadda-yadda, keep their mossy ears full, not nada.' I would have thought Anders would have taught you that one already."

A soft chattering sound began, and the moss almost looked like it perked up some as he started back down the ladder.

"I'm not really magically inclined," he said when he was back on solid ground.

"Oh, really? How interesting. Did Anders read the incantation for the soup, then?"

"No, that was me." Sil brushed the dirt and loose thatch from his apron and pulled off his gloves.

"Then you do have *some* magical inclination," she said. "Then again, most people do. They just don't exercise their casting muscles, so to speak. By the way, you have a little stow away there."

Petting the pipe dragon's head, Sil shrugged. "It's nap time. I don't mind him."

"Good, then hopefully you won't mind helping me clear out the jumping mouse infestation I discovered under the kitchen sink?"

Anders had promised to try and convince the mice to move on, but apparently, that hadn't happened.

Holding a sigh in check, Sil said, "Yeah, I'll try."

He didn't bother taking off his apron as he followed Auda back into the kitchen. It was full of steam and the musky smell of herbs and tea. And it was clean. Sil could see the full surface of the worktable for the first time since he'd begun working for Anders. There were counter tops, too, and no dishes piled in the sink. He didn't think it was possible to have it all cleaned up so quickly.

Auda had gone over to the sink and was opening the

cupboard with the end of a wooden spoon. "All of you are going to shoo now."

Sil went to the ice box to retrieve some bribery in the form of a block of cheese. He crouched down in front of the cupboard and held out the morsel of cheese. "Come on, there's gotta be somewhere else better you can live than under the sink."

There was no sign of any of the jumping mice, only little bits of fluff and sawdust they'd collected to make their nest.

Crumbling up the cheese, Sil made a little trail from the cupboard to a box he'd been trying to lure them into.

"Can't you just magic them out of there?" Sil asked Auda who was standing well clear of the sink.

"Yes, but I hate mice."

"I guess we'll have to wait, then."

"I suppose I can get working on the rest of the cottage in the meantime. Unless you'd like a cup of tea?"

"I should probably head out. I've got some packing to do back home."

Auda sat down at the worktable and conjured a steaming cup of tea in front of her, in a proper teacup with a saucer, not the mismatched mugs Anders kept. "Stay for a bit. I promise I don't bite."

Reluctantly, Sil sat down across from her. A second porcelain cup, which was filled slowly with a reddish tea that smelt of raspberries, appeared in front of him.

"What sort of packing?" she asked. "Going on a trip?"

It was a bit awkward to be sitting across from a stranger in Anders' cottage. And the topic of discussion did nothing to ease his nerves. "No. My lease is up at the end of the month."

"Ah, I see. Hopefully your new place doesn't have an infestation. I'm sure you've checked."

Sil sipped at the tea, a mild green that wasn't half bad. "I haven't found a new place yet."

Auda had the same calculating look that Anders got when he was in the middle of recording new data. "Is that so? Having trouble with it?"

"There aren't many available apartments in my price range."

"Is my brother not paying you enough?"

"No, no, he is! And I'm the manager at the plant shop in town, too. There's just nowhere to rent right now. My parents will probably let me move back with them at least."

"But you don't want to do that."

"Not particularly."

"Independence is important. I remember my first place alone was a wonderful little cabin up in the mountains for about three years. Nothing but nature for miles and miles."

"So, you're not really close with Anders or your family?"

She smiled, "We have our own quirks. Anders was never fond of the farm; he much preferred his little kitchen garden. And I was far more interested in developing new spell work and traveling. So, we drift about and eventually bump into each other when the wind decides we should. I'm sure as a garden lover you understand."

"I guess."

Though he wasn't certain she'd answered his question. Admittedly, no one else in his family was really a plant person.

His parents were far more on the "normal" side of things as far as people came. They'd met in high school, dated in university, and then had him. No magic. Non-magical jobs. Boring house in a little suburb with expectations that Sil would grow up just like them to repeat the cycle.

"Pity Anders doesn't have room for you here," Auda said. "A roommate might do him some good. You might actually be able to convince him to keep the place clean for a time."

Sil turned his tea cup around, finally noticing that the pattern painted around it was a dragon intertwined with oak leaves. "It would be a little strange to live with my boss."

"He's a little more than a boss, though, isn't he? You were trying to take care of him," Auda said, her smile visible even when she was sipping at her own tea.

"You saw him. He wasn't doing it on his own."

"True. But all the same. I think it's perfectly natural to be roommates with a friend you happen to work with. It would save on your commute, too."

"But I have the plant shop, too…" He wasn't about to just quit on Beren, she'd been too good to him over the years he'd worked for her.

"Oh? Beren's shop?"

"You know her?" Somehow it was unsurprising that Auda knew her. Especially with how small the village was. The whole high street was all of a couple blocks and an alleyway.

"Of course! She's an old family friend. We blame her for Anders' plant obsession. You can join us in that."

Sil smiled a bit uncomfortably as the pipe dragon started trilling for snacks. "I should get this one fed and get back

home."

"Not to worry. I'll keep an eye on Anders. I suspect you'll be back throughout the week for your other garden chores?" Auda asked him.

"Yes. I usually come by a few times a week."

"I'll see you then," she said.

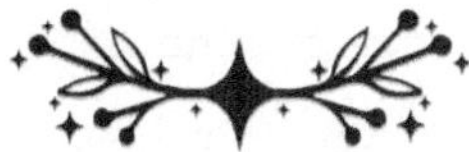

Sil's tiny kitchen was mostly packed up except for the essentials, like his kettle. The little pipe dragon had claimed the kettle lid as its new napping spot since it had snuck into Sil's backpack. At least the warmth had put an end to the little dragon's sniffling. So that was one illness sorted.

All his other belongings had been making their way into boxes and milk crates, but he still hadn't gotten up the courage to ask his parents if he could move in with them temporarily. Part of Sil was still holding out hope for a response to one of the housing inquiries he'd put out.

Grabbing his apron and a sweater, Sil nudged the little pipe dragon awake with a finger. "I've got to get to the plant shop now."

It huffed and tried to curl up tighter around the lid of the kettle.

"I can't leave you here alone all day," he said, picking it up gently and placing it on his shoulder. The little dragon nuzzled under his collar and settled with its head perched on the wooly fibers. Poor little thing was still feeling under the weather.

Once Sil arrived at the shop, his glum mood wasn't

helped by the huge shipment of plants outside. The pallets had been seemingly abandoned by the delivery driver near the front door, and a few of the more temperamental flowers were starting to wilt. Checking the delivery schedule, he confirmed that the delivery wasn't supposed to arrive until later in the morning. He'd have to give Beren a call and ask if she'd been notified of the change. For the moment, though, he started to shuttle plants inside onto open tables.

Plants were generally shipped without being watered so they weighed less. But by the look of this poor selection, it had been days—if not a week—since they'd last had a drink. Cacti and some heartier, more established plants would be fine going that long without water. But this order was mostly ornamental flowers that thrived in damp environments.

"Once I've got you all inside, I'll water you all," Sil assured the plants, carefully separating tangled stems and leaves.

He'd moved most of the order before Magda walked in, sunglasses perched on her head, iced coffee in hand, asking, "Why is there a pile of plants out front?"

"I'd love to know as well. The delivery was supposed to be at ten, but they were there when I got in this morning. Will you help me get the rest inside? I need to double check the inventory and get them watered."

"Sure. Shitty of them to just leave an order laying around," Magda said as she pulled her timecard out of the cracked terracotta pot next to the register and scribbled down the hour on it.

"Yeah, as if I don't have enough to worry about right now."

"Oh? Trouble in the garden?" Magda asked with an amused tone.

Sil gave her an annoyed look. "If you mean with Anders, then no." He moved a couple of flats of plants over on one of the benches to make room for the remaining plants.

"Then what else do you have to worry about? Besides being overworked and trapped in a contract with a wizard, I mean. Or is this just a new level of grump?"

Picking up the hose, Sil resisted the urge to spray Magda with it. Such childish behavior wasn't becoming of a manager, even if it would wipe that smug look off her face. Everyone seemed to have strange assumptions about his working arrangement with Anders. It was a perfectly normal situation.

"I got notice that my landlord is selling the building," he said, "so I have to move at the end of the month."

"Ugh, landlords are the worst. My school tried to tell me that cats weren't allowed in the dorms. I showed them the requirements for my familiar studies course, and they finally let me keep Marvin."

The comparison wasn't exactly the same, but at least Magda hadn't made some smartass comment about sleeping on someone's floor.

"Your cat's name is Marvin?"

Magda shrugged. "Yeah, why?"

"No reason," Sil quickly responded, starting to water the morning's delivery.

"I keep asking Beren to let me bring Marvin to work with me, but she says it would just encourage the strays to try to come in the shop."

Sil fluffed up his collar to make sure that the pipe dragon was still hidden under his shirt. "I mean, a lot of animals aren't really good with magical plants. Cats and jays like to torment them."

"Marvin isn't really interested in plants. He just lays in the sun most of the time."

"Shouldn't a familiar be more, I don't know, interested in magic and things?"

Magda leaned against one of the tables and sucked on the straw in her iced coffee. "He helps when I need him. Not all familiars are active ones like in stories. Some are there just to support their practitioner. Since I study wards, I don't need a super vigilant familiar."

"Oh." He'd never taken any of the magic related classes in school.

"Guess you aren't a know it all about everything," Magda said with a slight smirk.

"Magic isn't my forte."

"Unless its plants."

"Magically enhanced plants are a completely different subject. And plants are still plants, magical or not."

"And magic is magic, Sil. If you didn't have some aptitude for the mystical, then you wouldn't be so good at your job," Magda said.

Sil was almost certain it was a compliment, but the bell above the front door rang before he could confirm if it was meant to be one.

"Welcome, let us know if you have questions or need any assistance," Sil blurted out as the customer ducked into

the shop.

"Oh, just browsing," the man said without looking in Sil's direction.

Their usual clientèle didn't wear business suits, unless it was close to a holiday and they were gift shopping. With no holidays coming up, though, the man was certainly out of place.

Magda rolled her eyes and wandered over to the register to open it on the off chance that the man bought something. Meanwhile, Sil hurried to the office to grab the inventory checklist for the morning's order. Most of it seemed to be there, but there were a few missing flats of posies, and the shrinking violets weren't in the proper plastic wrapping. As far as damaged plants, the hellebore and daises seemed alright, but the petunias and cosmos had wilted. The irises and lilies were probably a lost cause without some kind of magical intervention. But there was a chance he could save them if he made sure to pay them close attention over the next few days.

"Those flowers look a bit worse for wear," the strange customer commented as he typed out something on his phone.

"Were you looking for flowers?"

"Not anything as mundane as those. I heard this shop might carry an unusual and exotic selection."

"Did you have something specific you were looking for, then?" Sil asked the man.

He smiled, dimples appearing on his cheeks. "What would you suggest for a collector?"

Pushing his glasses up the bridge of his nose, Sil countered with, "What's your experience level?"

"I have a large selection of orchids, including a few carnivorous varieties."

"We don't usually carry orchids. Or carnivorous plants. We can do a special order if there's something specific you're looking for. And you have the proper environment for it."

The customer just shook his head. "No, that's alright. I thought I'd come and browse a little. I did also see you have some vegetable starts. Is that all you have?"

"For now. We get in the more tender stuff later in the season."

Nodding, the man in the suit crossed his arms. "Are there any other gardening or plant shops in the area?"

"Not unless you go up to the city," Magda said.

"Well, thank you for your assistance, then."

As the man left the shop, Magda swirled the watery remains of her iced coffee. "That was weird."

"Well, we can't cater to everyone."

"Yeah, but we're obviously just a country garden shop. Not some specialist store. I bet he was scoping out the shop."

"Why would someone do that?"

"I dunno. Maybe he's some real estate guru trying to buy up the street? Or he owns his own garden shop and was spying on our setup."

"You've been listening to too many radio dramas," Sil told her as he finished separating out the worst-looking of the plants. "Next you'll claim there's a writer-turned-detective holing up in the coffee shop down the road."

"The old lady *has* been asking a lot of probing questions," Magda mused.

"I'm going to call Beren about the delivery, I'll be back in a few."

He didn't wait for a response from Magda before closing the door to the little office. The phone rang a few times before Beren answered with, "This is Beren; who is calling?"

"It's Sil—"

"Oh, hello. Is something the matter? You don't usually call so early."

Sil leaned back against the little desk and absently rubbed the pipe dragon's head. "The order that was scheduled for today…did you get an updated delivery notice for it?"

"No. Why do you ask?"

"It was all stacked up at the door when I got in. I double-checked our records, and it shouldn't have been here until ten this morning."

Beren was silent on the other side of the line for a long moment. "Why don't you let me give them a call."

"Alright, thanks…"

"I'm certain it was just a mistake. Don't fret, Sil. Thank you for letting me know."

"Alright. I've marked down everything that was damaged or missing from the order."

"Good. I'll take a look once I get in later. See you then."

"Of course," he said, setting the phone down after Beren had hung up.

Usually, the old shop owner confided in him if anything was amiss. She was prone to gossip, so anything that happened in or out of town was bound to end up in Sil's ears eventually.

Cooing, the pipe dragon tickled his neck with its tongue

as the door creaked open. One of Magda's eyebrows lifted as her gaze focused on the dragon.

"So, you can bring in a pet, but I can't have my familiar?"

Sil quickly pulled his collar up again. "It's not a pet. It's an endangered species. And besides, I think it's sick. I couldn't just leave it at home alone. Even though it needs to stop sneaking into my apron from Anders' garden."

Magda sighed and leaned over, offering the pipe dragon her finger to taste. "Hey there, little guy?"

The dragon poked its head out and licked Magda's finger before slinking back to hide in Sil's sweater.

"His scales do look a little dull. I'm not really an expert in animals, though."

"Maybe what Anders has is catching," Sil said, pinching the bridge of his nose. "The last thing I need is to try to find a vet that will take a look at a pipe dragon when I still need to pack up the rest of my apartment."

"One of my classmates is taking some magical creature courses. They might be able to take a look at the little guy."

"Do you think they'd mind?"

With a shrug, Magda sucked on the dregs of her iced coffee. "Put in a good word about me bringing Marvin into the shop, and I'll ask."

Sil chewed his lip. "I don't know how up to suggestions Beren will be..."

"Why? Did she say something was wrong when you talked to her?"

"No, but she was a little odd on the phone."

"She has been a little stranger lately."

"Do you think she's mad that I started working for Anders?"

"What? Scales, no! I think she was relieved. I swear she's been trying to get the two of you to get along for a while now."

He blinked her dumbly.

"He's one of our best customers, and you were always so antagonistic to him," Magda explained. "But now you're his apprentice. I think Beren figures it would be good for the shop to have a wizard on."

"I'm not his apprentice. I'm an *assistant*. I just help around the garden."

"Uh huh. Sounds like what an apprentice to a wizard that focuses on plants would do. What's your hang up with magic, anyway?"

"I don't have a hang up with it. It's just…not for me."

She snorted. "I hated wards and sigils before my apprenticeship started. But I read some books about them and met my wixen, and they showed that wards could actually be really fascinating. Oh, did you know Anders' sister is pretty good with wards? She has a couple papers that I read last year in one of my classes."

"If you're fishing to meet her, I can't help you. Ask Anders the next time he comes in."

"Oh, come on! I know she's in town. Beren mentioned it."

"Then ask Beren to have her for tea or something," he told her in an exasperated tone. "I've only barely met her."

A grin started to widen on Magda's face, which was usually far more sullen. "But if she's like Anders, she'd probably be up for meeting a student interested in her work."

"I'm not a matchmaker for your studies. Get back to watching the shop while I finish up this paperwork. I don't have time for scheduling teatime between wixen."

"There's the grumpy old Sil back. I thought Anders might have finally killed him off," she replied before slipping back into the green house.

He leaned back in the chair and let out a huff. Nothing about him had changed since he started to work for Anders. Except sleeping a bit less. And trying to practice silly watering spells. The pipe dragon sneezed, and Sil gently pet its head.

"And of course, I have you clinging to me now."

Anders peered through the open crack of his doorway before carefully pushing it open. She wasn't anywhere in sight, though, and neither was Sil. Blanket trailing behind him like a cape, Anders started for the kitchen to retrieve a new cup of tea. He certainly could live on tea and biscuits if he so pleased. As he was refilling the kettle at the sink, he heard a throat clear behind him.

"I see you're still with us," his sister commented.

Turning to glare at his unwanted company, Anders snapped his fingers to light the stove. "Of course, I am. It's just a cold."

The gas flame flickered and guttered out a few times before it finally caught. He pulled the blanket up on his shoulders to hide his annoyance. Magic could be fickle any day; it had nothing to do with his illness.

Auda smiled and said in a cloying tone, "Just a cold? With how your apprentice has been fussing over you, I would say it's serious."

He quite liked the idea of Sil fussing, even if that wasn't what the young gardener had been doing. "He's not my apprentice. Just an assistant. To do the watering. And the weeding..."

There was a twitch in his nose, and Anders sneezed violently. It was one of those sneezes that twinged the back and caused the head to go a bit fussy.

"Oh, sod it," he grumbled. "When are you leaving?"

"Once you're well again," Auda said, clearly amused by something.

"Don't you have...witchy things to do?"

"And leave my poor baby brother here with just an errant apprentice to help him get well? No."

"I'm all of two minutes younger than you, and he's my *assistant.*"

"For now." She sipped at her tea. If her grin grew any wider, she was in danger of being mistaken for the Cheshire Cat.

He rummaged through the cupboards before finding a forgotten tin of biscuits shoved in the back of one and sat down at the table across from Auda. As he pried open the lid, he was disappointed to discover that it was stuffed full of half empty thread spools, a pincushion resembling a hedgehog with its back full of pins, and a tiny pair of scissors.

His sister chuckled. "Ah yes, thread for breakfast. I always knew it was your favorite, Ande."

"I need to do some mending," Anders replied defiantly, pushing the tin aside and tapping his thumb and middle finger together three times. A plate of biscuits appeared on the kitchen table in front of him, along with a steaming cup of tea. The smell of it was enough to help him forget about his sister for a moment. It was earthy, with just a hint of peppermint to soothe the sinuses.

"I can imagine," she said, "given the literal rats' nest I found under the sink while I was cleaning."

"Jumping mice," Anders corrected, inhaling the steam as it rose up from the cup.

"Whatever."

"And you didn't need to clean—"

"There wasn't a clear surface in this entire kitchen, Anders. That poor apprentice of yours was up to his elbows in tea mugs!"

"We get along just fine here."

"And yet, here I am. Summoned to help."

"I knew I should have thrown that soup spell out years ago."

"I'm honored that you forgot to throw it away, then. Now, when are you going to register him as your apprentice?"

"He's still an assistant."

"I know you've taught him a few little spells. Well, attempted to," Auda mused.

Anders picked up his mug and started drinking his tea, even though it was still too hot. A couple spells here and there didn't really make Sil his apprentice. Not officially. Hells, he and Auda had messed around with plenty of spells back home

before finding apprenticeships. Experimenting with magic was part growing up.

"You'll have to apprentice him eventually," his sister said, pushing a stack of folded tea towels aside. Anders wasn't even sure where they'd all come from.

"He doesn't want to be my apprentice. He's perfectly happy just helping in the garden."

Auda shrugged. "Perhaps. But I find magic a bit addictive. Once you get a taste for it, it's hard not to want more."

"Sil isn't like that. His passion is plants." Dipping a biscuit in his tea, Anders nibbled at it. At least his sense of taste was coming back. The worst thing was being sick and being unable to taste what you were eating. It made the whole idea of consuming food disgusting.

"And yours isn't?"

"Well, I mean… You can have the same passions and approach them differently. Besides, not everything is about magic. There are plenty of people who live their daily lives without magic."

"What a horrid idea," Auda said with a shake of her head. "Well, I'm planning to start on cleaning the sitting room today. Though I really wish you had a proper guest room. It's such a pain to have to pop over from town to make sure you're still alive."

"No, no no!" Anders yelled, brandishing his biscuit like a shield, "There will be no more cleaning!"

"Anders, you can hardly walk through a room without knocking over a tower of books."

"I know where everything is," Anders insisted.

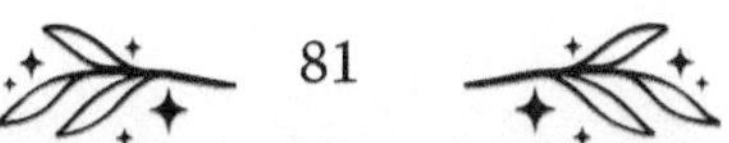

"I'm sure you can look up a finding spell if you need it." Auda said, then pulled out a hastily sketched out map of the cottage, "Now, about the cottage layout—"

"No."

"Shouldn't Sil have a place to stay? If he needs it?" Auda asked pointedly.

His eyes narrowed. "What do you think you know?"

"Nothing. Just thinking it would be a nice thing for him to have a space. You know…if he wants a nap."

"A nap?" What was she plotting?

"Yes. People do nap after a long day, Ande."

"I don't."

"You're abnormal."

"No, I'm not."

"Yes, you are. And I would know." She got up and strolled to the back door. "What about adding on here? I'm sure the garden can shift around an addition."

"The cottage doesn't need an addition. Besides, if I'm so ill that you can't leave, why are you tormenting me?"

"You enjoy our bickering," she said tilting her head to one side, then the other. "Yes, here would be good."

"The shed with all the supplies is through that door," Anders protested, gathering up his blanket shroud to stand firmly in front of the back door. "Besides, this roofline is the easiest to get up to in order to check on the moss."

His sister's eyes scanned the rest of the kitchen, finally landing next to his own bedroom door. "What about there? It's a north facing corner, so it won't interrupt any experiments." Her fingers were already twitching with spell work. "He'd still

have a nice view of the lane and plenty of room for a decently sized wardrobe."

"No! Don't you dare!" Anders tried to protest as the outline of a door began to appear on the wall next to his own bedroom.

"What is his favorite plant?"

"Tuft tails," Anders replied, mentally trying to reorganize the plants on that side of the cottage.

"Curious. Most non-wizards don't bother trying to delve into that level of difficulty."

"Well, he's very good at his job."

"Indeed. Well, I'll leave the decorations up to him. Until then, though, I would really prefer to leave that damp tavern I've been holed up in since I arrived. Would you mind getting the door when my luggage gets here? I'm going to tuck into the sitting room and attempt to find a home for all your mess."

The new door clicked open as his sister turned on her heel to storm the sitting room at the front of the cottage. Trying to get Auda to stop once she'd put her mind to something was nearly impossible. He stared at the wooden door carved with tuft tails twining up the sides. At least it matched the rest of the cottage. Shuffling over to the door, he nudged it open with his foot.

While the room itself was small, the light filtering in through the windows was nice. Some hardier house plants might do alright on the windowsill, even though it wasn't ideal. The furnishings were simple and blocky, and the bed looked comfortable. Anders still felt like his sister was up to something more with the addition. He would have received a panicked message from their parents if Auda were suddenly going to be homeless, though.

Whatever surge of energy he'd managed to muster seemed to escape his body all at once, and the pounding in his head came back from a quiet tapping to a roaring, thunderous banging. Or perhaps that was Auda "cleaning" the sitting room.

Leaving the cozy new room, Anders retreated to his own cluttered sanctuary. The lights dimmed as he kicked the door closed behind him.

An entire swath of the cottage's front garden was stacked with boxes of books as Sil biked up to the gate. Puffs of dust were emanating from the front windows like chimney smoke. And he was certain that the herbs were trying to escape the confines of the window boxes to avoid whatever commotion was occurring.

"Don't you dare touch another book, Auda!" came Anders pitiful cries from inside the cottage.

Sil was half tempted to avoid the sibling feud altogether and go home to finish packing his own apartment. But as the window was flung open, he was spotted by the witch at the heart of the argument.

"Ah, Sil! So good to see you. Come in and help me dismember Ande's archaic excuse for a filing system."

"It's perfectly organized!" Anders insisted. "Or it was—before you came and put your grubby fingers all over my books!"

Leaning his bike against the fence, Sil nudged the little pipe dragon. "You might want to stay out here. Out of the line of fire."

The dragon sniffled, and Sil sighed. The chill in the air wasn't going to help the pipe dragon get any better. Magda had suggested letting it simmer in a kettle, though. So, he hurried inside and made a beeline for the stove to put the kettle on before picking up the tiny black dragon and helping it coil around the lid.

"Just stay here," he told it. "I'll check on you in a bit."

It happily wrapped its tail around the warmth of the iron kettle and let out a soft chirp.

"Sil! She's completely ruined my organization!" Anders whined.

"I'm not getting in the middle of you two," Sil called from the kitchen, grabbing his gloves from their cubby.

Before he could run out into the garden to get started on his chores, though, he stopped in front of a door he'd never seen before. Anders was a wizard, so Sil supposed adding a new room wouldn't be that big of a deal for him. But the carvings along the door frame looked just like tuft tails.

He was tracing a carved tuft when Auda poked her head out of Anders' office. "Nice bit of work, isn't it?"

"Huh? Oh, yes. Guess Anders figured he needed more storage finally, huh?"

"Open it," she urged him.

"I should get to the watering."

Rolling her eyes, Auda crossed the kitchen and pushed open the door with a little flick of her fingers. "You men are so fickle. Just look inside. I assume it will be to your liking. Ande mentioned your apartment wasn't much to look at. So, I imagine a full kitchen and garden will be an upgrade."

Sil quickly noted the simple bed and wardrobe. A few plants had been crowded on the windowsill, but the room was otherwise a blank slate.

Then he finally realized what she'd said. "Wait...*my* liking?"

"You do need a place to live, don't you?"

"Auda, stop pestering Sil and let him get to the garden," Anders chided his sister. "He has his own apartment. He doesn't need to move into the cottage just to work for me."

A cheshire grin spread over Auda's face. "You didn't know your apprentice was having to move?"

Sil could see the gears all grinding against each other at once in Anders head as he asked, "You're moving? Where? When?"

"My landlord is selling the building," Sil explained. "So, I have to find a place by the end of the month. I was going to move back with my parents."

"Ooooor you could move in here," Auda suggested.

Both Sil and Anders glared at her.

"It's a perfectly suitable room," she said. "And it means you won't have to commute. And it might convince Ande to keep the place in order."

"It was in fine shape before you arrived." Anders crossed his arms firmly over his chest. "And I'm feeling much better now, so you can pack up that infernal carpet bag of yours and leave."

"Tch, you just don't like it because you could never figure out how to get the infinite space charm to work," Auda countered. "I'm set to have tea with Beren and that co-worker of yours, Sil, so I'll leave the two of you to work out the moving details."

Without any other warning, Auda popped out of sight, leaving behind an acrid smell and a puff of smoke in her wake.

"She's always so dramatic!" Anders complained. Though Sil was certain at this point that the dramatics were a family trait.

"Is that normal?" Sil asked. "Her just disappearing?"

"Yes. Though she rarely does it on command. Maybe you're having an influence…" The wizard trailed off in thought.

The two of them stood in silence in front of the new room, uncertain of what to say to one another. While it would be nice not to have to go very far to complete his chores in the garden, Sil wasn't sure about living at the cottage. *Anders'* cottage. He would never consider living with Beren. It was too strange to live with your boss. But Anders wasn't much of a boss. He was more of an eccentric friend that had somehow wormed his way into Sil's life in a short span of time.

"I'll get started on the watering," Sil said. "Oh, and I checked the moss the other day, and it seemed alright."

"Would you rather go live with your parents?"

"*Madcaps*, no! But I haven't found a place yet." It wasn't even that he didn't get on with his parents. He just liked his space, and his parents had a habit of still treating him like a child whenever he visited.

Anders' brain was doing those calculations again as his

eyes scanned the kitchen, flicking back to the new room occasionally. "It would be a waste to leave the room empty."

"I wouldn't want to impose."

"You're already here every other day. And you have free reign of the cottage and the garden."

Sil didn't really consider that the same thing, but he wasn't going to argue. "What would the rent be?"

"Rent? Oh…I mean you can cook right?"

Nothing was normal when it came to Anders, so why would he be a normal landlord? "Um, yeah."

"Good. You can handle lunch and dinner, then. That will be your rent," Anders told him with a nonchalant wave. "When do you have to move by again?"

"End of the month."

"That's only a few days. We can get you all settled in no time," Anders said and raised his hand to snap his fingers together.

Grabbing Anders' hand, Sil quickly said, "I can move everything! Don't worry about it."

"If you want to."

Sil nodded, jumping back and rushing to the garden door. "I'll get to the watering now!"

His face was flushed, he knew. But hopefully Anders hadn't noticed. At least there was plenty to do in the garden to distract him from over thinking that interaction. Instead, he could worry over the fact that he'd just agreed to move into the cottage and live with Anders. And somehow, he'd gotten off with just having to cook some meals to pay rent. Was grabbing Anders' hand considered a handshake? He'd need to

write everything out and have Anders sign it, just to ensure it was binding. Though at this point, the wizard hadn't given him any reason to make Sil doubt his word.

The garden seemed to breathe in relief as he turned on the hose to fill the watering can. Maybe he'd have more time to try to master that watering charm now? There was certainly less chance of causing a rainstorm in his apartment now.

Moving things the old-fashioned way had drug on for almost a week as, box by box, Sil slowly brought the contents of his life to the cottage. Anders tried to stay out of the other man's way, but he couldn't help himself when it came to peeking into the boxes stacked up in the kitchen. Mostly it was mismatched, mundane flatware and crockery that had been well loved and chipped or scuffed. But a box of books had nearly jumped at Anders when he walked by it.

A couple of old textbooks and worn-out cookbooks were scattered across the tile. Notes stuck out from almost every page of the volumes, and Anders couldn't help but think how alike he and Sil were in that respect. Even if their initial interactions had been less than pleasant, they were both hopeless bookworms. As he carefully replaced the books back in their box, his fingers hovered over a bright green book.

"Cershaw," Anders whispered angrily to himself, resisting the urge to step on the offending tome. Instead, he threw the book into the bottom of the box, quickly stacking everything else on top.

There were so many better researched and laid out gar-

dening books out there. Why did Sil have to have this one?

"Maybe it was a gift," he reassured himself. He still hated that one of those horrible green books had made it into the cottage.

He was debating if he should mention it to Sil when there was a knock on the cottage door. Sil had his own key, and even though Auda was still sulking around town, she would just barge in. Stepping over a few stacks of papers that he'd yet to put back in their place after his sister's rampage, Anders opened the door to a group huddled under his sister's over-sized umbrella.

Auda grinned at him and began explaining, "I brought along some friends for tea. Sil mentioned your poor little pipe dragon is still under the weather, so we figured we'd try to sort out the source."

Sil was at the back of the group and pushed his glasses up his nose while offering an apologetic expression. "I tried to say I would bring it to the garden shop—"

"Oh, tosh! Inside, everyone," Auda insisted as she pushed past Anders.

Beren hung up her coat on one of the pegs by the front door as Auda led the way towards the kitchen. "Auda insisted," Sil's boss said. "But I brought some biscuits and scones and a housewarming gift for Sil."

"You didn't need to get anything…" Sil said, balancing a box in his arms topped with the tin of biscuits.

"Everyone needs more amaranth in their lives," Beren insisted. "Oh, Anders, you know Magda. Our other employee?"

Nodding, Anders took Magda's jacket from her. "Yes. How is your familiar doing, by the way?"

"Marvin's enjoying hunting down all the pixies in the shop now that he's allowed to come in with me," Magda said with a satisfied smile.

"He's tormenting the shrinking violets," Sil protested.

"Maybe they need put in their place," Magda countered. "They did try to shrink Mrs. Parva the other day."

"Oh, then the stimulation is probably good for them if they're acting up like that," Anders said.

"This is Palla by the way," Magda said, tilting her head towards the bearded man behind her. "He's a classmate and knows a bunch about magical creatures. I thought he could help with Blip."

"Blip?" Anders asked, puzzled.

"Every creature should have a name," Palla replied, following Magda into the kitchen.

"I did not agree to 'Blip,'" Sil replied.

"It makes more of a 'bleep' sound than a 'blip,'" Anders mused.

"You're not helping," Sil told him, setting down another box in the hallway. "I'll move it once tea and snacks are all sorted out for everyone."

Anders shrugged and snapped his fingers without thinking, sending the box's contents to new homes throughout the cottage.

Sil pinched the bridge of his nose in the way he did when he was annoyed. "I'll go get the kettle on and try to contain the chaos coven."

Anders raised an eyebrow. "That's an ominous name."

"Its two university students who both want to grill your sister for magical information, your sister, which should be self-explanatory, and Beren."

"Fair. And fitting."

"I didn't invite them all over; it just…happened."

"It's fine, Sil. Company is nice once in a while. Even if it is the 'Chaos Coven.'" Anders held up his fingers in air quotes.

"What are you two up to out there? Dillydallying?" Auda's voice called over the din of conversation from the kitchen.

"We were just chatting," Anders said, pulling Sil along with him towards the kitchen.

The party had already settled at the table, and someone—Auda—had taken the liberty of adding a few chairs and extending the old wooden worktable to better accommodate them all.

Magda had a four-inch thick textbook open in front of her and was scribbling notes into the margins, while Palla inspected the cupboard under the sink.

"This is where the rodent colony was?" he asked in his rumbling voice.

"Jumping mice," Anders corrected, ensuring the bedroom doors were closed and locked in case any of the guests got brave enough to try exploring.

"Hm…they don't usually like it so damp."

"They were here before me," Anders said, sitting down at the table. "I just hope they're not scared half to death after Auda tried to eradicate them."

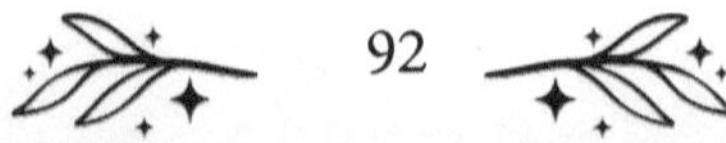

Palla nodded in understanding and rubbed his hands together. "So, where is the patient?"

Sil went to the stove and lifted the lid off an old pot. "It's been curled up in here. Poor thing can't seem to get warm enough."

Stroking his beard, Palla leaned over the pot, "Interesting. And you found it in the garden here?"

"Well, nearby, in a neighbor's field," Anders told him. "It became rather attached to Sil once he started working for me. Before that, it was more interested in chasing down worms and bugs in the herb garden."

Gently, Palla picked the pipe dragon up and ran his fingers along its scales. "I believe Blip is going to be fine. Garden pipe dragons often go through a spring molt once they reach maturity. But it takes a lot out of them. Hence the lethargy. She should get her wings and shed the black scales for brown ones in a few weeks or so."

"She?" Sil and Anders asked in unison.

Beren laughed. "You're both too cute. Most pipe dragons start off female and then, if needed, change genders to be able to mate."

"They're basically butch hermaphrodites," Magda added without looking up from her note taking. "Even I know that, and I'm not specializing in animals."

Palla set the pipe dragon back into the pot. "Just let her keep warm and make sure she gets some protein in her once she's done molting. Snails or slugs might be good. Or beetles and crickets, if you have some around."

Replacing the pot lid, Sil nodded. "Anything else we

should keep in mind?" He pulled the kettle off the stove as it was finally starting to spew steam out of the neck.

"If she sprouts spines along her back, I'd be interested in taking another look at her."

"I've never seen a pipe dragon with spines," Anders said, pulling out mugs and setting them out on the table for Sil.

"It's a trait that's usually found on the continental sub-species," Palla said. "But there's been some interbreeding recorded in this region, so I'd be curious to know if Blip produces them."

"I'll let Magda know if that happens," Sil told him.

Palla took a seat next to Magda and began munching on some of the biscuits Beren had brought along.

"Wixen Kessel?" Magda interjected.

Both Anders and Auda turned to her.

"Uh…Auda, I meant. You were saying that wards drawn in charcoal can have a similar strength to those made in blood?"

Anders sighed and started looking through the pantry for some additional snacks. He really needed to go to the market. Or, rather, *they* did. Sil had started serving the tea as if he'd done it a hundred times. The little gathering was strangely natural. Maybe it was because Auda always made it seem like she belonged wherever she went. She was good at forcing things to fall into place. It was part of her special magic.

Thankfully, as the evening dragged on, Magda and Palla excused themselves for a midnight astronomy workshop. And Auda surprisingly shuffled off back to her room at the tavern, complaining about the lack of wine in Anders' cupboards. Which left Beren to help clean up after the impromptu gathering.

"The two of you seem to be getting along well so far," she said, setting the sponge to work on cleaning the tea mugs out in the sink. It just took a wiggle of her nose, and the scrubbing started in earnest.

"Sil's been a great help in the garden," Anders replied, watching the young man attempt to shoo away one of the gnomes from the lily patch as he finished up the night pruning on some of the nocturnal varieties.

"But even when you were sick, he called Auda for help."

"Well, that was an accident. He didn't realize it was spell."

She followed Anders' gaze. "He's a good lad. We need to watch out for him."

"Is everything alright?"

"Hrm? Oh, yes! Everything's just fine. I just worry about him wearing himself out. He tries so hard to do it all."

"I'll make sure he's not overworking himself here," Anders promised. "Especially since he'll be living here."

"It is hard not to work all the time when you live so close to it."

"My editor would love it if that were true."

She laughed, and the sound warmed Anders' chest. "I bet! Don't you have a book you're supposed to be working on?"

Anders mumbled something about it just taking time. He'd been working on it. Slowly. And clawing for the moti-

vation to finish it. Which was nearly impossible, knowing it would probably be a failure.

"I saw Cershaw's new book at the bookshop the other day," Beren said suddenly.

"Ugh! Not you too!"

"It's popular. That's all. I declined the publisher's offer to carry a few copies, if that helps. If you get your book finished, you could even release it at the shop."

It was good to know that Beren would support his work. If he ever finished it.

"Sil might have some input on your manuscript if you're stuck," she continued. "He has a lot of knowledge stored up in that head of his."

Anders nearly said no, but it was out of habit more than anything else. Looking out the window at Sil, he nodded slowly. "Yeah. Yeah, that might be an idea."

Field Notes
2

Pan Fried Salmon

Recipe — Red Pepper Chicken + Potato Soup

Ingredients

- 1 white or yellow onion, chopped
- 3-4 cups cubed yellow potatoes
- 2-3 tbsp minced garlic

(or more, measure garlic with your heart)

- 1 tbsp thyme
- 1 tbsp oregano
- 1 tbsp marjoram
- 1/2 tbsp dried basil
- 1 tbsp garlic powder
- 1/2 tbsp onion powder
- 2 tsp pepper flakes
- 2 bay leaves
- 1 can chopped tomatoes
- 3 qts chicken stock*
- 2 cups chopped, cooked chicken
- salt + pepper to taste

*see Papi Lew's recipe

Optional

- 1 1/2 cups cooked rice (more carbs make you feel better)
- knob of butter
- chopped carrots
- chopped leeks
- chopped bell or sweet peppers**
- tsp sage

*Ask Auda for the stock recipe

**The peppers mi[s]
maybe add at the

Recipe

Instructions

- Combine all ingredients except chicken and tomatoes (and rice if adding) into a large pot

- Bring to a boil

- Cook on medium-low heat for 40-60 mins, until potatoes are cooked through

- Add chicken and tomatoes (and rice) 10-15 mins prior to soup being finished and allow to warm through

- Serve with toasted bread or rolls

Makes a large batch to last all week ~

Adding in cooked rice at the end prevents it from absorbing as much liquid & keeps it from burning on the bottom of the pot.

The New & Improved Cottage Layout!

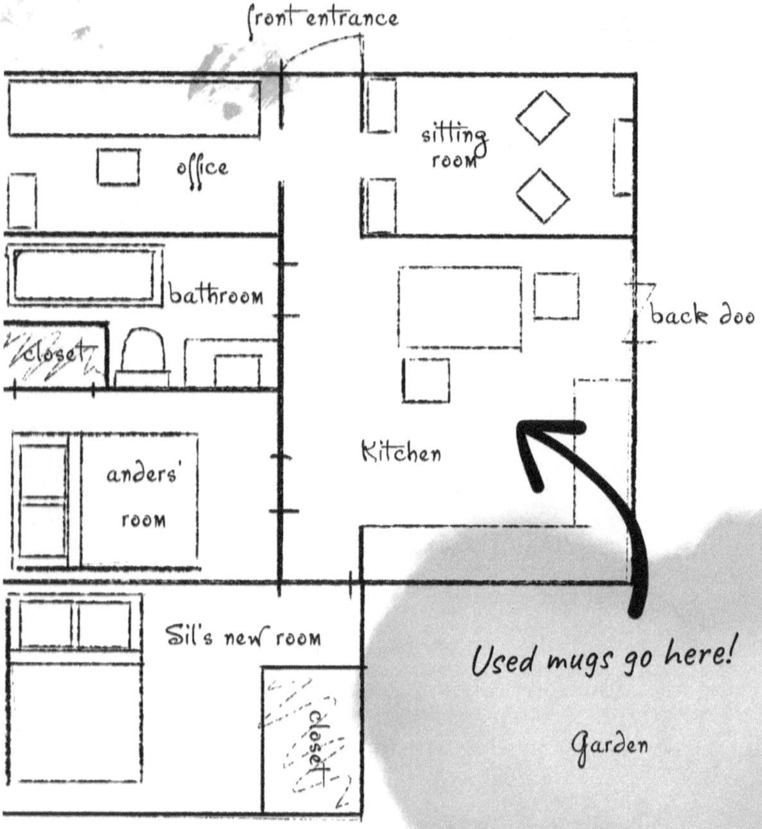

front entrance

office

sitting room

bathroom

back doo

closet

Kitchen

anders' room

Used mugs go here!

Garden

Sil's new room

closet

Chore List:

Collect mugs & put in kitchen - Anders

Garden things - Sil

Office & Sitting Room Tidying - Anders

Cooking - Sil

Grocery List - Sil

Dishes - Anders

Trim herbs - Anders

Sweep & Mop - Sil

Shopping - ~~Anders~~

If we ever want to eat, I'll do the shopping!

Pranks & Puddles

SIL'S FIRST NIGHT IN THE COTTAGE wasn't bad. It was just new, with all the creaks and thuds that came with sleeping in an unfamiliar place. There was Anders' shuffling in the sitting room until who knew when in the morning. And the breathing of the old wooden beams. Not to mention all the critters scampering about. At least Sil had gotten used to Blip curling up on his pillow at night. It was nice to have something a little familiar close by amongst so much change.

The tossing and turning had finally subsided into sleep, which was only interrupted by the first fingers of sunlight creeping in through the window, along with the calls of birds and everything else that lived in the fields around the cottage. But his new bed was cozy, staving off the early morning chill, so it was reluctantly that Sil finally got up, vowing to find a carpet to cover the freezing floorboards.

It had been since he'd still lived at home that he'd been able to start his mornings with a cup of tea in the garden, so while the cottage was still quiet, Sil pulled on a jacket with the full intent of breathing in the misty morning air. His boots weren't by the back door where he was certain he'd left them, but Anders probably wouldn't mind too much if Sil borrowed the dusty pair of yellow wellies that never got used. They were a little big for him, but he didn't plan to do more than walk around the garden and check on things while he woke up.

As he stepped out the garden door, he started to feel a little strange. The rain boots were too floppy. And his nose itched like when someone wore a down jacket around him. Sil sneezed, stumbling back a step, his feet coming out from under him.

When Sil blinked to get his bearings, the world seemed oddly far away. He'd have to scour the cottage to find the source of the feathers. There had been some pigeons hanging around the eaves. Or maybe it was because Auda had kicked up so much dust in her short stay. At least he hadn't hit his head.

Fluffing himself back up, Sil stamped his little webbed feet on the paving stones before looking around for his tea mug. Luckily, it hadn't broken, but he'd need to get some new tea. It wasn't until he tried to reach for the handle that he quacked in surprise.

Instead of his hand, a wing of white and brown feathers reached out towards his mug. He stretched his neck down past the fluff on his chest and spotted two webbed feet in place of the old yellow boots.

Feathers. Webbed feet. Quacking…

The horrible realization dawned on Sil that he was now a feathered waterfowl.

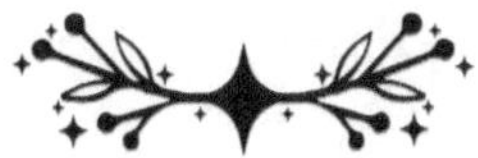

Anders had expected Sil to be up by now, but he hadn't seen or heard a peep from his assistant yet. He'd been up late again, trying to reorganize some papers and condense some notes, so he'd let himself sleep in. It was one of the few advantages of his job. Especially with Sil's help in the garden.

Wandering out of the kitchen and into the garden, Anders sipped his tea and mused about what he should get up to. He should probably wake Sil up, but he didn't want to be a bother. As he settled in one of the chairs near the kitchen door, he spotted a duck trying to lap up the remnants of an overturned mug. Its feathers were brown and white, and it had the most unusual dark round markings around its eyes.

"What are you doing? That can't be good for you," Anders said, moving to get up as the front bell rang.

He got to his feet and said to the duck, "Don't drink too much of that."

It quacked at him, wings beating excitedly.

"The caffeine would be too much for a little guy like you—"

The bell rang again, more desperately.

"Okay! Coming!"

He must have accidentally left the mug out there for the duck to have gotten into it. Tea was just roasted leaves, though; it couldn't be too bad for the poor thing. Hopefully

Sil wouldn't find out. He wouldn't think it proper for a duck to be drinking tea.

As he opened the front door, Anders was surprised to find his editor standing in the doorway with a briefcase bursting with papers.

"Torlind?"

Her trademarked bun was barely holding together on the top of her head. "Finally!" she held out her briefcase in front of her. "Take this. I have another bag."

Sure enough, she leaned over to pick up a carpet bag bigger than most dogs. She hauled it over the threshold and towards the sitting room.

"We have too much work to do, so I came myself," she said by way of explanation.

"The book isn't due for another month," Anders protested, stumbling after her.

"And how far are you on it?" she asked pointedly.

"Uh…"

"Exactly. Now you're going to gather everything you have up—notes, outlines, finished pages—and then we're going to go through it."

"I've got some things I need—" Anders tried to back away, hoping to escape out the back door.

But Torlind was quicker and grabbed his arm, dragging him across the hall into his office. "I want all of it. Even the bad stuff."

"But the garden?"

"You have magic and an assistant to do watering, if I remember correctly. You can't use magic to write."

A quack made both of them pause and glance at the hall.

The little duck was standing as if it expected something of them.

"Did you get a new pet? Or a familiar finally?" Torlind asked.

"No…the little guy was just in the garden," Anders said. There was something about it, though, especially the way its feathers ruffled up, almost in annoyance.

"Then maybe take it back into the garden?" she suggested. "We can't have any distractions on the path to a great book!"

He picked up the duck, which tried desperately to escape, and took it back into the garden, setting it down in a grassy patch. "There should be plenty of snails out here for you. I'll ask Sil to keep you company later."

The duck seemed very displeased by this and tried to come back in the door as Anders closed it. While he'd always lived around animals, he'd never had a "pet." The pipe dragon was the closest to being a pet that he had. Maybe he'd have to ask that classmate of Magda's about the little duck if it kept hanging around.

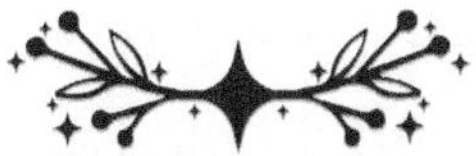

Sil flopped into a puddle in frustration. Apparently quacking wasn't translated into any common language. And even if he knew a spell to help him speak something intelligible, he didn't know how to start going about it as a duck. The sky began dripping, adding to his poor luck that morning, though the rain did roll off his feathers quite easily at least.

He was a little curious about the woman who had shown up with all the bags, though. She was a bit scary, like Auda. Maybe she was another witch?

Wriggling his feet, Sil huffed, wishing he still had the wellies on. How did you take off something that wasn't there anymore?

"Yoooooou've gotten into a mess, haven't you?" a hoarse whisper asked from the bushes across the path from Sil's puddle.

"What?"

A hissing laugh sounded from the bushes, which rustled against each other. "That spell. It's been a while since someone was dumb enough to fall for it."

Sil got up and stretched his neck and fluffed up his feathers to look bigger. "Come out here!"

The leaves shook as a goose strutted out of the bush. Three heads perched on long necks studied him. "Such a cute little duckling."

It was nearly twice Sil's size, not to mention the three heads. He waddled back a step. "That's close enough!"

"Is it?" one head asked.

"You might need our help," the second replied.

"Indeed. You might," the third added, a threatening note in its tone.

"I'm perfectly fine on my own. I was just...taking a stroll."

"It's not so easy being a little duckling out in the big, big world."

He flapped his wings as one of the heads tried to move

closer. "I'm not a duckling!"

"Suit yourself, duckling."

Another head hissed a laugh. "Good luck with the cat."

Sil glanced around quickly. "There's no cat that lives here."

"It stalks around the various properties."

The third head bobbed up and down before adding, "Along with the field dragon."

A shiver ran down Sil's back and shook his tail feathers. How had he not noticed an entire dragon? A branch behind him rustled, and he flapped his wings with a squawk.

"What was that?" he asked nervously.

The goose's heads bent back in laughter as a large toad hopped out onto the path.

"Just me," it croaked. "Ducklings should be careful 'round 'ere on their own."

"I am not a duckling! I'm a person!"

The toad's long tongue snapped out of its mouth, returning with a fly that Sil hadn't even noticed. "Duckling, person, they're all the same to me."

"*Heeeeee's* gotten himself into a *nassssssty sssssssspell*," one of the goose heads replied. "But he won't take our adviiiiiiice."

"Cerbs ain't half bad, duckling. They look out for the 'ittle ones. Don't wanna be a meal, do ya?"

"No, but—"

"Then stick with them," the toad said before hopping off down the path.

Sil glanced back at the goose and sucked in a breath. "I just need to figure out how to turn back."

"We can't help with that."

"No, but we can keep you from being eaten."

"If…"

He expected them to continue, but after the silence had stretched on, Sil asked, "'If' what?"

"If you help us out."

"With what?"

"Just a project of ours."

"*Yesssss*, a little project."

"*Sssso? Isss* that a *yesssss?*"

Did he have much choice? Not really. He had no thumbs to open the door with. And based on the smell of the wood smoke wafting from the roof, Anders had woken up the fire, so going down the chimney was out of the question. Not that he could get Anders to understand him to undo whatever jinx he'd been put under.

"Fine. I'll try to help you," Sil said.

"*Goooood,*" the middle head said. "Follow *usssss* then."

The goose started off across one of the lily beds. Sil gave the back door one more glance before hurriedly waddling after the goose into the garden. He desperately tried not to get distracted by all the plants that he noticed could use attention given his new vantage point. There was a colony of ants living in one of more overgrown herb beds. And some kind of caterpillars seemed to have decided the leeks were a good snack.

"Where are we going?" he asked as they got closer to the edge of the garden.

"Into the *woodsssss,* of course," the three heads responded in unison.

"That seems pretty far."

"*Thatsssss* because you have little *legsssss*."

His stubby little legs weren't *that* little, he thought. It was more that he kept tripping on his wide, webbed feet. Walking with duck feet was like trying to walk with pizza boxes tied to your shoes. Though it was also difficult keeping up with the goose's pace.

"What's in the woods?" he asked.

"You'll seeeee…" the goose told him, stopping at the old stone wall that marked the end of the garden. Flapping its wings, the goose alighted on the wall. "Come along, little duckling."

The wall had never seemed like much of a barrier before. It was only waist high and fairly easy to climb over. But to a duck, it might as well have been a castle rampart. He tried to hop up, but the results were pathetic to say the least.

"*Ussssse* your *wingsssss*."

If ducks could blush in embarrassment, Sil was certain he would be. Of course, he needed to try to fly. But how he was supposed to go about that, he had no idea. Flapping seemed like a decent start, but while it gave him a little lift, he very quickly crashed into the tall grass.

"He's not very good at being a duckling, *isssss* he?" one head asked the others.

Sil righted himself and shook out his feathers. He could try a running start. That might give him some momentum. Wiggling his tail feathers, he backed up several feet and began flapping as he ran towards the wall. After a few steps, he could feel himself lifting into the air, but it wasn't fast enough in relation to the wall. With a squawk, he collided into the stone and tumbled back to the ground.

The goose leaned over the edge of the wall and peered down at him. "*Perhapsssss* try flying the correct way?"

He glared as best as a duck could glare. "I'm not a duck! I don't know how to fly!"

"Every creature with wings knows how to fly."

"I'm a person! A regular person. Not a duck or any other kind of bird—a person."

Shaking its heads, the goose said, "Yet you have feathers and wings, a little bill and webbed toes."

"*Yesssss*, if it looks like a duck—"

"And quacks like a duck—"

"It must be a duckling."

If he'd had fingers, Sil would have pinched the bridge of his nose. Instead, he tried looking around for any other way up onto the wall. But all he could see was the grass swishing back and forth. Oddly, in a line coming towards him. He couldn't tell what was making the grass move, but something in the back of his mind knew it probably wasn't anything good. Running as fast as his little feet would go, he tried to put more distance between himself and the wall this time.

Putting more power into his flapping, Sil felt the air rush through his feathers, lifting him up higher and higher. As he started picking up more speed and height, he spotted the orange cat from its hiding place in the grasses and couldn't help but let out a triumphant laugh.

"I'm doing it!"

"Aye, now come down!" the goose called after him.

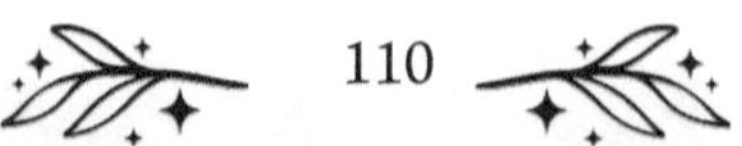

Sil hadn't thought about landing. Panic ran through him. If he stopped flapping, would he just plummet to the ground? But there wasn't too much time to wonder about the mechanics of stopping, as the branches of one of the large spruce trees acted like a net, tangling Sil up and effectively putting his first flight to an end.

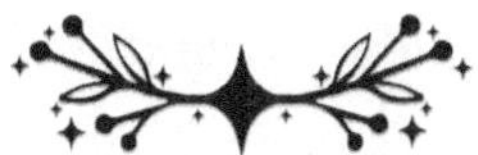

Camped out on the floor of the sitting room in front of the fire, Torlind looked half mad as she sorted through scraps of paper, notebooks, and endless piles of books with notes scribbled in the margins. Making sense of a manuscript was always the most difficult part. At least, after writing it. But Torlind always seemed fueled by the chaos.

She dropped another stack of notebooks in her lap and pointed to a pile of books. "Grab me that one on ancient gardening again."

Anders twitched a finger, sending the book floating towards his editor. He was bored. And worried that, even with all the noise that they'd been making, Sil hadn't stuck his head out to chastise them yet. But every time Anders tried to slip away, Torlind would chuck another book at him.

"Where did I put…" Torlind said to herself, tapping her chin with a red pen.

"I'm going to start another pot of tea."

"Oh no, you're not! You've got magic to refill your tea if you want more."

"Well, then, I really need to check on Sil."

Torlind blinked at him for a moment. "Who?"

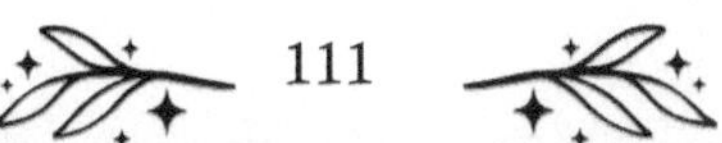

"Sil. My assistant. He just moved in. But he's not up yet. Maybe he caught the cold I had," Anders said, inching towards the back of the cottage.

"He's living here? Why the hell isn't he helping, then? Go fetch him! He can sort through these!" She held up a handful of little pieces of paper.

Anders didn't allow Torlind any time to change her mind and rushed to Sil's door. There was no answer after a few knocks, so he cracked the door open.

"Sil?"

The little pipe dragon yawned and curled up tighter on Sil's pillow, but there was no sign of him.

"That's odd…"

Maybe he'd gotten up early to do some errands? Or work in the garden? But he was certain there was no one in the garden.

"Do you know where he went, Blip?" Anders asked the pipe dragon.

She didn't respond, more than happy to be curled up in a warm spot for now.

He checked the kitchen, just to be certain Sil wasn't hiding in a corner with some tea, but he wasn't there, either. Going out the back door, he called out again, "Sil?"

But there was just the dripping of rain and the distant honks from one of the geese that roamed the area. He wasn't much of a fan of tracing spells and the like, but he was puzzled why Sil would disappear without leaving a note or something. It was so unlike him.

Returning to Sil's bedroom door, Anders gently tapped

the corners of the doorframe, then rubbed his thumbs and forefingers together. A yellowish glow began emanating from his fingers, then he snapped. Golden footprints slowly revealed themselves, leading from Sil's room to the kitchen. Then to the kitchen door. But when Anders opened the door, expecting to see the footprints leading off into the garden somewhere, there was nothing.

"He got up..." Anders muttered, retracing the footprints again. They led to the cupboard in the kitchen with the mugs, then stopped in front of the stove. "Then he got some tea. Went out and..."

"Well, where is he?" Torlind asked from behind him.

Anders jumped. "Geez!"

"Anders, I swear if you got distracted again—"

"No, I just can't find him."

His editor's foot began tapping impatiently. "You've misplaced an entire assistant that could be helping to make sense of your mess of manuscript?"

"I haven't misplaced him! He's just...gone."

"And you promise you didn't make him up to escape for a few minutes?"

"I swear!" He took Torlind's arm and pulled her towards Sil's bedroom. "See! Auda added on to the cottage 'cause Sil's lease was up, and he was going to have to move back home."

"Uh huh. Or Auda just wanted a bed that didn't stink of vomit to sleep in when she came through town."

"Sil isn't made up. Let me just make a portal, and you'll see."

Anders waved his hand in a circle, focusing on how

annoyed Sil was probably going to be with another portal showing up. The air shivered, then tree branches began to come into focus.

Torlind, as usual, was unimpressed and crossed her arms. "You've found a forest."

"Just hold on," he said, trying not to let worry ruin the spell.

It really was just a forest, though. And from the looks of it, they were up a tree. He highly doubted that, even if Sil had wandered off that morning, he'd decided to take up tree climbing.

"Maybe I should call Beren," he said. "Maybe he had to go into the shop today…"

"You do that. I'm going to make some more tea," Torlind replied with a sigh.

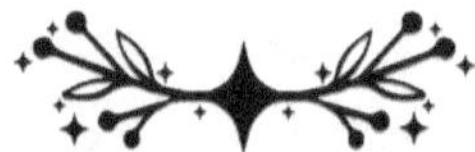

His recent dislike of heights was not improved by his current predicament. Sil peered at the ground from his precarious perch but quickly looked away. Flying had *definitely* been a mistake. Following the damn three-headed goose had been a mistake. This whole day was a mistake, and he should have stayed in bed!

"Duckling! We still have a ways to go!" the goose called up at him.

"I can't get down…"

"Don't be *sssssilly*."

"Just glide down," one of the heads insisted.

If he tried, he was going to drop like a stone and break

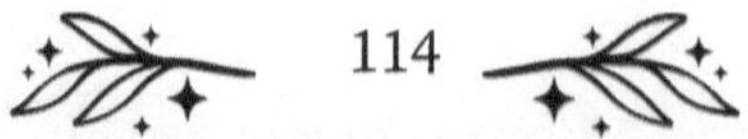

his feathery neck. He knew it. "I'll just…stay here."

"You're *sssssupposed* to help us."

"You did *promisssse.*"

"Leap off, flap a little, and don't think too hard about it."

"That's easy for you to say!" He huddled closer to the trunk. "You're a goose!"

"And you're a duckling. So, use your wings."

Sil stretched his wings out. It wasn't going to go well, but how else was he going to get down? Maybe the fall would wake him up from this terrible dream.

"Fly, little duckling!" the goose crooned at him.

He started flapping before he closed his eyes and jumped. The ground didn't rush up to meet him right away, but it was a shaky trip to the forest floor. His wings started to give out the closer the ground got, until Sil was falling the remaining few feet. He bounced on the pine needle carpet as the goose broke out into its hissing laugh again.

"*Sssssee,* everything turned out fine."

Getting to his feet, Sil used his bill to sort out his jumbled tail feathers. "It was *not* fine. I could have gotten hurt."

"But you didn't."

"Now, the perfect place should be just around the bend there."

"The perfect place for what?" he asked.

The goose bobbed up and down as it led the way, one head turning back to reply to Sil, "The pond, of course."

"Yes, do keep up duckling."

"You've been very tight-lipped about what you want help with," he said. "That's why I asked."

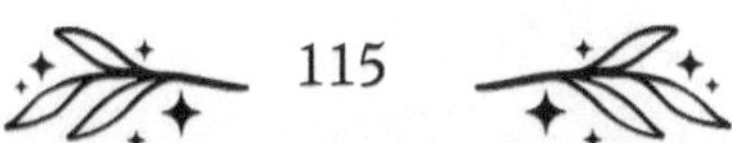

"Well, the pond needs to be somewhat isolated. We don't want all sorts thinking they can use it."

"But it's a pond. It should be open to anyone. Especially because no one owns the forest."

"We don't want other creatures mucking it up."

"Though I suppose ducklings would be alright, since you're helping to make it."

Sil paused as they came to a little ridge where the forest floor dipped down. "I can't make a pond."

"You've got water magic. Surely a pond isn't too difficult."

"What?" Sil shook his head. "No I don't. I haven't been able to figure that spell out. Besides, I'm not exactly in a form conducive to magic right now."

"I'm sure you'll figure it out."

"This really is the perfect place for the pond," another of the heads added.

"It will be nice and cool in the summer."

"And protected from the air as well."

He sighed; this damn goose obviously had seen him in the garden trying to make the stupid watering spell work but hadn't stuck around long enough to realize that it always went awry.

"I don't even know how to water plants," he protested, "let alone make water stay in a pool."

"Couldn't you just make it rain continuously?" the goose asked.

He tried to gasp, but it came out as a quack. "No. That could damage the ecosystem. The trees could fall if the ground gets too saturated. There's a pond on the other side of the

lane; couldn't you just use that one?"

"No, can't."

"Why not?" he asked, exasperated.

"The cows like that one."

"Couldn't you share?"

"We don't want to."

Crossing his wings, Sil tapped one of his feet "You're asking for an impossible, private pond."

"Yes."

"I knew this would be useless."

"Can't you just try to make the pond?" the goose asked. "You and the other wizard make all sorts of spells for the plants. Why not one for the animals—"

"You mean you?"

"Well, yes."

"Just try."

"Yes, try to make it rain duckling."

"You won't know you can't do it if you don't try."

"Fine! But nothing is going to happen," Sil told them firmly.

He spread out his wings like Anders had shown him to do with his arms and wiggled the tips of his feathers. The air was damp enough. And Sil could feel just the tiniest tingle of magic, but as usual, it felt out of reach. Closing his eyes, he whispered the rhyme that Anders had said could help.

"*Water wet, water dry, we haven't met, but hear my cry.*"

"*Ooooooh, magic words…*"

"Just like the wizard!" the goose replied to itself in a giddy tone.

Sil reached for the water again, but as he did, the magic dissipated. The spot in front of them was still dry. "See? I'm not any good at it! The only thing I can do is take care of plants!"

"And fly."

"Badly. But you did fly."

"How many ducklings that were human can say that?"

"Who's tromping around in our territory!?" a distinctly grumpy voice rumbled at them.

Sil barely flapped out of range of several very sharp sticks wielded by a troop of gnomes. About half of them were sporting Anders' homemade hats, while the other half used an assortment of mushroom caps, leaves, and other various bits and bobs from the forest.

"It's not your territory," Sil argued.

"'Tis. We cleared it nice and fair."

"You don't need more gnome huts, Veles," the goose hissed.

"We can have as many huts and houses and hovels as we want, thanks. And it is *Veles the Great and Tall* to you, horrible goose!" Veles spat. For good measure he stabbed his makeshift spear into the ground. "We've claimed all this. So out! The both of 'ya!"

"This is our new pond," the goose told him.

"Ain't no water, ain't no pond. So out."

"We have 'til at least next week to make it a pond before your contract goes into effect," the goose countered.

"Are you all fighting over this one piece of the forest?" Sil asked.

"Is the duck one of yours?" the lead gnome asked.

"The duckling is helping."

"I'm not a duck! For the last time, I'm a person! Now why don't one of you go over there and do whatever you need to?" Sil pointed a few yards away. "Besides, a location with a large dip in it wouldn't be very good for housing. And finding an actual pond would mean you have one year-round rather than trying to one make one with the help of magic."

"Hey, hey! We said no wizards involved!" the Veles said.

"He's not a wizard. He's a duckling."

"You're all somehow worse than Anders. I'm going back to the cottage," Sil said and started walking back towards the garden wall.

"But what if the wizard could help?" one of the goose's heads asked aloud. "Duckling! Could the wizard make a pond?"

"Probably," Sil replied, not slowing down.

"Then we shall ask the wizard."

"Hey! No wizards, witches, or wixen!" Veles yelled after the goose as it took off into the air.

The gnomes quickly surrounded Sil. "They can't get help from the wizard. That wasn't part of the deal."

Sil held his wings up. "Whoa, I'm not involved in all of this."

"You are now. So, move it!"

One of the gnomes pressed the pointed stick into his feathers, urging Sil to get moving.

He could attempt flying again, but it was likely to end in failure, or worse, some kind of injury. If the gnomes didn't stab him with rusty garden tools first.

As Anders was making his third pot of tea, there was a screech from the sitting room. He rushed in to see a rain cloud hovering over Torlind, dripping steadily but surely. She was desperately trying to save all the papers and books strewn around her.

"Anders! Who did you piss off to make it rain in your house?" she demanded.

"No one."

At least that he could remember. Though the stormy little gray fluff did look like some of Sil's attempts.

He waved the cloud away, then whipped up a spell to help the papers dry out. "It'll be a bit for all that to dry. Why don't you take a break?"

Torlind grumbled, wringing water out of her sweater sleeves. "Alright. No more rainstorms, though."

"The garden could use some water, actually. And the pipe dragon really should go out and get some sunlight."

"Don't get too distracted," she said, tapping her watch. "I want you back in thirty minutes."

"Alright," Anders called over his shoulder as he made a beeline for Sil's room again.

The pipe dragon was parked in the window, digging around in the mint pot for worms.

"Let's go out and see if we can't find Sil," he said, picking up the pipe dragon.

She made a little blipping sound and twisted around his

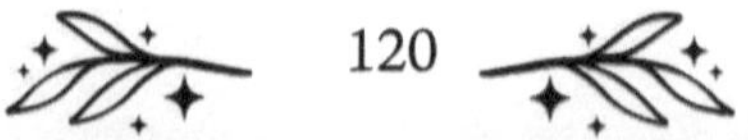

wrist.

He didn't bother hunting for his boots, but he was a little confused that his spare pair was missing from their home by the back door. The yellow galoshes had been there for years, so their sudden absence was suspicious. Especially with Sil missing. Heading out into the garden, Anders began making his rounds, watering plants absently. What if something had happened to Sil?

As he trudged along the paths, he pulled up a new portal and waved at Beren when she appeared on the other side, "Is Sil at the shop?"

Beren shook her head as she moved a flat of poppies to another table, the portal following her as she went. "No, he has a few days off to get settled. Is something the matter?"

"He might have disappeared," Anders admitted.

"Disappeared?"

"He's not in bed or in the garden."

"Have you checked in with his parents?" Beren asked.

"No, that seemed a little intrusive if it turned out he was just running errands or something. But he didn't do his morning chores. And he didn't leave a note or anything."

"That doesn't sound like him. Did you try a portal?"

"Yes, but it ended up in a tree."

Beren looked puzzled. "Strange."

"Agreed. Maybe I'll try again…"

"If he doesn't turn up, let me know. I'll reach out to his parents and ask."

"Thanks, Beren, I will." He let the portal fade and sighed. It was possible Sil was just fed up with all the changes. Or

working in the garden.

Tapping his chin, Anders whipped up another portal, focusing on Sil's glasses and the way they always slipped down his nose. It opened to show the little duck from earlier that morning, surrounded by a rather angry looking troop of garden gnomes.

It quacked loudly, flapping its wings as it made a leap for the portal. The gnomes began yelling after it in their squeaky voices, "Come back!"

"We knew you worked with the wizard!"

Falling through the portal into Anders' arms, the duck squawked louder. He quickly shut the portal before the gnomes could burst through as well and tried to calm down the poor bird. The gnomes usually left the local animals alone, so it was odd for them to be almost holding a duck hostage.

"It's alright, you're safe, little guy."

The duck began quacking loudly and nipping at Anders' cloak.

"Hey! Calm down! *Parse animalis!*"

"—and I'm going to kill that damn three-headed goose if I catch it! It just left me with those horrible gnomes! And of course, they hate you! Is there anything *good* about magic?"

Holding the little tawny duck up, Anders' eyes grew wide. "Sil?"

"Yes, it's me! I was quacking that the whole time before you tossed me back out into the garden!" Sil continued, his webbed feet paddling in the air. "Wait, you can understand me?" His head tilted adorably to one side.

"Well, now I can," Anders said, feeling a little sheepish.

If a duck could give anyone a sour look, it was Sil. His beady eyes narrowed.

Quickly changing the subject, Anders asked, "What happened to you?"

"I don't know! You're the wizard!" Sil flapped his wings angrily.

"Calm down. I don't want you to get injured."

"You try to be calm as a duck, Anders! Then you can tell me how to act."

Anders tried scritching the top of Sil's head, which resulted in Sil's feathers puffing out before he settled down into Anders' arms. "Is that better?"

"If you tell anyone about this…"

"I promise I won't. Now, let's get back inside and figure out how to change you back," Anders said.

The pipe dragon had slithered out of Anders' collar and was now inspecting Sil's feathers while coiled up on his back. If he thought he could get away with it, Anders would have taken a picture. But Sil certainly wouldn't have been pleased with that.

As he went to enter the back door, there was a loud honking and the pattering of feet running up one of the garden paths. Cerberus, the local three-headed goose, was tottering towards him.

"Ugh, not that damn goose again," Sil complained.

"Oh? What did you and Cerbs get up to?"

"Nothing! It was all a pointless escapade to try to get me to make a pond in the damn forest."

Anders couldn't hold back a laugh. "Well, that seems

very goose-like."

"And that's when the gnomes showed up. Because apparently there's a turf war going on in the garden between the gnomes and that goose. Let's just go inside."

"We should at least make sure Cerbs is alright," Anders said. "If the gnomes were fighting with them."

"The goose is fine," Sil insisted as said goose finally reached them.

One of the heads peered up at Sil while another looked behind them to ensure the gnomes weren't on their tail. "Wizard, we require assistance."

"What kind of assistance?" Anders asked.

"Oh, so you can understand the three-headed goose?" Sil said bitterly.

"Spells that allow you to converse with other species affect an area rather than a specific creature," Anders explained.

"Good to *sssssee* you escaped, duckling," Cerbs told Sil with a bob of its heads.

"With no help from you!"

"But all is well."

"Speaking of wells, we need a pond."

Anders nodded absently. "Sil mentioned you wanted him to make you a pond."

"Before the gnomes take our spot, yes."

"His efforts weren't very successful."

"Perhaps ducklings aren't very good at rain spells?"

"He may be a duck, but he's still Sil," Anders said. "Once he gets the hang of water spells, rain should be easy."

Sil nipped at Anders' hand. "None of it is easy!"

"So, the pond?" Cerbs asked again.

"I don't know... There's a pond right over in the field there." Anders pointed towards an expanse of grassland.

"The cows monopolize it."

"And the cat."

"We'd like a private one."

"Well, I don't own the forest," Anders told the goose, "so I don't think putting one there would be fair to everyone else that uses it."

"You wanted to expand the pond for the lily pads," Sil said.

"True..." Anders tapped his chin, "Do you have any idea why Sil turned into a duck?"

Cerbs eyed Anders suspiciously.

"I'll look at the garden and find a place for a pond for you and the other birds," Anders said, "but I would like Sil back to his human form. As adorable as he is."

"I'm not adorable," Sil huffed.

"You are," Cerbs and Anders replied in unison.

He puffed up again, wings folded in front of him.

"It was probably the gnomes."

"They do like their pranks."

"And they hate wizards."

"But I made them hats!" Anders said.

"It's not personal. They're trying to expand their huts and hovels."

"And we promised no wizard interference in our game."

"Yes, so they probably spelled something of yours."

"The boots!" Sil cried. "I put on those old boots that

are always by the back door to go out and drink my tea this morning!"

"I really don't know much about gnome magic," Anders admitted, wracking his brain for a solution.

"Kisses usually break spells," Cerbs suggested.

Without much thought, Anders kissed the top of Sil's head. But nothing happened.

"It has to be a real kiss," the goose scoffed.

"Don't humans know that?"

Sil blinked up at him. "I guess we could try? Unless you have any other ideas…"

Anders shrugged. "The kiss seems simplest. If that doesn't work, we'll go from there?"

"Okay…"

Under normal circumstances, Anders wouldn't be up for kissing someone who was working for him. But magic did tend to complicate things. Sil's little bill was cold as his lips pressed against it. At least the change was quick. Almost too quick. Anders found himself on the ground, with Sil in his lap, looking a little dazed.

Torlind, of course, had perfect timing, having stepped out of the kitchen to yell at Anders and instead seeing a duck transform into a person.

"Anders?" she asked.

"Uh, Torlind, I'd like to introduce my assistant, Sil. Sil, this is my editor, Torlind."

Sil was repositioning his glasses and trying to scramble to his feet. "So nice to meet you. Anders didn't mention you were coming."

"I've found it more useful not to announce my visits." She shook Sil's hand. "Now that he's found you, come inside and help me go through the mess in the sitting room. It's mostly dried out now."

"Dried out?" Sil asked her.

"Yes, assistants transforming into ducks isn't the only bizarre thing to happen to your cottage this morning."

"I'm not exactly the kind of assistant that knows about books," Sil tried to argue.

But Torlind didn't seem fazed.

Anders gave Sil a grateful smile as he was dragged back into the cottage, then he turned back to Cerbs. "Thank you for the suggestion."

"Of course. We'll miss our little duckling, though."

"He was spunky."

"And grumpy."

"I was positive he was going to get that rain spell to work."

The wizard had half a mind to tell Cerbs that he was fairly certain that Sil *had* gotten it to work. He just needed to work on targeting it a bit more carefully. But he didn't want to encourage the goose to keep pestering his beleaguered assistant.

It took a few days for Sil to feel like things had gone back to normal. Normal*ish*, at least. Torlind was entrenched in the sitting room and hardly let either Anders or himself out of her sight. Unless it was for "official garden duties," as she

called them. Sil was just glad the gnomes hadn't showed up at the garden door.

When he did manage to escape Torlind's demands, Sil retreated to the garden, where Anders had been busy moving flower beds around to create space for a hidden little pond. He was covered in mud and had wisps of grass hanging from his hair.

Sil held out a steaming mug of tea, resisting the urge to pull the grass from the wizard's hair. "How's the pond coming?"

"I managed to get the space cleared out and the pebbles spread. We can worry about plants once its filled," Anders replied, gratefully taking the mug from Sil.

"Has Cerberus 'inspected' it yet?"

"No, they were around munching on some of the slugs we uncovered."

"Well, at least that's useful."

Anders chuckled before sipping at his tea. "Did you want to try that water spell again?"

"It didn't work the last fourteen times I tried it," Sil said with a sigh. The pipe dragon chirped in his ear, and he shook his head. "I just can't make it work."

"Humor me?" Anders asked, a tinge of pleading in his tone.

Blowing out a puff of air, Sil spread his arms wide, trying not to spill his own tea and quickly whispered the spell words, "*Water wet, water dry, we haven't met, but hear my cry.*"

There was a distant rumble of thunder, but not even the hint of a sprinkle as the sun shone down brightly.

"See? Nothing," he said with a shrug, ready to trudge to the other end of the garden to take his frustration out on the weeds attempting to strangle some innocent marigolds.

Anders grabbed his arm. "Just one more time?"

"No matter how many times I do it, it's not going to happen, Anders." But Sil let Anders guide his arms into a more elongated pose, as if he were about to conduct at a symphony.

Standing behind him, Anders then adjusted his fingers slightly, and his breath ruffled the hairs on the back of Sil's neck when he said, "Now focus on exactly this spot. The daffodils swaying, poppies starting to bloom—"

"The smell of dirt and wet stones," Sil continued, letting his eyes close.

"*Rain, rain, come to play. Rain, rain don't delay,*" Anders recited as he conducted Sil's arms through the motions.

"*Rain, rain, come today. Rain, rain, come to stay,*" Sil continued, unable to ignore the earthy smell of foliage and soil that clung to Anders.

He felt a drip on his nose. Then another sliding down the lenses of his glasses. As he blinked up at the sky, it opened to a downpour. Sil wasn't certain he'd really done it. At least, not on his own. But there was a tingle in his fingertips, like static, which he hadn't felt before.

Anders was grinning like a fool, hands on his hips, seemingly immune to the chill that had come in with the sudden rain. "That is a first-class rain spell if I've ever seen one!"

"You helped," Sil said, scrunching up his shoulders to prevent droplets from running down the back of his sweater. The pipe dragon had already climbed up his arm and out of the wet.

"Not really," Anders said. "I just made some corrections. Hopefully it will let off once the pond is filled up."

"We should get inside. Wouldn't want your sister coming back if you get sick again."

With a shudder, Anders said, "Don't even suggest it!"

Field Notes
3

Cerberus (Cerbs or Cerbie)

The middle one is the only reasonable one

⭐ Three-headed common goose. Named for the Greek, three-headed dog Cerberus, guardian of the under world.

⭐ Perfers they/them pronouns and refers to themsleves as such. Each head does have their own personality afterall.

⭐ Willing to assist in the garden in return for either spellwork or ability to eat all the snails, slugs, and grubs they can find.

Who knew that Sil would make such an adorable duck? ACK! I should have gotten pictures!!! Next time…maybe.

If he wasn't so worked up about the whole situation, I might suggest some other transformations. Maybe once he gets more comfortable with magic in general he'd be up for it. Temporary transformations can be a lot of fun, and give you all sorts of new experiences. I bet he'd be brilliant at flying if he gave it a go.

We're lucky that the kiss broke the hex…  xoxoxo

At least Cerbs was there to help and tame the gnomes. I'll have to have Beren chat with them. And figure out why they're so hostile & seem to have a vendetta against magic.

Garden Gnomes

 Small statued, woodland dwelling creature with a penchant for collecting objects to be refashioned into clothing and accessories.

⭐ Commonly considered pests or nuisances.

⭐ Highly intelligent and social. Live in family groups or 'villages'.

FUNGUS & FRIENEMIES

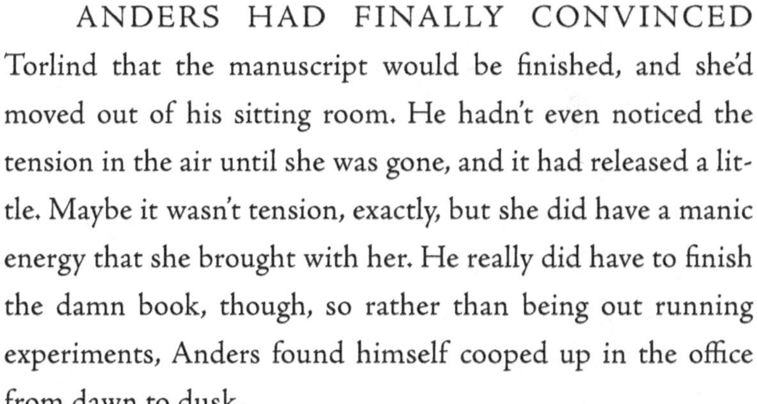

ANDERS HAD FINALLY CONVINCED Torlind that the manuscript would be finished, and she'd moved out of his sitting room. He hadn't even noticed the tension in the air until she was gone, and it had released a little. Maybe it wasn't tension, exactly, but she did have a manic energy that she brought with her. He really did have to finish the damn book, though, so rather than being out running experiments, Anders found himself cooped up in the office from dawn to dusk.

Luckily, Sil could take care of the watering and weeding and planting and all the other little tasks as the weather warmed up. He still had some issues with water spells not landing exactly where they were meant to, but at least they hadn't had another indoor rainstorm.

He glanced at the clock and groaned at the fact that it

wasn't even noon yet. While he'd made a lot of progress on the book, Anders was dying to get out into the dirt. A little break would do him good, he thought. And he might even get an idea of how to continue from where he was stuck.

Sil was curled up on a bench flipping through a book as Anders walked through the garden.

"I thought you were tired of reading?" Anders said.

"Only your scribbles," Sil replied. "I was going to get to the rest of the vegetable planting this afternoon."

"Good. It shouldn't be too warm, at least. So, what are you reading?"

"Oh, just one of Cershaw's older books. Did you see he's going to be at the bookshop for his new release?"

Anders couldn't help but wrinkle up his nose in disgust. "Is he?"

"Yeah, I didn't think he'd come to such a tiny village on his book tour."

"It's only to pester me," Anders said.

Finally looking up from his reading, Sil gave him a confused look. "You?"

"Did I say me? I meant—"

"You know Cershaw?"

"We only went to school together. And graduate school…"

Sil's eyes were shining with excitement. "Do you think he'd sign my old copies? I know they aren't in perfect condition, but surely that just proves how many times I've read them."

"I don't know. We haven't really seen each other in a

while."

"But you'll ask? It wouldn't be too much trouble, right?"

His assistant very rarely asked for anything unless it was directly related to his work in the garden, so Anders was finding it very difficult to say no to this request. "I guess it wouldn't be. But I can't promise anything."

Jumping to his feet, Sil hugged Anders before running back towards the cottage. "I have to figure out what to wear. And which books to bring…"

In his hurry, Sil had even forgotten his book on the bench. Part of Anders wanted to fling it into the pond and tell Cerbs to have at it. But that wouldn't solve anything. He was a bit shocked; Sil was not one to show gratitude with physical affection. But now Anders had to ask his sworn academic enemy to be nice to his assistant. Because the last thing Anders wanted was to disappoint Sil.

Picking up the worn book, Anders noticed a peeling book plate pasted onto the title page. Sil's name was written neatly on the yellowing paper, covering up another name: Taimi. Maybe it had been second-hand, and that was the previous owner. That at least meant Sil hadn't given Cershaw money.

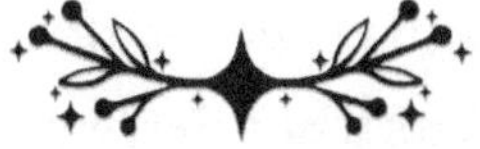

Sil had started to feel the strain of working for both Beren and Anders, but he didn't have the heart to let either one of them down. The work was easy when there was something to look forward to. Hours seemed to float by, and even the grumpy customers didn't bother him half as much as they usually did.

Magda was reluctantly tolerating his peppy mood. "Anders smooch you again?"

Sil didn't pause his sweeping. "No. And that was only to break that stupid spell."

"Then why are you so happy?" she asked.

"Anders is going to ask Cershaw to sign my books when he's in town this weekend."

"Is that supposed to mean something?" She took a sip of her iced coffee, unimpressed.

"Cershaw has one of the most popular gardening book series in the country! He's the one that hosts *Little Gardens*."

"I think my grandma watches that show. It's the one about keeping magic out of the garden, isn't it?"

"I wouldn't put it that way," Sil replied, clutching the broom. "He just sees the benefit of doing things without magic."

"Sounds lame. Magic is a tool, just like any other tool."

"Maybe if you have magic. But some of us don't."

"Beren told me you managed a rain spell."

Sil could feel his cheeks growing hot. "Only with Anders' help."

"Only people with magic can do magic Sil."

He started to retort, but Beren popped out of her office with a smile.

"What's all the chitchat about?" Beren asked.

Clearing his throat, Sil went back to sweeping. "Sorry, just discussing a book, Beren. Won't let it happen again."

"Oh, what book?"

"Cershaw's," Magda chipped in before going back to rearranging some of the pansies.

"Oh, dear. I see." Her brow furrowed, and the mushrooms in her hair seemed to sink into her curls.

"Is there something wrong with Cershaw?" Sil asked her.

"No, dear, him and Anders are just old rivals…" It sounded like she wanted to say more but didn't continue.

"Anders didn't mention that." Though Sil would admit that Anders had seemed strange about it when they'd talked.

"Well, I wouldn't worry too much, then."

But there was no stopping his spiral of worries that he'd somehow stepped into the middle of something he shouldn't have. Once he'd finished cleaning up and Magda had left for the night, Sil cornered Beren in the office.

"About Cershaw and Anders…"

"Yes?" she asked.

"They're not like 'hate each other' rivals. Right? Just competitive. Anders mentioned they went to school together."

"I think that's something you should ask Anders yourself. By the way, how are your parents?"

He wanted to push for more information, but Beren seemed determined to change the subject. "They're fine. Not exactly happy about the duck incident. But I wasn't hurt or anything, so…"

"They're just worried, I'm sure. Magic is new to them. And parents are allowed. Just give them some time. Now, isn't there a mycelium culture you're supposed to be helping Anders with?"

"There is." He sighed, not really looking forward to more work once he got back to the cottage. "Have a good night, Beren."

"Thank you, I will."

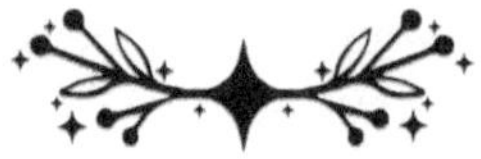

The days were stretching longer, so the sun hung around long enough for Sil to ride his bike back to the cottage. He left his bike under the eaves on the side of the cottage and walked around back. It still amazed him how the garden seemed to relax when he walked into it. Trailing his fingers along leaves as he strolled, he found Anders in a bed full of mushroom-laden logs. A few of the mushrooms were slowly inching away from the wizard, so Sil carefully scooped them up and replaced them on their designated stump.

"These were trying to escape."

"At least they don't get far fast," Anders mused, jotting down some notes.

"Have you eaten yet?"

"No, I wanted to wait for you."

"You didn't need to," Sil told him, trying to identify the various fungus. They looked similar to little button mushrooms, brown caps with white stems. It wasn't his specialty, that was for certain.

"You're home now, so we can eat." Anders smiled up at him.

Home. Someplace to curl up under a window during a rainstorm and watch the water stream down the windows with a hot cup of something in hand. The cottage was feeling

more and more like home by the day. Even if it still felt like Anders' place.

"I was going to call my parents really quick," Sil told him.

"Oh, go ahead. I'll figure out something to cook."

"I was still going to make dinner."

"Don't worry about it! I can handle the meals once in a while."

Sil nodded and let himself in the back door. The phone was in a corner of the sitting room, perched on one of those old, oddly shaped phone table-chair contraptions. Taking a deep breath, he dialed his parent's number and waited as it rang.

"Hello?" his mother's voice answered.

"Hey, it's Sil."

"Sil! Darling! Sil's on the phone!" she yelled, presumably to his father. "It's so wonderful to *finally* hear from you. Your dad and I were starting to worry something terrible had happened, since you didn't tell us you were moving. Beren had to tell us you'd turned into a duck!"

"You make it sound like turning into a duck was something I wanted to do."

"Well, my point still stands about the moving."

"My lease was up. And I'm an adult—"

"Sil! How's life with the wizard?" his father asked him, picking up the other line.

Sil sighed. "It's fine. Like every other time you've asked."

"Good, good. Want to make sure he's treating you well."

"Besides the duck incident?" Sil countered.

"That does put a mark against him, admittedly."

"It wasn't his fault. We're pretty certain it was the gnomes."

"Gnomes?" his mother cut in. "That doesn't sound safe. They can hold grudges, can't they? Oh, I didn't bother taking any of the magical curriculum in school, so I'm not as informed about all those things."

"Anders smoothed it over," Sil promised her. "It was all a big fuss over nothing in the end."

"You know we just worry about you, Sil," His mother said. There was a grunt of agreement from his father.

"Everything is fine. It's nice to have a roommate."

"Just so long as he isn't taking advantage of you, son," his father said.

"He wouldn't do that. Anders is a nice person. Just… different."

"It's the magic. It makes people strange," his father said.

As if on cue, Anders poked his head in the sitting room. "You could invite them for dinner," he whispered.

"Sil, dear?" his mother asked.

"Huh? Oh, Anders said you should come over for dinner." Why had he asked them over for dinner? It wasn't like having a new roommate was a big deal. People had been sharing rooms, houses, lodging for centuries.

"We could do that…" It sounded like she wanted to be enthusiastic. "I could bring my casserole—"

"You don't need to bring anything. I'll let you know when later. Bye!" Sil quickly dropped the receiver back on its stand and stared at it for a moment.

"Sorry, I didn't mean to butt in. I just thought you might be missing them," Anders said.

"No, its fine. I'll figure out a time for them to come by…"

"How about this weekend? My parents will be in town as well. And Auda, of course."

"Oh…" He wasn't certain if it was some milestone, meeting each other's parents. Was it normal to meet your roommate's parents? Somehow, that seemed like a "more than friends" sort of thing.

"I'll expand the kitchen and sitting room so there will be enough space for everyone," Anders said, "so don't worry about that."

"That sounds good."

"Fantastic!" Anders seemed rather excited to meet his parents, which was strange.

"Um…" Sil hesitated, then pressed on. "Beren mentioned that you and Cershaw were rivals. You…you don't need to bother about asking him to sign my books."

"I told you I would. So, I will," Anders said reassuringly. "Dinner'll be done soon, by the way."

"Thanks."

Was Sil the one making the situation weird? Anders didn't seem fazed about having his parents over. Then again, maybe it was just because he'd been lonely and was taking advantage of the promise of company. And if Anders' parents were there, too, the whole thing would be on much more equal footing.

Though it still felt as if they'd reached some kind of strange crossroads…

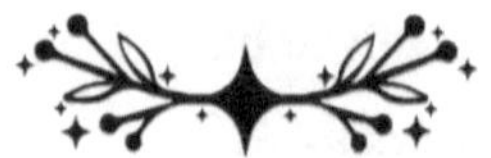

The mushrooms were becoming a problem. It had warmed up significantly that week, which had pushed them into erupting. Which was fine, really. Except that Anders hadn't anticipated dealing with them for another few weeks. Torlind would be thrilled, though. His study on mushrooms was the last part of the book, and according to her, that's what was holding it up. Maybe inviting their parental units for dinner on top of everything else wasn't the best plan?

Anders did thrive in a little chaos, though.

As he scribbled out notes and diagrams, Anders' thoughts started to wander. Sil had been rather subdued and far less spiky since he'd moved into the cottage. It had to be all the changes. And he was busy, not to mention exhausted. He'd nearly fallen asleep during dinner the night before.

Scanning back over his notes, Anders realized none of them were making sense, so he picked up his bucket of gardening tools and deposited them next to the back door. Sil was sorting seed packets or, rather, the mess of envelopes and baggies that Anders had collected over the years, at the kitchen table. The little pipe dragon seemed thrilled about this project, darting across the table to retrieve spare seeds and pull them into a little pile.

"Blip seems to be having fun," Anders said, rubbing her head with his finger.

"I think she's decided to hoard seeds."

Shrugging, Anders scooted a few errant seeds into her pile. "There are worse things for dragons to hoard. Back home, we had a mossy green that liked to hoard my mother's pies."

"I'm just glad she hasn't tried ripping into the packaged ones yet," Sil told him.

"Fair. I was going to walk into the village. Want to come with me?"

"I should really finish this up. Then I've got some more weeding I've been avoiding."

"That's alright." Admittedly, he was a little disappointed, but he didn't want Sil to feel guilty. "I'll be back later then."

He could have easily opened a portal and ended up right in front of the coffee shop, but Anders started the trek down the muddy lane, noting which local pollinators were out enjoying the wildflowers that had popped up along the fences and walls.

It was almost too warm for his cloak, but he felt a little silly without it. And it had a wonderful array of pockets to stash trinkets or little treasures he found along the way. With Sil around so much now, Anders had started to forget what it was like to always be alone. And that felt like a good thing.

As he came into the village, he noticed a gaggle of people huddled near the bookshop. Maybe a new novel had just come out? But as he passed the shop, he heard the grinding voice of Cershaw.

"It's been lovely to meet you all," his rival said, "but I really must be going. I hope to see you all at my book release on Saturday."

There was a chorus of disappointment, and Anders thought he'd escaped Cershaw's notice. But then…

"Anderson? Is that you, old boy?"

He flinched at the poor excuse for a nickname. "Cershaw. I didn't know you would be in town."

"Well, my editors gave me a little more leeway on my tour schedule this time. I couldn't pass up visiting such a quaint little village."

Anders rolled his eyes as Cershaw strode up to him, looking smart as ever in a dark suit.

"Now, we should get reacquainted. It's been years."

"Has it?" Anders said. "Grad school seems like just yesterday."

Cershaw barked out a dry laugh. "Oh, don't tell me your mind is finally going!"

"No. It's just as sharp as before. And I'm sure you're too busy—"

"Nonsense! I heard your new book is due out any time now."

"Yes, soon."

"Then congratulations are in order!" Cershaw took hold of Anders' elbow and steered him towards the pub.

Settling down into a booth, Cershaw flagged down one of the servers and ordered some drinks for them.

"Now, what have you been up to?"

"Research. Same as always," Anders told him.

"Ah, with that little mock garden of yours?"

"It's not a 'mock' anything. It's a state-of-the-art research garden. I was just working on a project with mobile bottle mushrooms this morning!"

"No need to get all riled up." Cershaw's grin curled up on one side of his face. Anders had once thought his grin was

charming. Right now, though, he wanted to throw his drink in the other man's face.

"Then don't be dismissive of my work." Anders curled his fingers around the edge of the worn wooden table so he wouldn't be too tempted to do something he might regret.

"Tosh! I was only joking! You never could take a joke."

He could take jokes just fine, he just didn't appreciate being belittled.

"How are your parents?" Cershaw asked.

"Fine."

"And Auden?"

He let his fingers uncurl a little, twitching out the start of a nasty blistering curse.

"*Auda*," Anders snapped coldly.

"Right, of course. I forget."

"She's only been Auda since before you met her." They might bicker like hell, but Auda was still his sister.

Cershaw's smile soured. "So mushrooms? Sounds more like student work."

"There's still a lot to be learned about mycelium neural networks. Especially of the more magically imbued species."

"Of course. If that's what you're interested in."

"It's better than writing another drab "make your best garden" book."

"And yet I'm the best seller, and you're the one fighting for scraps of funding," Cershaw said, leaning back in the booth with a smug look.

"I do just fine, thanks."

"Are you with anyone?"

"No. And that's a rather personal question, thank you."

"Guess I'm a bit difficult to live up to, huh?"

The server dropped off their drinks before Anders could say what he really wanted to. So instead, he said, "You were a bad decision in a bag of many bad decisions I made."

"Not many people would agree with that. I'm quite a catch. I've been on the front page of a number of magazines as the most eligible bachelor in the country."

Anders sucked in a breath to try to calm himself down. "That's because most people haven't spent more than five minutes with you."

"You're allowed to be jealous of me. I have the fame, the money..." He looked Anders up and down. "I have style and clothes that aren't falling apart, my dear Anderson"

"You're nothing special, *Marion!*" Anders spat back.

The grin sank from Cershaw's face. "I don't go by that. It's Michal."

"And I have *never* gone by Anderson!" Getting to his feet and dropping a handful of coins on the table, Anders put on a fake smile. "But really, I could care less. I hope you fall in a bog. Oh, wait, that would require you to *abandon your hordes of fans and go outside!*"

Storming out of the pub felt good at that moment, but the farther down the street he walked, the more guilty Anders felt for making a scene. It wasn't the servers' fault that Cershaw knew how to get under his skin, even after years of being able to avoid each other.

He found himself at the plant shop before long and was glad that it was Sil's day off. He didn't know that he could deal with Sil's level of snark at the moment. Magda was petting her familiar, a long-haired tabby called Marvin, at the register.

"Didn't expect you in today, Wizard Kessel," she said.

"I just needed some air. Is Beren in back?"

"Yeah. But she was on the phone dealing with suppliers."

"I'll be quiet, then. Thanks Magda."

He really wished she wouldn't be so formal. He wasn't one of her professors or anything, just a customer. But he didn't want to fight right then. Slipping to the back of the shop, he pulled the door to Beren's office open.

"Yes, that will be just fine," Beren was saying. "Add on the pallet of garden soil and that should be all for this week. Thank you." As she finished up her conversation, she was already pouring Anders a cup of tea. "You look dreadful. Something the matter?"

"Cershaw's in town early. I had the misfortune of running into him just now."

Beren shut the door with a flick of her wrist. "I see. Still a pompous ass, then?"

"A bigger one! Somehow!" Anders leaned back against one of Beren's overstuffed bookshelves, feeling deflated. "Now he's a best-seller, of course! And I'm just a scholar trying to do actual research! Why is that such a bad thing? I want to make sure my books are based on facts and will inform and teach people!"

"It's called morals, Anders. He just never had any."

"Ugh, how am I going to beg for him to sign Sil's books now?"

She paused for a moment, setting aside her tea and try-

ing to offer Anders an understanding expression. "You could always explain to Sil why you don't want to?"

"No, I already told him it was a promise. I'm not going to let my personal feelings about that asshole ruin something for Sil."

"That's very kind, but I think he'd understand."

"He'd still be disappointed." Anders set his tea mug down in mid air, as if her were placing it on a shelf, and pulled a tiny vial of honey out of his cloak. After dripping a few golden drops into the mug, he sipped at it.

"Disappointment is part of life, isn't it? But on a brighter, different note, I did have an interesting conversation the other day."

He appreciated Beren changing the subject. "Oh?"

She rummaged through some papers on her desk, finally pulling out a page with notes scribbled on it.

"Yes. A producer of some cooking show stopped by a few times. Apparently, they're filming later this year and looking for someone to provide produce for the show."

"That would be great for you!"

"I actually suggested you might be able to provide it. We don't really have the setup for a kitchen garden here. Your garden is far more suited. And your knowledge, too, with your climate spells and such."

"Me?" Anders nearly dropped his mug.

"With Sil's help, of course. They wouldn't be filming 'til the end of the summer, so there's still time to plant any special requests they might have."

Beren offered him the page of notes and reluctantly

took it, skimming through her looped handwriting quickly.

"I've never really done anything like that. I don't even watch TV that often."

"It might be a nice change of pace…from all that scholarly work," Beren said an air of knowing in her tone.

She was right, of course. Once this current book was finished, he didn't have any more research projects planned. It was worth a try, he supposed. "I'll have to talk it over with Sil."

"Of course. I'll get you the producer's contact information. But he sounded excited when I described your garden."

"It's just a garden," Anders said disparagingly.

"No, it is not. It's a well-loved, magical place that you've spent years working on. Don't sell yourself short."

"That's why I have you. To sing my praises."

Anders tucked Beren's notes into a cloak pocket.

Beren snorted. "I see. How is your little pipe dragon doing? Better?"

"Yes, much. She's started hoarding seeds."

"How perfect! I'll make sure to send you home with some jars or seed packets for her. She has become rather attached to Sil," Beren said with a smile.

Anders smiled and settled into the old armchair. "I noticed. She even curls up next to his head to sleep. It's adorable."

"It might be worth investigating if she might be his familiar?"

"That would take convincing him that he has a knack for magic."

"I'm sure you'll get through to him," Beren said, leaning back in her chair with a sigh. "He just needs more confidence in that area. Then he'll be casting like the best of us."

"I hope so. He has so much potential. If he'd just see it."

"Sometimes people have to come to conclusions on their own. He'll get there."

Sil couldn't believe how late he'd been running all day. No matter what he did, he couldn't seem to catch up. He was rushing to finish up everything in the garden before they needed to be in the village to meet all the parents and for Cershaw's book release. After some wheedling between him and Anders, they'd decided dinner at the pub would be easier for everyone. And yet, Sil still felt like he had a million things to do.

Yanking on one of the hoses, he backed into the wobbly little table they'd pulled out so Anders could take notes on the mushroom experiments more easily. The table tipped over, sending papers, notebooks, and the stack of reading Sil had foolishly thought he might be able to get to that week.

"Oh, for the love of…" He cursed, dropping the hose to pick up the mess.

Luckily, nothing seemed to have crushed the mushrooms. They had been quick enough to scamper out of the way.

"I'm sorry! I just—ugh!" Sil piled everything back on the table and grabbed the book he wanted Cershaw to sign before running into the cottage to clean up.

Anders had been quiet all day. Moping, almost. It wasn't like him, but Sil didn't have the time to coddle him with everything that needed done.

Before rushing into his room, Sil called to Anders, "I'll just be a couple minutes!"

"Don't worry about it. We can be a little late."

"No, we can't! Two minutes!"

He hurriedly stripped out of his muddy clothes and nearly fell over yanking on a clean pair of trousers. Luckily, he'd picked out his outfit days ago. With a quick comb yanked through his hair, Sil grabbed his shoes and skidded into the kitchen.

"Are you ready?" he asked, glancing at Anders quickly.

As usual, the wizard was wearing his worn out cloak over faded trousers and a shirt that had been patched more than once.

"Yes. I've been ready," Anders answered, sharper than usual. "We'll just use a portal to pop over; we'll be fine."

"Right. Let's go, then." With his shoes and sweater on, Sil hugged the book to his chest and tried to push any thoughts of forgetting anything out of his mind.

Swiping his hands in the air, Anders summoned a portal that opened up onto the village's main street. He motioned for Sil to go through first. There was a line winding down the street from the bookshop already. It looked like half the county had crowded onto the sidewalk. He tried his best to hide his annoyance, but Sil hadn't anticipated the book release to be so busy.

"Guess we should get in line…" Sil suggested as Anders came through the portal.

"Yup."

Sil slipped into line at the end. "My parents seem excited

to meet you."

"Hrm." He just wanted to get this over with quickly and painlessly. Then he could sit through dinner with their *parents*. This was a comedy of errors if there ever was one.

Pushing his glasses up, Sil sighed. "You can just go to the pub if you want to."

"No. It's fine."

"Anders, I can wait on my own."

Someone wrapped an arm around his shoulders, and Sil stiffened at the casual touch. "Anderson, who is this adorable waif?"

Anders ground his teeth. "Cershaw, leave him—"

Sil backed against the storefront, trying to keep his wits about him. "Mr. Cershaw?"

"Yes, now what's your name?" he grinned, his smile matching the author photo in the back of his books perfectly.

"Sil."

"Sil? Just that?"

"Yes…uh…I'm Anders' assistant."

Cershaw smiled wider. "I see. It's good to meet you. Come inside. No need to wait out here. Not when Anderson and I go back so far."

"I wouldn't want to jump the line. These people have been waiting—"

"It's fine; old friends can always skip the line." Cershaw wrapped his arm back around Sil's shoulders and began leading them to the bookshop entrance.

"It's nice to meet you," Sil said, heart racing. "I've been a fan for a long time."

"Have you now? That's so good to hear." Cershaw sat down at the table stacked high with copies of his new book and held his hand out expectantly. "I imagine you want me to sign that?"

"If it's not too much trouble…" Sil said, handing over the worn book.

"Not at all," Cershaw said, opening to the title page and signing his name with a flourish. Then he pulled a copy of his new book off the stack and signed that as well, adding a little note before handing both back to Sil.

"Oh, I can't—"

"It's a gift. To an old friend," Cershaw replied with a wink. "Have anything for me to sign, Anderson?"

"No. My parents are waiting at pub; we should go, Sil."

Cershaw's face tightened a little. "Too bad. Give them my love."

Anders grumbled something under his breath as he squeezed past the people in line to leave.

Sil thanked Cershaw again before chasing after him, finally grabbing the edge of Anders' cloak a couple blocks away. "Anders! What was all that about?"

"Nothing! Can we just go get dinner over with?"

He actually sounded angry, which Sil had never witnessed before. Even when Auda had appeared unannounced, it was clear that, while Anders was complaining, there was an understanding between them. But this was vastly different. His shoulders were slumped and Sil wouldn't be surprised if a tiny black cloud began hovering over his head. Though the starkest change was the stern quiet.

"You didn't have to come…" Sil began.

"I told you I would. Now it's done, and we can have dinner and forget about him."

"I'm not hungry anymore," Sil told him. He wished he'd never mentioned the damn book release to Anders, not if he was going to be upset over it. "If you can't deal with being around someone you went to school with… I just…I'm going home. Tell all the parents and Auda I'm not feeling well."

"Sil! Wait!" Anders called after him but didn't try to stop him.

Sil shook his head and walked on. Moving in with Anders had been a terrible idea. He should have just moved back in with his parents. Then he wouldn't be out the rent. Or have to deal with *whatever* this was.

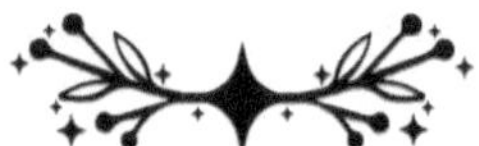

"Sil's not feeling well?" Lyssa, Sil's mother asked in a concerned tone after they'd settled in the pub for dinner.

Anders nodded, picking at the sticky film that covered the table. "He said to apologize."

"It's good to meet you both anyhow," Anders' mother, Odell, piped in with a smile. "Maybe Auda can drop by later with some soup?"

"I think he wanted to be alone," Anders explained. If the dinner was bound to be awkward before. it was worse now.

Auda nudged him. "I'll pop by anyhow. Just to check on him."

"It's good to know that Sil has made some friends, at least. He stopped talking to a lot of the friends he had from school," Sil's father said. It was clear that Sil had inherited his mousy features from his mother. But his matter-of-fact attitude came from his father.

"I agree, Wilton. I do wish he'd still go to see Taimi. They used to be so close," Lynna said, shaking her head.

"People do move on, dear. You know that," Wilton said, paging through the drinks menu.

Lynna tipped Wilton's menu down so she could give her husband a disapproving look, "Yes, but being around people his age might convince him to go back to school and finish up his degree."

"Oh, what was he studying?" Odell asked cheerily.

"Accounting," Wilton replied.

Auda gulped down half of her wine. "Accounting? He wasn't studying any magic? Or maybe botany?"

"We're not a magical family," Lynna said, adjusting her flatware so it was perfectly perpendicular to the edge of the table.

"Anyone can study magic. He's not half bad with the couple of spells Anders has taught him so far," Auda said.

"Our Sil? You're sure?" Wilton asked, actually setting his menu down for a moment.

"Seen it myself, right, Anders?"

Anders just wanted to escape this entire situation. He hadn't been angry at Sil, and yet he'd taken it all out on him. "Sorry, what Auda?"

"The spells you've been teaching Sil, he's not half bad at them, right?"

"Yeah…sure."

"Show me to the ladies' room, Anders," Auda told him, shoving him out of his seat.

"You know where—"

Auda elbowed him in the stomach and gave Sil's parents an apologetic smile, "Sorry, Mr. and Mrs. Fennen. We'll be right back."

"Can you ask the bar keep for another beer on your way back?" their father asked.

"Yes da—"

Auda proceeded to drag Anders to the back of the pub and corner him. "What the hell is going on?"

"Nothing!"

She shook her head. "*Nothing?*"

Anders stared at the dirt clinging to his old leather work boots. "Cershaw is in town."

"Why the hell is that bastard here?"

"He said it's for his stupid book release! I think he's purposely trying to torment me. There's no reason for him to come here."

Auda peered back towards their table and discreetly snapped her fingers. A hazy bubble surrounded the two of them, cutting out the noise from the pub.

"Okay, that still doesn't explain why Sil was upset, though. He was perfectly fine this morning when I dropped in, so what's going on?"

Taking a deep breath, Anders tried to level his voice before replying, "It's…Cershaw was being handsy with him, and I just…"

Disgust flashed across Auda's face. "That man needs to

be slapped."

"Be my guest."

"So, you lost your temper?"

"No, I just…was upset. Sil doesn't like strangers touching him, and Cershaw just wrapped his arm around him and—ugh! He's such a slime ball, but Sil is a fan, and I couldn't warn him he was such a jerk."

Auda raised an eyebrow and crossed her arms. "So what are you going to do about it?"

"Apologize?"

"And?"

"And what?" he asked, spreading out his arms in defeat.

"Some groveling might be required."

"That seems a bit much…"

"Anders, you're not acting like yourself. And you made your 'assistant' upset," she said with air quotes.

His shoulders hunched up in impertinence. "What's that supposed to mean?"

"That you need to figure out what's going on between you and Sil before either of you ruins it. I'll go by the cottage and stop in. You have fun entertaining the parents. Just try to cheer up a little, or Sil's parents might think you're hiding their son from them. Or you've turned him back into a duck."

"I'm not! And I would never do that! Without permission."

"I know that. Parents are just fickle, you know that."

"I'll do my best."

"Good." Auda snapped her fingers again to dissolve the bubble of silence. "Now, shoo, back to the table!"

Anders retreated to the booth and tried to smile. "Auda is going to go to the cottage to make sure Sil is doing okay."

"She really is the best at mothering," Anders' father mused. "We ordered for you."

"Thanks," he said, wishing for the evening to be over.

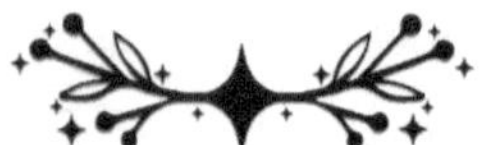

The banging on the front door didn't stop, so Sil finally pulled himself out of bed and opened it. Auda was stood on the front step with a cast iron pot in hand.

"I bring soup and chocolate," she announced.

"I'm not really—"

"Misery doesn't look good on anyone. Now, come on." She wedged herself inside and headed for the kitchen. Why she even bothered knocking, he wasn't sure.

"Shouldn't you be at dinner?"

Auda shrugged as she started taking bowls out of cupboards. "I bailed. Anders will live. Sounds like he needs some punishment, anyhow."

Sil wiped his eyes and knew that she'd noticed how puffy they were. "I'm not in the mood for company."

"Luckily I'm just Anders' sister, then. Go put your pjs on, and we can curl up by the fire."

With a sigh, Sil went back to his room. He'd rather unceremoniously dumped the books on the dresser when he'd gotten back to the cottage, but they'd tumbled off. As he picked them up, he flipped the new book open to see what Cershaw had written:

"*To my biggest fan, M.H. Cershaw.*"

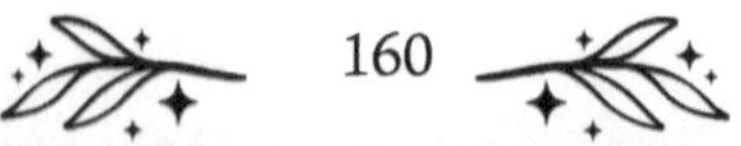

"He's always had a big head, you know," Auda said from the kitchen.

"Who?"

"*Marion* H. Cershaw."

"His name is Michal," Sil said.

Auda snorted. "That's what he tells everyone. That's just a penname. He has the nerve to get all haughty over people calling him Marion when he *refuses* to call anyone by what they prefer."

Sil pulled on a pair of flannel pajama pants before coming back out to the kitchen, "I thought it was weird that he called Anders 'Anderson.'"

"It was a pet name at one point."

"A pet name?" The idea of someone he'd idolized for years having a pet name for Anders seemed impossible. And given the upsetting encounter with Cershaw earlier that evening, it gave Sil the shivers.

She paused and started dishing up the soup. "Anders should really tell you."

"Do a lot of wizards have hangups about names?" he asked, allowing for the change in subject.

"More than most probably. We like knowing 'real' names." Auda said.

Sil curled into one of the kitchen chairs, hugging one of his knees to his chest.

"What makes a name more real?"

"Well, you know all that lore about fairies being able to do spells with your true name, right?"

"Yeah."

"It can make spells that involve that person easier, yes. But we also just like to know things."

He really shouldn't have been surprised it was so banal. "So, the answer is you're nosy."

"More or less."

Sil couldn't help but smile, "I guess that makes sense, if you're just trying to get to know someone."

"Exactly! Now, dessert?" Auda began pulling chocolate bars wrapped in brightly colored foil wrappers out of her bag.

"We haven't eaten the soup yet…" Sil said, even as he reached for a spiced chocolate bar wrapped in red and gold.

"It'll keep. But tonight seems more like a chocolate night."

"I can agree there."

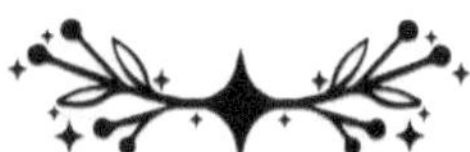

Somehow the hours had dragged on, and dinner had turned into dessert and drinks, and then more dessert and coffee. Sil's parents looked glad to finally escape. Though Mrs. Fennen did come away with Anders' mother's lemon tart recipe. So, it couldn't have been a terrible evening. When he popped back to the cottage via portal, Auda was still sitting by the fire in the sitting room.

"Where's Sil?" Anders asked.

"He went to bed a little while ago. Even with chocolate for dinner, he was falling over. You're working him too hard."

"I am not!" Anders whispered.

Auda waved her hand at him impatiently. "I already put up a quiet spell on his room."

Dropping into the other chair in the sitting room, Anders grumbled, "Thank you. Is he still mad?"

"I think he's more hurt. You need to tell him about Marion."

"I don't want to talk about him." Anders replied firmly.

"Too bad. It will explain things."

"Why do you have to be right?"

Auda perched a porcelain tea cup on her knee while she twirled open a raspberry truffle. "Because I'm an outsider who isn't as emotionally invested. How was dinner?"

"I think we scared Sil's parents," Anders admitted.

"The non-magical are so easily riled up. If they knew half the things we'd gotten into as kids."

"I think the fact they can imagine is what terrifies them. I was hoping having a normal dinner would calm them down so they wouldn't worry about Sil as much. But I think that backfired."

"He's an adult. They can't really do much," Auda said with a shrug.

"I guess so. I just wanted to make a good impression." Anders willed himself not to pick at the loose threads on the arm of the chair. Auda had always been better at reading him.

Auda sipped at her hot chocolate, suspiciously not commenting.

"What?"

"Nothing. I didn't say anything," Auda said.

"You're thinking something."

"Is that a crime?"

Anders leaned forward and squinted at her, wishing for

a moment that he could read her thoughts. "No, but you're still thinking it."

"You never told me how you broke the little jinx the gnomes put on your boots."

Anders knew his flushed cheeks gave him away. "It had to be done."

She grinned knowingly. "So you *did* kiss him."

"It was just to break the spell. It's a common way to break stupid little curses," Anders insisted, stealing one of the chocolate bars she had stacked on the arm rest of her chair.

"All the same. He let you, didn't he?"

"Well, yes. But he didn't want to be a duck anymore," Anders said.

"I bet he was so cute," Auda replied, grinning to herself. "He was…"

"And see, this is why you need to tell him about Marion and get all that out of the way. That jerk doesn't deserve any more space in your budding little relationship with Sil."

Taking an aggressive bite of the chocolate bar, Anders said, "Nothing is *budding!*"

"You should plan a date," Auda told him, giggling.

"No!"

"It would be good for you. Both of you. Oh! You could go to the Royal Gardens! They're having an exhibition soon."

Anders hadn't been to the Royal Gardens in at least a year, he'd just gotten so busy with the book, and his research.

"That's a long way away," Anders said.

"That's what portals are for."

"Sil doesn't really like them."

"Then a romantic train ride sounds like just the thing," Auda said, leaning over to dig a tattered leather notebook out of her bag. "I think I still have a couple old classmates that work there. I could see about getting you passes. Plus, it might inspire your next research project."

"Beren actually had a lead on that."

"Really?"

"Yeah, she said a producer from a cooking show reached out about growing stuff for the show," Anders said.

"Interesting. All the same, I'll talk to Yolanda about passes for you two," Auda said, scribbling something down in her notebook.

"Fine."

"Good. Oh, I was hoping you might be able to babysit Crusher for me."

Anders shook his head. "Oh, no! That dragon hates me!"

"Aw, he just wants a plaything. And it would only be for a couple of weeks. I have to go to the mountains for some research, and I really can't take him with me."

"No."

Auda batted her eyes, "*Plllllllease?* I'm helping you with Sil."

"If that dragon ruins any of the plants in the garden—" Anders began to say.

"I'll bring him by on Wednesday. Now I really should be off. Lots to do! I'll leave the soup for you and Sil." She kissed his cheek and grinned at him. "Just stop being such a grumpy puss. Only one of you can be a grump."

"Goodbye, Auda…"

"Totty-bye!"

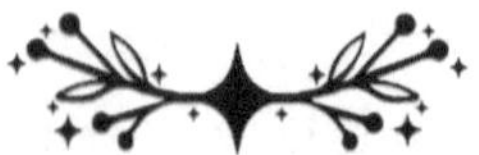

Why people had to ruin the peace and quiet of a perfectly good morning by pounding on the cottage door was beyond Sil. It went on long enough that he figured that Anders was still too groggy, so Sil shoved his gloves into his apron pocket and picked up the pipe dragon from where she was trying to steal the seeds he'd been planting.

He found a very disheveled Cershaw on the doorstep. His hair was sticking out at all ends, and it looked like he'd gotten dressed in the dark given how his shirt was on backwards.

"Mr. Cershaw?"

"You've infected me!"

"Excuse me?" Sil asked.

Cershaw pulled his shirt sleeve up to reveal a row of tiny mushroom caps dotting up his arm.

Sil pushed his glasses up his nose and leaned in closer to look at them. They did look similar to the ones in the garden. But Sil didn't know enough about fungus to tell for certain.

"I'm not really sure how you think I'm responsible."

"Then it was Anders! How am I supposed to finish my book tour infested with mushrooms? They even spread to my bed at the inn!"

Chewing on his bottom lip, Sil suggested, "Maybe you should look something up to fix it?"

"Oh, no! Don't you dare try to put this off on me! One of you did this, and you're going to fix it!"

"Or you could leave and never come back," Anders sniped, leaning over Sil.

"Anders, fix it, damn it!"

Anders just shrugged. "You're the best-selling garden book author, not me. Certainly you can find some vinegar solution or something to fix it. Oh! Maybe you'll get sponsored by a fungicide!"

"You—you'll be hearing from my people!"

"Suit yourself," Anders told him.

"Mr. Cershaw?" Sil asked.

"What!?"

Sil spread out his arms. "I just thought of something to try."

"Then do it!"

"You asked for it. 'Rain, rain, please pour down. Rain, rain, just don't drown the town.'"

There was a crack of thunder and what seemed like a tub of water dumped on Cershaw's head. He let out a shrill shriek. "Curse the both of you!"

The little rain cloud chased after him, finally disappearing once he opened a portal a bit down the road.

"Serves him right," Sil said, shutting the door.

Anders was trying desperately to stifle his laughter. "I can't wait to tell Auda about this."

"Yeah, she'd probably enjoy it. She didn't seem to have much love for him either."

"Did he have mushrooms sprouting out of his arm?" Anders asked, walking to the kitchen.

"Looked like it. I don't know why he thought it had

anything to do with either of us."

"I have a theory," Anders said. "Mind if I see those books you had signed?"

"Sure, if you really want to." Sil went to his room and grabbed them. A few tiny mushrooms had started growing from between the pages. "What in the world?"

Anders carefully took the books from Sil and turned them over. "You had this one out near my mushroom garden. A couple spores must have caught a ride."

"I did accidentally knock the table over when I was hurrying to go."

"That would do it."

Sil took the books back and strutted to the back door, shoving on his wellies before going out to Anders' mushroom bed. He unceremoniously dropped both volumes into the dirt. "Well the mushrooms can have them."

"Are you sure?" Anders asked, pulling his cloak tighter around himself.

"Positive. Auda might have alluded that the two of you were..."

"Exes?" The wizard sounded embarrassed.

"Yeah. If I'd known, I wouldn't have ever asked you to go, let alone gotten a signature from him."

Anders pulled him into a tight hug. "I didn't want to disappoint you!"

"It's fine. As they say, never meet your heroes."

"I mean, I wouldn't say that's a hard and fast rule..."

"No, I'm good without meeting any more famous people. *Ever.*"

Field Notes
4

Tips for the Care of Mushrooms & Fungi

Mycellium thrives in shady, cool places.

Once the spawn has inoculated a suitable growing medium, mushrooms can be harvested and regrown for 3-5 years. They will spring up after a good rain, or a shower in your case, Marion.

I believe the variety you were 'infected' with, is a variety of button mushrooms. They can be eaten raw or cooked. Store them in a paper bag in your ice box for up to five days, or dry them for later use!

Good luck! - Anders

MEET BESTSELLING AUTHOR, M.H. CERSHAW!

ONLY AT THE BATTERED PAGE BOOKSHOPPE; 3-6PM

M.H. CERSHAW'S GUIDE TO A GREEN GARDEN

A GREAT BOOK FOR BEGINNER GARDENERS.
- DONTEN MONTEGUE

IT'S A GARDENING BOOK I SUPPOSE...
- WIXEN BEREN AYTON

ake Beren cookies!

nders would also like cookies, please!

0!

cake?

Greenhouses & Grimoires

HE'D NEVER RIDDEN FIRST CLASS ON A train. They had their own compartment, like those old mystery serials his grandmother liked to watch. Anders was deep into his final copy edits on his book, so Sil had brought his own books to read through, including the copy of *Beginnings of Magical Learning* Auda had left with him. It was horribly dry, and he doubted he was going to get much of anything out of it. But he wanted to humor her. After all, she had arranged the entire trip for them.

Crusher snored loudly at Sil's feet, rolling over on his side, tongue lolling out of his mouth. He was incredibly affectionate for a bull dragon, much to Anders' annoyance. Though it had caused some trouble with Blip. Since her shed, she'd become very territorial over Sil, especially with the wildlife that frequented the garden. She was happily tucked around

Sil's neck, snoozing as well.

"Should I be concerned that lighting a candle is one of the first spells in this book?" Sil asked aloud.

"The theory is that if you learn to deal with fire early, you'll be less likely to burn something down."

Sil frowned, not sure that he should be trying half of the spells in the book, let alone ones involving fire.

Absently, Anders reached across the table between them and flipped to the middle of volume. "Try some growing spells with those sunflower seeds. That's more up your alley."

Propping his chin on his arm, Sil pulled a couple of sunflower seeds out of the packet and started reading through the instructions.

"Hold the seed pinched between two fingers. Give it warmth. Then water. And it should sprout."

He held the seed out, willing it to warm up. The first seed popped, much like popcorn, and catapulted against the window.

"Gentler," Anders said without looking up from marking his manuscript with a red pen.

Picking up another seed, Sil tried to dial it back. After a few more tries, he finally stopped exploding the seeds between his fingertips and burning his fingers. He tried dropping the seed in a glass of water, but it simply bubbled a few times before it lay at the bottom of the glass.

"You can't drown it," Anders told him, finally pushing aside his work. Holding his hand out palm up, he closed his eyes. A droplet of water formed in the palm of his hand. "You just need a drop."

"I don't think the train company would appreciate a rainstorm inside the train."

Anders cracked a smile. "Fair." He took Sil's hand and tipped the drop into Sil's palm.

Carefully, Sil placed the seed into the drop of water and watched as the shell protecting it began to crack open. A tendril of green began emerging from the seed, leaves unfolding and leaning towards the window.

"See, you're a natural."

"But doesn't germinating seeds like this mess up the process of growing for the plants? If the germination is accelerated, it could promote weaker plants that shouldn't have survived."

"And that's the conundrum with magic. What do you use magic on, and what do you not?"

"Soooo…?"

"You have to decide for yourself what you want to use magic for. Though never to harm someone. That's never a good path to go down."

"What about making it pour down rain on someone?" Sil asked sheepishly.

"Cershaw wasn't harmed. Wet, but unharmed. And I hear he still has mushrooms on his arm."

Sil couldn't help but snigger. "He really should find a fungicide to sponsor him."

"Not our problem."

"We shall be arriving at Paddington Place within the next five minutes. Please gather your belongings if you plan to depart. This train will continue onto Nix Farm. Thank you for traveling

with Albion Rail."

"That's us," Anders said, starting to collect his papers and shoving them into a pocket of his cloak.

Sil put his books into his backpack and double checked that he hadn't dropped anything. Once he was satisfied that he hadn't missed anything, he gently shook the potbellied dragon that was snoozing at his feet.

"Come on, Crusher; its almost time to get off the train," he said.

Crusher yawned and stretched out groggily.

"I still think we should have left him with Magda's classmate for the day," Anders said.

"It'll be fine. And magical animals of all sorts are allowed at the gardens; I double checked."

"Yes, yes."

Sil picked up the dragon's lead and nudged him towards the narrow corridor so they could disembark. The station was smaller than some of the ones in the city, and most of the other travelers looked to be tourists like themselves, with their noses buried in maps and pamphlets. The last time Sil had been on holiday was when he was still in grade school. Most of his free time was taken up by reading, taking care of his plants, or picking up extra shifts at whatever job he had at the time.

"You know the way, right?" he asked Anders. Of course, he'd looked up the winding route from the station to the Royal Gardens, but Anders had been there several times.

"Of course." Anders motioned at the hill behind the station. "It's up there."

"You usually portal there, don't you?" Sil asked.

"Well, yes. But I still know the way."

"Then you lead the way," Sil said.

Anders started on the trek, which consisted of a long, winding stone staircase that disappeared into the trees. Crusher was already huffing and puffing after about fifteen minutes, smoke rising from his nostrils.

"Maybe we should take the magical shortcut?" Sil suggested. "For Crusher's sake. I don't think Auda planned on her dragon passing out."

"That might be for the best," Anders agreed, opening a portal for them to step through.

The magic tickled as Sil shuffled through the crystalline portal. At least it wasn't as jarring as it had been the first few times. He'd been noticing that more, though, the feeling of magic, whenever Anders used it or Sil managed to complete a spell that wasn't completely wonky.

They arrived at the door of a greenhouse the size of a barn, the huge glass panels sparkling in the sunlight and distorting the greenery hidden inside. Sil's eyes widened as he turned to take in the grounds. He'd expected a more formal space, but there were garden beds overflowing with native wildflowers and clumps of vegetables. No wonder Anders had been so eager to visit; it was like the cottage garden but on a massive scale.

"One of Auda's old classmates said they'd meet us to give us a proper tour. Was there anything in particular you wanted to see?" Anders asked him.

"I didn't realize it would be so…huge!"

"It doesn't seem as big once you know your way around," a young woman with dark hair said as she approached them. She held out her hand and smiled. "I'm Yolanda. You must be Sil?"

"I am." Sil shook her hand, dragging his attention away from the expanse of foliage.

"Wonderful. Anders, it's good to see you again."

"Same. We have Crusher with us. That will be alright?"

"Oh, of course." She knelt down to scratch the scales under Crusher's chin. "We'll just keep an eye on him in the hot houses. Some of those plants can be toxic to native dragons."

"My...uh, *our*, pipe dragon came along as well. She's a little attached," Sil admitted.

"Perfectly fine. Familiars and creatures are all allowed—within reasonable limits."

"I wanted to see your vegetable gardens," Anders said. "If we have time."

"Sure. I thought you were more into ornamentals and mushrooms."

"Usually. But I'm curious."

"Well, we should get started then. We usually start in the big greenhouse here," Yolanda said, opening the door.

Sil walked into the sticky heat of the greenhouse, immediately wishing that he'd dressed in fewer layers.

"We don't use as many micro-climate spells here as Anders does," Yolanda explained. "But we do maintain the temperature in here very carefully."

"It's a huge space to keep heated," Sil said, taking out a notebook to jot down some notes. The whole greenhouse smelt like damp soil and lightly floral. Crusher had quickly busied himself with sniffing every leaf in range of his snout.

Yoland smiled. "Luckily, the sun does a lot of the work for us. Especially on nice days like this. We had to open the vents earlier."

"What do you use for temperature control then?" Sil asked kneeling down to get a closer look at an unusual lily. The plant leaned towards him, almost as if it were inspecting Sil. Blip chirped protectively from her perch under Sil's collar and the lily shrank back.

"Heated pipes, like in the front herb bed," Anders replied before Yolanda could.

"Exactly. We try to keep some things maintainable for our less magically savvy staff."

"You must have an army of caretakers," Sil said.

"Fewer than we'd like, but we make do. Oh, we don't normally allow it, but if there are any leaves or blooms that have fallen on any of the paths, feel free to take them. Just leave anything that's fallen in the beds or natural areas."

Sil turned to Yolanda, "Really?"

"Of course. Just don't brag to anyone about it," Yolanda said with a wink.

Anders pulled on Crusher's leash as he became a little too interested in one of the lilies. "How's your corpse flower doing?"

"We think it might be blooming soon, actually."

"That's good to hear. It never bloomed while I was studying here."

"I thought you just did some projects here," Sil said,

slipping a snowy white lily petal into his notebook to press later.

"Before I had the cottage garden set up, I used to run experiments here. But I worked here as a student, too."

"Anders is being modest," Yolanda said. "The micro-climate spells we do use are his design. And he helped facilitate opening our moss gardens."

Anders kept his attention on a patch of bluebells as he murmured. "There were plenty of native specimens around. I just suggested collecting and arranging them."

"We've expanded into some tropical species in here, too."

Anders' eyes grew wide. "Oh, I'd love to see that!"

"Torlind is not going to let you add anything else to the book," Sil warned.

"I can still keep it in mind for the future." His bottom lip threatened to slip out and form a pout.

"When is your new book due out?" Yolanda asked.

"Soon?" Anders said sheepishly. "We don't have a hard date yet."

"I'll keep an eye out for it."

Sil trailed behind them as they continued to talk shop about academia and recently published studies and papers. Anders' micro-climate spells had been novel to him, but he hadn't considered that the wizard had invented them himself. As far as Sil had been able to find, there wasn't any literature on them. Which meant that the Royal Gardens and the cottage garden were probably the only places the spells were in use. It felt even more special that he was allowed free rein of Ander's garden.

The greenhouse had so many varieties of flowers and bushes that Sil had never seen. It was a bit overwhelming. Really, there was no reason to add anything so exotic to the cottage garden, but it was nice to look. He was more than grateful to escape the muggy greenhouse and be back outside, though. Crusher seemed to agree, loafing in a patch of grass.

"You doing okay, buddy?" Sil asked him, rubbing his nubby horns.

He snorted in reply.

"I can leave you two to look around some of the walled gardens, then I'll take you to the food gardens this afternoon," Yolanda suggested.

"That sounds fine. Sil packed us a full picnic, so we'll probably eat that," Anders said.

"Oh, fantastic! Enjoy yourselves, then, and I'll find you both later." She winked at Sil before wandering off.

"What was that about?"

"I have no idea," Anders replied.

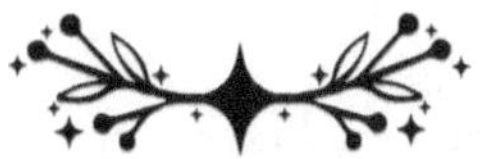

Anders knew exactly why Yolanda had left them on their own to explore the grounds. Because Auda had most certainly insinuated that the trip was a "date," not just a visit to somewhere both he and Sil happened to be interested in. Luckily, no one had leaked that insinuation to Sil. He probably would have been horrified, and his face would have been the shade of a tomato for days.

"Where do you want to see first?" Anders asked.

Prepared as always, Sil pulled a map of the gardens out

of his notebook. It was full of scribbles and circled areas. "It looks like we're close to the stream. I'd like to see the marsh and wetland plants they have."

"Your tuft tails are much more impressive," Anders assured him.

Sil cleared his throat and buried his face in the map again. "They have some other things I wanted to see there."

"Okay. It should be cooler over there, too. And maybe we can find a place to eat."

He led them to the path that wound around a series of orchards before running parallel to the little stream. Sil was careful not to step off the path but seemed more than happy to list off all the types of reeds and other aquatic plant life present.

"Oh, they have alisma mixed in with the cattails over there!" Sil pointed out some bunches of paddle-shaped leaves with wiry stems topped with white flowers.

"I didn't know you were such an expert on water plants," Anders admitted.

"My parents' yard backed up to a brook, and we used to trek around the marshes hunting frogs in the summer. I just kinda picked up the names and stuff."

"I know there used to be a wandering willow down a bit. It's probably still there. Or nearby," Anders said as he looked over Sil's shoulder at the map.

"Oh, I've never seen one of those. The streams around where I grew up weren't really big enough to support them." Sil said, nudging Crusher along. "Aren't they also called 'wishing willows'?"

"In some places. They're supposed to be lucky if you come across the same tree more than once since they like to move around." He'd never been that interested in tracking the tree down when he was working at the gardens, but it seemed like something Sil would like to see.

"What would you wish for then?" Sil asked.

"I don't know. I never really believed in that, I guess."

Sil started stuffing the map and his notebook into his bag with his free hand, "You're a wizard, but you don't believe in a wishing willow granting you a wish?"

Anders took Crusher's leash from Sil so the dragon wouldn't try to escape into the reeds. "No."

"You're so strange. How about wishing for your book launch to go well?"

"Even if I don't believe in it, I can't tell you what I'd wish for. It would ruin the wish. Besides, we'd have to find the tree first," Anders said, looking down at the stream flowing past. "I'm surprised it's something you believe in."

Sil shrugged. "I did when I was kid."

"And now you don't?"

"Well, when you grow up wanting to have magic and you don't, you kinda give up on things like wishing willows."

Sil held out his hand for Crusher's leash, which Anders gladly handed back. The oversized lizard at least pretended to listen to Sil.

"Magic is something you have to practice, just like painting or foreign languages. There's no 'having it' or 'not having it.'"

"Maybe when your parents are wixen. But mine weren't.

I had friends who took magic classes and stuff, but that was just never an option for me."

Anders resisted pulling Sil into a hug, even though he could sense it would be alright in the moment. "You have the option now, though."

"Yeah..."

"You do! All it would take is practice. And I think you'll be brilliant at it."

Sil frowned and fidgeted with Crusher's leash. "I'm kinda old to start."

"Nonsense! Some of the best wixen didn't start their formal magical education until their thirties or forties, or even later! Merlin was probably in his eighties..."

"I have enough going on with managing the shop and managing you," Sil said.

Anders crossed his arms, his cloak billowing out behind him for a moment. "I don't need managed!"

"Oh, yes, you do! You constantly get distracted from your work, and you forget to eat!"

"You were so much cuter as a duck," Anders teased, changing the subject.

"Because you didn't have to understand me?"

Anders chuckled. Even with the animal language spell making trans-species communication possible, Anders had thought Sil was cute. "No! Never! It's sad you didn't get to try out swimming as a duck..."

"I'm good without doing that, thanks. Flying was bad enough."

Spreading out his arms, Anders closed his eyes for a mo-

ment. "Flying is fun." Exhilarating even. Dragon riding could even be a cure for acrophobia, which might be something to keep in mind for Sil in the future.

"You've been a bird?"

The question jostled Anders out of his thoughts and back to Sil.

"What? No. Just ridden dragons." It was so easy to forget how "normal" Sil's upbringing had been.

"Oh! Just ridden a dragon?" Sil said teasingly.

"We had them on the farm. Sometimes they needed to stretch their wings."

"Most people don't get to ride dragons."

"Well, that's because most of the native species that aren't protected are little pig-sized monsters like Crusher," Anders said, glancing down at his sister's familiar.

"He's not that bad. He's been very well-behaved, all things considered," Sil said as Crusher tried to pull him into the stream.

"We should ask if we can see the library while we're here."

Sil's nose scrunched up, and he pulled out his map again. "There's no library on the map."

"It's not really open to the public," Anders admitted. He was certain that Yolanda or one of his old professors would give them permission to look around the research library for a while. So long as they didn't bother anyone. Sil would probably just find a corner and get absorbed in a book on cultivating curse resistant plants or something until it was time to catch their train.

"We're the public last I checked."

"But we do have certain connections."

"If it wouldn't get anyone in trouble, I guess," Sil said, nodding to himself.

Anders' grinned. Sil did love a library. Maybe this was a *little* bit like a date?

They'd nearly walked the length of the stream without passing the wandering willow, but where the stream pooled into a pond, the old willow stood leaning back and forth in the breeze.

"Is that it?" Sil asked him.

Nodding, Anders pressed his hand against the trunk.

"So how do you make a wish?"

Anders picked up a silvery-green leaf from the ground and twirled the spade shape between his fingers. "Like this."

Placing the leaf to his lips, Anders whispered his wish, then let the wind whip the leaf away. He watched it until it disappeared into the nearby woods.

"I hope your wish comes true, then," Sil said.

Anders hoped so, too.

"We should eat," Anders said quickly, starting to dig around in the pockets of his cloak for the food that Sil had given him to carry.

Sil watched with mild curiosity as Anders pulled out wrapped sandwiches. "So is there just infinite space in the pockets?"

"Not 'infinite' but a lot. The key is to have everything partitioned so you can find where you put things," Anders replied, fingers trying to figure out where the marmalade jar had gotten.

"There's a recall spell I was reading about that can pull objects to you..." Sil suggested.

"Well, if you want to do things the easy way." Anders spread his fingers out to keep the pocket open for Sil. "Try your hand at it."

"Me?"

"You have to start practicing. Might as well give it a go."

Sil shook his head no. "I just read about the concept of the spell—"

"Yes, and if it's in a beginner spell book, you should be able to figure it out. So, give it a whack so we can eat lunch. And do it before Crusher starts trying to climb into my cloak in search of food."

Pushing his round glasses up his nose, Sil locked his eyes on the pocket. Blip squeaked encouragingly from her perch wrapped around Sil's shoulders. He opened his hand, and a sandwich wrapped in brown paper flew from the depths of Anders' cloak and into Sil's hand.

Glee spread over Anders' face. "See! You're a natural!"

Sil was inspecting the sandwich as if it might be something poisonous. "How did that even..."

"You're the one that studied the spell. How is it supposed to work?"

"You picture the object, then imagine it in your hand. But there has to be more to it than that. Otherwise, everyone would use magic."

"It's an art, Sil. Some people are naturally better at magic than others. It doesn't mean it isn't work. It just means you have some natural skill at it already. And a lot of people just don't *want* to use magic."

"The sandwich is a little warm," Sil finally said.

"Oh, I figured they'd be okay at room temp for a while."

His assistant rolled his eyes. "We're going to talk about food safety later."

Crusher had started pawing at Sil's leg in an attempt to reach the sandwich he was holding, so Anders quickly extracted the remainder of their picnic, laying it out on the bank of the stream for them so they could watch the leaves float by. His sister's dragon immediately tried to stick his snout into the spread that Sil had prepared them. But Anders didn't mind if the dragon got into something. Sil was laughing as he held back the little monster from devouring their entire lunch in a few mouthfuls.

After finishing up their lunch by the stream, Sil and Anders found their way to the vegetable gardens before Yolanda tracked them down again. While they waited for her, Anders had been scratching away in a tattered notebook, sketching out the telltale rows of new beds. He hadn't mentioned wanting to start anything new to Sil, so maybe it was just an idea. But he did proceed to grill Yolanda on what she knew of edible plant varieties.

"I've heard that carrots can be difficult," Anders said.

"You mostly leave them alone," Yolanda said. "Once you thin them out and make sure they're kept moist during germination. You do want to be wary of gophers and moles and that sort of thing, though. Especially with root vegetables."

"I don't know that we have a problem with the typical rodents, but I'm sure the gnomes or Cerbs will know if any have moved in. I try to use natural deterrents or physical barriers in most of the garden."

"The gnomes would probably encourage the gophers," Sil said.

Crusher had climbed into his lap on the bench he'd been sitting on and settled down, snoozing after stealing half of their lunch. For how small the dragon was, he weighed enough to match a wet bag of potting soil. Or a boulder.

"They said they were sorry."

"Having trouble with them?" Yolanda asked.

"They, uh…were fighting with one of the neighbor's geese, and Sil got roped in the middle of it," Anders admitted, scratching the back of his head nervously.

"Oh, dear. I have always marveled at the fact that you have so few problems with your local wildlife," Yolanda said, leaning back on her heels.

"I try to leave them alone and give them their space. Did you by chance have time to make a list of the garden's edible plants? I know I mentioned it to Auda."

Yolanda nodded. "Yes, I was going to grab it for you before you left. I am curious as to what you're plotting with all this sudden interest in the world of vegetables."

"So am I," Sil commented, trying to shove Crusher off his lap.

"I'm just…thinking…" Anders said.

"And sketching things out."

Anders looked a little guilty as he closed his notebook. "It's just ideas."

Sil huffed. "And more work for me. You hardly even use the herbs you do have. They're just there to look pretty and smell good at this point."

"You did sign up to be my assistant," Anders pointed out.

Sil really couldn't argue with that even if the idea of more work annoyed him. Their rent and payment agreement was still rather loose. His parents would probably have fits if he admitted to them that there was no official contract or lease in place.

"Oh, before we leave," Anders said, "I wondered if it would be possible to pop into the library?"

Yolanda scratched the back of her neck. "I'd have to ask."

"Would you? If you don't mind?" Anders asked.

"Of course."

"Thanks. I think Sil would really enjoy seeing it."

Yolanda started heading towards one of the stone buildings, "My boss will be leaving shortly, so I should go grab him and ask. If you want to meet me by the big greenhouse again?"

"Sure thing." The wizard called after her.

Sil tried again to move Crusher off his lap "Come on, boy. My legs are falling asleep."

Anders bent over to help him up.

As they headed towards the greenhouse, Sil noticed that an old man was digging around in one of the beds that outlined the greenhouse. He stopped what he was doing as they passed and tipped his hat to them.

"Would the two of youse mind taste testing something for us?"

"So long as it's not that black licorice mint, MacGregor," Anders replied.

The old man chuckled. "No. We scrapped that when you were still a student. This your apprentice? 'Bout time you got one."

Before Sil could correct the old man, Anders did. "No, just a friend. Sil, this is Old MacGregor. He's been a gardener here since the dark ages."

"Aaaah, not that long, Kessel. Well, you see I've got this tea here. And I need some volunteers." The old man held up a dinged-up thermos.

"Sure," Anders said, taking the thermos from him and using the cap to pour some of the tea out. He took a swig, then passed it to Sil.

Sil sniffed the sweet tea and tasted it. "What is it?"

"Violet and honey. Supposed to be good fer 'ya. How's the taste?"

"A bit sweet but not much else. It kinda sticks to the back of your mouth," Sil replied.

"Hrm, I'll have to work on that. The sweetness should fade eventually. Maybe add in something earthy. You staying much longer, Kessel?"

"No, we were hoping to poke into the library really quick, then head home on the evening train."

"Good luck in your travels, then," MacGregor said, taking back the thermos and pulling out a packet of waxed paper. "Take some of these tea cakes with you for your trip."

Anders took them with a smile, shoving them into one of his cloak pockets. "Thanks."

"Another old teacher?" Sil asked as they walked away.

"Sort of. Not officially at least. But MacGregor was always cooking up all kinds of experimental treats. And broke students are usually willing to be guinea pigs."

"The tea wasn't half bad."

"Yeah, that was fairly normal given what MacGregor normally cooks up."

"What does he *normally* cook up?" Sil asked, dread suddenly puddling in his stomach.

Shrugging, Anders began ticking things off his fingers as they passed by rows of immaculate garden beds with little plaques planted in front of them. "There were the fizzy lemon drops that made your mouth numb. And the brownies that made a couple of exchange students invisible for a week. Oh! The polka dot peppers gave everyone spots. And a classic: pixie dust."

Sil could feel his eyebrows raising. "Pixie dust?" Some days it felt like there was a whole other world he had never experienced until he started working for Anders.

"I mean he didn't come up with that one so much as collected it and distilled the stuff into a syrup. It was great fun once you got the hang of it."

"So, he was just giving out a syrup that could make you fly?"

"Well, only on moonlit nights. That's when pixie magic works best."

Sil opened the door to the big greenhouse and wished

they'd planned to meet Yolanda somewhere else. Sweat was already dripping down the back of his shirt, and they'd only been inside a few seconds.

"How is it more humid in here than before?"

"The afternoon is always the warmest part of the day," Anders said, pulling off his cloak and draping it over his arm.

Sil knelt down to make sure Crusher's harness was still tight so he couldn't go rummaging in things he shouldn't be. He didn't remember the straps being so thick before. Maybe he'd just been tired. They had gotten up early to make the train. Then again, Crusher was also a bit bigger than Sil thought he should have been.

As Sil turned to Anders, the plants suddenly looked a lot taller as well. Even with acceleration spells, they shouldn't have grown so much in the course of a few hours. Unless they were part of some special experiment. And Sil was certain that Yolanda would have mentioned that. The pipe dragon which had been snoozing on his shoulders most of the day wriggled her way down Sil's arm and perched on Crusher's back.

"Anders?"

The wizard was glancing around as well. "It's not just you…"

"What do you mean?" But as Sil asked, he realized that nothing was getting bigger—they were shrinking.

"Not again!"

"You don't have feathers this time," Anders said, trying to be helpful.

"If I did, I could fly at least!"

Crusher was watching them curiously as Sil shrank to

being barely as tall as a dandelion.

"The key is not to panic," Anders said.

"I'm not panicking! I want to know what the hell did this!" The grass and weeds resembled trees. *Scales*, he couldn't even see past the bend in the path through the greenhouse! Cracks between the flagstones weren't just an inconvenience you had to walk over, they were big enough to fall into.

Anders winced. "Shrinking violet tea…maybe?"

Sil glared at him. "You mean one of Mr. MacGregor's random experiments?"

Crusher tried to bat at Sil, but he crossed his arms and told the dragon firmly, "No! Anders, how do we change back?"

The wizard shrugged. "He said the sweetness would wear off?"

"We are six inches tall!"

"The library might have something…"

"Great! Where's that?"

"Across the yard."

Sil looked up at Crusher and Blip, who was very curious about her new, tinier companions. "You've ridden a dragon. Think we can ride Crusher?"

Anders frowned. "I have no idea, but I sense we're going to try."

"Unless you can portal us into the library?"

"That might be faster. No offense, but I don't think Crusher has done this much walking in ages."

"Portal it is, then," Sil said.

He really hoped these situations weren't a regular occurrence.

Getting to the library had been the easy part. Crusher had waddled along behind them, and Blip had been cooing over Sil, clearly glad that her favorite person was the same size as her. She still wanted to wrap around poor Sil, though, more resembling an overly long scarf than a pipe dragon as she coiled around Sil's body.

"Anders, how are we supposed to get to any of the books if we're six inches high?"

Admittedly, Anders hadn't thought that far. "I could portal up onto a shelf and push the book off…"

"That could damage the book!"

"I'm just putting ideas out. I don't even know where to start. Let me look around and see what I can find. If they haven't moved the section on jinxes, we can start there."

Sil huffed and sat down next to the corner of the first shelf. The shelves normally towered over everyone, but from the perspective of the floor, it really was a massive library.

Anders leaned down and ruffled Sil's hair. "Either we'll find a spell to fix it, or it will wear off. No big deal."

"I just wish this sort of thing would stop happening."

"It comes with the territory. Magic works in mysterious way. Or is it 'magic does as it pleases'?"

"I should have become an accountant. Accountants don't turn into ducks or get shrunk by tea." Sil pouted, hugging his backpack on his lap.

"Just stay here so I can find you again."

"Noted. Don't get lost in the library."

"Oh, and watch out for the bookworms."

Sil glared at him again. Setting down his cloak next to Sil, Anders hastily opened another portal, really hoping his memory of where the books on jinxes were kept was accurate. Or that shrinking violet tea qualified as a jinx. Maybe he should start with the effects of medicinal plants? Or try to find a section on shrinking potions. He shook his head; even the library at the Royal Gardens didn't have everything! Though plants were used in potion making. All this was much more in line with Auda's knowledge base. Potions and jinxes were far more complicated than plants. Most of the time.

He walked along the bottom shelf where he thought he remembered the jinxes might be shelved, tilting his head to the side to read the embossed titles. He was much more used to crouching down to read the lower shelves.

"*Jinxes, Hexes and Spells of Annoyance*, no… We should have tried kissing. For all I know, that would work again."

Anders tried pulling another book off the shelf, but it was wedged in tightly. He yanked as hard as he could but just ended up toppling across the aisle. Rubbing the back of his head, which had connected with the edge of the shelf, he grumbled. Maybe it would be better just to wait it out. Though, he did remember one of MacGregor's previous experiments turning the Head of Planting's hair into string for weeks before they figured out how to reverse it. It would be impossible to get all the work they needed to get done if they were tiny.

Grateful that their clothes and what they'd been holding had shrunk with them, Sil dug the beginner's spell book out of his backpack and started flipping through it. Maybe there was something useful in the book, but Sil had no idea what. There wasn't a chapter called "So your employer's old acquaintance shrunk you." But why would there be? That might actually have been useful rather than six different spells to get rid of dragon rash.

Blip nuzzled his ear, nearly toppling Sil over.

"Ack! Careful!"

The pipe dragon didn't seem to care, wrapping around Sil's waist just in time for Anders to pop back through another portal.

"Any luck?" Sil asked.

"Not really…" He nodded at the spell book. "You?"

Sil replied dryly, "I can solve your dragon rash problem."

"Luckily I don't have that," Anders said, his eyes scanning the titles of the books on the shelf behind Sil.

"So, we're just stuck like this?"

"It'll wear off," The wizard promised.

"You hope."

It could take days or weeks for the effects to wear off. Especially since it was a random gardener's strange, experimental tea.

"I'm pretty sure."

"Don't you know some spell that could help? Like a growing spell?" Sil asked.

"Those are for plants. People are complicated."

"Uh huh…"

Anders grabbed the spell book and turned to one of the first chapters, pointing out a passage that read, "*Great care should be taken with spells not meant for humans.*"

"Couldn't we test it on something?" Sil asked.

"I don't think Auda would ever forgive me if we accidentally blew up Crusher."

"*We?* I'm not helping with any spell we think might help! I would just ruin it."

"You wouldn't ruin it."

"Why do you have so much confidence in me?" Sil asked him. "I flooded the cottage before I got that watering spell anywhere close to correct."

"You retrieved our lunch just fine." Shrugging, the wizard started rummaging through the pockets of his cloak. "And because I know you have potential."

"To run amok maybe."

"If every witch, wizard, or wixen that didn't get their first spell one hundred percent correct the first time gave up, then we wouldn't have any. Magic takes practice. And work. And believing in it. Hungry?" Anders asked him, taking out a bag of snacks.

Crusher's nostrils flared, and he tried to use his tongue to pry the miniature treats out of Anders' hand.

"No! No! Not for you!" Anders scolded, then he held the snacks out to Sil.

"I'm fine. I can't believe he's still hungry."

"I'm pretty sure he's got a bottomless pit for a stomach."

Reaching deep into another pocket, Anders pulled out the bag of Crusher's food they'd brought along. The two of them looked at it for a moment and then at Crusher.

"That's not even the size of a treat," Sil said.

"Nope." Anders set down the bag of food out of Crusher's reach and made a series of hand motions over it until it grew in size.

"And you couldn't try that spell?" Sil asked him as Crusher started devouring the enlarged dragon chow.

"It's strictly not for humans. I never studied much magic to do with humans."

"Wish you had."

Anders sat down next to him and started munching on a biscuit. "Sadly I'm shite at time travel spells, too."

"Those aren't a thing," Sil said, stealing part of one of the biscuits.

"How would you know?"

Sil turned to the end of the beginner's spellbook and jabbed a finger at the page. "It says so right here."

Smiling, Anders shrugged. "You never know. Maybe there are and they just don't want beginner wixen getting into them."

"This book may be for children, but it's not for idiots."

"Alright, as far as I know, there are no time travel spells."

"And yet I've been turned into duck and shrunk in the same month. That has to be a record."

Anders offered him another biscuit. "Maybe."

Crusher's snorting as he ate didn't allow for much contemplative silence.

"At least it was nice seeing the gardens today."

"Good. I'm glad you enjoyed it."

"Why are you interested in vegetables all of a sudden?" Sil asked, nibbling at the biscuit. They were bland, but at least they were absorbing the after taste from the tea concoction.

"Oh…just something Beren suggested."

"If it's something that would increase my workload, you should tell me."

Anders pulled a notebook from his cloak. "Apparently there's some show that's looking for a farm or something to grow produce for them."

"But we're not a farm," Sil said. Vegetables were a whole other beast when it came to gardening. The closest he'd been to that type of gardening was his little windowsill herb collection. Or going to the farmer's market as a kid.

"No, but it might be an interesting project. I haven't done much with edibles besides the mushrooms and herb garden. It could be fun."

"Isn't it a little late to get started on that? Especially without much experience. And where would we be putting all this? What if the plants don't survive?" There were a million things that could go wrong.

"It's not too late. The producers are okay with a little magical help to get the starts going. And they want some specialty things that most farms don't bother with," Anders explained and flipped to another page to show Sil a diagram. "We'd add on another set of beds on the north side of the cottage. We might have to use a location spell to squeeze in everything on their list, but I think it will work. And I highly doubt that, between the two of us, we can't handle vegetables."

"Seems like a lot of work for something silly like a show,"

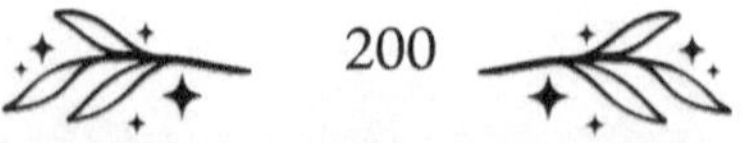

Sil admitted. Though he'd have a nicer view from his bedroom if there were rows of vegetables.

"At least we're not dealing with an orchard! They have another little farm that handles all the fruit. But their usual supplier for other things retired and sold," Anders said, his tone getting a little excited.

"I guess it would keep you busy since the book is nearly done."

"That's what Beren and Auda thought."

Sil sighed, "That makes me think that if you have too much time on your hands, mischief happens."

"No! Why would you think that?"

If he didn't like Anders at this point, Sil would have been seriously considered quitting. But the little dash of chaos was refreshing. Just not this much chaos.

"We are currently six inches tall because an old man ran out of students to experiment on. And you said he was an inspiration," Sil said.

"Okay, that's not entirely fair!" Anders replied.

"Yes, it is!"

The wax paper packet of tea cakes that MacGregor had given Anders slipped out of his cloak.

"I don't think we should try those. Given the circumstances," Sil said.

Opening the packet, Anders sniffed them, "They smell okay."

"That doesn't mean anything!"

Taking one out, Anders inspected it. Sil had to admit they looked good. And fairly normal.

Crusher leaned over and licked Anders, the tiny morsel ending up stuck to the dragon's tongue as he swallowed.

"Shit!" Anders shook the slobber off his hands and arms and jumped to his feet. "Don't swallow that, Crusher!"

"I really don't think you're getting it back at this point."

"They're probably normal tea cakes…right?"

Blip cooed.

"For your sake, you better hope so," Sil said, warily eyeing the dragon. "I do *not* want to see your sister angry."

Crusher burped and gave them a puzzled look.

Anders took a step back. "Sil…I think you should get up."

The pipe dragon seemed to agree and started pulling Sil away from the bull dragon.

First his feet started to expand. Then his stumpy tail. His belly. His mouth. And finally, everything else. As he grew, Crusher tipped over the bookshelves around them, sending books everywhere.

Grabbing his backpack and the rest of the pastries, Sil ran after Anders and Blip. Why Anders wasn't just opening a portal was beyond him. Sil grabbed onto Anders' arm and shut his eyes.

"Open a portal, Anders!"

"Oh—"

A series of thuds reverberated through the room when Sil opened his eyes to find the two of them in another part of the library. Anders was staring at him. Then he started to smile.

"What?" Sil demanded.

"You just used a translocation spell!"

"No. You opened a portal…" His fingers were tingling, though. "That couldn't have…"

Anders pulled him into a hug. "That's incredible! See, this is why I believed in you! Working out a translocation spell on instinct."

"I didn't do anything. If I did, I have no idea what I did."

The wizard was grinning from ear to ear as he started digging through Sil's backpack. "Where did that spell book go?"

Sil sighed, pulling it out. "It's right here."

But instead of the brightly colored illustrations on the cover, the book was wrapped in dark green leather with a tiny leaf engraved on it.

"I knew it!" Anders exclaimed.

Turning it again in his hands, Sil blinked at the grimoire. "But I'm not really a magic user."

"And yet, having your spell book turn into a grimoire is the first step to becoming a fully-fledged apprentice," Anders said. "I didn't think it would happen so quickly. I'll have to write to the board and see what tests you need to apply for—"

"Wait! Slow down, Anders. I never said I wanted to be an apprentice. Actually, I'm pretty sure I specifically said I didn't want to be one."

"Don't be silly. You have the talent. Think of all the things you could do."

There was a lot he couldn't do without magic. His mind raced through the list of restricted plants for instance. He'd be able to get a license to cultivate some of them, even as just an apprentice.

"Just 'cause I can, doesn't mean I should. And when would I have time?"

"I'm sure Beren would work with you on your schedule. And I would, of course."

"There already aren't enough hours in the day. Or days in the week."

"I'll handle the garden chores if you want to do this."

"But you hired me because you needed the extra help."

"Yes, but I won't have to worry about research for a bit. And the vegetable garden should be easy."

"Should. There's a whole host of new pests to worry about—"

"For *me* to worry about. Sil, don't you want to know what you're really capable of?"

He looked down at the grimoire—*his* grimoire. "Yes..."

Anders kissed his cheek, and Sil could feel his cheeks growing red.

The moment was cut short by someone screaming, "What? What happened here! Why is there a dragon in the library?"

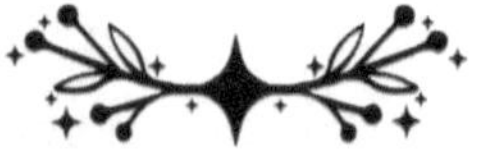

Anders' mood couldn't have been better. Even after getting yelled at by Auda. And guilt tripped by her. He hadn't even minded taking care of Crusher for another few weeks while Auda extended her work trip. Anders had so many plans for spells that Sil could start learning. There was, of course, the outline of coursework put forward by the Board of Wixen, but he hated being confined to lists.

Sil's grimoire was already full of notes sticking out at odd angles. And his stream of questions hadn't let up since they'd returned to their regular sizes and gotten home. He was eager, and that was one of the most important parts of learning magic. If a wixen were curious and willing to try new things, it was hard to reach the limits of what they could do.

Blip had been "helping" Anders plant squash in the new vegetable garden. Though Anders was fairly certain she'd stolen half of the seeds for her hoard in the corner of the windowsill in Sil's bedroom. They'd already had to give her a second jar to keep them in.

"When they talk about wands, they mean actual, like, wooden sticks?" Sil asked him as he paced up and down the rows, mounding dirt over the seeds with his feet.

"Historically, yes. But you can use whatever works for you," Anders said only a little distracted by Sil walking along the fresh rows of dirt with his nose down in his grimoire.

"You don't use a wand," Sil countered.

Anders paused mid seed drop, "I like feeling the magic more directly."

"So, you don't *need* a wand, then?"

"It's recommended for learning purposes," Anders replied, hoping he wasn't sounding like a kill joy. Pressing a finger knuckle deep into the dirt he dropped a seed into the new hole, covering it with his hand so Blip couldn't swoop in and take it.

Sil's nose wrinkled up in annoyance. "But I don't have to use one. Right?"

"You don't *have* to do anything. Everyone's magical journey is unique."

"And yet there are rules and course outlines and classes and—"

Anders wiped the dirt off his hands onto his cloak. "You're getting caught up in all that rather than just learning. Pick a topic and read about it. Practice some of the spells, and if it doesn't jive with you, move on to the next topic."

"I like having a plan."

Shrugging, Anders tossed a handful of seeds across the ground. Blip darted over to one, discreetly picking it up and dragging it off into a pile. "Nature may have rules, but a lot of those 'restrictions' can be bent and molded. You're already pushing at the boundaries of those rules by not wanting to use a wand. And there's nothing wrong with that. Some gardeners prefer digging with their hands rather than using a spade."

He could tell that Sil was having a hard time resisting the urge to pick up the scattered squash seeds to realign them into neat rows.

Anders slipped the bag of remaining seeds into a cloak pocket and began picking up the tools that were laying around.

"Now, we should finish this up before Blip or the goslings try to undo all the work we've been putting into these vegetables. Besides I need to try to show you a growth enhancement spell. Plus, we need to decide what other varieties we should try out," Anders said.

"We have a list of varieties," Sil tried to say.

"Yes, but we could have more. Besides the show, I was interested in some unusual things. And Beren already sourced some of them for me."

Sil finally closed his grimoire and pushed his glasses back up. "Of course, she has. You know that this little corner isn't nearly enough space for everything you have planned."

"This is only stage one, Sil. We can expand all the way up to the fence line there," Anders said, pointing off towards the rickety wooden fence that marked the end of the property.

"Isn't that a bit big for a first attempt?" Sil asked. "And if I'm studying, then how is all the watering and weeding and mulching—"

"Oh, I found us some interns," Anders replied happily, dropping the spades and hand rakes into a bucket.

Sil took a deep breath, quickly squashing his own objections. "Did you?"

They'd just started falling into a sort of routine between the two of them. And while he knew that they couldn't handle everything on their own, he didn't love the idea of other people encroaching on the peace of the garden.

"Yes. Cerbs was very interested in helping with pest control. They even enlisted some of the wild ducks to help with that. Especially with the slugs and snails. And the gnomes agreed to help with weeding in return for some spell work."

"Gnomes and a bunch of ducks are your interns?"

"I think 'gaggle' is more appropriate than 'bunch.' But Magda and her classmate—Palla, I think it was—agreed to come by in the mornings or evenings. I talked to their professors to work out some extra credits for the help."

"Next you're going to say that Auda and Crusher will be dropping in from time to time," Sil said, rubbing his temples.

Anders grinned at him. "The more the merrier!"

Sil made a mental note to decline any future "dates." Anders got too many ideas, and they had far too much work to do.

Field Notes
5

Crusher

Swine-Sp...

✵ Domestic Draconia ✵

Three years old
Will eat anything, but loves dog treats
Favorite passtimes: sleeping & eating
Auda's familar

The ROYAL GARDENS

Est. 1452

by the Royal Wixen Council

Spanning nearly <u>on</u>e hundred acres, the Royal Gardens pride ourselves <u>on</u> featuring native and exotic plants of all types for the purposes of study and c<u>on</u>servati<u>on</u>. Our gardeners and researchers work in tandem to learn about and develop new and innovative techniques in the world of horticulture.

<u>The</u> Royal Gardens' library is <u>on</u>e of the most extensive libraries <u>on</u> plants, horticulture, gardening, plant medicine, herbological studies and poti<u>on</u> making <u>on</u> the c<u>on</u>tinent.

HIGHLIGHTS

The Royal Gardens contain a numbe[r]
highly rated attractions:

The Tropical Greenhouse

Royal Garden Library & Archives

Research Garden

Kessel Grant Experimental Garden

Wandering Willow

Pan Fairy Garden

MacGregor Edible Garden

And many more!

Open daily, excluding holidays.
8am - 4pm

Tour availablity
varies by season.

I should check in with the staff about the state of the bequest.

I knew when I first met Sil at Beren's shop that he'd become a wizard someday! There's always been something about him. And now I get to teach him. After he passes his requirements at least.

To Do List:

 Sign Sil up for classes at the university

★ Ask Beren if she can assist in the garden a bit and let Sil have some extra time off

 Figure out a way to tell Auda that Crusher might have eaten too much

★ Send thank you note to Yolanda

★ Ask the rest of the Chaos Coven if they'd like to help in the garden too!

 Send MacGregor result write-up of his violet tea

DANDELIONS
&
DISASTERS

SIL WAS WONDERING WHY HE'D ALLOWED himself to be signed up for what was essentially more school. In his haste to get Anders to leave him alone about all the apprenticeship "stuff," Sil had let the wizard handle picking out what coursework he should be doing at the university. Not that Sil really knew what he should have signed up for anyway.

The campus was enormous, and Sil's navigation of it wasn't helped at all by the "map" that Anders had scribbled out for him. The little community college Sil had taken a few classes at after high school had been mostly focused on mundane subjects, like maths and literature. So being at a proper university, with full magical degrees, felt completely bizarre to him. He was running late by the time he found the correct room, which looked more like a gymnasium than a classroom.

Most of the students were in various clumps and cliques scattered about, while the professor stood on a circular, raised platform in the center of the room.

"This looks like our new student. Welcome to summer term," the professor said as Sil tried to close the door without it slamming.

"Um, yes. Sorry, I don't know my way around."

"Not to worry. Wixen Kessel briefed me with your current levels. Please take a seat if you are able." The professor motioned towards the floor. "Today, we'll be covering converting energy and thoughts into focused spells. Please take out your wands."

Sitting down on one of the overstuffed cushions on the floor, Sil pulled out his grimoire so he could take notes.

"The professor prefers more hands-on learning," a girl whispered to him. "Do you have a wand yet?"

She looked overly friendly, with her hair tied up in two wheat-colored buns on the top of her head and a cardigan covered in embroidered blobs of color. Freckles dusted her nose, accentuated by tiny rainbow stars that spread onto her cheeks. Everything about her screamed pastel-golden retriever who adopts the grumpy main character. Right down to the friendship bracelets clacking together on her wrists. In high school, she was just the type of person Sil would have avoided as much as possible. But he had to admit, she was just trying to be helpful, and *he* was the duck that couldn't figure out flying, so to speak.

Sil shook his head, "No. A wand feels kind of silly."

The girl smiled at him. "You can use your pencil. It just

helps to keep things flowing until you really get a hang of things."

"Thanks," Sil said, and held his pencil out in front of him, feeling like a kid pretending to cast spells in the backyard. He would have felt less ridiculous if he'd just grabbed a stupid stick from the woods before leaving that morning.

Taking out a long, slender, intricately carved piece of wood, the professor began to wave it around in circles. "Loosen up your arms. You can stand if you need to in order to let the magic flow through you."

While Sil followed the professor's instructions, the whole thing felt silly. The professor ran them through stretches and "focus sessions" and instructed them to feel the magic pulsing through the air and through them. But Sil didn't *feel* any of that. When the class was over, Sil wasn't really sure what he was supposed to have gotten out of it. If this was how most of the magic classes were going to be, he didn't have high hopes of completing them, let alone achieving the required levels of proficiency needed to continue on as an apprentice in the future. He'd expected something more direct, like being given a formula in chemistry and being expected to prove it out.

"I'm Greta by the way." The girl next to him held out her hand in greeting as they collected their things.

"Sil. Thanks for the tips."

"Of course! You're more of the bookish type, though, aren't you?"

"Yeah. I mean I know this sort of thing helps some people, but I'd rather just be told how to do a spell."

"I figured," she replied, shouldering her bag, which was dripping with keychains and ribbons. "Did the wixen you're studying under sign you up for all your classes?"

"I wasn't sure what to sign up for, so I let Anders do it," Sil explained as they left the "classroom".

"Well, you can always transfer to other classes. I'm sure they won't mind. And the entry level stuff doesn't have student limits, so there's always room."

"How long have you been studying magic?" Sil asked her.

"Oh, off and on since I was kid. I wasn't sure I was going to go into the craft until last year, though. That's when I finally found a witch to apprentice to."

"And you're still in the beginner classes?" he asked, surprised.

"I'm a slow learner! And I did a lot of self-study, outside of formal classes like here. But plenty of my friends have moved on to higher levels already! So don't worry, you'll be ahead of me in no time."

A group of younger students ran past them, twinkling stars following in their wake. The amount of magic being used so freely almost made Sil's skin itch. He'd only ever watched his friends and classmates goof off with the spells they'd picked up.

"I doubt that," Sil told her.

"I don't. I learn at a glacial pace according to my uncle. But I don't care. So, what did you think of your first Magic in Motion class?"

"It's the first magic class I've ever taken." He hated the

name of the class. and how pointless it had felt. If he'd wanted exercise, he would have just walked the country lanes around the cottage.

Greta whistled. "Really? I wouldn't have guessed. You have pretty good form already."

"That wasn't form. That was me attempting to keep up with everything the professor was saying!" Sil told her.

"You're going to be fine! Do you have another class right now?"

Sil replied, "No, this was the only one for today."

He honestly wasn't sure how much magic he could handle in one day. At least magic performed by other people. And by "other people" he realized he meant anyone who wasn't Anders.

"If you want to pop in on my cooking class, that might be fun. It's definitely more books and instructions."

"There are magical cooking classes?" Cooking was one of the few things he might be willing to stick around the campus a little longer for.

"Of course!" Greta pulled out a little booklet and flipped to a dog-eared page to show Sil. "Enchanted Foodstuffs 101 is the class I'm in. But there's a whole list! I took Classic Cauldron Cookery and Potions last semester; that one was a lot of fun. And if you're wanting more on the potions side of things, Thaumaturgy of Potion Craft is a great class. The professor really knows their stuff. And lets you take the potions home after."

"I don't think I'm ready for potions…" Sil admitted.

They passed an older looking stone building that Sil was

certain they'd already passed before. He was going to have to take another look at the damned map to make sure he could find his classes for the rest of the week.

"Oh, no worries! I do think that Conjuring Baked Goods and Remedies is full for the term. But come to my class with me!"

Sil turned the booklet to another dogeared page. "There's gardening classes?"

Greta prattled on happily, "Mostly during spring term. Though sometimes Healing through Herbs is taught at other times in the year."

"I guess I missed them, then. I actually work at the plant shop in the village. And Anders' focus is in plants," Sil said.

"Oh, then you really should try signing up for the Seeds of Magic track; that's all to do with the magical side of plants. They send out notifications whenever classes open up."

"I'll take a look at the catalog again when I get home." Sil had a feeling that Anders had mostly signed him up for "basic" classes, at least if the list of course names was anything to go by.

"Well, for now you can sit in on my cooking class. It's at least plant adjacent," Greta said.

"I do most of the cooking at home," he admitted. It was still odd to call the cottage home.

"You'll fit right in, then!" Greta said, pulling him out the door and into the quad.

By the rule of coincidences, as they walked towards Greta's next class, Sil noticed Magda spread out under a tree

with her iced coffee and feline familiar, Marvin. She spotted him immediately and waved them over.

"Anders said you were starting your magical education."

Sil resisted rolling his eyes. "Yes, well…I am."

Marvin rolled over in her lap, yellow eyes watching Sil carefully, as Magda said, "Guess I'll see you even more, then."

"Probably."

"I'm Greta. We're in the same Magic in Motion class," she said brightly. "Is this little fluff ball your familiar?"

"Yup, Marvin," Magda replied, scratching Marvin's fluffy ears as she told him, "Sil doesn't have the pipe dragon. Stop trying to stalk the poor thing."

Greta knelt down and shook Marvin's paw. "It's very good to meet you, Marvin. And you're…?"

"Magda. I'm going into my second year focusing on wards and sigils. Sil's my manager at the plant shop in the village."

"Oh! That's wonderful. I was making him tag along with me to a cooking class since he just had the one today."

Magda snorted. "Careful, he's already been adopted by one wizard. I think Sil might explode if more try whisking him away."

Sil crossed his arms. "Anders did not 'adopt' me. I started working for him. It's a completely professional relationship."

"You live with him, too, now."

"That…that's for convenience!"

"And you two went on a date to the Royal Gardens."

His cheeks started growing warm. "It was not a date."

Magda leaned towards Greta. "They're in denial. Don't

pay it any mind."

"I think that's sweet," Greta said. "And you don't need to worry. Any of your secrets are my secrets."

"It's not a secret that I work for Anders! We're going to be late if we don't hurry up," Sil said, hoping to end the embarrassing conversation.

"Oh, yes. It was good to meet you, Magda! And Marvin. The kitchens are over this way."

Sil let her drag him across the campus to where the kitchens were attached to the dining hall. He certainly hoped that he wouldn't be participating in the class because he did not trust himself to inject magic into any food and have it be safe for consumption.

As they shuffled into the old kitchen and sat down at a long wooden work bench, Sil couldn't help but suddenly feel starving. The kitchen resembled a greenhouse in some ways, with huge windows that formed one side of the roof and walls. Terracotta tiles covered the floors, and the worktables were huge chunks of butcher block on worn posts. Iron hooks suspended pans and bundles of dried herbs, peppers, and braids of garlic. There were pots simmering happily away on a huge wood-burning stove at the front of the room, and the scent of herbs and garlic wafted through the whole room.

When the teacher entered, dressed in a stained and singed apron, Greta raised her hand and said, "Wixen Cooke, I brought a new student with me."

Stalking over to where they'd sat down at a couple of stools, the teacher eyed Sil up and down. "Greta, you can't keep bringing new ones."

"I think he'll be a great fit! He loves plants and cooking. And he likes hands-on magic."

Wixen Cooke sighed. "What experience do you have with cooking?"

"I blend my own tea?" Sil offered.

"So, none."

"I mean I cook for myself and my roommate. But nothing with magic. Except that soup that summoned Auda I guess."

"You summoned someone with soup?" Greta asked with interest.

"Uh…it was an accident. I just read the inscription and, well, a spell kinda triggered."

"You can stay if you keep the chitchat down. Grab an apron off the hook over there." Wixen Cooke pointed to a row of aprons.

Sil nodded and wished he could turn invisible as the rest of the class gave him furtive glances and whispers. He grabbed an apron and hastily tied the straps around his waist. At least the apron gave Sil a little bit of normalcy.

"Today, we're tackling nettles and octopus brambles," Wixen Cooke barked. "Neither is dangerous per se but can be unpleasant. So careful handling is imperative. Understood?"

"Yes, Wixen Cooke," the class droned together.

"Good, open your books to the section on nettle tea. New one, you can share Greta's book."

Greta scooted closer to Sil, opening her textbook with a flourish. She frowned at the blank page for a moment, tapping it with a finger impatiently.

"Come on, don't be faulty on me now," she said to herself.

"Did something happen?" Sil asked her.

"Oh, its just one of those universal textbooks. So I only have to carry around one. But it's getting on the older side, and the magic is a little slow to make the pages appear sometimes."

Sil asked, "May I?"

His new friend nodded. "Go ahead."

Without really knowing what he was doing, Sil closed the book again, then opened it back up to the middle of the book. The ink lines of botanical drawings of the spiky leaves of nettles began to appear, before finally, the text bubbled up from the worn pages. He flipped to the next page, and the ink was filling in there as well.

"You really do have a knack for this stuff," Greta said with a smile.

"It's just luck."

"Hush! You can chat on another wixen's time!" Wixen Cooke said from the front of the room.

Greta had to stifle a laugh before pulling out a pink, glittery notebook and a matching pen.

Digging into his bag, Sil pulled out his grimoire, very aware of everyone's eyes on him. Why had he let Anders talk him into this?

Flowers often sprung into bloom all at once in Anders' experience, so he shouldn't have been surprised to find himself suddenly required to go into the city for the finalization of his book. They'd just gotten started on the vegetable planting.

And that was already a bit late, all things considered. Not to mention Sil was starting some beginner magic classes at the university to fulfill some of the more basic apprenticeship requirements. Anders was beginning to think that a cloning spell might be useful.

"Sorry I'm late!" Sil called as he finally came through the cottage door.

"Did you get lost on campus?" Anders asked. It wasn't uncommon to walk through the wrong door and end up in one of the secret libraries.

"No. I met someone in my Magic in Motion class, and she invited me to her cooking class. It was called something like Enchanting Foods or something. I need to find that catalogue so I can look it up."

A little pang of jealousy bubbled up in Anders' gut at Sil's casual statement. "Oh?"

"Yeah, she noticed I wasn't really into the focus class cause of how 'woo-woo' it is. I really liked the cooking one, though. I might sign up for it if the professor lets me."

"Just don't put too much on your plate too fast."

Sil's classic eyeroll was accompanied by him saying, "It's just one more class. And it's not boring."

"I never said that the basics would be fun."

"I know, but that Magic in Motion class felt like I was in some surrealist's idea of a yoga class."

Anders coughed to cover up his laugh. That sounded exactly like how he remembered that class. Then he said, "Ah. Well, I have to go to the city for a few days to finish up the last things on the book."

"Torlind can't come here?" Sil asked him.

"She's got some other work to do, so it would be a hassle. And I've already put her through enough. But don't worry, I spoke with Cerbs, and they can handle all the pests. The gnomes just need pointing in a direction for weeding. And I'm sure Beren could come over and help with some of the growth spells, if you want help with those."

Sil appeared to consider it while he unpacked his bag. "That would probably be for the best. I really don't trust myself with spells on my own yet."

"You'll have to trust yourself eventually."

"I've been doing magic for all of a couple months. Growth spells aren't even on a first-year apprentice's curriculum."

Anders snorted. "Everyone learns at a different pace and in a different order. The curriculum is just a guideline. If you're a little advanced in places, it won't hurt anything."

"But I should learn the foundations first, then build on those. That's what you said when we went to the Royal Gardens. And isn't that why you signed me up for only the most basic courses?"

"Well, if you want to bring that up," Anders lamented, crossing the kitchen to the little broom closet. He rummaged around until he found a dusty, long forgotten crate of books. Pulling them out, he dropped the crate on the kitchen table, sending a puff of dust in all directions. "These are the beginner magic books. You can read through those if you want."

His apprentice coughed but looked a little too eager about diving into magic that was far too elementary for him.

"Your grimoire is the best tool to guide you where to

focus your studies," Anders said. "Don't forget that."

"Reading a book never hurt anyone," Sil argued, flipping through a book Anders hadn't seen since his childhood.

"Not entirely true. Just don't get too sidetracked. Apprentices are usually given a year of grace period before having to pass their first level requirements."

"The girl I met in my class said she's been taking first level courses for more than a year."

Anders shrugged. "Maybe her wixen asked for an exception."

"She doesn't seem very good with magic. She couldn't get her textbook to work."

"Oh?"

"It was interesting. Apparently it's a universal text book. You spell it to show which coursework you're working on."

"Those are awfully experimental for a beginner to have," Anders muttered.

"I thought it was pretty cool, and she seemed to think they were pretty normal. I would have loved one in high school."

"We should go over all the chores for while I'll be gone," Anders said in an effort to change the subject.

He stood up and went over to the backdoor where Sil had hung up a pin board filled with lists and calendars. The color-coding was far beyond Anders, but he appreciated all the effort Sil had gone through. His eyes quickly scanned for anything that he might have forgotten to tell Sil about.

"I know what chores need to be done by now," Sil replied, rolling his eyes.

"I wasn't implying—" Anders tried to correct.

Sil began ticking off his fingers as he recited the various garden tasks. "Water everything, per the schedule I put together. Make sure the weeding is done. Fertilize the new vegetable beds. Prune back the spring annuals. And corral the local goslings and ducklings into Cerbs' pest control patrol."

"Do they all get little badges that say, 'Pest Control Patrol'?" Anders asked.

The glare Sil levelled at him said no, sadly. "We should also trim the herbs for drying."

"Then I'll trim the herbs, too."

Anders frowned and started picking up some papers he'd left strewn on the table. "I guess I should pack, then."

"I'll go check on things before I get to bed," Sil said, closing his bedroom door behind him.

Sighing, Anders wished he knew why Sil always took things so personally. He just wanted to make sure everything was alright while he was gone. Taking his tea and stack of papers, Anders wandered into his office to make sure he had all his notes packed. The miscellaneous papers were tipped into an open leather case, where they sorted themselves. He tossed in some other bits and bobs until he heard a chiming sound.

"What the—?"

He reached into the bag, digging around until his fingertips found a vibrating, spherical object. Blinking into the croquet-sized glass orb, he tapped the side gently.

"Took you long enough," Auda said as her head appeared within the orb.

"When did you slip that in there?" Anders asked her.

"Years ago! Looking glasses are so much more convenient than other communication."

"This is more of a crystal ball." He set the ball down on his desk where it hovered gently just above his mess of notes and papers.

"It's glass, and I'm looking at you through it."

Anders rolled his eyes. "We have portals for good reason. I can close them when I wish."

"I see Sil is rubbing off on you."

"Ugh, I have to pack to go into the city. So, what do you want Auda?"

"Someone is grumpy."

"This trip just has me on edge," Anders said, slumping into his chair. There was a to do list as long as a dragon's tail for the garden, and chores he'd been neglecting around the cottage. He hadn't looked in on the wildlife in some time now. And while they could take care of themselves, Anders liked to check in. Not to mention Sil's classes. If he had questions, Anders figured he should be there to answer them.

Auda actually looked concerned. "That's not like you."

"It's just the first time Sil will be alone at the cottage…"

"Just bring the cottage with you, like you normally do."

"No. We've got too much going on. And he's just started magic classes. And he's still working for Beren."

"Sounds like a lot."

"It is. I just think he's taking on too much."

"Has he said that?"

"No, but—"

"And didn't you sign him up for those classes?" Auda asked.

He could sense that Auda thought that all this stress was their own faults, and while it might have been true, Anders was loathe to admit it.

"Well, yes, but he has to start on his first-year requirements."

"Give him some space. He's still getting used to all this. Magic is new to him."

"What if something goes wrong while I'm away?" The last thing Anders expected was for things to go wrong. But the worry had still been gnawing at him like a griffon with its favorite log.

"Beren could check in on him, I'm sure. Or I could. I think Crusher buried his favorite bone somewhere in the garden, anyhow."

Anders desperately wanted to tell Auda to come by, but he knew that would be too much. "He already thinks I'm being overbearing."

"Maybe you are? Look, I'll drop by as a sisterly courtesy. But don't worry. It's just a garden; nothing terrible is going to happen."

"Alright. What did you call about?"

"I forgot!" Auda said cheerily.

He shook his head. "Then I guess I'll talk to you later."

"Crusher sends his love!"

The orb went blank, and he set it aside. Maybe it would be a good idea to get Sil one? He was still skittish around portals, and it would be useful in emergencies. Taking the glass orb with him into the kitchen, Anders stared at Sil's bag for a long moment before setting it on a shelf by the stove.

The cottage was eerily quiet after Anders left through a portal the night before. Sil hadn't realized how accustomed he'd become to the wizard's shuffling around in the mornings, or the whistling of the kettle when Anders went out into the garden and forgot about it. Even with Blip curled around his shoulders, the cottage felt lonely.

Work always kept his mind off of his feelings, though, so with a mug of tea in hand, Sil trudged out to the garden to inspect the new vegetable sprouts. Cerbs, the three-headed goose, seemed to have been keeping the insects at bay. There was a pile of empty snail shells next to one of the plant labels. There were a few weeds enjoying the newly-tilled ground. He pinched a few of them, but he'd have to make some time to properly come through and weed everything. Even though the gnomes had agreed to help, he wasn't eager to trust them.

Sipping at his tea, Sil admired the fog lingering in the dips of the surrounding fields. He'd always lived closer to or in town, so the great expanses of farmland and woods were far more peaceful than he was used to. Blip tensed on his shoulder, the end of her tail flicking back and forth.

"So, the wizard really left you in charge?" a squeaky voice asked.

Several of the garden gnomes had climbed on top of each other, creating a precarious tower of beards and mushroom cap hats.

"Yes?" Sil said uncertainly.

"Hmph," the gnome at the top of the tower grumbled. "We've been assigned weed patrol."

"It's really not that bad. Don't worry about it."

"If you let them get their roots in, the dandelions will wreak havoc on these carrots."

"I'll take care of it," Sil insisted. It was just a couple weeds. He could handle that.

"The whole garden will be overrun by tomorrow if you're not careful!" another of the gnomes warned.

"I'm pretty sure I can handle a couple of weeds."

"Pft, humans think they can do all kinds of ridiculous things! You don't '*handle*' weeds. You destroy them!"

"With fire!" another gnome piped up, a dangerous glint in his eye.

"No! No! No fire!" Sil said. "The last thing we need is for all the vegetables to be scorched."

One of the gnomes nodded up at Blip. "She could help us with the fire bits if the duck-wizard is too scaredy-cat to do it."

The tower of gnomes began leaning to one side, then collapsed, sending the gnomes scattering across the ground.

"Leave the stupid duckling. He'll find out the hard way."

Gathering up their mushroom cap hats, the gnomes began hiking back towards the edge of the garden.

"I'm not stupid, and I'm not a duckling," Sil called after them. "I just don't need help. Make sure you tell Veles I have it handled!"

"If you say so. You do squawk like a duck, though."

Blip chirped as if to disagree with them. Part of Sil wished that Anders' translation spell was still working. But at least the gnomes were leaving. Reciting the watering spell, he directed the tiny rain cloud to rotate along the vegetable bed. He needed to get ready for class and ride to campus, then he could finish up the chores once he was back.

Before retreating back into the cottage, Sil sent the little rain cloud off to another part of the garden. Blip huffed, tickling his ear.

"Stop that. It'll get watered. The wind will move it around while we're gone. And I'll water everything else when we get back."

He hadn't really tried any other elemental spells yet. But he figured that if the magic followed any kind of logic, the breeze would help out. Sil made sure everything was locked up before he headed to school.

The university campus felt even more impossible to navigate on his second day. Sil was certain they must have moved the buildings around when he passed the dining hall twice without taking any turns. The maps posted in the quads were as unhelpful as Anders was before he had his morning tea. Eventually, Sil came across a modern-looking, glass-faced building, with "Jones Department of Magical Theory" written on a large placard. He didn't have time to internally debate the fact that he was certain he'd walked past it at least three times before noticing the sign.

Inside the building was easier to navigate at least. Trails

of colorful sparks spread out from the doorway and disappeared around corners and down hallways. The green path seemed to light up as soon as he stepped inside, so Sil took a chance and followed it to a large slab of a door, which opened into a lecture hall.

A bespectacled woman with frizzy white hair paused mid-sentence as he opened the door. "Can I help you?"

Sil tried to ignore the eyes of the other students boring into him as he cleared his throat. "I think I'm supposed to be in this class?"

"Are you or aren't you?"

"Sorry?"

"Be in the class? Are you or aren't you?"

"I am…"

"Then take a seat, please. I trust you have your grimoire?"

"Yes, ma'am."

"Professor."

"Uh, sorry, professor," Sil said as he slunk up the steps of the lecture hall to find an empty seat.

Greta waved at him from one of the rows in the back of the room, and he sighed in relief. At least she'd be able to catch him up on anything he'd missed.

Once he was settled, Greta leaned over and whispered, "Get lost again?"

"I swear the buildings move around here."

She giggled. "Are you surprised?"

"I guess I shouldn't be." Anders moved the cottage around with him, so a few shifting buildings wouldn't be that strange to wixen.

"We'll be covering everything from elemental spell work to designing your own spells in this course," the professor said. "We meet twice at this time every week, in addition to extra classes during the new moon. It's important not to miss any extra classes or you'll have to take the course again. Understood, class?"

There was a garble of acquiescing from the students and the scraping of pencils.

"Now, I need to gage where everyone is in their studies," the professor continued. "Please raise your hand if you have managed any elemental spells. That includes lighting a candle or moving a stone."

Most of the students raised their hands.

"Good. Keep your hand up if you've successfully cast a spell from opposing elements."

Sil lowered his hand along with a handful of other people. Greta kept her hand raised. Even as a self-proclaimed "slow learner," Greta was still miles ahead of him.

The professor went through an exhausting list of other types of spells, like levitation and communication, and the number of hands raised slowly decreased. Finally she asked, "And has anyone done a translocation yet? Don't worry, this is fairly advanced."

Nervously, Sil raised his hand again.

The professor scanned the room and met his gaze, "You've managed an elemental spell and a translocation?"

"Yes, professor."

She scribbled something on a notepad. "Interesting. Who is the wixen you're training under?"

"Anders? Um, Anders Kessel…"

"Unsurprising. He doesn't like to stick to the proper order of things. Would have been better if it was the sister," the professor remarked dismissively.

Sil felt his cheeks turning red. "It's not Anders' fault. The translocation just kinda happened."

"*Did it?*" the professor asked dryly. "Then perhaps you should pay attention in this class so you can fill in the many gaps in your magical education."

Before he could argue further, Greta kicked him under the table.

When the professor was confident that Sil wouldn't be talking back any further, she continued, "As I was saying, elemental magic is foundational to every wixen's practice. If you can boil a cauldron, you can brew a potion. Being able to control the earth means you can grow the ingredients you need, etcetera."

"Fighting with Professor Hildegaard won't gain you any favors," Greta whispered to him.

"I wasn't fighting with her—"

Greta raised an eyebrow.

He huffed and flipped to a blank page in his notebook and started scratching out plans of where to plant the next batch of vegetables. While Anders might not be everyone's cup of tea, he was a great wizard. And he'd managed to teach Sil of all people a few spells already. So that had to speak to something. If anyone had the right to complain about Anders' methods, it was him. He was the pupil, after all. *And* the one who had to deal with all of Anders' eccentricities. Not to mention cleaning up a week's worth of tea mugs from the wizard's office at a time.

The professor droned on about drawing water out of the air for most of the remaining class time. Of course, the first class would be covering the one spell he'd managed to cast fairly consistently. And by the end of the two hours, Sil had a fully planned-out vegetable garden to squeeze in next to the fence in order to grow some extra squash and maybe try some potatoes.

"Before I let you all go for the day," Professor Hildegaard said, "I'd like to see some attempts at water spells. Bricol, Yantes, Cershaw, and Kessel, come down here."

Greta had started gathering her things, but she too a moment to nudge Sil. "Come on."

"What?"

"*Kessel* is you. She refers to her students by their wixen's names."

Shoving his notebook into his bag, he followed Greta down to the front of the lecture hall. "Wait, then what's your wixen's name?"

"Edalyn Cershaw, my aunt," she replied and grabbed his hand.

"She's not related to..."

"The famous author? He's my uncle. My mom's their little sister. The family magic kinda got watered down by the time it got to us."

"You're M.H. Chershaw's niece?"

"Yeah," Greta shrugged. "Are you a fan?"

"Not anymore," Sil mumbled.

"Kessel, you can start us off," the professor said.

Sil's mind was still wrestling with the bubbly Greta being related to that horrible man, but he held his hands up and began hurriedly reciting the watering spell, "*Rain, rain, come to play. Rain, rain don't delay. Rain, rain, come today. Rain, rain, come to stay.*"

A few drops of water appeared and splashed on the tile floor before fizzling away. But there was no sign of the little rain cloud that usually accompanied the spell.

The professor wrote a note down then turned to Greta. "Cershaw, your turn."

"It worked just this morning!" Sil insisted. "I was watering the garden—"

"It needs to work now, Kessel."

Greta had raised her hands and was about to start, but Sil repeated the rhyme.

"*Rain, rain, come to play. Rain, don't delay. Come today. Rain, rain, come to stay.*"

"Kessel, you had your turn for today," the professor told him impatiently.

"My name is *Sil*, not Kessel!" he yelled at her.

His outburst was followed by a crack of thunder and a bright flash that made the air in the lecture hall buzz with electricity. As the other students looked around the room, it suddenly began to downpour on them all.

Holding her fist above her, the professor made quick work of dissipating the rainstorm. "Are you done with your tantrum, Kessel?"

"No," he spat out. The tips of his fingers started to tin-

gle, and he wished he was back home in the garden. "But I am done with this class."

With a rush of cold air, Sil blinked at the flooded rows in the new vegetable patch on the north side of the cottage.

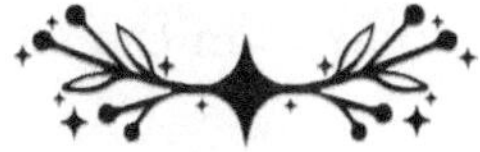

Torlind waved her hand in front of Anders' face. "Those edits done yet?"

"Huh?" Anders started shuffling the papers in front of him as if he'd been working.

His editor leaned on the edge of the worktable and crossed her arms. "You're more scatterbrained than usual. Which I didn't think was possible. Something wrong?"

"I don't know." He sighed and absently checked off one of Torlind's notes. "I just don't like being so far from my work, I guess."

"This *is* your work. And we're almost done, so can you *please, pretty please*, focus for a just a little bit longer?"

"What if something happened?"

"Nothing has happened. Otherwise Sil would have called you."

"But I have a feeling—"

"No, no! You are going to finish these edits *today*!"

Scooting his chair away from the table, Anders grabbed his latest cold mug of tea and sipped at it. "Sometimes he doesn't want me to worry, though."

"There isn't anything you can't fix up with a snap of your fingers. Why don't I make some more tea?"

"Your tea is better cold."

Torlind grumbled. "Then I'll make more cold tea! You stay there and approve those edits."

Picking up the top page, Anders pointed to one of Torlind's edits. "But this one is wrong."

"You're the researcher. I'm the editor. You do your job, and I'll do mine."

"So…I can go home, and you'll finalize the edit, then?" Anders asked.

"What? No!"

"But you just said—"

"So help me, I will call Auda if you don't stop trying to shove this all off on me! *You* have to approve the edits. That's how this works."

"She actually might have some input on the alpine section."

Torlind crossed her arms, "Finish in the next two days and then you can go home, and I'll even tell the publisher you don't want to do a book tour."

"Promise?"

"Final offer."

Anders held out his hand. "Deal."

The mud was so thick, Sil had nearly lost his galoshes several times as he tried to dig out the ends of the rows to drain them. Why had he trusted that magic would be the way to do anything? He'd been just fine gardening the hard way his whole life. Sprinklers could be set on timers. Or drip lines! But as soon as he thought he knew how to handle a watering spell, he'd let it go to his head!

Blip had retreated to the herb garden as he rushed around. And before long, Cerbs was honking at him incessantly. Sil was doing his best to ignore the three headed goose, but their squawking was giving him a headache.

"Can you please stop that?" he called over his shoulder before slipping and falling squarely on his back in the mud. At least the ground was soft when the back of his head connected with it.

"Is this a new gardening trend?" Magda's voice asked, followed by her telltale sip of iced coffee.

Sil winced as he pulled himself up and searched around for his glasses. "What are you doing here?"

"Making sure you're not dead."

"Why would I be dead?" Sil asked, deciding not to put his mud-covered glasses back on until he'd cleaned them.

"You completely disappeared from class!" Greta said, poking her head around Magda. "I didn't know if you were okay or not. So I found Magda in case she knew where you might have gone."

"Well, I'm not dead. And I'm busy."

"You know, translocation is a pretty complicated—"

Glaring at the blob he was pretty sure was Magda, he yelled, "I don't want to hear anything about magic! Just leave me alone!"

"The duckling has been angry all day," one of the gnomes added.

"Not you, too!" The mud squelched as Sil got up, minus one boot, and hobbled towards the cottage's backdoor. He

shut his eyes tightly as muddy water tried to run into them. "Just stop talking to me! All of you!"

Sil knew he'd screwed up. He didn't need Magda and Greta and the gnomes and Cerbs and everyone else in the country knowing about it. At least they listened, going surprisingly quiet as he stormed away. Sil's head started pounding as he rushed to the door and beelined to the washroom. Normally he would be worried about tracking in mud, but he frankly didn't care at the moment, eager to wash the mud off of himself and make a pot of tea.

When the water in his bath had finally turned icy, Sil reluctantly dried off and put on a sweater and pajama pants. Filling up the kettle, he figured he would have to clean up the rest of the mess outside before Anders got back. But he didn't feel up to tackling that at the moment—or the muddy footprints he'd left through the kitchen. He very nearly dropped the kettle when he went to put it on the stove only to find Auda sitting at the kitchen table with a sour look on her face.

"What—?"

"When I told Anders I'd check in on you, I didn't expect to find so many things out of sorts."

"Anders asked you to check in on me?" Sil could feel his earlier anger flare up again. He didn't need a babysitter.

"No. I offered to. Because he was worried about you."

"He doesn't need to be worried about me."

"Doesn't he? Just today you've flooded one of your lectures and the garden outside, *and* you managed to mute at

least two people and a handful of animals and garden gnomes."

"Mute?" he asked nervously.

"Yes!"

"I didn't…it wasn't on purpose."

"If all magic were on purpose, we wouldn't have half the spells we do."

"I was just angry."

"Clearly. Put the kettle on and sit down."

Sil set the kettle on the burner, which sprang to life on its own. He would have been ecstatic if it had been any other day, but instead, he hardly noticed it and slumped in the chair across from Auda.

"You're lucky your friends are understanding," she said.

"I doubt that professor will be, though."

Auda shrugged. "You won't know until you apologize."

Sil had been trying to figure out how he could avoid ever seeing that particular professor ever again, and he grumbled a little at the thought of apologizing to her.

"Are you able to unmute Magda, Greta, Cerbs, and the gnomes?" he asked.

"Luckily, most spells cast in anger fade when the anger does. But yes, they're all back to speaking now."

He sunk lower in his chair.

"You and Anders are a lot alike you know," she said. "He turned a dragon into a dandelion once."

"On accident?"

She nodded. "It kept getting into the garden and eating all the sprouts he was experimenting on, and he finally lost his temper one day. Not sure if the dragon was worse as a dragon

or a dandelion. It roared and spread seeds around constantly until the spell wore off. Where's that little pipe dragon of yours, by the way?"

"She was somewhere… Blip?"

Sil leapt up and retraced his steps in the cottage. She wasn't in his pile of muddy clothes. Or curled up in his lone boot. Rushing outside, Sil finally found her curled up under the fire curry plant in the herb bed.

"Blip! You scared me!"

She made no effort to climb up his arm and wriggled out of his grasp when he tried to pick her up.

"I'm sorry. I shouldn't have been so angry."

The little dragon stuck her tongue out at him and coiled up into a tighter ball.

"Familiars do tend to mirror their wixen," Auda said, leaning over his shoulder.

Sil nearly jumped out of his skin. "Don't sneak up on me like that!" When he caught himself, he added, "Please."

Auda smiled and tickled the little dragon's head. "I'll try."

"And she's not my familiar. She just likes me."

"To think a witch of my caliber wouldn't know a familiar when she sees one! Sil, dragons—let alone rare ones like her—do not just follow people around willy-nilly. She likes tea pots, right?"

He nodded.

"Then fetch one and bring her inside. That should help with the pouting."

As Sil went back inside to get the old tea pot they'd set aside for Blip, he noticed that Magda and Greta were both sat around the fireplace in the sitting room. He nodded to them, and Greta at least smiled at him. Magda just sipped loudly at her iced coffee, flipping the page of her book in a distinctly annoyed fashion.

"I'm sorry," he said. "I didn't mean to mute the two of you."

"Funny way to treat people who try to help," Magda said offhandedly.

"I didn't really want help. I was trying to fix it on my own," Sil said, leaning against the doorframe as if it might help him feel less like melting into the floor.

"Things usually go faster when you have help," Greta added.

Sil rubbed his arm uncomfortably and said, "Yeah, I know. But I've always done things on my own."

"Classic know-it-all boy problem," Magda huffed.

"Probably," he admitted.

Magda actually looked up in surprise. "You're agreeing with me?"

"Yeah. I messed up. And I shouldn't have lashed out."

His coworker leaned forward, in case she hadn't heard him correctly still. "You're hearing the same words I am, Gret, right?"

Greta nodded. "We accept your apology, Sil. Maybe next time just let us help you out?"

"I'll try to."

"Are you ill?" Magda asked.

"Not last I checked," Sil replied, wishing that flooding the garden and then freaking out at others had been a passing illness.

"Why would he be ill?" Greta asked.

"Because he's never admitted he's wrong—about *any-thing*," Magda explained.

"Even silly boys can admit they're wrong sometimes, Magda."

"I was wrong about Anders," Sil said.

"Well, you're just in denial about all of that."

"About all of what?"

Auda thankfully butted into the conversation. "Gals, what do you fancy for lunch? Then we can get dug into that mess out in the vegetable patch."

"I have my packed lunch still," Greta said, pulling out an aluminum lunch box covered in pink and purple stars.

"Magda?"

Holding up her iced coffee, Magda said, "I'm good. Thanks, though."

"Coffee isn't a meal," Sil argued.

"I don't trust your cooking."

"My cooking is just fine! Its far better than Anders.'"

"Snacks to munch on it is, then," Auda sighed, snapping her fingers. "Now, before those plants drown, we should try to mop up all that extra water."

"I'll be right out," Sil told the three women as he retreated to his room to change into something more garden work appropriate before fetching the teapot for Blip.

#

Some of the plants were a complete wash. Broken stems and wilted leaves meant they were better off in the compost pile. And without Anders there, Auda wasn't comfortable attempting to revive them. With most of the water drained and new mulch put down, Sil mentally tallied up how much had been lost due to his errant watering spell. It was probably a good third of the vegetables, unfortunately. He wasn't sure that they'd be able to make up the difference in time for the show, even with all the growth spells in Anders' arsenal.

While the gnomes, Cerbs, Greta, and Magda took care of the watering and weeding in the rest of the garden, Auda helped Sil sort through the remaining seeds.

"I don't think this is really enough," Sil said. "I'll have to ask Beren if there's any leftover stock from the shop we can have. Or even some starts, maybe."

Blip nuzzled his ear; she'd seemingly forgiven him for now.

"Yeah, maybe if you hadn't hoarded half of the seeds," he said to the pipe dragon, "we'd have a few more plants?"

"Awww, she's been collecting seeds?" Auda asked.

"While we were trying to plant them."

"Such a clever little dragon, helping you out."

"Were you helping or were you just taking the seeds so you'd have a pile of them to lay in?" Sil asked, rubbing her head with a finger.

She purred.

"Would you mind if we used them?"

Winding around Sil's arm and down his leg, the pipe dragon slithered off to the corner of the cottage where she'd stashed some of her hoard and chirped at him.

"I would take that as a yes."

Sil followed Blip over to her stash of seeds, which she was helpfully making into a pile. "This will be a really good start."

Chirping happily, the pipe dragon wiggled back up Sil to perch on his shoulder again.

"Hopefully there's still enough of Anders' growth spells in the soil to give these a head start," Sil said as he began sorting through the handful of seeds.

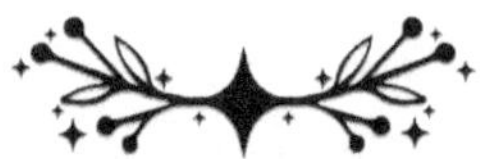

When Sil dared to check on the vegetable garden the next morning, it was still a bit disheveled. But the plants that were still there hadn't died in the night at least. Unfortunately, it did appear that Anders' growth spells were in full force, at least if the forest of little dandelion sprouts were any indication. Some even had flowers trying to bloom already. Battling dandelions for most of the day would at least keep him from having to go back to the university, though.

Grabbing his tools from the little shed attached to the back of the cottage, Sil dug into the weeding as the sun crossed the sky. It was a slog to say the least, with dandelion leaves strewn across the vegetable rows behind him. The company the day before had been nice, even if the extra work had been his own fault. He glanced towards the fence line and sighed to himself. There were still apologies to be made.

Sil was unsurprised to find the gnomes hauling a pile of stones towards the woods.

"Hello?" he said.

A couple looked up at him, but most kept on with their rock relocation.

"What does the duckling want?" one of them asked.

"To say sorry for yesterday…and to ask for your help."

"Help?" one of the gnomes asked suspiciously.

"With the weeding. You were right; the dandelions did get out of control."

"Humph! Serves the duckling right!" Veles spat at Sil in response.

"Would you help me with the rest of the weeding? I did about half, but I still have my other chores…"

They huddled together for a few minutes before a handful of the gnomes began heading towards Sil.

"We're only doing this because the wizard asked."

"That's fine," Sil said.

"Good, good day, duckling."

"Some help is better than nothing," he said to himself as he fetched the hose. Sil was done with watering spells for now.

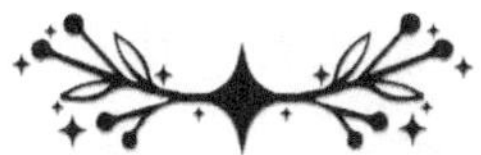

Anders didn't even wait for Torlind's feedback on the final edits before drawing up a portal back home. Sil was probably at school, but all the same, he wanted to be in his own cottage, with his plants and…

The muddy boot prints in the kitchen were strange. As was the stack of unwashed dishes. For a moment, Anders began to panic that maybe Sil had packed up and left, but his bespectacled assistant came through the backdoor with a kettle in hand.

"I thought you weren't supposed to be back for another day?" Sil asked.

"I finished the edits early," Anders replied, fighting the urge to hug Sil. He was still getting used to the other man's distaste for affection.

"That's good then, right?"

"It is…"

"I'll clean up. I just…" Sil trailed off, like he was waiting for Anders to get angry.

"You finish whatever you were doing, and I'll clean up. How about that?" Anders offered with a gentle smile.

Sil blinked at him, "But you didn't make the mess."

"You cleaned up after me, right?"

"I did, but I'm your assistant."

Anders felt like Sil had left out a "just" in that sentence. "We're friends," he replied.

"Yes, but—"

"Not to mention, roommates. Partners really! In a sense. So, I really should do my share of the tidying up. Even if a visit from Auda isn't imminent."

Without bothering to put down the kettle, Sil wrapped his arms around Anders in a hug. "I didn't think I'd miss you, but I did."

"Did something happen?" Anders asked, suddenly concerned.

"I'll understand if you don't want me as your assistant anymore…"

"Sil? Are you okay? If you're alright, then you have

nothing to worry about."

"I used a watering spell on the vegetable garden," Sil said, biting his lip.

"That's good, though. You must be close to not needing to recite the rhyme anymore."

"Ifloodedit!" Sil spat out. "And I insulted one of the professors at the university and muted everyone…"

"You muted everyone?" Anders asked, his brain picking just the last bit to focus on for now.

Nodding, Sil started absently putting mugs into the cupboard. "Magda, Greta, Cerbs, and the gnomes. It wore off pretty quickly, at least. But the garden—"

"Sil, it's alright. So long as no one was maimed or died, its fine."

"The plants though…some of them did die. And the dandelions sprung up, so I spent half of yesterday weeding them. Then the gnomes finished it off. But the flowers were back this morning."

"Weeds are just determined plants, and dandelions can actually be used in salad and teas and such." Anders shrugged. "I accidentally turned a dragon into a dandelion once you know."

"Auda mentioned."

"Of course she did. But did she tell you that she managed to turn our goat into a mushroom for a week? Mum was not happy that her goat cheese making was interrupted."

The hint of a smile started to form on Sil's lips, and his shoulders relaxed a bit.

"If we need to, we'll call on some help from Beren and

company to take care of the dandelions and get some extra things planted," Anders said.

"You mean the Chaos Coven? That's bound to turn into more of a garden party than anything."

Anders shrugged. "I'm game for it. The work will go faster if folks are having fun."

"My parents have been asking to come see the garden. Maybe they can come help, too," Sil offered.

"If they want to."

"I'll call them and ask."

Field Notes
6

Binding Circles

PICTI SPELLWORK UNIVERSITY

Sil Fennen

Anders Kessel
WIXEN

NAME

CLASS BLOCK	SUN.	MON.	TUES.	WED.	THUR.	FRI.	SAT.
8.00AM		ELEMENTAL THEORIES IN MAGIC		ELEMENTAL THEORIES IN MAGIC			
9.00AM			MAGIC IN MOTION	ELEMENTAL THEORIES IN MAGIC	MAGIC IN MOTION		
10.00AM			Enchanted Foodstuffs 101		Enchanted Foodstuffs 101	FAMILIARS & MAGICAL TOOLS	
11.00AM			↓		↓		SPELLWORK FORUM
			INTRODUCTION TO SPELLWORK	INTRODUCTION TO SPELLWORK			

IF FOUND: 982 PICTI AVE. CAMDEN VILLAGE, URSHIRE,

To Do While Anders is Away

★ Water & Weed veggie patch

★ Show Cerbs where to direct the ducklings for pest control patrol*

★ Double check micro-climate spells (Beren said she'd help!)

★ Take care of yourself

made of flower peta
remember to be preci

Woven Sigil
Best sewn with a blu
wooden needle. One of
strongest binding circ
masterable by novic
students of magic an
spellwork.

Always ask your Wixen for assistance during your intial attem

Practice Circles

ase use this section to practice drawing binding
circles under the supervision of your Wixen.

y out the spell to bind a
tering spell to lo...n!

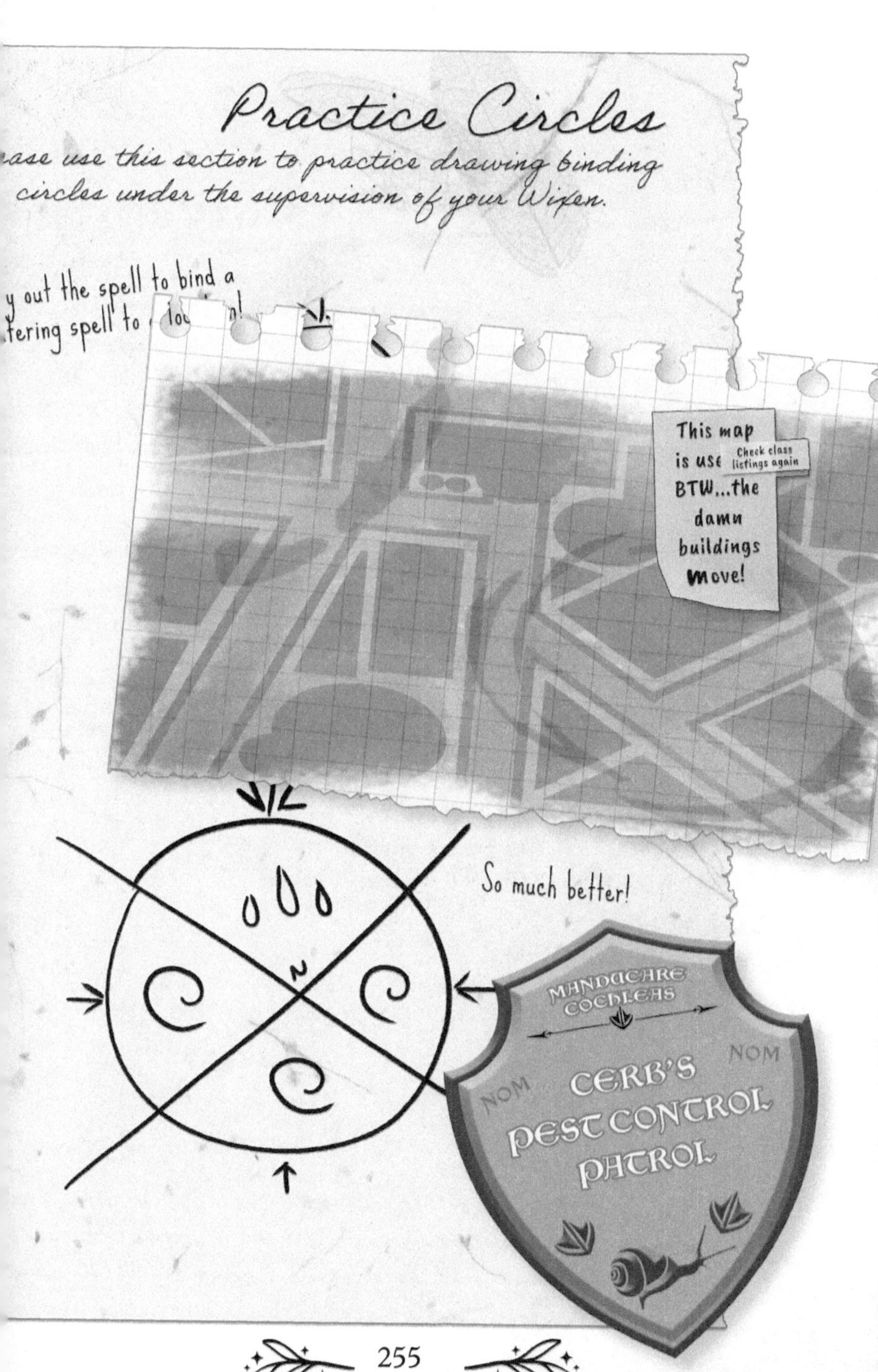

The Elements

...ments are fire, water, earth and a...

PICTI SPELLWORK UNIVERSITY

Sil Fennen
NAME

Anders Kessel
WIXEN

CLASS BLOCK	SUN.	MON.	TUES.	WED.	THUR.	FRI.	SAT.
3.00PM		BUILDING SPELLS		CALCULATING SIGILS	CALCULATING SIGILS		
4.00PM		BUILDING SPELLS		INTRO TO WARDING SPELLS & SIGILS		INTRO TO WARDING SPELLS & SIGILS	
5.00PM		HAND MAGIC			HAND MAGIC		
6.00PM	SPELLWORK FORUM						
7.00PM						SPOKEN MAGIC	SPOKEN MAGIC
8.00PM							
9.00PM	THE STARS & SPELLWORK				STARS & SPELLWORK		

* MAGICAE EST PRO OMNIBUS * PLEA...

...CTI AVE. CAMDEN VILLAGE, URSHIRE, ALBIO...

If there are other classes you want to take, I can send a message to the professors!

... Sil Fennen ... of ... is a ... admitted to ... regular student ... rom: ...shire Community College ...

...der the supervision of:

...ixen .. Anders Kessel ...

...or a degree in:

...eneral Wixen Studies ... w/ a specialty in plants ...

...ntering program at level indicated below

Attested by:

...vice ...vel	Intermediate Level	Advanced Level	Proficient Level	Expert Level

Anders Kessel

Once you believe you have found the element you hav... affinity towards, confirm with your Wixen & registe... element with your local Wixen Council.

SEEDS & SPELLWORK

WHAT HAD STARTED AS WEEKLY "GARDEN parties" to help manage the work in the garden and expand the vegetable patch even further had quickly turned the usually peaceful, misty mornings filled with birds chirping as they caught breakfast into chatty affairs sharing news and recipes over tea and coffee. It reminded Anders of summers full of cousins and friends coming and going for festivals or firefly catching or to help with the berry harvests at the farm. And the local wildlife seemed to have adjusted to all the extra humans tromping around. Cerbs was practically preening at the attention from Palla whenever the student dropped by. And Beren had befriended the gnomes, praising their millinery work, which Sil seemed grateful for.

The vegetables had mostly recovered from being flooded, and the weeds had been reined in. Anders didn't think the garden had ever looked fresher or more alive. As comfortable as he was on his own, having other people in the garden made it really bloom.

Sil was already dug into the newest addition to the vegetable patch, hoping to start some lettuce and other greens. He'd pulled up all the grasses and roots with the help of Cerbs and some of the local ducks and was working on evening out the bed.

"Do you have any classes today?" Anders called over to him.

Without glancing up, Sil replied, "We really need to get this finished up."

Anders hadn't pressed about Sil's resistance to return to university. After the initial excitement, his assistant had seemed rather anxious about having to go back.

"We can work on some spells here this afternoon, then. It might be good to start on the other elements."

"If you think we have time for it."

Surveying the state of the new garden bed, Anders nodded, "Beren was going to stop by and work with the gnomes on some fencing."

Sil stopped raking the soil for a moment. "But I haven't finished marking out—"

"It's alright. I think Beren and the gnomes can manage for the afternoon."

"But I'm your assistant. I should be doing the bulk of this."

"Sil, the more you're able to learn, the better assistant or apprentice you'll be to me. We all need help from time to time."

"Like when you were sick?" Sil asked dryly.

Anders let out an uncomfortable laugh. "Yeah, like that."

Giving him a stern look, Sil crossed his arms. "You can't tell me to accept help if you won't."

"I never said I wouldn't."

He was perfectly capable of accepting help. Just when it was convenient.

"You never said you would, either."

"I'll ask for help when I need it, then. Happy?"

Cerbs butted into their conversation with a squawk. "We should like help in acquiring more worms for breakfast!"

"Don't you have a bill perfectly suited for that?" Sil asked suspiciously.

"Your spiky tool is much faster at it. And the other ducklings are hungry, Duckling."

Sil huffed and tilled up a section of the new bed. The helper ducks flocked to the spot to gobble up as many worms and grubs before they burrowed back into the earth.

Waddling to a new section, Cerbs' heads inspected the patch and nodded to themselves. "This one next, Duckling!"

"Looks like you've got your work cut out for you for the rest of the morning at least," Anders told Sil.

"Palla is absolutely spoiling them. And you have micro-climate spells to adjust for the tropical beds in the back."

After delaying with extra chores until they ran out, Anders finally cornered Sil in the kitchen.

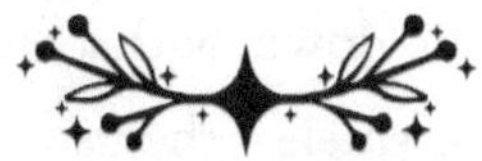

"So, elemental spells…"

"We've still got work to—"

Anders cut him off. "Avoiding them doesn't make them just fade away. You have to know the basics, no matter how annoying it is, to pass your entry level tests as an apprentice."

"I have almost an entire year to learn them, though, right?"

"Technically. But you're going to have trouble doing other things if you can't at least manage a fire spell on command."

Sil grumbled and set the kettle back on the stove. The burner burst to life, little blue flames licking at the black iron. Blip chirped happily from her perch.

Kneeling down to examine the flames a bit more carefully, Anders licked his fingers, then passed them through the fire swiftly, catching a tiny piece of it. The flame fought to escape his pinched grip before burning itself out.

"Don't touch fire!" Sil yelled at him, ready to douse Anders hand with his tea.

"Maybe we should move on to earth?"

"I didn't… Blip's been doing that, I thought?"

Shaking his head, Anders rubbed the little pipe dragon's chin. "That is 100% Sil magic. No Blip involved."

She chittered angrily and nipped at Anders' sleeve.

"Okay, maybe a little pipe dragon help was at work."

"How can you know it was all my magic?" Sil asked, reaching up to calm Blip down. with a few strokes of his hand.

"Taste, feel, look, smell—the usual."

"You can figure out if magic is done by a certain person by the taste or smell of it?"

"Of course!" Picking up a clean mug, Anders tapped it so it refilled with warm tea. "Try this, then the tea you made."

Sil took the mug and sipped it, swirling the tea around in his mouth for a moment before swallowing. Then he tasted his own and frowned.

"The difference is just 'cause its different tea. You like yours earthier. Like mushrooms with a touch of honey and herbs."

"It's the same tea. I just magically pull it from the tea cupboard."

In disbelief, Sil yanked open the cupboard door and pulled out the tin, quickly counting the tea bags. He counted them twice more before setting the tin aside and staring into the mug Anders had brewed.

"So what is my magic like?"

Anders nearly choked. "What?"

"Your magic is earthy and a little sweet, so what's mine like?"

Shrugging, Anders took Sil's mug and swirled it around before sipping. "Sharp, almost bitter. But in a good way! Then warm, which turns almost spicy."

"I don't taste any of that," Sil said. "It's just cheap black tea from the market."

"You asked, and I told you what I think."

"So it can be different for everyone?"

"I suppose so. Everyone has preferences, I guess. So something like bitterness might be good to one person and acrid to another."

"But you like my bitterness?"

"You do tend to warm up once you're comfortable," Anders replied, a soft smile on his lips.

"You're being sappy."

"And yet, you like me."

Sil glanced away, but Anders could see the red spreading on his cheeks.

"So! Earth spells!" Anders said, changing the subject. "There's a lot that falls under earth. And we should probably head out to the field, just in case anything goes awry."

When Beren arrived as the afternoon heat was settling in, she had an extremely overdressed man in tow. Sweat was beading at his temples, and his suit jacket was slung over his arm. He was desperately trying to avoid stepping in the dirt as Beren led him to where Sil was cleaning up piles of pulled weeds.

"Sil, dear, is Anders around?"

Wiping the sweat from his own forehead with his sleeve, Sil glanced towards the back garden. "He was a few minutes ago. Some of the tropical plants have been revolting."

"It is that time of year when they tend to act up," Beren said. "Oh, this is Mr. Vox. He mentioned he dropped by the shop some time ago."

"You were looking for carnivorous orchids," Sil responded, eying him suspiciously.

"You have a good memory."

"Most people that visit the garden shop in this area are

looking for vegetable starts or perennials for local pollinators."

The man laughed uncomfortably.

"Mr. Vox is a producer for Cookery & Curses. The show the vegetables are for," Beren said.

Sil let out an unamused snort. That certainly explained the suit and shiny shoes.

Beren clucked her tongue. "I thought he might want to see the progress?"

Pushing his glasses back up the bridge of his nose, Sil glanced towards the back garden. "I can see if I can find Anders, then. Hopefully he didn't pop off somewhere."

"I'm sure you can show Mr. Vox around in the meantime, and I'll go find Anders," Beren said as she disappeared into the swath of greenery.

Looking back at Mr. Vox, Sil sighed. "Most of the beds are on the north side here. It's where we had the extra space. But with Anders' micro-climate and growth acceleration spells, we haven't seen any noticeable difference in the growth patterns."

Attempting to avoid the largest dips and crevices in the yard, Mr. Vox followed Sil towards the vegetable garden. "That won't affect the taste or anything, right?"

"No. The acceleration spell works like a time pocket, allowing the plants to mature more quickly within the boundaries of the spell."

Mr. Vox stopped at the makeshift willow branch fence and asked apprehensively, "What about the aftereffects when consumed? I don't think any of our judges or contestants would want to start aging prematurely."

"The spells are crafted so they only effect the plant material. And once the vegetables are harvested and washed, the spell is washed off as well." Sil absently pinched off an errant tomato stem.

"That's a little more technical than I expected," Mr. Vox admitted.

"Surely not so technical that someone with carnivorous orchids can't understand it," Sil commented dryly.

"Well, no, of course, I understand it! We just want to ensure that our audience does." Mr. Vox wobbled as he stepped on a softer patch of earth and made a show of brushing invisible specks of dirt from his jacket. If the man knew about dust sprites down at the end of the garden, the man would probably have a stroke and run from the cottage as quickly as his loafers would carry him.

"Right." Crossing his arms, Sil stared at the man. "Any other questions?"

"We did have a list of items we were hoping for. Can we go over that and make sure that everything is accounted for?"

"I've triple checked that we have everything. We even planted extra amounts just in case something happened," Sil said.

"Like what?" Mr. Vox blinked.

"Insects or weather."

"I thought you had the climate thingy spell?" Mr. Vox asked.

Sil rubbed the bridge of his nose before saying, "Micro-climate spells can only do so much. Nature is still nature. And pests are still pests."

"So there might be bugs on the vegetables? We can't have that!"

No wonder this man had seemed so out of place at the plant shop. He probably watered his orchids with ice cubes!

"Insects live in gardens and farms. A lot of them are beneficial for plants. But Cerbs and the ducks have been doing a good job of controlling the ones we don't want."

"Cerbs?"

"Short for Cerberus. They're a three-headed goose."

"Oh…"

Sil could see the slight panic in Mr. Vox's eyes. If Sil were a malicious person, he might have had Anders call Cerbs over. Any goose, especially a three-headed one, seemed to put most people on edge. While they could be loud and territorial, it wasn't as if most geese would chase people around, or steal their things. In that regard, Cerbs was a perfect gentle-goose.

"Sorry! I was trying to sort out the tiger lilies out back!" Anders called out as he appeared with Beren.

"Mr. Vox wanted to go over the planting list," Sil said. "It's inside, so I'll go get it."

"Of course. Good to meet you, Mr. Vox." Anders replied with a smile. He stopped Sil before he could escape back into the cottage, though, taking the corner of his sleeve and dabbing at Sil's nose. "You have some dirt."

"I have dirt all over me," Sil sighed, letting Anders attempt to brush it away. The worn fibers made his nose itch, and he pulled away from Anders to rub at his nose.

"Well, now you have dirt freckles," Anders lamented.

"I'll wash up when I'm done out here," he replied, resist-

ing Anders' additional attempts to remove the specks of dirt.

Running into the cottage, Sil took a deep breath as he searched for the planting list. He must have been getting too much sun because his cheeks felt warm and his heart was pattering faster. The list was pinned to the door frame of the garden door, and Sil couldn't help but scan it again as he headed back outside. He was certain they'd managed to plant everything on the list, plus a few additional varieties of things like beans, lettuce, tomatoes, and peppers. Once they'd started planting vegetables, trying out new ones was hard to resist. Even if those extras weren't used by the production, they'd be eaten or given away to friends. Or the neighbors would find zucchini left on their doorsteps.

Blip chirped at him from her pot on the stove. They'd been finding black scales all around the cottage over the last week, and a pair of spindly wings had started sprouting from her back. The wings looked more like the skeletal veins of a leaf, coated in an iridescent film. With all the changes to the garden, it was unsurprising to Sil that she had decided the old cast iron tea pot was a much better place to molt.

Holding out a hand to her, Sil rubbed her head, which she leaned into with a few happy chittering sounds.

"That guy in the suit that visited the shop a while back is here," Sil told her.

The little pipe dragon was far more interested in Sil's scratches and pets than in what he was saying.

"You should come out and get some sun today."

Sticking out her black tongue, Blip curled back up in her pot.

"Well, I can't blame you for not wanting to deal with Mr. Vox."

There wasn't a good reason to delay going back outside any longer, so Sil trudged back out to the garden. Anders appeared to be attempting to show off some of the cabbages to Mr. Vox.

"Once they fully head up," Anders was saying, "they'll look much more similar to what you're used to seeing in the super market."

"What about the yellowy part on the outside, though?"

"You can just take off the outer leaves. Same with lettuces. Sil, did you find the list?"

"Yup." Sil held it out for Anders. "I'm going to take this wheelbarrow back to the compost."

"Sure." Anders smiled at him, then turned to their guest. "So here's everything you requested, Mr. Vox, and the number of plants we put in and such. Sil made sure everything was mapped out so it was easy to know where everything is."

Beren took Sil's elbow as he started pushing the wheelbarrow, "I wanted to chat with you a bit," she said

"Oh? I know I haven't had a lot of extra time to be at the shop..."

She shook her head. "Don't worry about that. Magda and I have the shop handled. I do wonder if it would be easier if you took a few things off your plate, though?"

He nearly tipped over the wheelbarrow. "What? No! I'm fine. I can find some time for the shop this week—"

"And what about your magical studies?"

"I don't really think some of the professors will let me

back into their classes at the university."

Beren patted his arm gently. "Formal classes aren't the only way to achieve your apprenticeship merits," she told him. "I'm sure Anders would be more than willing to help you with independent studies. Auda might, too."

"They both have their own careers, though," Sil replied.

"Anders wants you to be his apprentice. He wants you to succeed," Beren insisted.

"I have no idea why."

"Because you're his friend. And he sees that you're passionate about your work." The moss in Beren's hair quivered as she tilted her head to one side.

Parking the wheelbarrow next to the little tool closet, Sil made a mental note to tidy up their tools later.

"I still don't even really know what being an apprentice to a wizard means," He said.

"It can be a lot of things. Sometimes they're just assistants. Other times they help with research. It's whatever you and Anders decide for it to be. Most importantly, it's a type of partnership. He teaches you and helps you learn whatever magic you want to focus on, and you help him in return."

"He doesn't need that much help."

Linking her arm with Sil's, Beren easily guided them along one of the twisted garden paths. With how chaotic everything had been, Sil hadn't just enjoyed the wild explosion of color and foliage that had happened over the summer. When he was pruning or weeding, or watering, Sil was so hyper focused on each individual plant that he'd missed how the ferns had uncurled their lacy leaves. Or that the blue bells had spread from one corner of the garden to the other, even though their season should have been done weeks ago.

"Before you stepped in to help with the garden, Torlind was about ready to drop his latest book. I know that means a lot to him."

"Anders didn't mention that."

Beren wrinkled her nose. "He doesn't like to worry people. Much like another young man I know. Now, when are your parents coming to visit again?"

"I hadn't really arranged it yet. I wanted to make sure the garden looked good before I invited them."

"Garden work is never done, Sil. You know that."

It was as if she could see the list of plants to prune or clean up growing longer in his head by the step.

"Yeah, but still. I didn't want them to judge what I've been doing."

"They'll love it, no matter what state it's in, I'm sure." Beren stopped them underneath one of the towering oak trees and smiled as a squirrel darted out across one of the branches. The leaves vibrated and a couple of green acorns pattered to the ground.

"I hope so. They really wanted me to go back to school, but I kept putting it off," Sil said.

"Maybe that type of higher education just isn't for you?"

"Almost everyone else I know went, though. My best friend went off to Pendragon College at Oxenbridge."

"That's a very prestigious program."

"I know. They were always good at magic and stuff, and I was just the regular kid in our group," Sil said.

"You're hardly regular. You have a near encyclopedic knowledge of common garden varieties."

"Ah yes, my 'special interest.'"

Another shower of acorns rained down on them and Sil glared up at the squirrel that was chittering loudly. They weren't interrupting its meal time at all, so Sil didn't understand why it was being such a pest.

"Special interests can often inform what a wixen specializes in later in life," Beren said.

"What was your specialty?"

Beren smiled fondly. "The magical properties of the mundane."

"That's a bit…vague."

Brushing the moss in her hair, Beren shrugged. "Perhaps, but there is magic in all sorts of mundane places that people often forget. Like a little village shop. Or a good meal." She looked over his shoulder at whatever Anders was doing with Mr. Vox, then she smiled at Sil. "Even a well-loved garden."

Sinking into one of the armchairs in the sitting room, Anders stretched out his legs towards the fire. The evenings were still chilly enough to want the fire going, at least, even with the afternoon heat peaking. He was just about to summon up a cup of tea when he caught a whiff of his sister's telltale perfume of lavender and sea salt.

"Auda, I thought I told you to call before you showed up?" he began berating her, turning to find Sil holding two mugs.

Sil's eyebrows raised slightly above his glasses as he held out one of the mugs. "Just me."

"Sorry," Anders admitted, taking the tea and inhaling the lavender scent. It must have been a new blend Sil was trying.

As his assistant curled into the other armchair, Anders settled back into his own, saying, "She keeps threatening to show up."

Nodding, Sil scratched Blip's head absently.

"Everything seemed to go alright with that producer," Anders continued.

"He seems fake."

"He's just city folk," Anders mused. "You should have seen Torlind the first time she came to visit. I thought she was going to try spraying the whole place with disinfectant."

"A little dirt and a few bugs never hurt anyone."

"Not everyone is as understanding as we are."

"Do you think the Wixen Council would count some of my work in the garden towards my apprenticeship?" Sil asked him, still staring down at his tea.

"I would think so. Especially if you can work out the micro-climate spells. Or something along those lines. Why?"

He fidgeted in the chair for a moment before replying, "I don't want to go back to the university classes. They weren't really for me. But if you still want me to be your apprentice, maybe we can come up with some other way for me to get my credentials?"

"Of course, I still want you to become my apprentice! There's all sorts of different things you can do to satisfy the requirements. We just need to go over the list and figure out what will work."

Sil seemed relieved. "Oh, good."

"So long as you still want to try out learning magic, of course. If you don't want to, we can stop," Anders told him.

"No, I like a lot of the theory. It's just…the way most of the professors try to teach things just isn't very useful for me. *Feeling* for something that I can't see or touch is…difficult."

"Don't worry, we'll come up with something that does work." He was half tempted to go across the hall into the office and start putting together ideas right then. But his joints were protesting. "It'll just have to be approved by the Wixen Council to ensure it covers all their requirements."

"Fair. You didn't have any trouble with magical classes, did you? Or Auda, I bet…"

Anders sucked in a breath. "I mean, we did. But we had the advantage of growing up with magic. Our parents are a witch and wizard, so magic was normal for us. But just like you might have trouble on a math or spelling test, we had trouble with spells, too."

"Like turning a dragon into dandelion?"

"Harlow knew just how to get on my bad side!"

"Your dragon's name was *Harlow?*"

"What sort of name should a dragon have? Blip?"

Sil peered down at Blip curled up on his shoulder and brushed a few loose scales away. "*I* didn't come up with that. It was Magda and Beren."

"Anyway, yes, I had trouble with magic. Fire has always been my weakness. It took me ages to get the micro-climate spells to work because of that."

"So you could balance the temperature correctly? Couldn't you have focused on another element to do that part?"

Anders hadn't even fully explained the micro-climate spells to Sil and he was already figuring them out on his own. He wished he had someone else to gush to about how clever Sil was.

"Tried a lot of different ways, but pure fire was always better. And yet you just put the kettle on the stove and—boom! Instant flames! Just like that!" Anders snapped his fingers creating a tiny flame that appeared and disappeared in a flash.

"Maybe its cause I'm more comfortable in the kitchen?" Sil suggested.

"That could be it. And having a little dragon familiar helps, I'm sure."

"Have you ever had a familiar?" Sil asked him.

Anders shrugged. "No. Auda's had several, but I never clicked with one."

"Must have been pretty lonely here, then."

"I've had the garden and all the animals around. Plus, the village, Beren…and now I have you."

Sil reached over and squeezed his elbow. "And don't think you're getting rid of me anytime soon."

Wrapping his fingers over Sil's hand he replied, "Wasn't planning on it."

He hadn't been procrastinating talking to his parents per se. But Sil was definitely avoiding it. His fingers twirled in the air absently as he sat in the back garden under the canopy of the expansive willow trees. The slight tingling at his fingertips didn't pull him from his thoughts, so it wasn't until his mother yelped that Sil realized that there was an open portal floating in front of him.

"Sil! What's going on?" his mother yelled through the hole in space as batter dripped from the spoon in her hand.

Running his fingers through his hair quickly, Sil cleared his throat. "Um...hi?"

"Tell that wizard of yours that he can't just make portals appear in someone's kitchen without warning."

"It wasn't Anders..."

Her eyebrow twitched. "It's very rude to intrude in on someone with magic. No matter who did it."

"Sorry, I didn't even realize I was... I was meaning to call."

"Well, *finally*, dear. You haven't called in weeks!"

He bit back a retort. "Anders wanted to make sure you and dad were invited to come see the garden."

"Oh?" his mother asked, setting the spoon into the bowl finally. "Seems a bit of a drive just for a garden, dear. You haven't even been home in ages."

"Well, Anders could make a portal so you wouldn't have to drive. And I've been busy here and at the shop."

"I do wish you would have gone into something a little more stable."

"The garden shop is stable. People have always liked

growing things. And working for Anders is stable. He wants me to become his apprentice, even."

Rolling her eyes, his mother went back to stirring. "We don't have magic in our family, dear. I'm sure that he's a very nice wizard for humoring you, but we don't have any talent in that. Your father was going to have some friends from work over next week. Why don't you come home and see if one of them knows of any jobs open at the firm?"

"I have a job. Two jobs, actually!"

"And what happens if that wizard wants to retire?"

"He's only a couple years older than I am." Out of sheer nervous habit, Sil began picking at the fuzz on his sweater. Even though he knew that his mother would be dying to slap his hand to get him to stop.

"It's still a valid concern. Your predecessor at the garden shop was attacked by that plant and had to retire."

"That was an accident." Sil said.

"We all know that accidents and bad luck tend to find you, dear."

Sil's nose crinkled at the reminder. At least she didn't know about being shrunk to the size of a mouse. Or nearly being crushed by a dragon with a snacking problem.

"I should get going," he told his mother as the silence dragged on.

"You called *me*."

"Goodbye, Mom!"

Sil waved his hands, hoping that was enough to dissolve the spell. The portal rippled under his fingers and began to fade along with the disappointed look on his mother's face.

He groaned as he fell back against the willow tree's trunk, waking Blip from her nap nestled in the collar of his shirt. Her serpentine tongue tickled his chin and caused a shiver through him.

"Hey, stop that!"

The little pipe dragon blinked at him innocently, stretching out her new wings like a cat clawing at the carpet.

Some of the willow's branches moved aside to reveal Anders crouching at the edge of the canopy. "Oh, there you are."

Anders' usually carefree tone was a bit damper, and his smile felt forced.

"I was just finishing up my tea," Sil told him as he got to his feet, joints protesting.

"You don't have to get up. I just wasn't sure where you were."

Sil didn't want to read into it, but he wondered how much of the conversation with his mother Anders had over-heard. "I'm not planning on going anywhere. I just didn't want the damn gnomes bothering me about when Beren is bringing them more hats."

"Of course," Anders replied, his forced smile straining at the corners of his mouth.

"I should get to the weeding before it gets too warm out."

"It is supposed to get hot this afternoon," The wizard stood, and they were both covered in the dappled light fil-tering through the long shards of dusty green willow leaves. "Don't forget to put on a hat yourself. And make sure Blip stays out of the worst of it. Wouldn't want her overheating."

Anders reached out and gently scratched under her chin until she chirped happily. For as closely as they'd been working together the last few months, Sil couldn't remember many times he and Anders been in such close proximity—Alone. Sure, they'd worked on prepping the vegetable garden and planting seeds side by side. But usually someone else had been helping and filling the air with chit-chat. Sil half expected the fireflies to start blinking around them, even though it was still before noon.

He pushed past Anders and out of the willow's canopy, sucking in a deep breath. Dawdling wouldn't get his work done for him. Especially if he wanted to finish the bulk of it before the afternoon heat.

Planting himself near the edge of a row of lavender and rosemary, Sil rested his fists on the dirt like Anders had shown him. If he screwed up, the woody plants wouldn't be too damaged—he hoped. A couple of honeybees buzzed around lazily, hopping from purple bud to purple bud. They didn't seem bothered by the slight vibrations that began moving through the soil.

Some of the dirt shifted, and a few worms surfaced in confusion, but overall, the ground looked unchanged. Nothing like the trenches Anders had created with just a few motions. Sil picked up a stone and dropped it in the dirt, and again, nada.

"I'm just useless at this," he said to himself.

Blip slithered out of his sleeve and began rooting around the earth with her nose. She didn't seem all that interested in the worms and was instead making little trails in the dirt. At first glance, it just looked like a bunch of swirls, but as Sil began absently tracing them with a finger, it reminded him of the motions the professor of the Magic in Motion class had made them go through.

Anders had mentioned that he'd be able to do the watering spell without reciting the rhyme eventually, so maybe he needed training wheels on the earth spells he tried as well. He moved his hands in large circular motions, mimicking what Blip had drawn out and what he remembered from that one class before planting his fists firmly in the dirt. It trembled before tiny dips began to form on either side of his hands. Pressing harder into the earth, the dips widened into miniature valleys, plenty big enough to plant in.

"Did you have some seeds you wanted to plant, Blip?" Sil asked the pipe dragon, who was happily investigating his work.

She chirped in response and rushed to scamper back up his arm.

Leaving Sil to his own devices for the day was torturous. Anders wanted to ask if Sil's mother really didn't like him. Or if he had considered leaving, even though Sil had said otherwise. Sometimes it was easier to placate someone than have an honest conversion. But Anders wanted to know the truth. There were spells to compel someone to speak their true mind, though those were never a good idea, no matter how desperate Anders was—especially since it mixed people with magic.

One the sun moved to its peak, he'd peeled off his worn old cloak and rolled up his shirt sleeves to work through some better solutions for the tropical plants. The tiger lilies had been especially distressed with all the weather fluctuations, and the micro-climate spells were having a hard time keeping up.

The front bell rang, and Anders was more than happy to put down his notes in favor of avoiding the problem a little longer. He went around the side of the cottage rather than track mud all through the kitchen and hall and spotted a pair of people waiting a bit impatiently on the step.

"Hello?" he asked, waving to them as he came around to the front path.

A mousy woman and a stern looking man both turned towards him, and it took a moment for Anders to place them as Sil's parents.

"Anders, was it?" Sil's mother asked, pushing her glasses back up on the bridge of her nose.

"Uh, yes. I didn't realize you were coming."

"Can't we drop in to see Sil?"

"Of course. I just would have planned—"

"Is he around?" Sil's father asked, leaning over the herb bed.

"Somewhere out back or in the vegetable garden. Careful, the fire curry has been a little aggressive with the heat lately."

"Fire curry?" the other man asked without a note of curiosity.

"Yes. It can be a bit volatile with new people."

"Hrm, we'll see Sil now."

Anders had half a mind to tell them to leave, as Sil was working, but that nagging voice in the back of his mind with Auda's tone told him it wouldn't be a good idea.

"Sure," he said, walking towards the vegetable garden.

"I thought maybe we could have tea," Sil's mother stated.

Biting his tongue, Anders nodded. "You can, but he's probably in the middle of something, so…"

Sil's parents didn't leave the front step. He waited for half a beat before lamenting, "Why don't the two of you go inside and I'll find him? The kitchen is straight down the hall in the back."

They nodded and cautiously opened the front door. No wonder Sil was so stubborn. As he'd predicted, Sil was hunched over in the vegetable garden, sprinkling seeds from one of Blip's hoard jars along a trench.

"Your parents are here."

Sil waved him off. "Uh huh…"

"They want to have tea apparently. I sent them into the kitchen."

Turning to look up at Anders, Sil asked, "You're being serious?"

"Yes."

Squeezing his eyes shut and pressing his fingers to his temples, Sil grumbled, "Oh for the love of biscuits…"

"We might be out of biscuits. I think the mice got into

them."

Throwing his spade in the general direction of his weeding bucket, Sil shook his head as he stalked back towards the cottage. "Why do they think they can just show up whenever they like?"

"It's fine. You can finish that up later. Just enjoy your tea, alright?"

"You're not coming in?" Sil asked him.

"I didn't think you'd want—"

Sil grabbed his arm firmly as he headed toward the kitchen door. "They'll leave much faster if you come in. Then we can get back to work."

Anders couldn't argue with that. Sil's mother didn't seem to hold any warm, fuzzy feelings for him. And he was rather glad that Sil wanted him there, even if it was just so they could finish the day's work.

Sil's parents were hovering in the kitchen when they came in the back door, as if they'd been ignored by a waiter with too many tables to serve. But Sil didn't waste a moment in directing them to sit down at the little wooden table.

Instead, he said, "You can sit down you know."

"We didn't want to assume," his mother replied.

Anders could imagine Sil's snarky response of, "*You butted in without notice.*"

"I'll put the kettle on," Anders said, busying himself at the stove and trying to discreetly check if there were any biscuits that had survived the mice's midnight snacking.

"Are there other chairs?" Sil's father asked no one in particular.

Snapping his fingers, Anders smiled at the solid clatter of wooden legs settling on the wood floor as two more chairs appeared. "Sorry, I usually bring them out when we're expecting company."

"Is that your room?" Sil's mother asked without missing a beat.

Setting the tea pot on the table along with a plate of biscuits, Anders picked up a stack of papers and notes to make room for a few more mugs on the table.

"Yes."

"Seems a little small."

"It's fine, Mom. It's just my bed and a wardrobe. There doesn't need to be a lot of space."

"All the same, dear, it's a bit of a downgrade from your apartment."

"He's saving on rent, though," Anders interjected.

"Oh?" Sil's mother asked with fake enthusiasm.

"Anders doesn't charge me rent," Sil explained. "I just handle most of the cooking. And, of course, I'm helping with the garden."

"I thought it was one of your 'jobs.'"

"It is. But he's still not charging me rent."

"How lucky. What if you want to change careers?" she pressed. "Or go back to school?"

"I'm not going back to school. And I'm not going to change careers."

Sitting next to Sil, Anders casually wrapped an arm around the back of Sil's chair. "Even if he wanted to change careers, I wouldn't put Sil out or suddenly start making him pay rent. He's a friend."

"Retail isn't so much a career," Sil's father said, adding some sugar to his tea. "And no offense, but not having any kind of monetary agreement between the two of you doesn't seem very sensible, business-wise."

"It doesn't need to be," Anders insisted. "We're friends, and he needed a place to stay when his lease was up."

Sil nudged Anders' with his knee, and the wixen realized how combative he was starting to sound. His parents were just worried about their son. That was perfectly reasonable, Anders supposed. Though they didn't need to be so pointed or accusatory about it. His own parents had been wary of Cershaw when they'd met him. Though that was with good reason, as it turned out.

Anders took a moment to breathe, then said, "I'm sure you'd like to see the garden and all the hard work that Sil has been putting into it. He's been heading up the new vegetable patch."

"Vegetables? Like a farm?" Sil's father asked.

"Kind of. But we're not selling the produce," Sil said with a shrug.

"Then what are you doing with it?" Sil's mother asked.

"It's actually a contract with a cooking show. They wanted to source from some new providers this year and contacted Beren, who referred them to us."

Sil's mother's lips pursed at the word "us." "I see. Would I know the show?"

"It's *Cauldron Cookery*," Sil answered. "I know nan watches it sometimes."

"Ah, yes. That garden book author you like hosts it. What was his name?"

"I don't really like him anymore."

"Pity, he's rather handsome. Was his name Cray-some-thing?"

"No, its Cershaw," Sil corrected.

"That's it. You had all his books. I thought you still liked him."

"Tastes can change, Mom."

"I can't ever keep up," she said with a sigh.

Sil shifted in his seat. "Well, I do need to get back to work."

"Can't you do that later?" his mom asked. "We're here right now."

Sil got up. "I have a lot to do. And just because you think it's a hobby, doesn't mean it's not my job. Anders has work to do, too. If you want to look around the garden real quick, that's fine, but I can't just sit and have tea all day."

"Erasil, that's no way to speak to your mother," Sil's father said, his voice tinged in annoyance.

Anders looked between the three of them, wondering who would speak first. Or, rather, blow up. But before Sil could say something he might want to take back, Anders got up as well and said, "He's right. We do have a lot of work to get done. Sorry, it's just not a convenient time. Maybe you could come over for dinner sometime?"

"We're here—"

"Unfortunately, garden work can't really wait. If we do, the plants might suffer, and that could jeopardize this con-

tract or my research, and I won't let that happen. Thank you for coming, though. It was nice to see you again."

Sil's parents shared a look, then gathered up their belongings to leave. There were no goodbyes as they closed the front door, but Anders felt like he could breathe again. Sil was frozen behind his chair, mug still in hand.

"Hey? Are you alright?" Anders asked gently.

"I told them not to call me that," Sil's voice was low.

"They're gone, okay?"

"It's not okay. It's not my name anymore."

"That's fine," Anders replied quietly, offering him a hug if he wanted it.

Sil didn't move for a long moment, but finally, he wrapped his arms around Anders, his glasses pressing into the wizard's chest.

"I didn't lie to you when I told you my name was just Sil."

"Hey?" Anders ruffled Sil's hair gently, "I know that. You're just Sil."

"Thanks…"

"Of course."

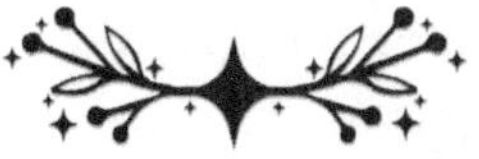

A part of Sil wished he could just run past the garden fence and hide. Or melt into a puddle of non-existence. He knew that Magda, Palla, and Greta were due to show up to help in the garden, but he didn't have the energy to deal with more people, even if he could mostly work in a corner on his own.

Every time he heard Anders' footsteps in the hallway, he snuggled deeper under the covers as the clock ticked along. He had to get up. But he could ignore things if he stayed in bed. Or pretend that his tiny room was a little bigger. That he wasn't terrified about failing to meet all the requirements for an apprentice. Maybe Anders would find someone better suited? With more time or that was better at magic? Magda and Palla were both miles ahead of him in that department. And they'd been coming over to help more and more.

Blip tugged at his ear, trying to nudge Sil out of the worry spiral he'd found himself in.

"Stop that," he told her, pulling the blankets tighter over his head.

She chirped and pulled and scampered down the back of his night shirt, sending Sil jumping out of bed with a yelp.

His door creaked open, and Anders poked his head in, worry on his face. "You okay?"

Sil managed to pull Blip out from under his shirt and held her at arm's length. "She's being a menace."

"She probably just wants attention. Or breakfast…"

A gurgle from Sil's own stomach answered Anders' unasked question. "I'll be out in a few."

"No need to rush."

"I should have been up ages ago."

"Blip, why don't we go find you some worms while Sil wakes up?" Anders asked, holding his hand out for her to perch on. The little pipe dragon wiggled out of Sil's grasp and curled around Anders' arm, chittering.

"The kettle's on for you."

"Thanks, Anders…"

"Of course."

The wizard had been saying that a lot. "Of course." As if he didn't expect anything in return. Which was a difficult thing to accept when so much of life was transactional. His mother's and father's critiques and jabs were worming their way into his own thoughts. Anders had *offered* to let him live there. Had *offered* him a job. Had offered to make him a wizard's apprentice. He'd even put together that welcome display in the garden not long after they'd first met. All of it just made Sil feel like he wasn't doing enough. Or giving enough.

Wrapped in a sweater and loose-fitting pants and a t-shirt, Sil poured himself a mug of tea. Anders had been better at keeping his papers from being so spread out over everything. They were mostly contained to his little office across from the sitting room. Somehow the overstuffed bookshelves crammed around the cottage had managed to accommodate Sil's odd collection of books. And Anders had even created a little nook next to the stove to house his cookbooks. They each had a fraying wool blanket draped across the armchairs in the sitting room for when it got chilly, and there were enough cubbies for Sil's gloves and work boots next to the kitchen door. It was almost like he'd been there for years already.

He pulled one of the cookbooks out and flipped to the back where the pastries and desserts were. Sil felt he hadn't been holding up his end of the bargain to cook in lieu of the rent since he'd moved into the cottage. Anders had a habit of just snapping a meal onto the table when they were too busy with work. Though Sil had insisted on doing dishes and tidying up the kitchen after they'd eaten, at least.

They had all the ingredients to make a chocolate cake. And he'd been craving something spicy now that the weather had started warming up. Sil started pulling things out of the cupboards and the ice box, measuring out ingredients.

"You don't have to cook," Anders told him when he returned from making sure Blip got breakfast. "I could have figured something out."

"It's for later," Sil said.

Peering over Sil's shoulder, Anders tried to see what he was making. But Sil quickly closed the cookbooks with a wave of his hand. "It's a surprise."

"Have you been practicing that?" Anders asked him.

"No…it just—no. Now shoo, or you'll ruin the surprise."

"You don't like surprises."

"When they're for me, I don't. This is a surprise for you."

One side of Anders' mouth tugged up in a smile. "So I should leave you alone for the day, then?"

"Yes," Sil replied firmly. "I'll bring out some juice and snacks when the others get here to work in the garden."

"Alright," Anders said, ruffling Sil's hair. "Don't work too hard."

"Out!" Sil pointed to the back door.

Anders poured himself a fresh mug of tea and snickered as he left the kitchen.

With Anders out of the way, Sil pulled the kitchen table over towards the counter to act as a secondary workspace. Then he cracked open all the windows to let the breeze in. He popped out to cut some herbs from the bed by the front door as Magda and Greta were walking up the path from country road.

Greta waved enthusiastically and called, "Hey, Sil! I brought lunch to share today!"

"So long as you don't mind if it's pink," Magda said, sipping at her iced coffee.

"Only the crackers are pink."

"And the cheese. It's unsettling," Magda replied.

"It tastes the same. And green would have looked moldy," Greta insisted.

"Palla's on his way. He got sidetracked with a West Country were-hound that was surrendered to the local Humane Society," Magda said.

"The poor little thing. It looked so scared."

"It's as big as a horse. It's not little."

"Anders is out back already," Sil told them, absently clipping a few extra sprigs of the fire curry.

"Oh, good. I also brought some mushrooms for him," Greta said, already walking back towards the kitchen. "Are you planning on something special? All this looks like a lot of work."

Rushing into the kitchen, Sil set the herbs aside and tried to minimize the organized chaos laid out across the various surfaces.

"I was just starting on some dinner. For later."

"What are you making?"

"Curry."

"Mmmhm, I can already smell it."

"You should pick some of the onions and garlic from

the vegetable garden," Magda said, setting her bag on one of the kitchen chairs. "There's probably some that could pass for ready,"

"I don't want Anders to know what I'm making."

Magda and Greta shared a conspiratorial look. "We can assist with that."

Sil wasn't sure if he should be concerned at how in sync the two of them were. But he was grateful for the help.

"Okay, just don't tell him," he said.

"Our lips are sealed," Greta proclaimed.

Magda wrapped an arm around Greta's waist and directed her towards the back door. "Just keep cooking, and we'll take care of the rest. Peppers? Tomatoes? Potatoes?"

"That would be great, thanks."

The tips of Sil's fingers began to tingle as he turned back to the pile of herbs he'd collected and started chopping them up. He had no idea if Anders would like it. But the wizard did have a sweet tooth, so at least the cake would be eaten. He pulled out a few recipe cards from a box on the counter to round out the meal and got to work.

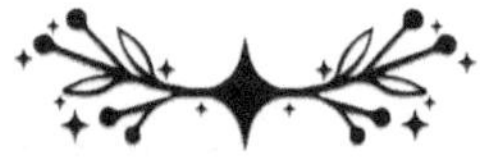

The girls had spent most of the morning giggling and whispering to each other once they'd come out into the vegetable garden. Not to mention their secreting away back into the cottage every half hour or so. Magda had been very firm about Anders working within eyesight of them—probably to keep him from sneaking inside to steal a look. It was near torturous not knowing what Sil was up to. Maybe Anders didn't like surprises, either, after all.

"How have your classes been going?" Anders asked them in between trips of hauling the wheelbarrow over to the compost bins.

"Good, though I miss Sil's snarky comments," Greta replied. "I still think he'd like the Enchanted Foodstuffs class."

"Mr. Know-it-all would rather spend his time here with Anders. And we stan that," Magda argued.

"The structure just wasn't working for him," Anders said.

Magda leaned against the wooden fence and grabbed the remains of her iced coffee. As she swirled the cup, it slowly refilled. "Hey, whatever works for him. It is a little lonely at the shop, though."

"Even when I drop by?" Greta asked with a grin.

Magda rolled her eyes, and pulled Greta close. "You're a brat."

"Only for you." Greta arranged Magda's arms around her waist and leaned back against the other young woman.

"Are you two…?" Anders didn't want to pry exactly.

Snorting, Magda kissed the top of Greta's hair. "Obviously."

"Hey, I didn't want to assume! Some people are just really good friends."

"Like you and Sil?" Magda asked, a knowing glint in her eye.

"Yeah…like us."

"I've worked with him for almost three years, and he's never mentioned dating anyone," Magda said, taking a long sip

of her drink. "But he'll go on about you for hours."

That made Anders' chest warm and fuzzy, like a hoard of dust mites nuzzling together.

"He does seem to really respect you," Greta added. "He was all flustered when some of the professors were kind of dismissive of you."

"What? He didn't mention anything about that."

Anders knew he wasn't the favorite wixen among the faculty of the local university. He was a bit of an oddball when it came to the rest of academia. Auda was the people person of the two of them. And she spent most of her time alone halfway up a mountain.

"I don't think he wanted you to worry about him," Greta said.

"Well, of course, I worry about him!"

Magda gave Greta a smug look. "I told you."

Anders looked between the two of them suspiciously. "Told her what?"

"Nothing!" Greta replied a little too quickly.

"Oh, it's just a…conspiracy we have," Magda said.

Anders pushed some of the mulch back around the base of a tomato plant he'd been weeding around and said, "I thought the two of you might want to stay for dinner."

Magda grabbed the shovel next to her. "We would, but I have a paper about runic mantras to finish up."

"That's not due 'til next week, I thought," Greta said, titling her head to the side like a confused puppy.

Magda raised her eyebrows conspiratorially. "Yes, but I have a lot of work to do on it still."

Greta practically jumped as the implications sank in. "Oh! Right, no, we should definitely finish up here. I have some papers to go over for my wixen, too."

"College students turning down free food?" Anders shook his head in disbelief. "Now I *know* something is up."

He moved farther down the row of tomatoes, sneaking a couple of cherry red snacks when he thought the girls weren't looking. They popped into sharp sweetness, the juice nearly drippling down his chin.

"Nothing needs to be 'up.' We're just being responsible students." Magda smiled. "Isn't that what you would want?"

"I feel like no matter how I answer that, I'll be wrong," Anders complained, glancing between the two of them.

"It's alright to be wrong," Greta said. "My uncle is wrong all the time."

"What about you and Sil?" Magda asked Anders pointedly.

"Us? Wh-what about us?" he stammered and stared at the mulch in his hands.

"You like him. Right?"

"Of course, I do! What kind of question is that?"

"And you like him as…what?"

He knew what she meant, but admitting it felt like finally crossing a line. "We're friends. And he's my apprentice now…"

Greta had stopped pretending to shovel more mulch into the wheelbarrow. "'Friends' only goes so far. Sometimes you grow into more than that. And it's okay to feel weird about it at first."

"No, that's not…"

"Who would you want to talk to if something was wrong?" Magda asked.

"Well, Sil…but we live together, so that's easiest."

"Oh, you're both so cute and stupid," Magda groaned. "Just confess to him and feel all the nice warm fuzzies."

"The warm fuzzies are the best part," Greta agreed. "Though, actually, the kisses might be. Or the snuggles… Oh! No, it's definitely waking up with someone next to you and just listening to them breathe as the sunlight peaks in through the curtains."

Anders go momentarily lost in the thought of his fingers curled up in the fabric of Sil's oversized shirt he slept in. Or nudging Sil's foot under a table during dinner until he finally leaned against him. The way he smelt like dirt and herbs after a long day in the garden.

"Anders?" Magda asked.

"Sorry! What would I be confessing?" Anders replied.

Greta tsked. "He's farther gone than I realized. But still cute! And dumb."

Magda snorted mid iced coffee swirl. "Emphasis on the dumb."

"This is why I don't bother trying to date boys," Greta said dreamily. They might have been an odd couple, but they did fit together well.

"Girls can still be dumb, Greta."

"Maybe, but we're pretty at least." Greta pointed out.

Anders blurted out, "Sil is pretty."

Both of the girls looked at Anders with amused looks.

If the ground had swallowed him up right there, Anders wouldn't have complained. The only way it could have been worse, is if Sil had been around to hear him. But, and Anders glanced around to be sure, his assistant was still no where to be seen.

"He's *very* pretty. You should tell him that," Magda chuckled.

"I am not going to tell Sil he's pretty. He knows that," Anders insisted. It was impossible for Sil not to know how cute it was when his glasses slipped down his nose. Or how his grumpy expression was lifted as soon as Sil walked out into the garden.

"It's always nice to hear it from someone you like."

"That implies he likes me."

"Yes! That. Is. The. Point." Magda ground out.

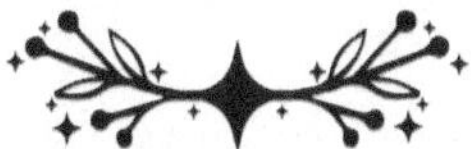

The magic of cooking was that measurements could be adjusted to personal taste. Sil's curry recipe was almost never made per the exact recipe. He estimated the spices and added in extra vegetables when he had them. But it always came out perfect: rich and just spicy enough to sate that craving for hot food when it got warmer outside. The key was to let it cook low and slow for most of the day, filling the house with the distinct aromas of curry powder, ghee, and garlic.

When Sil had finished putting all the ingredients to-gether, including the ones secreted from the garden by Magda and Greta, he set the stove burner to a simmer and placed a lid on the pot. He quickly went about clearing up all the jars and swept the vegetable ends into the bucket for the compost, though he was sure that Cerbs would want some for their gaggle of duck companions. Once the strawberries started ripening, they'd have to keep an eye on them so there were actually some left to eat.

The cake didn't really need to be started yet, so after raiding the cupboard for the promised snacks and taking out a pitcher of lemonade from the ice box, Sil headed outside. Overall, the vegetable garden looked so much better than when Anders had left it to him. The rows were all neatly weeded and watered. And there were hardly any signs of slugs or other insects munching on the lettuce.

"Oooh, snacks!" Greta declared when she spotted him. She was always quick to abandon the work in favor of a break. But Sil could hardly blame her; she was volunteering her time and energy to helping out.

"We're nearly out of biscuits," he said, "so I just put together what we had."

Anders was entrenched in the tomatoes, trimming and tying them up and making certain there were no hornworms in sight.

"Anders, I got out those crackers for you," Sil said, setting down the tray and the lemonade on a little iron table that they'd moved to be closer to the vegetable patch.

"Thanks! I'm nearly done with this row." Anders' silly grin caused Sil's eyes to lock on the wizard little too long.

Magda gave Sil a knowing smile. "We're actually nearly done here, so we can probably start making a dent on some of the tropical beds out back later in the week."

"Oh? Already?" Sil asked, staring back down at the snacks.

Greta nodded and said between bites of biscuit. "It goes so much faster when there's a lot of us working on things."

"Palla might even be able to focus on the wildlife," Magda added.

"That would be nice. I know plants aren't his favorite thing," Anders said.

"Though I'm sure he'll still help with harvesting everything for the show," Greta reassured him. "I nearly forgot to tell you all! My uncle is one of the judges this season. So you'll see him I bet. He's been a judge before, but I've never gotten to visit the set."

Wiping some of the dirt from his hands as he came over to join the rest of them, Anders asked, "We'll make sure to say hi. What's his name?"

"M.H. Cershaw. He's the same one that sometimes teaches that gardening class I told you about, Sil."

Sil had tried to signal to her not to keep talking, but his flailing clearly hadn't translated.

"Cershaw?" Anders repeated dryly.

Greta nodded obliviously. "One of the judges got a case of mulberry spots, so they asked my uncle to come back. Luckily, the fungal infection he had cleared up. He was really stressing about it."

Sil stifled a snort, "Fungal infection?"

"Oh, yes! It was like an army of tiny mushrooms all up his arm. I thought it was kinda cute."

Magda said, "Not everyone can pull off mushrooms like

Beren can."

"Luckily, I don't think they'll have much room or time for us on set," Anders said.

"I'm sure they can make time! Especially if I ask Uncle."

"It's fine. We wouldn't want to be in the way," Sil assured Greta. As Anders poured a few glasses of lemonade, Sil casually said, "The dust mites seem to have settled in the back near the creek."

"To the annoyance of our garden gnomes," Anders said, latching onto the change in subject. "Though I think Marvin is enjoying himself chasing the dust mites."

The cat had quickly discovered the joy in hunting down the little mites by the water. Even if his paws sometimes got soggy when he was too enthusiastic.

"They aren't *our* garden gnomes," Sil said. "They just live here. And steal my gloves."

"Borrow! They give them back," Anders said.

"Yes," Sil said. "But with holes in them."

"Why would there be holes in your gloves?" Greta asked, interjecting into Sil and Anders' banter.

"Cause they cut them up to make gnome sized gloves," Sil complained.

"That sounds adorable!" Greta said.

"It's not. It's frustrating."

"But tiny gnome gloves!"

Magda patted Greta's shoulder. "Don't even think about inviting them back to my place. Gramma would kill me."

"*Gnome gloves...*" Greta whispered to herself between bites of another biscuit.

"Okay, I think we should be taking off," Magda said.

"But we still have—"

Magda wrapped an arm around Greta's waist. "A paper to write."

"Mags…" Greta whimpered, reaching for the plate of biscuits.

"Besides, Sil and Anders probably wanted some alone time."

"Alone time?" Anders asked.

Grinning at Sil again, Magda added, "Yup. So we're gonna go."

Greta looked between Sil and Anders and nodded slowly, as if she was finally in on the joke. "Ohhhhh, yeah. We have to go. But we'll come back later—"

"Tomorrow," Magda corrected.

"Yes. Tomorrow!"

"But I haven't finished the…"

"I'm sure Anders will help you." Magda assured Sil.

Hugging him, Greta whispered, "Good luck! Bye, Anders! Have a good night."

As Magda and Greta disappeared around the side of the cottage, Sil turned to Anders. "I feel like I'm missing something."

Anders groaned. "They have some weird assumption that I…well, that we…that I…"

Like me? Sil thought, feeling icy sweat drip down his spine.

"Are we friends?" Anders asked. "*Just* friends?"

"You're my Wixen…and roommate," Sil said cautiously.

"But is that it?"

Sil waited a beat to see if Anders would elaborate before saying, "I don't know, are we anything else?"

"I'm asking you."

"And I'm asking you, Anders!" Why was the damn wizard being so obtuse all of a sudden? One of the nice things about Anders was how plainly he said things. Sil didn't have to worry about if he was being honest or not. Anders just said what he thought, when it came to mind.

"Do you want to be more?" Sil asked him.

"Of course, I do!"

The buzzing of insects was suddenly very loud in Sil's ears. "So...that's a yes?"

"Yes? Yes!"

It felt like a weight had been lifted off Sil's chest. The relief melted the tension out of him.

"Why didn't you say so sooner?" Sil asked Anders.

"I did just now. Why didn't you say something sooner?"

"Because I was terrified you didn't feel the same way, and I'd ruin everything!"

"You couldn't possibly ruin *anything*."

"Oh, I'm very good at ruining things." Sil motioned to the recently drowned vegetable garden.

Anders shrugged. "We fixed it. So, it's not ruined."

"Next time, it might be!"

Putting his hands gently on Sil's shoulders, Anders met Sil's eyes and said, "Then we'll fix it again."

"I don't want to ruin what we have," Sil admitted, his eyes tearing away from Anders' gaze. His chest was tightening, and the corners of his eyes stung as the thousands of what-ifs all tried to file through his mind at once.

"You won't." The wizard started to reach out a hand to him. Hesitant. Testing to see if their proximity was okay.

"You're biased," Sil countered.

Anders hand was gentle as rough, dirt stained fingers traced Sil's wrist.

"Sil? I promise you won't. Okay?"

"But—"

"No 'buts.' I forbid any 'buts.'" Anders leaned in closer and kissed Sil's forehead.

Sil felt stupid that tears were welling up. There was no reason to cry. Grabbing Anders' lapels, Sil pulled the wizard close and pressed their lips together. After a moment of confused immobilization, the wizard wrapped his arms around Sil's waist, and the two of them relaxed into the kiss until they eventually pulled apart.

"I think I really like you, Anders."

"I'm pretty sure I feel the same."

Sil choked and wiped at his eyes.

"Did you not like the kiss?" Anders asked him, panic starting to bleed into the wizard's tone.

"No, I did. Really, I did. I'm just…happy. And relieved."

Anders let out a sigh of relief. "Oh, good." They stood there for a moment longer before Anders asked, "What's for dinner, by the way?"

"Curry. And chocolate cake for dessert?"

Leaning in again, Anders nuzzled their noses together. "Sounds perfect."

Field Notes
7

Auda would like to know when the Chaos Coven is invited over for curry?

If they come help with the harvest, that might be a good time.

Recipe *Chicken Curry*

Ingredients

- 2lbs chicken cut as desired
- 2 tsp salt
- 1 tbsp olive oil
- 1 1/2 cup chopped onion
- 1 tbsp garlic
- 1 1/2 tsp ginger
- 1 tbsp curry powder
- 1 tsp cumin
- 1 tsp turmeric
- 1 tsp coriander
- 1 tsp cayenne pepper
- 1 tsp garam masala*
- 1 tbsp lemon juice
- 15 oz crushed toma[toes]
- 1/2 cup water

Optional
- 2 cups chopped potatoes
- 2 tbsp butter or ghee
- 1 cup chopped bell or sweet peppers

*see recip[e]

Double or triple recip[e] for large group gathering. ← 'Chaos Coven'

Cake for dessert?

Fine.

Recipe

Garam Masala

Ingredients

- 2 tbsp coriander
- 1 tbsp cumin
- 1 tbsp cardamom
- 1 tbsp black peppercorns
- 1 tsp fennel
- 1 tsp mustard seeds
- 1/2 tsp cloves
- 2 tbsp tumeric
- 2 dried chili peppers

Instructions

- If using whole spices, toast lightly first

- Grind all ingredients together

Recipe

Oh! My mother has a great flat bread recipe that would be amazing with this!

Instructions

- Combine all dry ingredients (spices) together.
- Put garlic, onion, ginger & peppers in pan with olive oil & cook until onion is golden.
- Add chicken, tomatoes, potatoes, spices, lemon juice and water into pot.
- Bring to a boil, then lower heat to medium-low and cook for 45-90 mins; until chicken and potatoes are cooked through

- Can also be cooked in a slow-cooker or pressure pot

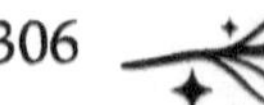

Cauldrons
&
Cookery

"Unger! Check those lights again! Sound, can we have another test once we have our host out of makeup? Robin, how is set dressing? Are we ready to go?"

Sil tried to shrink out of the way of another assistant rushing by with a clipboard and headset. Given that the show hadn't even started filming yet, the studio was a swarm of caffeinated teams wrapping up final details. Anders had lucked out and been cornered by someone in charge of food presentation and was in the middle of helping to find the "best" looking vegetables out of the harvest.

"You!" the director or producer, aka the scary person in charge, pointed at Sil.

"Am I in the way?"

"Why aren't you in wardrobe?"

Blinking at the man in confusion, Sil tried to explain,

"I'm just here with…"

"Donna, can you get him in the right wardrobe? And some makeup? Can hardly see his eyes behind those huge glasses."

A woman in a black apron covered in splatters of various colored powders nodded and touched Sil's arm gently. "This way."

"I'm not with the show."

"It's best to just stay out of his way until the cameras are going," Donna assured him. She led Sil back to a hallway with various rooms splaying off it. A few doors had name placards, including one labeled "Cershaw" in gold letters, but most just had a couple cards with "Contestant #___" scrawled across them in thick black marker.

"In here," Donna said, opening the last door in the hall. "Once we get first shots he'll calm down and it's easier to see all the *magic* happen."

"Uh, thanks."

"You're with the wizard, right?" she asked him, fluffing her hair in one of the mirrors surrounded with huge light bulbs.

"I'm his apprentice."

"That sounds exciting."

Sitting in one of the makeup chairs, Sil resisted the urge to spin around in it. "Well, I'm brand new at magic, so I'm not exactly good at it. Have you been doing this long?"

"Been on the makeup team since series one. This is only my second run as head of the department, though."

"I didn't realize that a show like this would need a whole

makeup team."

"There are still plenty of things that magic doesn't handle when it comes to TV. Good makeup is an art, just like casting a spell."

"Or not burning your cake."

"Just wait until you see how many things get messed up while we're filming. TV will be ruined for you for good!"

"Thanks for letting me hide in here."

"Of course, and good to meet you. I should get back to it. Craft services should be set up across the hall if you get peckish."

A voice came over the building speakers, announcing, *"Host and judges to set, please."*

"The mysterious voice calls." Donna waved as she left the room.

This seemed to be the dressing room where random items were left so they wouldn't be in the way. A few racks of clothes were shoved in a back corner, and hair and makeup tools were scattered across one of the dressing tables. A few of the mirrors had clippings of past contestants and stories about the show taped up. He recognized a few smiling faces in the photos from episodes he'd watched while cooking in his tiny apartment kitchen. The show never really shared full recipes, but that was nothing the show's devoted fanbase and a few key interviews from contestants sharing their grammie's crab-apple crumble recipe couldn't figure out.

Draped across the arm of one of the chairs was a green apron. He figured it was probably an extra or rejected color. The show's famous cauldron was embroidered on the front pocket. Double checking that no one was in the hallway, Sil slipped it on over his head and snorted at his reflection in the mirror.

"Good thing I'm not planning on being a TV star." He tried to flatten a few wiry curls, but they wouldn't behave.

A tickle on the back of his neck nearly made him jump out of his skin as Blip wrapped around his shoulders.

"I told you to stay at the cottage!"

The tiny dragon just happily bopped her snout against Sil's nose.

"I don't think they'll want a pipe dragon around all this food." He sighed and sat back down. "Just stay out of sight when we go back out, okay?"

For such a large studio, Anders was finding it nearly impossible to avoid Cershaw. The man was seemingly everywhere Anders turned, clips in his blond hair to keep curls in place and a plastic cape around his shoulders to keep his tailored suit spotless. He looked like a manic superhero from a children's show. Usually, Anders didn't care that his own clothes were worn or that he had dirt under his fingernails, but around all these people worried about how things looked, he was suddenly very subconscious, even though he'd dressed in his least threadbare shirt and trousers.

"Anderson, I feel like you're avoiding me," Cershaw said.

Placing a final head of lettuce on a pile in the show's pantry area, Anders shrugged. "Hadn't noticed you."

"Of course, you did. You glared at me when you walked

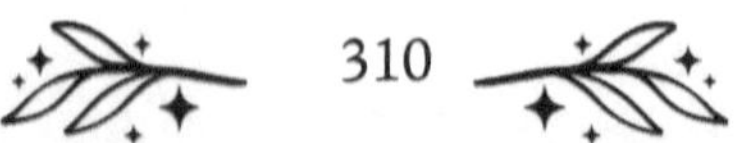

in."

Turning to face him, Anders crossed his arms over his chest. "Must just be my face."

"I saw Sil with you—"

"You leave him alone."

"Touchy. I just wanted to say hello to a fan. I'm allowed, aren't I?"

"Leave. Him. Alone."

A grin spread over Cershaw's lips. "You do have feelings for him. And here I distinctly remember you swearing never to love another after me."

"Sil is none of your business. *I'm* none of your business. Now, excuse me, I need to make sure the fire curry is playing nice with the other herbs."

"He's never going to come to much without proper schooling. He may pass a level or two of his apprenticeship, but then he'll get bored of you."

Anders took a deep breath. Cershaw was baiting him. All he needed to do was ignore him, and he'd eventually move on.

"Let him know I'll tutor him if he decides he wants to become a *real* wizard," the odious man said. "Even though he infected me with that fungus."

A voice over the speakers prevented Anders from lunging at him. "*Host and judges to set, please.*"

"Oh, that's me. Chat later, Anderson." Cershaw turned on his heel and headed towards the main set, grinning.

The head of lettuce Anders had placed suddenly split into pieces and toppled to the floor.

The food presentation supervisor threw up her hands. "That was the hero lettuce!"

Bending down to help pick up the scattered lettuce leaves, Anders said, "Sorry."

I was imagining it was Cershaw's head, he thought.

"There's another one that looked alright."

"The one that looked like it had a butt?" the food presentation supervisor asked.

"We'll just make sure that side isn't to camera?"

"And cross our fingers we don't have a rugby player with the humor of a twelve-year-old on the cast."

Anders offered her an apologetic smile. "I'm sure it'll be fine."

"The first day of shooting is always a mess. Twelve hours of no one knowing what's going on. Tomorrow is always easier."

Nodding, Anders glanced towards the main set where it seemed the director was in another flurry of angry-panic.

"What do you mean we're missing a contestant? Did they vanish?"

"They never showed up to their call time this morning."

"Then call casting and figure out when our backup can get here!"

The assistant sighed. "I told you already, casting has been making calls, but no one is available."

"Are you telling me no one wants to be on TV?"

"We're working on it, Jay. If we focus on filming the host and judge intros, hopefully we can get someone here before lunch."

"That will put our whole schedule behind!"

"We can re-order the shooting schedule. It's not the end of the world."

Cershaw had been sitting next to the two other judges and piped in casually, "There might be someone who could fill the spot. Since all the contestants are home cooks, it doesn't particularly matter who, right?"

The director turned to him, "So long as it's not a relative, friend, or business associate and can be here in less than half an hour, they have the spot."

Anders just knew that whatever Cershaw was cooking up was bad news.

"They're already here."

"Great. Get them into wardrobe and makeup…Donna?"

He'd already started marching towards the set when Cershaw locked eyes with him and smiled that crooked smile that Anders hated.

"Anderson, you can find out where Sil ended up, can't you? He's about to get an amazing opportunity to be on national TV."

Anders knew there had to be some malicious intent behind Cershaw volunteering Sil, but screaming at the man in front of a bunch of strangers wouldn't do any good.

Sil winced under the huge lights on the set. Even the sun in the dead of summer wasn't this bright. The assistants kept motioning to him to stop squirming on his stool in the line of other contestants. He hadn't gotten a chance to object before he'd been made-up and plopped right into the lineup.

"Welcome to this season of *Cauldrons & Cookery*! I'm your host, Corina Broom. This year, we have a brand-new batch of eight excited and magically endowed home cooks eager to battle it out for the coveted golden cauldron!"

A camera swooped by all the contestants, and most of them did their best to look cheery or smug. Sil, on the other hand, just tried not to look terrified.

"Our judges, Chef Nulus Tran and Rickland Pauls are rejoined by bestselling author, M.H. Cershaw. Now, let's find out what our contestants will be brewing today!"

Purple and green sparks erupted behind the host, matching the colored streaks in her hair, but she managed to keep her perfect smile as the cameras rolled.

"Cut!" the director yelled, and the fake smiles relaxed.

"Corina, we'll do that one more time to get a few extra angles. Though pump up the sparks a bit. Can we get another few passes on the contestants, too? Then some close-ups?"

Camera and sound people shuffled around as the shot was reset, reshot, and the director approved it.

Robin had been put in charge of handling the contestants, and once the close-ups were finished, she shooed them off the set to the craft services room.

"When do we start cooking?" Sil asked her as she scrolled through her phone.

"Probably not 'til tomorrow. Eat while you can."

An arm slung around his shoulders and pulled Sil towards the tables of chips and sandwiches. "They always get the 'clean' shots in the first day or so of shooting these shows. I'm

Khulan, by the way."

Sil discreetly separated himself from Khulan's much taller frame and grabbed a juice and some biscuits. "Oh."

"You're the guy they got to fill in last minute, right?" Khulan asked him as he filled a paper plate with sandwiches.

"Yeah."

"You'll get into the swing of it in no time."

"Have you been on a show like this before?" Sil asked him.

"Oh yeah! I've been on *Kitchen Spells*, *Homegrown Recipes*, *The Great Bread Battle*, and I had a couple spots on some web shows, too. Faro and Errol over there, the twins, they were on *Kitchen Spells* with me a couple years back."

Khulan waved at a pair of blond young men who were paging through a stack of index cards. One of them nodded, but the other was more intent on whatever he was studying to be bothered.

"They're pretty serious competitors. Not super chatty."

"Khul, are you bugging the newbie?" a woman with short, bouncy lavender hair asked between bites of an apple.

"Just introducing him to everyone, Quina. She's one of the top magical food bloggers in the northern counties."

"I'm not just a blogger. Hi, I'm Quina. Don't let this big guy get in your head." She nudged Sil's shoulder and hooked a thumb at Khulan.

"I'm not trying to get into his head! I'm being friendly," Khulan insisted.

Crossing her arms over her chest, Quina asked, "And trying to warm him up to you so you can glean info out of him because you weren't able to do any research ahead of time?"

Khulan gave Quina a sheepish grin, "I can be friendly and trying to glean information, can't I?"

"So, what do you do?" Quina asked Sil.

"I'm the manager of a plant shop. And Anders' assistant—well, apprentice now." Sil said, trying to slink out of the little group towards a corner of the craft services room.

Quina's eyebrows raised. "Like an actual apprentice? Shouldn't you be taking classes or something?"

"I'm just going to study with Anders for now."

"Does your wixen have other apprentices?"

Sil shook his head. "No, it's just me."

Khulan and Quina gave each other a surprised look as Sil realized that escaping the conversation wasn't going to be that easy.

"Is that weird?"

"I mean…my friends that got apprenticeships were all in groups under a wixen. But I guess it might not be uncommon," Quina replied.

"So, you're not a witch?" Sil asked. He'd just assumed that everyone on the show had some level of schooling or training.

Quina laughed. "Nope, I just know a handful of spells that are useful in the kitchen. And to really get a great face of makeup for a photo."

Her eye makeup glittered and shifted from a neutral brown color to bright green and then back again with a swish of her hands.

"Yeah, this is an amateur show. Can't be a pro in cooking or magic," Khulan added. "Latif is probably closest on the edge of the rules for that, though. She's in her last year of her apprenticeship. And Hoa is an intern at a restaurant."

Khulan pointed out two more of the contestants who were talking at another table.

"But competitions make a lot more of an even playing field. Everyone has a bad day on a show. So don't stress out about all that," Quina assured Sil.

The eighth contestant stepped into their circle and leveled their gaze at Sil. "And here I thought you were going to rot in that plant shop forever."

His hair was longer than Sil remembered, and he'd clearly grown into his lanky build since their school days, but the freckles and mossy brown hair were the same. The scraggly beard was new, however.

"Taimi?" Sil asked, shocked. "It's been a while."

"Oh, you do remember me. How nice of you."

Sil's former classmate gave Khulan a once over, but didn't even bother glancing in Quina's direction.

"I didn't recognize you—" Sil tried to say.

"Some of us do grow up once we leave school," Taimi said, flipping a loose strand of hair over his shoulder.

"You also moved away to go to university…"

"So, I just didn't exist anymore?"

Khulan cleared his throat. "I'm gonna grab another sandwich. Quina, you want some water?"

She nodded, and the two of them quickly retreated to a safe eavesdropping location near the food tables.

"I mean I called a few times," Sil said, "but you were

busy with classes and stuff."

"Being busy doesn't mean we can't be friends anymore. At least it shouldn't."

"We drifted apart. It happens."

"I guess it does. Better warn your *new* friends there that once this show ends, they'll never hear from you again."

"They were just being polite and talking with me. We literally just met."

Taimi crossed his arms and shook his head. "Same old Sil. Making excuses."

"I'm not making an excuse! Look, I'm sorry we stopped talking. But you didn't exactly reach out either. Communication has to be worked on by both parties."

"How did you even get on the show?" Taimi asked him pointedly. "There was someone else cast originally, right? Someone with a better personality."

"I happened to be here, and they needed someone..."

"'*Happened to be here?*' What does that mean?"

"Anders grew and provided the produce for the show."

"Who is Anders?"

"He's my—" Sil nearly said boyfriend but managed to catch himself. "Wixen. I started working in his garden earlier this year, and now I'm his apprentice."

Taimi snorted. "Wixen? *You* have a wixen?"

"His name is Anders."

"Never heard of him."

"That's because he's busy with research most of the time."

"Or maybe because he's never going to amount to much. Like someone else..." Taimi trailed off with a smirk. "So, they just threw you into the competition."

"Yup."

"Well, then you won't mind losing to me."

"Sorry?"

"The show. You won't mind when I beat you. It's not as if you're any good at magic. You couldn't even lift a rock to get into the magic basics classes when we were kids."

"That test was flawed. It didn't consider other learning styles."

Taimi shrugged. "No, it just showed you couldn't learn magic."

Sil balled up his fist at his side. He hadn't really thought about making it past the first week or two of the show. But with Taimi's challenge, he was willing to at least try to outlast his childhood friend. If only to rub his newfound talents in Taimi's smug face.

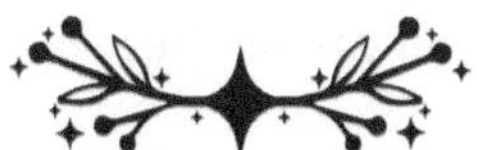

Filming had gone late into the morning, far past Anders' usual bedtime. But he didn't want to leave Sil alone, no matter how much he protested. By the time he portalled them back to the cottage, his eyes were slipping closed.

"You didn't need to stay the whole time," Sil was repeating again as he fidgeted with dishes in the sink.

"I wanted to make sure you got home safe," Anders said, stifling a yawn.

"Go to bed."

"Aren't we going to snuggle?"

Sil's ears turned bright red, and he nearly dropped a

mug in the sink. "You're going to pass out as soon as your head hits the pillow!"

"That wasn't a no."

With a dramatic sigh, Sil clanked the dishes in the sink and turned to Anders. "Isn't that a little fast? Sleeping together...?"

"Sharing a bed and snuggling isn't 'sleeping together.' It's fine if you aren't ready for that."

"Then we're setting ground rules; snuggles only, with pajamas on."

Anders grinned in victory. "Fair. My bed is bigger."

"Go!" Sil shooed him out of the kitchen.

Anders didn't have to wait too long for Sil to knock gently on the door carrying an old, chipped tea pot.

"Blip was fussing," he explained.

"That's fine," Anders said, motioning towards a little table in one corner. "You can set her there. Or on the window-sill."

Climbing into bed while Sil settled Blip's teapot on the windowsill, Anders fluffed a couple of the pillows. He'd been alone in the cottage for so long that even Sil casually popping his head in asking if he wanted tea in the mornings had quickly become something he looked forward to. Once Sil was satisfied that Blip wouldn't knock the teapot over, he sat down on the edge of the bed, farthest away from Anders.

"You can't snuggle if you're all the way over there."

Sil in the meantime was lifting up the corner of one of the quilts gingerly, revealing the layers of blankets. "Do you have enough blankets?"

"I like being cozy."

Anders leaned over and gently lifted Sil's dark rimmed glasses off, setting them aside. Sil's eyes sparkled in the low candlelight, dark and warm and hiding his apprehension. He tried to give Sil a reassuring smile and laid down, propping his head up on his arm.

"Did you 'snuggle' with Cershaw?" Sil asked.

Opening and closing his mouth to respond a couple of times, Anders finally formed the right words. "That wasn't really the type of relationship we had."

Sil started nodding, but then seemed to come to some kind of conclusion he wasn't thoroughly happy about and cleared his throat. "Right, of course…"

"What about you? Have you ever dated anyone?"

"No," Sil replied, staring up at the ceiling.

"Never?"

"Nope."

Anders pursed his lips and continued with his questioning, "Have you ever had a crush?"

"Of course! But they were just silly school crushes. The likelihood of ending up with someone you met at school and having it work out are very low."

"Didn't your parents meet school?"

Sil's nose crinkled up cutely. "Yes, but that's different. It was more of a thing then."

"Get comfortable."

Shoving a few of the blankets out of the way, Sil finally nestled into the bed, hugging a pillow to his chest. "Did you always know you were going to be a wizard?"

"I did. Farming wasn't really my passion. But I learned a lot about plants and creatures from growing up on one."

"It's hard to imagine you on a farm still," Sil admitted.

"Even when I tell you we primarily raised dragons?" Anders asked. He did really need to take Sil out to the farm. Once everything settled down again.

"I mean, that sort of makes sense. But still, you getting up early in the morning to do chores and not get distracted by some new kind of lichen seems impossible."

Chuckling, Anders replied, "Well, Auda and I traded chores a lot. And I ended up distracted a lot."

"Auda definitely seems too fabulous to have grown up on a farm, too."

Anders was creeping closer to Sil in the bed. He didn't want to move too quickly, but his eyes were drooping and he kept having to fight off a yawn.

"You do know she lives halfway up a mountain, right?"

Sil shrugged and smiled. "Yes, but now she has magic to help her."

"She wasn't always like that; she was skinny and nerdy when we were growing up."

Bursting out laughing, Sil shook his head. "No! Auda is the least nerdy witch I've met!"

"We were nearly identical as kids!" Anders tried to argue.

"You'll have to show me pictures to prove it."

Anders could only imagine his mother's excitement to get out the old photo albums full of muddy pictures of him and Auda. There had to be some similarly embarrassing pho-

tos of little Sil with his glasses askew.

"Only once I get to see old photos of you."

"Weren't you tired and nearly falling asleep?" Sil asked him.

"It's hard to sleep when I haven't had any snuggles yet," Anders said, making a show of stretching his arm across Sil's pillow.

"Okay! Fine! Snuggle me and go to sleep already!"

Sil rolled over and wiggled into a more comfortable position.

"If you command it," Anders replied, wrapping his arms around Sil and pulling him close against his chest.

They laid there in silence for a few minutes before Sil squirmed and readjusted so his head was cradled in the crook of Anders' arm. Pressing his lips to the back of Sil's neck, Anders inhaled the earthy scent that clung to him.

Sil froze and said, "I thought I said snuggles only."

"Sorry, I'll stop."

Stretching out his neck a little, Sil whispered, "No, don't."

"You're sure?"

"Yes, I'm sure," Sil replied and twined their fingers together.

"Alright," Anders said, nudging Sil's collar down a little with his chin. He kissed Sil's neck more firmly, parting his lips slightly and letting his teeth drag gently along skin.

Shivering, Sil curled his legs under the blankets. "That's…nice."

Anders pulled Sil's night shirt down a bit more, reveal-

ing a peek of shoulder, and planted kisses along it, one after another. As Sil uncurled along Anders' body, Anders let his hand rest on Sil's hip. The tension in Sil's shoulders and limbs was slowly melting away the longer they laid there, pressed together.

Sil's breathing slowed, and as Anders kissed just behind Sil's ear, Sil mumbled, "Keep like that…"

"Good night, Sil," Anders whispered to him before whispering for the candles to go out.

"Mmm, night."

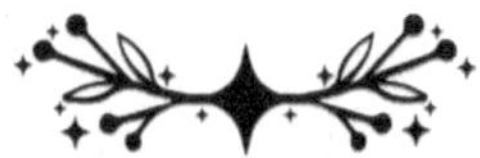

The teams for the show's first challenge couldn't have been random as the show's narrator would surely claim. Team Purple consisted of the twins, Faro and Errol, with their culinary focus. Latif was their magic specialist. And rounding it out was Taimi.

On Team Green, Hoa and Quina starred as the stronger cooks. Khulan had the charisma and competition experience. And then there was Sil. Even without watching many reality shows, Sil could tell they were going to be billed as the underdogs. Skill-wise, the other team was just better balanced. Latif was nearly a fully qualified witch. And while Taimi didn't have a background in spells for the kitchen or cooking, he was enrolled at Oxenbridge, not to mention much farther along with his magical education than what Sil had managed to learn in the past few months.

Sil found himself smoothing invisible wrinkles in his apron as they waited for their next instructions and an idea of what the challenge would be. Anders gave him a thumbs up from behind the camera with the cluster of assistants. Sil gave the wizard a tight smile as the host finally walked onto the set.

Corina's white pant suit was accented with purple and green trim to match the show's theme. "How's everyone this morning?"

There was a rumble of "good,," "tired," and "ready!" from the contestants.

"Fantastic! We're going to do a couple run throughs of the episode's challenge intro and then we'll get to the first round of cooking. Sound good?" she asked.

"Our first challenge's theme is 'Herbaceous'!" Corina gushed to the cameras even though it was the tenth take. "The special ingredient is a spicy one: fire curry. And our teams will need to follow the 'magic card,'" she said, holding up a large card with a cauldron printed on one side.

Turning the card around for the "audience" to see, it read, "Must heat everything with magic."

Every time the card was turned around, Sil's stomach plummeted farther. He was the designated wixen for the team, which meant *he* was the one his team would be counting on to provide the required magical heat over the course of the filming day. At least his humiliation would be nice and short—even if it was going to be broadcast across the country.

"It's going to be a hot episode, right, teams?" Corina called out. "Let's cook some magic!"

"Cut! Let's wrap that and film some cut aways to the

two teams planning their meals out," the director said.

Khulan clapped Sil on the back with a grin. "Can't wait to get into the hard stuff."

Hoa shared a look with Quina before turning to Sil. "You can manage the magic card, right?"

Pushing his glasses up his nose, he tried his best not to catch Anders' eye. "I'm still pretty new at all this."

"Meaning?"

He made the mistake of glancing up at the wizard, who gave him another thumbs up. Sil cleared his throat and replied, "I'll do my best."

"So…we're fucked?" Hoa commented dismissively.

"Don't be so sour. We'll get into the groove of things in no time. Just give him some time to warm up," Khulan told Hoa.

"I'm not being sour; I'm being realistic," she argued.

"We can plan on something that doesn't rely on precise temperatures or cooking techniques," Quina commented.

"This is a *magical* cooking competition, and we have a novice on our team."

Shrinking back from his teammates, Sil did his best not to bolt off the set and towards the little table with water laid out. The only times he'd managed fire were when he wasn't thinking about it. People were expecting fire from him: on command and for long enough to cook a full meal. Not to mention, Blip had been banished to Anders' custody for the duration of filming. Familiars were considered an unfair advantage for the wixen on the teams.

He could sense someone hovering over his shoulder.

Turning on his heel, he was about to chide Anders but found Taimi looming over him.

"Thinking of quitting already, Sil?"

"No. I was just thirsty," he lied, downing a gulp from the bottle.

"You could still back out and not have to worry about failing so publicly."

Sil pushed past him as Anders approached. "Perhaps you should worry about your own performance. If I remember correctly, you tend to choke up if you miss a step in a spell."

He could tell he'd hit a nerve as Taimi clenched his fists at his side. "Excuse me. I should get back to my teammates."

Anders was quick to wrap a protective arm around Sil's shoulders as he walked away. "You alright?"

"Yeah. Just an old classmate of mine."

"Really?" Anders sounded mildly curious.

"We lost touch," Sil replied dryly.

"Ahh, well, um. I just wanted to wish you luck."

"I'm going to need more than just luck."

"You'll be fine. It'll come to you."

"Just because I've managed to light the stove for a kettle a handful of times, doesn't mean I'm going to master fire spells in the next twelve hours."

Nodding slowly, Anders shrugged. "Just remember to feel out what you want to do. And don't overcomplicate it. Elemental magic tends to come pretty easily to those with strong emotions."

"I have a temper, so that means I can bend the elements to my will? That's a load of bull—"

"Contestants back to set please!"

He sighed, and Anders kissed his temple, saying, "I'm rooting for you."

Sil's face felt tight, and he really just wanted to hide it in the folds of Anders' worn-out robes.

"I know. Just don't get your hopes up."

Taking his hand, Anders' moved Sil's fingers so they all came together in a point. "Just draw the fire out."

The wizard mimicked the position with his own hand, closing his fingers and pulling his hand down. A few wisps of blue flame appeared at his fingertips before going out. He always made things look so simple. Why couldn't the first challenge have had some kind of water related magical element?

"Sil, we're just about to start again," one of the assistants called out to him from across the set.

The walk back to his teammates felt like he was about to be failed in a group project, even as Khulan gave him a big smile.

"Any ideas on what we should make?" Khulan asked.

Quina shook her head. "Plenty of ideas. But a lot of them can't be done in the time limit or with our…limitations."

Sil bit his lower lip. "Whatever your best idea is, let's try it."

Tucking a lavender strand of hair behind her ear, Quina asked, "Are you absolutely sure?"

"Worst thing that can happen is I can't manage it, and I go home. Right?"

"That's the spirit!" Khulan declared.

"Well, the judges will no doubt be expecting some kind

of curry dish, given the special ingredient. But I was thinking we could instead make a curry leaf chutney," Quina explained.

"Will that have enough of the fire curry leaf flavor?" Hoa asked.

"We won't know until we make it. We'll need some kind of flat bread or something to go with it."

Khulan already had a notepad out and was writing things down. "Hoa, do you want to focus on the prep of the chutney with Quina? And I can make some dosa and other toppings?"

The women nodded in agreement.

"So, we'll need a few pans heated for the dish. Sil, can you manage that?" Hoa asked.

"Yeah," Sil said, feeling his palms getting sweaty.

The production required several takes of them going over their cooking plans, collecting the ingredients and such before they were able to move onto the actual cooking portion. Sil tried to ignore everything happening on the other side of the cooking set, instead focusing on the cast iron pans that Hoa had selected. Each had a stand, under which a flame or other heating device could be used to cook on. He'd only ever made fire from the stove, with the gas or wood just needing a spark to light. But it was going to require him to create a flame from nothing but air and maintain it for the duration of the cooking time.

Pinching his fingers together like Anders had shown him, Sil tried to feel the fiery elements and pull them out of the air. But nothing happened, and he caught Hoa watching him with an annoyed expression. The motion felt much more like how Professor Hildegaard had tried to teach pulling water out of the air. He'd never made it past that one class, so he didn't know if maybe the elemental spells all had similar hand magic or not.

"Sil, I need one of these pans heated up," Hoa told him. She was already cutting up vegetables while Quina measured out whole spices to toast.

"We need to toast these before we do anything else," Quina added.

"Right," he replied, staring at the cast iron pans in front of him.

He felt wiggling under the collar of his shirt and closed his eyes, begging Blip silently not to poke her head out right now. She chirped a few times, still nestled under his shirt, body wrapped around his arm. Sil hadn't even noticed that she'd slithered back to him from Anders' shoulder. Taking a deep breath, he tried to focus on fire—not too big or too small, just enough to heat the pan evenly so they wouldn't completely fail this first challenge.

"Wow, that is some great control on those flames there, Sil. What is the Green Team planning on cooking up for this challenge?" Corina asked.

Sil opened his eyes and realized there were several cameras huddled around, along with Corina leaning casually against the counter.

"Um...what?"

Khulan came to the rescue. "He's still kinda shy. Quina's come up with a chutney recipe to feature the fire curry, and I'll be crafting some dosas and other toppings to pair with it."

"That sounds delicious," Corina gushed. "Sil, are you going to be showing off any fancy magic for us today?"

He was still trying to focus on not losing the flame now that he'd managed it. "I just want to make sure we get everything cooked properly."

"I see, keeping your secrets for later. We'll have to keep an eye on the Green Team!"

Khulan laughed along with Corina as Quina dumped her spices into the first pan.

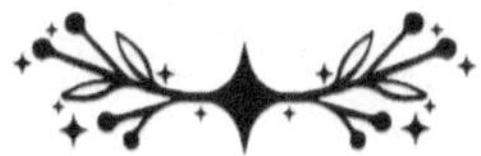

Everything seemed to move at a glacial pace as Sil tended the little flames under each pan his three teammates needed. It was a dance between the four of them as Hoa and Khulan checked on dishes and Quina flitted around tasting and adjusting. His arms were cramping, and he was sweating like crazy when time was finally called.

Assistants rushed in with cameras in tow to film each dish and spirit them away for the judges and final beauty shots. Sil opened and closed his aching hands a few times as his teammates absently cleaned up a little.

"At least you managed to keep the fire going the whole time," Hoa told him, offering him a towel.

Wiping his forehead, he shrugged.

"That's practically a compliment, Hoa," Khulan declared.

She snorted. "Hardly. We'll see how things fall when the judges come back."

"How long does the judging usually take?" Sil asked.

"Hours," Quina replied. "Let's grab something to eat. It

won't be half as good as anything we cooked, but it's food."

"And the first rule of showbiz is always eat when you can," Khulan added.

"The second rule is sit around and wait," Quina said.

"Ignore them," Hoa told Sil, putting her knives off to the side in a little bin with her name. "They have far too much energy for most anyone."

Sil laughed a little, at least now that the challenge was over, his nervousness had dissipated a little.

"Ah, so your face isn't frozen in terror," Hoa said off-handedly.

"No, it's not. I just never imagined doing anything like this..."

"Cooking on TV?"

"Or doing magic," Sil admitted. The sad looking craft services sandwiches didn't look great, but he shoved one onto a paper plate all the same.

Hoa had opted for the wilted looking salad and some kind of protein bar.

"You are a little old to be just starting," She said.

The purple team had spread out at different tables in the makeshift cafeteria, but Khulan and Quina had pulled over a few extra chairs so they could all eat together. It was nice to feel like he belonged on their little ragtag team, even if it was probably just for this one episode.

"I've been learning magic for all of a couple of months," Sil said.

"We're really fucked when things get more complicated, then," Quina said, though Sil wasn't sure if it was more to

herself or not.

"Again, I'll try my best. But I don't make any promises."

She sighed. "At least the judges pretty consistently don't send home other team members if the wixen fails a challenge."

"But don't you need one to compete?"

"The rest of the team has to fill in that spot as best they can. All the contestants have to have a little experience with magic under their belts. Same with the cooking bit."

"I see..."

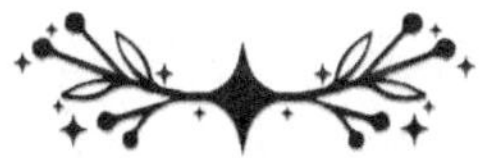

It was hard to read the judges' expressions. And the contestants hadn't been able to see all their feedback. So Sil had no idea what to expect when the host turned to them and asked who would be eliminated. Part of him also didn't care after three hours of waiting on the judges, then another two hours of filming the food, the team's explanations of their dishes, and more.

"Today we're sending home Quina from the Green Team," Rickland Pauls replied. "It was splitting hairs, but we felt her recipe didn't fit the brief as well as the Purple Team's."

"Quina, I'm very sorry, but that means you'll need to hand over your apron," Corina said.

Khulan already had Quina wrapped in a big bear hug, but she nodded. "Someone has to go home first. The Purple Team's eggplant curry looked really good."

"It really was a hard choice," Chef Tran said, not sounding all that sorry.

Quina removed her apron and handed it off to Corina.

And then the director made them reshoot the moment twelve different times and had Donna give her eye drops so she'd look like she'd been crying. Donna had been right; TV was completely ruined for Sil.

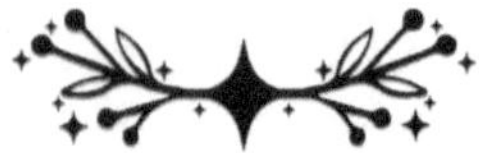

"He survived the first round, though, that's good news," Auda said, chasing a cherry tomato around her plate with her fork.

There were going to be so many salads in their future. The production probably only needed half of what they'd managed to grow.

"It is, though it means more filming. And stress."

"And you miss him?" Auda smirked.

Anders was too anxious to know if Sil had made it to the next round to eat. Crusher had noticed and had planted himself next to Anders' chair, waiting for him to discard parts of his meal.

"Of course, I miss him. That's allowed," Anders said. He knew he didn't have to say a word for his sister to infer that he and Sil had taken "official" next steps in their relationship. Auda had clocked the shift as plain as the rain on an autumn day.

"I'm happy you're happy, Ande. And Sil will do amazingly. He's a wildcard, and TV producers love that."

"What do you know about TV?"

His sister shrugged. "I dated that producer in uni, and they took me around set a few times."

"I don't remember this."

He tried to wrack his brain for any memory of this supposed love interest. The last person he remembered Auda bringing home was a hair dresser that smelt of bleach. Or had that been the professor? She went through flings at least once a quarter; Anders had never been good at keeping track of them.

"That's because you were too focused on your latest mushroom experiment up at the Royal Gardens. You don't notice much when your head is in the dirt. When will Sil be home tonight?"

"Late, probably. They've gone past midnight nearly every day," Anders said.

"Ah, yes, the horrendous hours of TV. Absolutely nothing like the long hours of academia."

"You're making fun of me."

Auda grinned proudly. "And myself. I'm an academic, too."

"When is your next study finishing up?"

"Oh, you know, when its finished," She said and waved her hand amorphously.

Maybe Anders could sic Torlind on her. That would get Auda to finish her current project. Though he did worry about them spending too much time together. No, it was best to keep them apart in case of potential plotting.

"So, you're stalling," Anders said.

She shrugged. "I was thinking of finding an apprentice."

"Now you're copying me?"

"I'm a witch; I'm allowed to have an apprentice."

He did know firsthand how lonely it was living on your

own. Even as independent loners.

"You never wanted one before."

"And now I do. So deal with it. I've put out some feelers at the university and with Yolanda at the Royal Gardens to see if there are any eager students looking for a wixen."

Snickering, Anders said, "If they know it's with you, you'll have about a hundred applications before Monday."

Auda wrinkled her nose. "Maybe I should take back a few of those feelers…"

"You're popular; don't let that get you down." Giving up on his dinner, Anders set his plate down on the floor next to Crusher. The dragon promptly nudged the lettuce with his snout and looked back up at Anders expectantly. He'd clearly been hoping for something a bit more on the savory said.

"A popular academic, who would have thought?"

"You're also an inspiration to a lot of young magic users looking to become wixen. You graduated with honors and have been a positive influence on your field ever since," Anders said.

"Science shouldn't be influenced. Even science imbued with magic."

"You know what I mean!"

Chuckling, Auda leaned back in her chair, a wine glass appearing in her hand. "It always amazed me how little you cared about what other people thought."

"That was all for show. I cared."

"We're horrible at the twin thing, aren't we?" Auda said.

"Twins aren't carbon copies of each other."

"Thank scales Mum never tried to dress us identically!"

"Agreed!"

Sil tumbled into the hall with a clatter, and Anders was immediately on his feet to help him up.

"Are you alright?"

"I'm fine. Just caught my foot on the damn portal, that's all."

"But you managed a portal? That's amazing!" Auda called from the kitchen.

"She popped in for dinner to keep me company," Anders explained.

Sil looked exhausted but forced a little smile.

"Did you get booted already?" Anders asked.

"No, no…Khulan did. The judges didn't like his sweet cap ice cream."

Anders perked up at that. "Mushroom ice cream? That would actually be interesting…"

"I thought it was okay. Not my favorite. But Cershaw especially hated it. I'm pretty sure he was the driving force for us losing."

Anders wrapped a comforting arm around Sil's shoulders and kissed his head. "You get another episode, though."

"There's only two of us left on the team. I really doubt I'll make it another."

"Why don't you get to bed?"

"Yeah, I'm wiped," Sil admitted.

"We'll try to keep it down," Auda said.

"Or I'll just put a quiet spell up."

Auda giggled. "Oh, yes! Those!"

"How much of that wine have you already had?" Anders

asked, not really wanting to know the answer.

Sil kissed his cheek before disappearing into his room.

"Not enough to forget that cuteness," she cooed.

Tracking down Cershaw around the set wasn't hard. Especially not with the all-access badge Mr. Vox had given Anders and Sil as part of the contract for the show. Anders didn't bother knocking on the door of Cershaw's dressing room, but he did cast a handful of spells upon closing the door so they wouldn't be overheard or interrupted.

"What in the—? Anderson, what are you doing here?" Cershaw's attention was pulled away from plucking the errant hairs from his eyebrows. He had a makeup cape draped around his shoulders and a hoard of products cluttering the dressing table with little labels marking them as "Cershaw's personal cosmetics. DO NOT USE!".

"Anders! It's Anders, for the hundred millionth time. I always hated it when you called me that when we were together, and I hate it more now," Anders said.

"Tch, what do you want, then?" Cershaw spun his chair back to face the mirror.

"Don't take your dislike for me out on Sil."

"I'm the one that suggested him for the show."

Anders met Cershaw's gaze through the mirror. Somehow the man had become even more vain over the years. Anders replied, "Yes, so you could ultimately humiliate him and, by association, me."

"You're so dramatic."

"No, I'm not. I'm asking you to leave him alone."

"Or what?" Cershaw spat back.

"Or I'll take your 'best-selling' spot away from you."

Cershaw started laughing, nearly falling out of his chair. "Oh Anders! That is—you're kidding, right?"

"No, perfectly serious, Marion," Anders said sternly.

"I'd like to see you try."

"You will. And when my book surpasses yours, you'll have to admit to yourself that you're just a snobby, second-rate author that couldn't make it as a wizard, one who writes books about gardening even though he hates dirt! Now, excuse me, I have people that actually give a shit about me I'd rather be around."

He stepped back outside Cershaw's dressing room and unclenched his fists. At least he hadn't agreed to any duels against Cershaw. Now he had to write a book that was somehow a best-seller. Torlind was going to murder him.

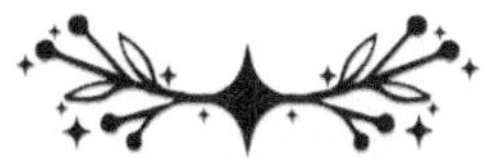

The cooking arena was getting emptier and emptier as the days stretched on. With Quina and Khulan as the first two contestants off the show, that just left Hoa and Sil on the Green Team. But with the third challenge, they finally snatched their first win, with Errol, one of the twins, eliminated.

Hoa had won the challenge with an amazing concoction containing burrowing crickets and hornworms. It was actually really good, so long as Sil didn't think so hard about the fact he was eating bugs. Not that he would go out of his way to ever eat them again. All the same, Hoa completely deserved the win.

Huddled at their cooking station, Hoa flipped through a notebook. Both Quina and Khulan had left them recipes to work with, so they'd each taken a stack to go through as quickly as possible while they waited on production. The reading helped the minutes go by at least.

"Do you want anything to drink?" Sil asked, finishing off his coffee.

"Some black tea would be good, thanks," Hoa replied without looking up.

As Sil went to pick up her cup, it started getting heavier. When he didn't leave their workspace, Hoa gave him a puzzled look. "Black tea?"

"Yeah, sorry…it's refilled for you."

She took the cup from him and breathed in the slightly bitter steam. "This smells so much better than the stuff they serve here."

Sil watched as his coffee mug refilled as well, black and tangy, just how he preferred it.

"Don't waste time fretting over whatever it is," Hoa said. "Get back to reading."

"Right…"

"Okay, contestants," Corina announced, "we're gonna get into the thick of it here in a few minutes. One of the judges is running a little late, so we're handing over the challenge cards while we wait on them."

Hoa snatched the card from Corina and scanned the text on it, flipping to a whole other section in the notebook she'd been reading through.

"Under the Sea? Gag me."

Leaning over Hoa's notebook, Sil asked, "What's the magic card?"

"Must conjure all liquid."

"I hope they don't mind flooding..." Sil muttered.

"Flooding? Come on, Sil; we just had a win let's not ruin that," Hoa said, stopping mid way through a note.

"It'll be fine. Do you have an idea?"

"'Water vegetables' is pretty vague for an ingredient, but that gives us some flexibility."

Flipping through the stack of recipes Quina had given them, Sil pulled out a card and slid it over to Hoa.

"Um, how about lotus flower?" Sil asked.

She nodded. "Good, and kelp or seaweed can help punch up the salt."

"Adding any seafood might take away from the challenge."

"Agreed. We'll stick with the plants and make it vegetarian to really drive it home. Have anything out of left field that might be interesting?"

Sil was a little taken aback that Hoa was asking for his input, he banished every poisonous thought. It was a little strange, and niche, but Sil replied, "I mean, tuft tail seed pods are edible. They're a little fibrous, but they're nutty. And they can go sweet or savory."

"We can walk the line and roast them with a little honey or maple syrup."

"The honey would be better; the maple syrup would

hide too much of the flavor."

Hoa jotted down a list of dishes and began breaking down each into various steps. "You'll do the tuft tails, then. And we'll need all our liquids as early as possible 'cause we're going soup for the lotus and konbu."

"Does honey count as a liquid?" Sil asked.

"I actually don't know," Hoa replied and flagged down Robin. "Clarification: does honey count as liquid?"

"I'll have to check," Robin said. "Go ahead like it is for now to be safe."

Hoa frowned. "Not the answer I wanted, but okay."

Sil began making their list of items that probably weren't already in the pantry so the production team could acquire them. In addition to the tuft tails, he added water plantain and a handful of flavorings Hoa listed off to him. Blip was getting restless under his collar and popped her head out.

Spotting the little pipe dragon, Hoa quickly put her hand on Sil's shoulder to hide Blip from the wandering assistants and producers. "*You have a freaking snake with you?*" she hissed.

Adjusting his shirt and carefully pushing Blip back into hiding, he whispered, "She's a pipe dragon…"

"That is somehow worse. Is she a familiar?"

"Technically, no…"

"Technically? Sil, this could get you disqualified."

One of the assistants stopped next to their worktable and held their hand out for their ingredients list with a bored expression. "List?"

"Oh, it's right here," Sil said quickly.

"What are 'tuft tails'?" the assistant asked.

"They're like cat tails. Kinda…Anders can get them."

The assistant raised an eyebrow before wandering off.

"You're certain he can get some?" Hoa asked.

"Yeah, the seed pods on the ones at the cottage are just about perfect."

"Nice to have a wizard with a garden, I guess."

"It is nice. You and the others should come visit once the show is done. And we have plenty of extra produce. I think Anders is dying to get rid of the lettuce so I stop making salad for every meal."

Hoa snorted. "I appreciate it. And maybe in exchange, I'll teach you some non-salad lettuce recipes."

"Please do!"

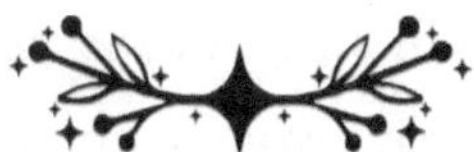

"We are halfway through our cooking time here in the cauldron!" Corina gleefully explained to an army of cameras. "So we're going to check in on them and see how they're getting on. Team Purple, what are you concocting for us today?"

"We have an urchin soup going and a couple surprises we think the judges will enjoy," Faro replied.

Sil glanced over at the other team momentarily and met Taimi's gaze. His former friend narrowed his eyes and spoke up, "Yes, Mr. Cershaw especially, I think."

"Interesting!" Corina cooed. "How are you getting on with the magic card today, Latif?"

"Water has never been my forte, but the rest of the team is helping out, so I think we'll be back on top this week."

Sidling over to their workspace, Corina made a show of taking a big sniff of their soup. "I see we have soup over on the Green Team's side as well. We're having a really treacherous battle here under the sea."

"Hopefully a delicious one," Hoa countered.

"I'm sure the judges agree after last week. Any bugs this week?"

"No, we're cooking a lotus, water plantain, and wild rice soup topped with roasted tuft tail seed pods."

"Oh, really going for theme this week, aren't we?"

"There's only two of us left," Hoa replied. "So we have to hedge our bets in that regard."

"Very true. Now, Sil, how is all this magic treating you? I hear you've only been practicing for a few months?"

"It's a bit of a challenge, but I've been managing alright."

"Fantastic! I'll leave you to it, then!" Corina told the cameras, nearly deflating once the lenses turned on the judges.

"Good luck, you two."

"Thanks," Sil said.

"It smells heavenly."

"You're sounding a little biased there, Corina," Hoa said, offering her a spoon to taste.

"I'm allowed to be; I'm just the host." She gratefully took the spoon and melted as the soup hit her pallet. "Oh, that is good. So good."

One of the camerapersons caught Corina's attention, and she mouthed *"thank you"* as she set the spoon back down.

The average judging time had run anywhere from two to four hours thus far. But when the judges came back a mere hour into their allotted time, Sil felt his heart sink. Surely, they'd found something wrong with the dish, or Cershaw was ready to finally kick him off. He was certain they had met all the challenge requirements, at least.

"That was one of the fastest judging sessions we've had in the show's history. Care to shed some light on why that might be?" Corina asked the judges.

"We all agreed," Chef Tran said simply. "Tonight's winner is Sil for helping create such a diverse and subtle dish. But we do want to give credit to his teammate for helping to focus in on the heart of the challenge."

Sil was certain he'd misheard. Or there was a mistake.

Hoa wrapped a triumphant arm around him. "Great job. Khulan was right that you just needed to hit your stride."

"I won a challenge?"

"And you get immunity next episode. The last immunity of the series, actually."

"But that means…"

"And who will not be going into the semi-finals?" Corina continued.

"Unfortunately, today we need to eliminate Latif. While she did contribute with her magic, that was all she did today," Rickland said.

"Magic sadly isn't everything," Cershaw added.

"And there you have it! From Team Purple, we have Faro and Taimi going to the semi-finals next week. And from our underdogs, the Green Team, Hoa and Sil!"

Taimi met Sil's gaze again from across the room and then wandered off the set towards one of the producers. Sil was too elated to let it bother him, though.

Sil had been holed up in the kitchen all weekend while the show was on a break from filming. He wasn't allowed to say what the challenge was, but given the amount of flour covering everything and the double boiler melting heaps of chocolate, it was dessert. Anders had tried to give him space, but he was worried that Sil hadn't slept or eaten.

"Want to take a break?" Anders offered.

Groaning, Sil shook his head. "Not really. But yes."

"A break would be good. I think the kitchen needs one, too."

"I'll clean it up…"

Anders wrapped his arms around Sil from behind, looping his hands together at Sil's waist. "I wasn't trying to make you feel guilty. Let's go for a walk."

"Out in the garden?" he asked as he leaned his head back against Anders' shoulder.

"To the village," Anders said.

Sil tried to grab the recipe cards he'd been fussing over, but Anders hugged him tighter.

"I have to figure this out, Anders!"

"Sil, it's a chocolate cake. It's delicious, but you've made five, and we're running out of people to gift them to."

Why did the stress start to melt away the longer Anders held him? It made him want to stay intertwined with the silly

wizard forever.

"You're right." Sil admitted. "I'm just stuck on the damn magic card bit."

"I know you can't tell me…but you'll figure it out. Besides, their best magic person was sent home. So you're not going against a nearly graduated witch."

"I have immunity, and that makes me feel guilty. Cause I feel like I kinda get a free pass on this one now that I'm really stuck."

"Don't think of it as a free pass, then," Anders said. "Think of it as a way to experiment."

"Maybe," Sil replied and untangled himself from Ander's grasp.

"Come on, the fresh air will help you get out of your head."

The breeze had cleared away the afternoon heat, so it was actually a pleasant walk into the village. They passed a couple of people, and Anders was happy that Sil didn't try to hide their clasped hands.

"I wonder if any of this stuff for the show would count for any of the apprentice requirements?" Sil asked as they walked past the bookshop.

Anders tapped his chin thoughtfully. "It might. I can write and ask. Though it may have to wait till the air date since we signed all that legal paperwork."

"That's fine."

"Oh, I do think we should register Blip as your familiar soon, though. Just so she's all official."

"I didn't know you had to register familiars," Sil said,

leaning closer to Anders. Even just a walk around the village made him feel warm and fuzzy when Anders was around.

"It's just another hassle with the paperwork, honestly. There's few requirements for them. I think it's more for demographic data purposes."

"I would hope so."

"I wouldn't fret about it. And Auda can help with any questions we have."

Wendy waved at Anders as she was bringing in her café sidewalk sign for the evening. "Nice to see you around so late."

"We needed the air," Anders replied.

"Well, everyone is excited to see you on *Cauldrons & Cookery*, Sil. It's exciting to have someone from the village on a big show like that! Maybe we can trade some recipes sometime? I'll throw in some free coffees for your trouble."

"I can't talk about it until it comes out, if you're fishing for gossip."

"I don't even get to know, and he lives with me!" Anders said with a chuckle.

"Oh, always, but I understand. Take care you two!" If she noted their intertwined hands, she didn't mention it, shooing Brandr back inside. The fox chittered happily as he rushed past her feet.

They made it to the plant shop and stood under the sign in the growing dark and quiet.

"I've got the key with me," Sil said.

"Oh? And what might you have planned?" Anders asked in a joking tone.

"Resigning…"

"What? But you love that job!"

"I do, but that's why I think its best if I leave it for someone else."

"Does Beren have any idea?"

"I think she knows. I've been here less and less. Especially with the filming. And if I'm going to be serious about my apprenticeship, I have to take something off my plate," Sil replied, unlocking the door to the garden shop.

The lights flicked on as they entered, and Sil made his way back to the office. Anders stood amongst the tables of plant pots, resisting the urge to wake up the snap dragons. When Sil had first started working for Beren, he'd been so quiet, Anders hadn't been able to get more than three words out of him at a time. He was glad he'd kept trying. And grateful that Beren had finally intervened.

A crackling sound got Anders' attention, and he looked up to see the words "I love you" written out in bluish flame above the potting benches. Sil was peering at it, like it was some experiment but seemed pleased with it all the same.

"When did you have time to learn all this?" Anders asked in amazement. It wasn't lost on him that Sil had been improving exponentially due to the show and being pushed to his creative limits.

"Oh, you know, sleep is overrated," Sil said with a shrug.

"Is this why it's smelt like something was burning in the mornings?"

"I fireproofed everything. Well, Auda did, actually."

Anders scooped Sil up in his arms and spun him around. "I love it. Thank you."

"You made a silly gesture, so I had to try it, too."

Pressing their noses together, Anders grinned. "I don't care if you win or not, you know that, right?"

"I do...but I'd kinda like to at this point."

"Because of Cershaw?" Anders asked.

Shaking his head, Sil said, "No, because of Taimi."

"I thought that name sounded familiar..."

Leaning back against one of the planting benches, Sil explained, "He was my first crush...and he never really felt that back, so I let us drift apart."

"Sorry..." Anders offered Sil a smile.

"It's nothing to do with you."

"I know, but I know how hard it can be to walk away from someone like that."

"After this stupid show, I don't plan on ever talking to him again," Sil said.

"Good." He placed a hand over Sil's, just to reassure him that he meant it.

"What about you and Cershaw?"

Biting his lip guiltily, Anders said, "Well...about that, actually..."

"What?"

Anders rubbed the back of his neck and laughed as he replied, "I might have threatened to outsell him with my next book..."

"Don't you essentially write textbooks?"

"I may need some help?"

"You're going to need a *lot* of help," Sil said.

"Luckily I have you," Anders told him with a grin. "The

target audience for gardening books!"

"I'm just one person…"

"One brilliant, amazing person! And right now, all mine." Anders scooped Sil into his arms again.

"We still have to walk home," Sil said.

"Or you could portal us. You've been getting better at those, by the way."

"Walking is good for us."

"But portalling means we get to cuddle up in bed sooner," Anders countered.

Sil groaned but leaned in to kiss Anders. "You're a ridiculous wizard, you know that?"

"Oh, I do. Now lock up so we can cuddle!"

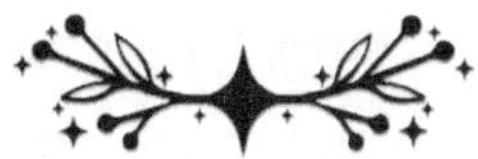

Taimi approached the Green Team's work bench and leaned over it, palms planted on the edge of the butcher block. Hoa didn't bother looking up from the collection of recipes and handwritten instructions. Matching Hoa's energy, Sil kept his head down as well, re-reading the same line of ingredients over and over as he hoped Taimi would just leave.

"So…" Taimi said, expecting their attention.

Finally, Sil looked up, "Can we help you?"

"I just wanted to wish you both good luck. Though I guess since Sil has *immunity*, it would take him completely ignoring the challenge parameters to be sent home. Or something else."

"Why would I just ignore the challenge now?" Sil asked dryly. "Maybe you should be more concerned about your own

cooking today?"

"The producers already know who they want to win. And it isn't *you*, Sil," Taimi replied sharply. "Why would the nobody with no formal higher education or prospects even be on their radar?"

Tapping his pencil against his chin, Sil shrugged. "Why are you so worried, then? If they don't want me to win, then I won't. I'm here, I'm doing my best, and I'm trying to actually enjoy it. Why are you here?"

"Why am I here? To win, obviously!"

"So, you think the producers have chosen you to win? Why?"

"Because I'm the most well-rounded of the contestants."

Setting down her notes, Hoa glared up at Taimi. "You're not. Khulan probably was the most well-rounded. And he had the most experience competing on these types of shows. Producers are always trying to eke out the best narrative to keep people engaged. Audiences like underdogs. Your team was stacked with the more polished contestants. So, like Sil said, maybe you should be more concerned about your cooking today than what you think the producers have decided. Especially since you won't have your teammate to lean on."

Taimi was visibly flustered, but he lunged towards Sil and whispered, "Someone who just started learning magic yesterday is never going to beat me."

He stomped off back to his own worktable, leaving Sil and Hoa to share bemused glances.

"He's a piece of work."

Sil nodded and said, "I somehow had a crush on him in

high school…"

"Teenagers are dumb. You've been holding your own just fine. University degrees and prestigious internships don't mean much if you don't like what you're doing."

"Aren't you in a prestigious internship?"

"Yes, and I'm privileged enough to take it. And to take time off to be on this show. It helps that my boss is an uncle, and I live with my grandma, so no rent."

"Fair enough."

Holding out her hand, Hoa offered Sil a smile. "No matter what happens today or going into the final, it's been nice cooking with you."

"It has."

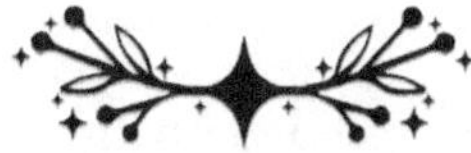

There was very little magic being cast on set. Everyone seemed far more concerned with their desserts and the magic card, a surprise presentation of some kind. Sil expected that would be where the magic truly shined. Which made him wonder if his presentation was going to be too simple.

His cakes were already in the oven, so he could focus on the surprise portion. He started crushing ginger snaps and mixing in melted butter and brown sugar and forming the mixture inside little terracotta pots he'd brought to form a crust. Resisting the urge to watch the cakes bake from the floor in front of the ovens, Sil tried to spend the waiting time prepping the rest of his decorations.

The chocolate cake was eventually layered into the bottom of the ginger snap pots, chocolate ganache spread in between. The molten centers would hopefully flow out properly when the cakes were cut. But Sil could worry about that bit of magic later. Green colored sugar was heated and molded into stems and leaves—or, at least, Sil's best attempt at stems and leaves—and stuck into the pots to make them look like real plant pots. He couldn't imagine anyone buying them out of a shop windows, but he knew it all tasted delicious, at least.

When the timer rang and their dishes were ferried off to the judges, Sil wiped his hands off on his apron. Just one more marathon day of filming, and it would be all over. Minus some extra filming for those silly "confessional interview" portions they always inserted into these shows to ramp up the drama. He'd be able to really dig into magic and his future plans for the cottage garden.

He supposed he needed to figure out what his focus would be as a wixen. Plants were obviously going to be a part of it. But he really did enjoy cooking, too. Combining the two was clearly fairly simple. After all, he was on an entire TV show based on mixing plants as food and magic. There were so many possibilities.

As he was wiping down his station, Mr. Vox and Robin walked up with stern expressions.

"Is everything alright?" Sil asked.

Mr. Vox cleared his throat. "There's been an allegation, and we need to investigate it."

Hoa crossed her arms. "An allegation of what?"

"Cheating," Robin said. "Sil, do you have any kind of animal with you?"

Sil's hand automatically went to his shoulder where Blip

was snoozing under his collar. "I…"

"Familiars are strictly forbidden in the competition for designated team wixen. I know that you had to rush through all the paperwork, but I'm fairly sure we made that clear," Robin continued, shuffling through papers on her clipboard.

"No, you did," Sil admitted.

"She's not his familiar," Hoa said.

"Sorry?" Mr. Vox asked. "How's that?"

"A familiar has to be properly registered."

Robin and Mr. Vox shared a look.

"So, she wouldn't be considered a familiar. Technically…" Hoa added.

"Hoa, it's okay."

"No," Hoa hissed. "It was that snake, Taimi, I know it. He's terrified he's going to lose."

"We can't verify who the accusation came from," Mr. Vox said.

"Hoa is actually correct," Chef Tran said, cutting into the conversation. "If an animal isn't registered as a familiar, it's not recognized as needing to be compliant with rules or regulations related to familiars. Can we see the animal in question?"

Sil gently nudged Blip awake, and she poked her head out from under his collar. "She's a pipe dragon. She lives in the garden at the cottage."

The disruption had drawn the other judges and Corina over as well. "Oh, she's the most precious little garden noodle, isn't she?" Corina gushed.

Mr. Vox sighed. "All the same, production is very clear—"

Rickland was looking over Robin's shoulder at the contracts. "About familiars, not animals in general. Magical or otherwise. Not all dragons have the ability to cast spells innately. And Mr. Fennen is so new to all this, I doubt the little thing really did anything."

"What are your thoughts, Cershaw?" Robin asked him.

"I think there should be some consequence."

Sil hadn't really expected anything else from Cershaw of all people.

"Then we strip him of immunity," Chef Tran said. "It wouldn't be too hard to clip the mentions out. Right?"

"Well, I mean…I suppose not," Mr. Vox replied.

"It is strange that someone has immunity going into the semifinal," Rickland said, nodding. "I think it's fair."

"If our judges feel that's fair…" Corina said with a smile at Robin and Mr. Vox. "Maybe we can continue. We've still got a long day to get through."

"Agreed," Chef Tran said.

"We should really run this by legal…" Robin said.

"Mr. Vox can handle that and explain why it would be good for business to just keep things moving," Rickland said. "Right, Cershaw?"

"Sure," Cershaw said in defeat, clearly outnumbered by the other judges.

"Great!" Corina said, clapping her hands together.

"What do you think about me writing something with a little more market appeal?" Anders asked Torlind.

She popped her head up from Anders' desk. "Why? And what?"

"I just think maybe I should feature the garden in my writing more. And gardening is really where Sil shines. With plant care and all that."

"Soooooo, you want to write a book with your assistant, now?"

"Well, he's more than an assistant."

Torlind sighed. "Apprentice, whatever!"

"More like boyfriend?"

Crossing her arms, Torlind frowned at him. "You want to write a gardening book with your assistant/apprentice/ boyfriend? For the general market? Are you trying to kill me?"

Anders picked up the mushroomy remains of one of Cershaw's books. "If he can be a best-seller with this nonsense, then between Sil and me, I think we can come up with something people will really connect to!"

"I don't want to know why that book looks like it was eaten by mushrooms, do I?"

"Probably not."

Downing the rest of her tea, Torlind got up and started pacing. "It's a completely different style of writing you know."

"I know."

"And it's a hard market to break into. People always want something 'new,' but so much has already been done."

"Yes, but I want to try."

"Write me a proposal, and I'll pitch it to some friends and see what they think."

Anders smirked. "Deal."

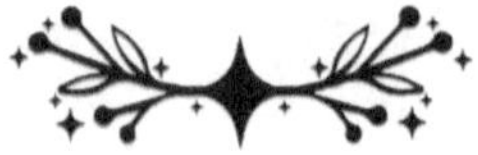

"The judges would love to hear from everyone about their desserts today." Corina's voice broke into Sil's wandering thoughts. "We'll start with Faro from the Purple Team."

"I created a flavored snowflake which doesn't melt," Faro explained as the judges examined his dish. Additional sugary crystals seemed to fall from the air above the snowflake, dusting the plate with a kind of edible glitter.

"Taimi, could you explain your dish?"

"I baked a chocolate cake," Taimi replied proudly.

Corina smiled and asked, "It's a chocolate cake? It looks almost exactly like a log."

Grinning wider, Taimi waved his hand over his log, and little mushrooms and moss began sprouting out of it. Sil noticed Cershaw's sour look at the reveal, but Sil was more annoyed that Taimi had created something so similar to his own dish. It could have been a coincidence, but Sil highly doubted his former friend didn't remember his favorite dessert.

"Hoa, you're next."

Hoa stepped forward, lifting the cloche off of her creation. Delicately baked golden brown petals unfolded, forming a lotus. She carefully pulled off a petal revealing a greenish cake on the inside. "Its a honeycomb cake flavored with pandan."

"I think that's one of the most beautiful desserts we've had on the show!" Corina exclaimed. "And finally, last week's winner, Sil. What do you have for us today?"

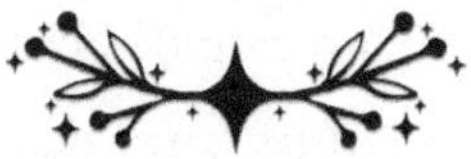

Laughter peeled from the garden as Anders brought out another tray of drinks from the kitchen. Lights had been strung across the flagstone patio they'd somehow made room for, and at one end, a large screen had been set up between a couple trees.

"Poor Faro's face when he lost out on going to the final," Khulan was saying as the judging for the penultimate episode played out on the screen.

"His dessert was the weakest," Hoa stated matter of factly.

"I'll drink to that!" Quina added, clinking her wine glass against Magda and Greta's.

"You're just saying that because your honeycomb cake won," Khulan said.

"Well, the mushroom's on Taimi's really didn't help," Greta added in mysteriously.

Khulan shook Sil's shoulders. "Way to go on staying in the game, though! All that bluster over little Blip was a big nothing."

"But you killed the stupid semi-finals immunity!" Quina cheered. "Hopefully they'll keep that for the veterans' season."

"Veterans' season?" Khulan asked.

"Oh, did you not get called for that?" Quina teased.

"Okay, bets on who won the final though," Magda said above the clamor. "Between Hoa, Taimi, and Sil?"

Sil caught Anders' eye and couldn't help but blush a little.

"And Hoa and Sil, no hints!" Greta called.

"There shall be no hints from me," Hoa declared.

"Or me," Sil promised.

"Good! Now, write down your bets, and they go into the jar before we start the last episode. And no magic, that's cheating." Magda was very at home giving the party orders and keeping the games on track.

Beren nudged Anders' arm gently. "Thank you again for hosting all of us. I know this is a lot more noise than either of you prefer."

"Actually, it's been nice having people over more," Anders admitted. "Sil agrees, even if he'll want to swear off company forever after tonight. How are things at the shop?"

"We've all been missing Sil, but Magda is really blossoming, and our newest hire is learning the ropes."

"I'm glad Magda was able to step up."

Beren nodded as she helped clear some of the plates and said, "She wanted the hours and the responsibility. I know I'll probably lose her in another year or two when she's finishing up her studies, but such is life. You youngsters are always flitting about, chasing your dreams here and there."

"Well, I'm not going anywhere," Anders assured her, tapping the lid of a pitcher so it would refill itself with raspberry lemonade.

"You never know. I think Sil has big ideas for that book of yours."

Anders chuckled. "Oh, I'm aware. But travel is just temporary."

"There's a lot of world out there to explore. And a lot of

magic to learn," Beren said, a knowing glint in her eye.

He knew they wouldn't stay rooted to the spot, but Anders liked to think that even if they did go off for some adventures, the garden would always be their little oasis. "Maybe, but this is home."

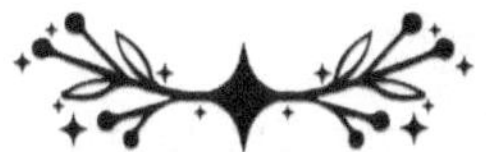

"A cottage meal! It's like they made this last challenge just for you, Sil!" Greta said, giggling. The wine had definitely gotten to her after a few glasses.

"That's all producer stuff. We didn't get the last challenge until the day of filming," Sil replied.

Khulan nodded. "I like it better when they give them out ahead of time. But alas, producers think they know best."

Sil leaned back against Anders', watching his own face up on the screen. It was surreal to see, especially now that, after the fact, he would have done so many things differently. Why had he wasted precious time watching his vegetables simmer when he could have been prepping other things? He also could have tried whole spices, but it wasn't what he was used to, so he didn't want to risk it. But risk was part of the game.

It was nearly dark out as the final episode wound down, and the fireflies had started to come out, and the frogs and crickets were singing around the pond. Surrounded by friends in the garden, he felt at home.

"*Why curry?*" Corina was asking him in the episode.

"*I know it's not what a lot of people would think of, but it's one of my favorite meals, and it feels cozy. That's what I think the*

heart of a 'cottage meal' is. Something you eat to feel warm and safe."

"I hope the judges agree," Corina said, "because it smells amazing."

"Isn't that what you made for Anders?" Magda asked.

"Yeah…it felt right."

Greta was curled up next to Magda, nursing the cup of water she'd been given. "You need to make it for all of us."

"We could have a stew-off," Khulan suggested.

"Not everything needs to be a competition, you goof!" Quina said.

"But it'll be stew and soup season before we know it! And I spotted some squash in the vegetable beds that are dying to go in a stew. It could be called the 'Chaos Coven Stew Competition'!"

"Someone else gets to plan it," Sil said. "I have to focus on getting some of my apprenticeship stuff done."

Greta raised Magda's hand for her. "We volunteer as tribute!"

"Shush, it's almost the end!" Magda said.

Cershaw's face appeared on the screen as he tasted Sil's curry. He was clearly fighting to keep his expression neutral. *"It's not fully to my taste. A bit too spicy."*

"Booooooo!" several of their friends hissed at the screen.

"I disagree. I think the spice is well balanced," Chef Tran said.

"It's just the right amount of kick, and you can still taste all the flavors," Rickland agreed.

"I think I might have to go back for more of the potatoes,"

Corina said. *"But we'll let the judges go and deliberate."*

The show cut to the judges around a little table with all three dishes in front of them. Taimi's shepherd's pie and Hoa's beef stew were far more classic "cottage meals."

"All three of our contestants gave us an amazing meal today," Rickland said. *"I like Taimi's traditional take on the shepherd's pie. But it was a little dry."*

Chef Tran nodded. *"I wish Hoa had given us more complexity like she did last week. Her stew was good, but for a finale dish, it was a little boring. Especially for someone wanting to go into the restaurant business."*

"But shouldn't a cottage meal be simple?" Cershaw argued.

"It should be hearty. Something you want to come home to after a long day," Rickland said.

"So do you have a winner in mind?" Corina asked the judges.

"We do," Chef Tran replied.

"Every contestant cooked their hearts out this season," Corina continued back in the competition kitchen. *"But we can only have one winner. Judges, who do you think made the best cottage meal?"*

"The three dishes were all well thought out. And we all liked parts of all of them," Rickland said.

"We're excited to award the golden cauldron for the season to Sil for making one of the…"

The rest of the dialog was drowned out by cheering and screaming from the party. Greta shot off a flurry of green sparks, and Anders hugged him tighter, planting a kiss on the back of his neck. Sil was fairly certain the party would be going on into the wee hours of the night at this rate. Luckily, they'd forewarned the gnomes and Cerbs, so the wildlife wouldn't be too disturbed.

As the cheers finally started to wane, and everyone had taken turns hugging Sil, Palla reappeared from wading along the pond, checking in on all the new fauna that had moved in.

"So, who was the winner, then?"

Magda shook her head and pulled a few strings of water cress from his beard. "Sil obviously. That's why we were cheering."

"Ah. I still have the hedge mice to check in on. Congratulations, Sil."

"Thank you, Palla. I'm sure the mice will enjoy the visit."

"What are you two planning next?" Greta asked Sil.

"A trip to a bad theme park?" Khulan joked.

Anders slipped his arms around Sil's waist and planted a kiss on his neck. The wizard replied, "Definitely not."

Holding up a glass as if to toast them, Auda said, "Well, Sil needs to finish off his training."

"There's that," Sil admitted. "And Anders' next book."

"*Our* book," Anders countered, nuzzling Sil's neck.

"Oh, the two of you are disgusting!" Magda called from down the table. But Sil saw her wrap an arm around Greta and pull her close.

"I guess you'll all just have to wait and see," Sil said.

Field Notes
8

**Confessional Interview Excerpts:
Cauldron Cookery**

Series 7; Episode 1

PRODUCER

So you're brand new to magic and
cooking?

SIL

Well, I'm new to magic. But I've
been cooking most of my life.

PRODUCER

Why did you start cooking?

SIL

I started cause I was kind of a
picky eater. So I taught myself to
make the things that I liked to eat.
And I try new recipes now all the
time.

PRODUCER

How are you blending the theme with

the required ingredient today?

                    QUINA
We're making a curry leaf chuntey,
which is all about blending flavors.

                    KHULAN
It's also delicious.

Series 7; Episode 2

                    PRODUCER
How do you feel about
today?

                    TAIMI
I'm grateful that th
what the Purple Team put together.

                    PRODUCER
They were especially impressed by
your smoked violet ice cream. How
did you come up with that?

                    TAIMI
Oh, I love making strange things
into ice cream. You get a lot of
unexpected flavors that way.

                    PRODUCER
Faro, which recipes of yours were
used today?

                    FARO
We relied on Taimi's flavors this
time.

                    PRODUCER
Isn't that a risk for you?

These questions are so boring. Couldn't they have asked some more interesting questions about the food, or magic or something?

Do we get to approve what they put in the actual show?

That would be a lawyer question. I'll ask Torlind then.

FARO
paid off in this case.

PRODUCER
ou ever made ice cream ore?

ERROL
We've done floral ice creams, yes.
Similar to tea based ice creams you
steep the flowers in the mixture to
draw out the flavor.

Series 7; Episode 3

PRODUCER
Your dish today includes burrowing
crickets and hornworms, why those?

HOA
Crickets and hornworms are both
considered pests in many places.
They attack various plants. So
turning them into a dish fit for a
competition seemed like a great
challenge. Besides, insects are
consumed in many cultures. They're
great sources of protein and can be
foraged.

PRODUCER
Hornworms are what eat you
tomatoes, right?

SIL
Yes. I didn't know until H
suggested it, that you can
once they've been cooked.

We should ship off all our hornworms to cooking shows in the future!

I dobut they will want them.

PRODUCER
Fascinating.

Series 7; Episode 4

PRODUCER
Urchin soup? Will the urchins
overpower today's required
ingredient?

TAIMI
Urchin is subtle enough, we think it
will be fine.

PRODUCER
We heard that you were friends with
another of the contestants?

TAIMI
Oh, you mean Sil? We went to school
together. We haven't seen each other
for some time.

PRODUCER
Must be nice to see an old friend
then.

TAIMI
It will be even better to beat him.

Series 7; Episode 5

PRODUCER
You have a familiar.

SIL
She's not registered as one.

Sowing Spells

PRODUCER
Well, she is cute. What type of
dragon is she?

SIL
A garden pipe dragon. Though
technically she's a type of wyrm.

PRODUCER
Did you feel the judge's descision
was fair, Hoa?

HOA
The whole thing was laughable
really. Most magic users don't
become proficient with using a
familiar until their third or fourth
year of study. Sil's been learning
for all of a couple months.

PRODUCER
It seems to have worked out in the
end. Both of you are proceeding to
the final.

HOA
It did. Luckily. I'm excited to know
what else Sil has up his sleeves.

SIL
I'm sure I don't stand a chance.

HOA
Are we done now? I've got other
things to do.

PRODUCER
Yes we're done for now.

<u>HOA</u>

Great. Coffee Sil?

<u>SIL</u>

Oh, sure. Thanks.

Envelopes
&
Epilogues

The new loft got much more light than Anders' little office. It helped that the hedges around the cottage had been trimmed in preparation for fall. Blip was enjoying the extra wide windowsills, both for basking in the sun and for her growing hoard of seeds. Sil had started labeling the jars with the dates they'd been filled. Hopefully, she'd let them use some of the seeds come spring.

His desk looked out over the back garden, and he sometimes felt like he was up in a tree house. Part of him had fantasized about planting a tree below the window so he could eventually crawl out on its branches. It was a little childish, but he couldn't wait for spring.

Anders clomped up the stairs, paging through a stack of envelopes. "I guess I should have checked the mail before that trip down south."

Sil held out his hand for his portion. "Probably. But if there was anything important, I'm sure someone would have called. Besides, mushroom season won't wait."

"You really need to make those roasted mushrooms again."

"We've had them three times already this week!"

"So?"

The wizard paused and pulled out one of the envelopes, giving Sil a serious look. "Now, don't worry if they say no. We still have plenty of time…"

Snatching the envelope, Sil scanned the gold print on the front listing the Wixen Council as the return address. "It would be thinner if it was a no, though, wouldn't it?"

"Maybe?"

He held it back out to Anders. "You open it."

Anders set down the rest of the mail and took the letter back. He tore it open, moving his eyes back and forth across the page but not saying anything.

"Well?" Sil asked, leaning forward to try to read the letter upside down.

"*The Wixen Council officially awards Erasil Fennen, here on known as Sil Fennen, credit earned towards his first year of apprenticeship to the Wizard Anders Kessel,*" Anders read out.

Sil jumped up and wrapped his arms around Anders' neck. "They did it!"

"You did it," Anders countered. "Now, how does it feel to be a wizard's apprentice?"

"Good." Sil pressed their noses together.

Anders mock gasped. "Good? Who are you, and what

have you done with my grumpy Sil?"

Sil kissed him. "A silly wizard befriended him."

The End

Glossary

pst! Spoilers ahead!

TERMINOLOGY

"**madcaps**" – recklessness; used as an expletive

"**scales**" – used as an expletive

Familiar – creature with an affinity for a particular wixen

Micro-climate Spell– a spell created by Anders to control the weather of a specific spot

Portalling – way of travelling via opening a magical portal from one location to another. Can also be used for communication.

Translocation Spell – a spell to transport a person or object from one place to another instantaneously.

Wixen – gender neutral term or title for witch, wizard or collective

LOCATIONS

Anders' Cottage – Originally a one bedroom, one story cottage tucked in the fields of Urshire county. Another room, for Sil, and a second story study are added on.

Bookshop – Another shop in the village

Café – Owned and operated by Wendy

Picti Spellwork University – University that Magda, Greta, and for a short time, Sil attend. Mascot is a pixie

Plant Shop – Owned by Beren

The Albion Railway – Railroad system in Urshire

The Royal Gardens – Collection of world class gardens open to the public for tours. Anders used to run experiments there as a student.

The Village – village located in Urshire county. Close to Anders' cottage

Urshire County – the county where Sil & Anders live

CHARACTERS

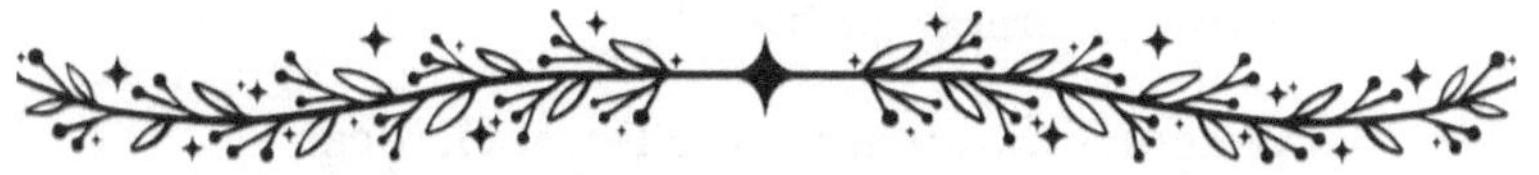

Sil (Erasil) Fennen – Plant lover, plant shop manager, assistant and later apprentice to Anders

Anders Kessel, Wixen – Eccentric wizard who specializes in magical plants

Auda Kessel, Wixen – Anders' twin sister

Beren Ayton, Wixen – Owner of the plant shop

Ceri Kessel, Wixen - Anders and Auda's father

Chef Nulus Tran – Judge on Cauldrons & Cookery

Sowing Spells

Corina Broom – Host of Cauldrons & Cookery

Donna – Makeup artist on Cauldrons & Cookery

Errol – Contestant on Cauldrons & Cookery

Faro – Contestant on Cauldrons & Cookery

Greta – Friend of Sil's from the university and Cershaw's niece; becomes Magda's girlfriend

Hoa – Contestant on Cauldrons & Cookery

Jay – Director for Cauldrons & Cookery

Khulan – Contestant on Cauldrons & Cookery

Latif – Contestant on Cauldrons & Cookery

Lynna Fennen – Sil's mother

M. (Marion/Michal) H. Cershaw – Best Selling garden book author; Anders' ex and rival

Magda – Sil's co-worker at the plant shop and university student; becomes Greta's girlfriend

Mr. MacGregor – Gardener at the Royal Gardens

Mr. Vox – Producer for Cauldrons & Cookery

Odell Kessel, Wixen – Anders and Auda's mother

Palla – One of Magda's classmates with a specialty in magical animals

Professor Hildegaard – Teacher of Elemental Theories in Magic

Quina – Contestant on Cauldrons & Cookery

Rickland Pauls – Judge on Cauldrons & Cookery

Robin – An assistant on Cauldrons & Cookery

Taimi – Contestant on Cauldrons & Cookery; Sil's former best friend and crush

Torlind – Anders' editor

Veles – Leader of the gnomes

Wendy – Café owner in the village

Wilton Fennen – Sil's father

Wixen Cooke – Teacher of Enchanted Foodstuffs 101

Yolanda – Worker at the Royal Gardens and Auda's friend

ANIMAL CHARACTERS

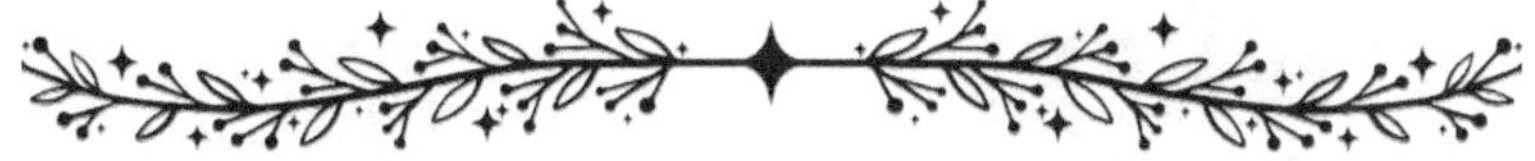

Blip – Garden pipe dragon and Sil's familiar

Brandr – Wendy's firefox/tulikettu

Cerberus (Cerbs) – Three headed goose that belongs to one of Sil & Anders' neighbors; Uses they/them pronouns

Crusher – Auda's bull dragon familiar

Marvin – Magda's tabby cat familiar

Sil Fennen

plant lover & ~~assistant~~ apprentice

Taimi
Sil's former classmate &
Cauldron Cookery
contestant

Green Team
Hoa - Cooking
Khulan - Cooking
Quina - Recipes
Sil - Magic

Purple Team
Faro - Recipes
Errol - Cooking
Latif - Magic
Taimi - Magic

Wilton Fennen
(Dad)

Lynna Fennen
(Mom)

Blip

pipe dragon &
Sil's familiar

Beren
Plant shop owner
& Sil's boss

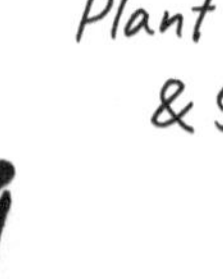

Magda 
Sil's Co-worker
& Uni student

Odell Kessel
(Mom)

Ceri Kessel
(Dad)

Anders Kessel

wixen & lover of tea

– ♥ – ♥ – ♥ – ♥ – ♥ – ♥ – ♥ –

Auda Kessel
(Sister)

Crusher
Auda's familiar

Torlind
Anders' editor

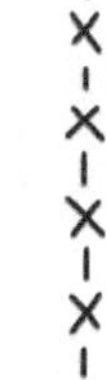

Cerbs
three-headed goose that lives
near the cottage

M.H. Cershaw

– ♥ – ♥ – ♥ – ♥ – ♥ –

Greta
Uni student
& Cershaw's niece

(Marion)
Anders' Ex & author

*Sil, Anders and the rest of
the Chaos Coven will
return in*

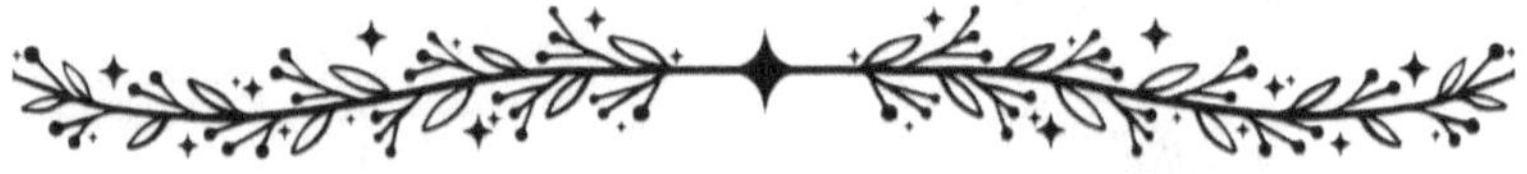

CULTIVATING CURSES

ABOUT THE AUTHOR

Cay Fletcher is a Queer author with a passion for fantasy and science fiction. Crafting rich landscapes and memorable characters in new and exciting worlds.

Living in the Portland metro area, Cay spends their free time in the garden, cooking, or making a mess, aka crafting. She spent over fifteen years volunteering at fan conventions across the US and still occasionally assists at events in the PNW. As a writer, Cay strives to create relatable queer characters, giving them the titles of hero and protagonist.

They also love to use their crafting and graphic design skills to make products such as patchwork book sleeves, TTRPG journals, stickers, bookmarks, and more. She lives with her wife Sam, their two roommates, and pets: cats Daphne and Tir, and keeshond, Lakota.

Cay uses She/They pronouns.

You can connect with Cay on social media or Goodreads.

www.cayfletcher.com

@cayfletcher

NEWSLETTER

Want to be the first to get the news?

Stay up to date with new releases by

subscribing to my newsletter.

www.cayfletcher.com/newsletter

ACKNOWLEDGEMENTS

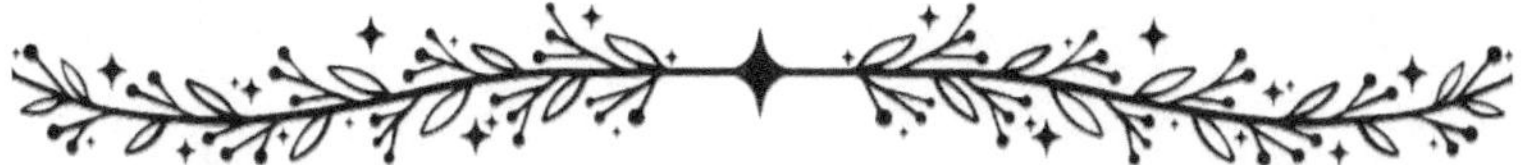

Huge thank you as always to my wife for reading, re-reading, suggesting edits, and complaining about the slow-burn romance between Sil and Anders. I shall never stop writing slow-burn.

Special thanks to all my readers who write, message, or come see me at events. I love hearing about your favorite moments, or who you've lent my books out to. I'm so lucky to have such a wonderful community supporting me and my work.

Thank you to Naomi for helping to proof the Field Notes. And to Gabe for editing for me.

And as always, thank you to the indie bookstores, book sellers and librarians that support me and share my work with their communities!

Spoke & Word Books

Always Here Books

Epic Quest Books

Cierra, Bonnie, Gere, Rafael, John, Artemis & Kel

...and all those I don't have the names of!

9 781959 916369